The

Peter Meredith

Peter Meredith

Fictional works by Peter Meredith:

A Perfect America
The Sacrificial Daughter
The Horror of the Shade Trilogy of the Void 1
An Illusion of Hell Trilogy of the Void 2
Hell Blade Trilogy of the Void 3
The Punished
Sprite
The Feylands: A Hidden Lands Novel
The Sun King: A Hidden Lands Novel
The Sun Queen: A Hidden Lands Novel
The Apocalypse: The Undead World Novel 1
The Apocalypse Survivors: The Undead World Novel 2
The Apocalypse Outcasts: The Undead World Novel 3
The Apocalypse Fugitives: The Undead World Novel 4
Pen(Novella)
A Sliver of Perfection (Novella)
The Haunting At Red Feathers(Short Story)
The Haunting On Colonel's Row(Short Story)
The Drawer(Short Story)
The Eyes in the Storm(Short Story)

A warning about the contents of *The Apocalypse*:

As Americans in the year 2014, a warning about graphic violence, political correctness, and sexual situations in a zombie novel would seem completely misplaced and yet I still have complaints!

Warning: In this novel there is violence; both zombie on human, and human on human. There are also some sexual situations. Read at your own risk!

I also need to warn people with preconceived notions. *The Apocalypse* is not about an ex-Navy Seal with a fallout shelter filled with canned goods, MREs, and a personal arsenal rivaling an infantry battalion. Sorry. Instead this novel is about real people, some of whom stay alive by their wits, or by their strength, or their speed. Some are just plain lucky and some are ruthless, making decisions based on the necessity of survival. Quite a few are downright evil. Yes, with the complete breakdown of civilization, evil will flourish!

And these people, both the good and the bad are represented by every race and every creed.

If you are the kind of person who is easily offended you may not like *The Apocalypse*. You may not like it that a black character speaks in the dialect of her environment and not as though she strolled out of the upper west side of Manhattan. In fact if you think the word Ebonics(African American Vernacular English) is insulting rather than descriptive or if you have called someone racist more than once in the last six months please go onto another book. You will not be happy with this one. You will see racism instead of reality.

Finally a word about the women in *The Apocalypse*. I know some of you would like to think that if push came to shove in a zombie apocalypse you would instantly become like Sarah Connors from Terminator 2: ruthless, hard as nails, and a cold-blooded killing machine. And I'm sure a few of you would. Once again I'm not writing about the few, but of the many. Most women don't have your heretofore-unknown Kung-fu skills, they have their brains, their looks, and the weak survival skill set that the comforts of modern civilization has left all of us. This is another hard reality that some people find unpalatable. Just as above, if you use the word misogyny with any regularity, you will find yourself hating this book.

You have been warned.

Peter Meredith

Chapter 1

June 27th

Rostov-on-Don, Southern Military District, Russian Federation

Under the neon lights, Yuri Petrovich seemed a sick, pasty white, however since this was normal for almost everyone at the facility, it went unremarked if it was noticed at all. From his office, he passed through the agriculture research section—what once was the façade of the operation, and took the secure elevator to the lowest sub-basement.

There he grunted a 'hello' to the aged guard, Beria, and signed his name on the log board. "Time for my monthly checks," Yuri said affecting a bored voice despite the tremor in his hands.

The guard didn't look up from his magazine, a German rag that was two months out of date. "Better you than me," Beria replied, as he always did. Though the man wore a gun at his hip, he was extremely disinterested in anything concerning the facility and no one knew who or what he actually guarded.

"Key me?" Yuri asked.

Once upon a time it would have been a sharp-eyed and sharply dressed political officer who had to match keys to get into the *White Room*. Now it was only fat, put-upon Beria. He sighed heavily as he heaved himself out of his creaking chair.

"On three," he said, taking up his position on one side of the door. "One, two, three." They both turned their keys and the door opened with a hiss. Beria beat a hasty retreat to his beloved chair, where his fat rear had only wiggle room left.

Yuri went into the next room and donned his bio-suit, ran down his checklist, inspected his filters twice, and then went first through one air-lock and then a second. Despite his years on the job, the *White Room* always gave him a shiver down the spine when he entered however today the shiver went to his guts and wouldn't leave.

"Fifty million rubles," he whispered to himself. "Fifty million fucking rubles..."

This helped. And so did the fact that he knew Beria was completely ignoring the cameras. To be on the safe side however, Yuri went through the dull routine of cataloging the various strains of bio-weapons stored there and he did so as slowly and methodically as he could.

Though it was called the *White Room* by the sad few who knew of its existence, it was officially unnamed and not at all associated with the Department of Agriculture housed in the building above. Instead it had grown as an offshoot of the Stepnagorsk Scientific and Technical Institute for Microbiology. It was what the Soviets had called a Biopreparat facility and thus very illegal in the eyes of the world—for good reason.

Yuri glanced down the rows of steel and glass cabinets that were clearly marked: Anthrax, Ebola, Marburg Virus, Plague, Q fever, Junin Virus, Glanders, and Smallpox; each had to be numbered and their dates checked. He worked, with clipboard in hand, in the tedious manner he had cultivated ever since he had become chief of scientific research at the facility.

The term 'research' made him want to gag. There hadn't been a *kopek* of new research money in a decade, and every year his budget shrank. There was even talk of ending the bio-weapons program altogether.

And then what would Yuri do?

The struggling Russian government wasn't hiring many scientists, and the private sector wasn't eager to be associated with a man who had made his living producing and maintaining weapons of mass destruction. His legal options were few, and his illegal options were even fewer, but they were oh, so lucrative –fifty million rubles worth of lucrative. The promise of the money was the single reason he had taken to going to the one locked drawer in the room on every visit.

With a quivering in his chest that wouldn't stop, Yuri undid the stout combination lock, opened the door to the locker, pulled back on the stainless steel slab, and then forced himself to breathe in a normal manner: in and out, in and out. The body lay beneath a sheet and as always, Yuri uncovered it with gritted teeth, while his gorge rose in the back of his throat.

The body was that of a man, or rather it used to be a man, now it was something else.

He took the right arm of the thing, it was grey and stiff, and set it to hang as far as the handcuffs would allow, letting the black blood pool in the extremity. Yuri then went through, what had become a routine and completely unnecessary check up. The thing on the slab should have been dead. It was quite literally ice cold since the refrigeration unit was kept at a constant zero degrees centigrade. And yet it was already moving.

The hands spread and the muscles around its mouth began to work, opening and closing. It was in the eyes where it was most "alive". Somehow they were hungry and furious, but also glassy and empty of any intellect. Lately Yuri had begun to dream about those eyes, and lately Yuri had become an insomniac. He couldn't sleep, knowing that those nightmare eyes would be worn by everyone he knew— if things went wrong.

Still he had a job to do and after a deep breath of stale bio-suit air, he began his check-up, starting with the hated eyes. He then peered into its ears, and nose, and its horrid, dank mouth. Then, making sure his body was completely blocking the camera, Yuri pulled a syringe from one of the zippered cargo pockets that adorned his suit and jabbed the needle into the crook of the thing's arm where a fat vein had begun to bulge.

The thing didn't flinch. According to every report the creature that once had been a man, couldn't feel the slightest pain.

Yuri filled the syringe with black blood, and then very carefully pocketed it. The virus was blood born and though he could bath in it if he wished, a single prick from the infected needle would kill him in hours.

With sweat running down his back, he covered the body, slid it back into the freezer where it belonged and then went on to his next chore which was to switch out the attenuated viruses in their little plastic pipettes. There were a total of twenty doses of the vaccine—he took six, leaving normal saline in their place. No one would notice, not until it was too late for them.

Of the six doses, he would inject himself with one of them that night, just in case; three were part of the bargain that would make him rich, and the final two he would keep for himself.

These last would guarantee him a position of power if his clients, the North Koreans, were ever foolish enough to release the virus. Given the right conditions he could churn out vaccines in as little as four months, while he had to wonder if the Koreans would ever figure it out. They were pathetically behind in all aspects of technology, as everyone knew.

Yuri closed the last glass case and breathed a sigh of relief. He was done and not a single alarm had gone off, which meant that one wouldn't. Beria had been as poor at his job as ever. Moving quickly, now that the toughest part of his job was past, Yuri breezed through both air-locks, and with the utmost care he transferred the syringe from his bio-suit to his jacket pocket. It felt like he was carrying a bomb with a hair trigger as he made his way up to his office, however nothing untoward happened and he was able to take the needle off the syringe without mishap.

The now capped syringe and the clear pipettes he bagged and then placed inside his thermos, while the needle he dropped onto the open face of the sandwich his wife had made him for lunch; it would go to waste anyway, he could never eat after a visit to the *White Room*. Very carefully he wrapped it back in the brown bag it had come from and this he gently put in a medical waste container.

One last item: Yuri took the container, which was nothing more than a plastic bag, and walked it personally to the incendiary chute and tossed it in. Now he was done. He went to his desk and sat there picturing everything fifty million rubles would buy, sighing happily.

Chapter 2

Rostov-on-Don, Russia

The second link in the chain of disaster occurred the following day when Yuri met with the North Koreans, who were far more adept at espionage than they were at biochemistry. Somehow they knew all about the dreadful creature locked away in the *White Room*, but knew almost nothing about science—though they did make a great show of it. They had surgical masks, pristine plastic Bio-suits and gloves that ran halfway up their arms. The lone microscope they had brought looked as though it had come from an eighth-grade science class. They took turns peering at the virus and jabbering away.

Without notes or images to compare it to, each agreed that this was indeed *The Virus*. Yuri had to hide a look of incredulity. He couldn't help wondering if he could have passed off a different virus, something far less deadly. Their incompetence gave him a nervous chill; however this was swept aside when they produced a briefcase full of rubles. The sight was so full of promise that his fears for the future left him and he became all smiles as he counted the money.

When he was satisfied, he handed over the remaining blood as well as the three vaccine filled pipettes and neither side knew that they were part of some grand cosmic joke for a few more months. That night, as Yuri planned his permanent vacation, the North Koreans, not a one of whom was a scientist, boarded a plane set for Pakistan. The following day, as Yuri began making deposits in the various bank accounts he had opened, the North Koreans started to bargain with the Pakistanis: shale oil contracts in exchange for a virus of untold potential.

The North Koreans were out of hard assets to purchase fuel, while the Pakistan scientists were bristling with excitement to get hold of the fabled Super Soldier Virus, confident that they could pare back its negative side effects. If they could, it would give them an edge in their endless armed rivalry with the Indians and perhaps even a super power status.

Their excitement made the bargaining tougher than the Pakistanis had foreseen, but in the end everyone came away with what they were looking for.

The head of the North Korean delegates, General Choe kept his face rigidly impassive as he handed over only a portion of what he had been given: a half-filled tube of blood and a single pipette. He was prepared to hand over the other two pipettes and the rest of the blood, yet no one asked and he didn't offer. Instead he remained perfectly calm despite that his insides were leaping with excitement. He was going to be rich!

The following evening, when Yuri was transferring his money to a Swiss account, General Choe was in Cairo meeting with a group of Saudi extremists, ensuring that he too would make a handsome profit from this dirty deal. He had seen too much of the world to go back to the prison that North Korea had become.

"I need proof," Kahled Marzouq, the chief financier present demanded. They were in a dusty warehouse where the desert ran up against the edge of the city, and Choe, despite that his flat features twiched not at all, was more than a touch nervous. To extremists like these everyone outside their little circle of hate was the enemy.

Kahled went on, "Twenty-million U.S is too much money to hand over without proof that this virus will do what you say it will."

A dog was called for, and a gun. The gun was the easier of the two to produce, though eventually a little mutt was brought in and tied to a girder. Choe pricked the dog and then came a four hour wait where it gradually turned from healthy to sick—its breath grew labored and its head went back forth with a long string of drool swinging below.

Eventually, its whining ended and it slumped and ceased to move. There were seven men in the warehouse and all waited to see what would happen next. Just as the Saudis were beginning to grow irritated, the dog reawakened into a mindless beast with blank, staring eyes and bared teeth, whose sole aim was their death.

"It no longer feel pain," Choe said in his broken English. He had been chosen for the Foreign Desk due to his ability in languages—he spoke six well enough to be understood. He gestured to the man with assault rifle and said, "Shoot in the back quarter."

One of the men had an AK47 and he put a well-placed bullet into the cur. The little dog didn't so much as yelp; it only turned on the shooter and pulled at the end of its leash desperate to kill, making a low moaning sound that seemed more human than canine.

"Now shoot in thorax. You know this word?" Choe asked, pointing toward the chest of the dog. The man again aimed his weapon and shot. The bullet staggered the dog, but after a pause it came on just as before, unrelenting despite the gaping wound that went through its body. The Saudis were wide-eyed now. "Next in head," Choe said. "Is only way is kill."

This last bullet did the trick. When the dog finally ceased to move, one of the extremists came forward; he stared down at it, lying in a puddle of its black blood and asked, "Ami, how long before you can get that vaccine into mass production?"

"Two years with my current funding," Ami Khalifa answered. He had the lilting cadence of an Englishman in his voice and the soft hands of a man unaccustomed to manual labor. "Eight months if my budget could be quadrupled. Of course your definition of mass production may be different from mine. If you are talking about millions of doses then I will need fifty times what I have and a hundred more men...and a much better facility."

"That I cannot do," the financier said. "However I think we can begin..." He paused suddenly and would not say more with General Choe present. Instead they made arrangements to pay the North Korean and then ,when the man went his way, the Saudis began a general discussion concerning the implications of the virus that went on for hours—and the body of the dog was forgotten. As the Saudis made plans to bring the west to its knees, rats began to feast on it. Many of them had open wounds and these became sicker by the hour, snapping at their brothers in a fever-driven delirium, further spreading the virus.

It became a slow motion chain-reaction that spread across the Middle East, and before Ami Khalifa reproduced even a single vaccine, infected rodents began to show up on cargo ships heading all over the Red Sea and beyond.

And on October first, as Yuri Petrovich came off the plane in New York City in a dapper new suit, he was only three days ahead of a cruise liner that would put into port in Miami carrying a great many sick passengers and a number of dead ones as well. The company tried to keep it hushed up, but very quickly it got out that cannibals had been aboard the ship.

By then the Saudi extremists were well aware that their designs had gone awry and though they had only managed to create two-hundred doses of the vaccine they put their faith in Allah and put their murderous plan into action.

Chapter 3

Sarah

Danville, Illinois

Sarah's cart shimmied to the right, while one of the wheels thumped with every rotation; that little bump ran up her arms and right to her head where it pulsed in a dull ache.

Why don't you just get another cart?

She knew the answer. It was the same reason she had only dropped hints to her daughter instead of just coming out and stating plainly exactly how upset she was. Sarah Rivers didn't like to make waves, or even ripples, like returning a cart. Some of her friends thought of her as a pushover, and she wouldn't have argued the point.

"Hey look at this," Brit said, grabbing up a tabloid as they took a turn near the front aisle. She was a bright and sunny girl of sixteen and like her mother was strikingly beautiful. Unlike her mother, however, she was more than a little gullible. She held the tabloid up for her mother to see the headline. "Zombie monkeys are invading India. That's messed," she said.

Sarah smiled. It was thin and forced, but it was what the situation called for and Sarah was always very aware what every situation called for. "It's probably not real," she said.

Brit looked closer at the tabloid picture and replied, "You don't know that. Maybe they have, like, mad cow disease or something."

The thin smile stayed in place and to it she added a little shrug, as if Brit's theory was actually possible. They turned up the next aisle and Sarah swept her blue eyes past the soup cans, Brit was the soup eater and it didn't make sense to buy more if she was leaving. Instead, she grabbed up four cans of French-cut green beans and a tin of fried onions, thinking they would have green bean casserole for dinner that night.

"Again?" Brit asked, eyeing the beans.

"You're the vegetarian," Sarah answered. She wasn't a good cook to begin with, but when her daughter had announced earlier in the year that 'Meat was Murder', her limited skills were really put to the test. "Just be happy that you won't be getting Mad-cow by eating my casserole. Though, I think only cows get mad cow disease; not humans or monkeys."

"You don't know that," Brit said again; it was a phrase she used frequently when talking to her mother. She held up the tabloid and tapped on the picture. "Maybe this is what happens when a monkey eats a cow that has the disease."

"Do monkeys eat cows?" Sarah asked—and was JFK really an alien, as the next headline suggested? She didn't ask this, though she wanted to. It would mean more waves and with her daughter on the verge of moving eight-hundred miles away to live with her father, Sarah was afraid to make even the tiniest of ripples.

However with a teenage girl even the smallest ripple could be made into a tidal wave.

"Of course they don't, duh!" Brit said, rolling her eyes. "But, you know, they like to eat anything a tourist will throw their way. McDonalds and shit like that."

"Brit, we're in public," Sarah said in a whisper as she looked about, ready to unfurl an apology if anyone had overheard the word.

The girl breathed out loudly as though it was an effort to exhibit the least manners, "Fine: *stuff* like that. You don't know."

Sarah didn't know, though she thought she did.

Chapter 4

Ram

Los Angeles, California

"Oh, this is going to suck big time," Victor Ramirez said, running a hand through his thick black hair. He was sitting in a van parked just down the block from the mosque with three other agents, though none were sweating like he was.

"You got that right, Ram," one of the men agreed. "But it's the job."

"But is it my fucking job?" he shot back. "We're DEA, not FBI, or NSA. This should be their shit job." The Special Agent in Charge, Ron Fillmore only continued to stare out the window, which had Ram getting angrier. "Look, I knew going in that I'd be monkeying around in Mexico, trying to get into a cartel, but this? Do I look muslim to any of you?"

The senior agent, who looked like he had just strolled out of the whitest section of Whitesville, Connecticut only glanced his pale blue eyes away from the window for a second, giving Ram a look. "You're closer than I am."

Ram pointed his deeply tanned hand at another agent and asked, "What about Shelton? He could be a black muslim. They have them you know."

Fillmore shook his head. "Not at this mosque. Trust me. Those sand-monkeys are the most racist people imaginable."

"Is that right?" Ram asked, dryly. "The *sand-monkeys* are racist?"

"What the hell's your problem?" Fillmore seethed, slamming a hand down on his chair. "This is the job. It doesn't matter right now that it should be FBI. Do you know how many mosques there are in this country? The Director has asked for our help and out of courtesy and damned love of country you're going to do this!"

"And what happens when this is another false alarm?" Ram asked quietly. "Who gets hung out to dry? Am I going to get thrown overboard as a supposed rogue agent?"

"This is nationwide, so no," Fillmore replied, calmer now. "And for Christ's sake I hope it is a false alarm."

In his gut, Ram didn't think it was going to be and that had him doubly nervous. In his seven years with the agency he'd had guns shoved in his face, he'd been beaten nearly to death, and he had dined with stone cold killers who made Ted Bundy look like a chump, but there was something about the ethereal and invisible nature of biological weapons that made him shiver at the very thought.

Was he even then infected? Or was his next breath going to be the one that killed him?

"What about clothes?" he asked, thinking that maybe he would like to wear one of the long robes he had seen Middle Eastern Muslims wearing. Sometimes they wore scarves, which would go a long way to hiding the fact that he was latino and not muslim, and which he figured he could breathe through in the hope of lessening any chance at catching the disease.

"What you have on is fine," Fillmore answered after a glance. "Here, study these while you can."

The senior agent handed over four photographs; all were of Middle Eastern men. Dreadful rumors had been rippling from every Intel source and only in the last few days had they firmed up. An Al-Qaeda spin off group was thought to be bringing a weaponized form of Bubonic plague into the US. However the group was so secretive that only eighteen of them were even named and just four of those had ever been photographed.

The others were described in the most useless fashion: Arabic; olive skin tone; black hair; brown eyes.

"This is impossible," Ram griped. "The pictures could be of anyone and I know it isn't PC to say this, but these descriptions are pathetic. They probably describe everyone in that damned building."

Fillmore nodded, thin lipped. "They aren't all the same. Not all of them are Saudis, Fuad Mehdi, he's from Kazakhstan, and Shehzad Bhanji, he's from Qatar. Maybe they'll stand out. If you don't see anyone who matches the pictures, look for someone who's alone, or a pair who don't belong. Use your training."

"My biggest worry is that I'll find fifty people who look like these pictures."

Fillmore tried a smile; it wasn't his strong suit under the best of conditions and this one was watery. "You're going to be fine, Ram. Now it's time to get moving. They should be calling the people to pray any minute and you should be in there before they do."

Ram took a shaky breath, felt the pistol in the holster under his jacket, tapped the tiny two-wave radio in his pocket, and then stepped out of the van. "Wait, is it salmon aleekum?" he asked, fouling up the traditional greeting.

"No, hold on." Fillmore looked at a folder and said slowly, "As-salam alaykum. Say it to yourself as you go." With that the van door was closed in his face and Ram was left to walk down the street alone.

He tried again, "As salamun malaikum? Oh, Jesus! This isn't going to work."

The mosque, a white rectangle of a building with a domed minaret in its center was fast approaching. He tucked his chin down and kept his eyes up, watching as men in twos and threes came up the street. Most were smiling easily, others seemed tired since the sun was already set. He followed a pair as they entered the front door, then stepped to the side in a lobby lined with shoes. Everyone who entered took their shoes off so Ram did as well, though he took his time, deliberately.

Going to one knee he scanned the faces around him and as he did his training, as well as his natural inclination as an adrenaline junkie, kicked in. His nervousness disappeared and his eyes were sharp. He took in every detail of the men who drifted through the lobby, most of whom jabbered in this-or-that language.

Quickly he realized two things: one, the pictures and descriptions were as useless as he had supposed they would be, and two, he didn't need them either way. There was another man lingering in the lobby.

He was dark complected, even compared to the other Middle Eastern men, and his clothes were odd: stylish, but outdated as only foreigners seemed to wear them. He and Ram locked eyes and the DEA agent *knew* this was his man. Unfortunately the man realized this as well, and without hesitation, he broke for the door in his stockinged feet.

Ram was right behind him at first, however the man was fleet of foot, while Ram, though tall was more of a bulldog in form and in style. Still he ran as hard as he could with his shoeless feet slapping on the pavement as he yanked out his two-way.

"Suspect running north…on ninth…in pursuit!" He yelled this between gasping breaths. The middle-easterner sprinted up the first street he came to and Ram was just putting the radio to his lips when the DEA van appeared and came roaring toward them. It slewed to the right and out of it jumped two agents.

The man turned first one way, and then the other, but by then it was too late. "One move, dip-shit and I'll drop you," Ram threatened as he came up with his gun drawn and the trigger half pulled.

"You have the wrong man," the Middle Easterner said in a thick accent. There was fear in his face, but anger as well.

The senior agent frisked him from behind and pulled a gun out of his jacket pocket. "My ass we do," Fillmore said, holding it up. In a second Shelton cuffed the man and hustled him into the back of the van.

"I'm glad that we won't have to worry about a

translator," Fillmore said, with an evil glint to his eye as the van took off in a screech of tires. "Or about rendition either. There'll be no playing around this time. No lawyers, no judges, none of that crap. You understand what I'm saying?"

"Like I said you've got the wrong man. Check my pocket! I'm Iranian not a Saudi!"

"Oh, you're Iranian? Well Mr. Iranian, do you care to explain what you're doing here in the States?" Fillmore asked, searching the man's pockets and finding a number of photographs. "Meeting some friends? Who are they?"

He held the pictures up to the Iranian's face and Ram caught sight of them—two looked very familiar. Way too familiar. Ram dug out the four photographs that he was carrying and stared with a growing realization.

"My name is Sayyid Nosair and I'm doing the same as you," the Iranian answered. "Trying to stop the world from ending. We're after the same people and you just ruined any chance that I could've had to stop them!"

"He may not be lying," Ram said, holding up the matching pictures side by side. His insides felt greasy.

Back at the mosque a man slipped from the prayer line and hurried outside to intercept another two men before they could come in. With quick steps they walked to a late model BMW and drove away, losing themselves in the night.

Chapter 5

Neil

Montclair, New Jersey

The train into Manhattan was right on time—according to Neil Martin's watch, and his watch was an Omega; a point of pride. He slid his newspaper into the briefcase he always carried and then commenced to bob up and down on his toes as the train slid by, going ever slower. The door, his door as he thought it, stopped precisely in front of him.

Neil was always precise; another point of pride.

He stood on the platform exactly three feet back from the door. It was plenty of room for anyone departing to walk around him, either left or right, and just close enough so that another passenger looking to board would have to wait behind him.

Unless they were rude, that is. The doors opened and with no one exiting, Neil started forward, only to be jostled aside by a rather average man pushing past him.

"Excuse me!" Neil said in anger.

With a snide look to his blonde features, the man turned on the top step of the train and stared down. "Yeah? You got something to say?" he asked. His Jersey was thick and menacing on his tongue.

"I was just here first," Neil said in a softer tone. The man might have been average in size, however Neil wasn't. Even with the inch tall heels on his loafers, they barely boosted him to five-foot-five. And no amount of eating seemed to ever push him over the one-hundred and forty pound barrier.

"You were here first?" the man asked. "Good for fuckin' you."

Neil's chin dropped on its own and the man walked off, snorting in contempt. "Troglodyte," Neil whispered, moving to the car on the left; the opposite direction of the rude Jerseyite.

He sat himself down and fumed, staring out of the window as the train commenced its journey and he didn't notice the pretty girl across the aisle until they ducked through a long tunnel. Then he could see her just fine reflected in the train's window: auburn hair, pert features, a trim little figure, and what was more, she was a good size for him, probably only a hair over five feet.

He turned with a shy look and was surprised when her smile broadened. "Hi," she said, scooting over to the aisle seat.

"Hi," he replied in kind, feeling that nice warmth in his chest at meeting a pretty girl. It was a rare event for him.

"You shouldn't worry yourself about that guy," she said, her smile turning sympathetic. She tilted her head to add to the effect.

"That guy?" The warmth in Neil's chest turned to ice.

"Oh yeah. That idiot. How on earth do those people get to walk around on this planet with the rest of us? You know what I'm saying? Homophobia is a disease on this society." She said this far too loudly for Neil's tastes.

His head clicked up and down and his smile went crooked. "It's a bitch," he agreed and then pretended to read his newspaper. The headline blared: *Super-flu Strikes Russia!*

"It's a real fucking bitch," he whispered. Neil Martin wasn't gay at all and he very much wanted to say something, but what good would it do him? None whatsoever. Instead he hid himself in the paper and when the nearly empty Sunday morning train pulled into Penn Station, he lingered in his chair, not wanting to see the rude man. Nor did he want to be around if the woman was going to fight his battles for him.

That would be embarrassing beyond anything he could contemplate.

So he hung back as they disembarked and as chance would have it they preceded him through the maze-like terminal.

"This can't be happening," he said under his breath. The ill-mannered blonde man was walking right for the 1 train. Heading south, and a few steps behind him, clacked the small woman in her four-inch stilettos. Neil groaned and actually considered the idea of taking a cab down to his office.

It would cost him twenty dollars and most of the remaining shreds of his ego to do so. Instead he took a deep breath and went through the turnstiles, hoping against hope that the pair had moved down the platform so that he would be spared their presence. It was not his lucky day it seemed. The rude man stood exactly fifteen feet from the beginning of the tunnel, right where the first car would come to a halt. It was Neil's spot. He always stood there.

Not that day. Keeping his head down to avoid eye contact he went past the man who made a loud business of it to hock up a big ball of snot and spit down into the tracks. Neil made a face of disgust and, unfortunately the auburn-haired woman, who was just a little further on, happened to notice.

"That's so foul," she said, shaking her head. "I'm sorry you have to put up with it. I have this co-worker, yes he's a bit of a flamer, but..." Just then the blonde man spat again even louder and the woman turned on him. "Do you have to be so gross?"

He didn't yell or make snide comments as Neil expected, instead he squatted at the edge of the platform and pointed down at something unseen. "I ain't gross. That is. I've never seen anything like that before in my life."

The man was at a safe distance so Neil inched up close to the edge as well. "What the...what is that?" he asked stepping back in alarm. Gradually, curiosity had him moving forward to look a second time. "Is that half a rat? And it's alive? How is that possible?"

It was indeed one of the huge sewer rats New York City was famous for, only this one was torn in half. It pulled itself along by its front limbs and all the while it made a doleful squeaking sound. The woman took one peek and then looked away touching her palm to her mouth lightly. The blonde spat on the rat again and Neil had to turn away as well.

The man smirked and said, "You're going to have to grow a pair or *Red* will never sleep with you."

Neil couldn't argue the point mainly because it was true; however the woman wasn't going to be constrained. "Listen pencil-dick. This guy's got far more of a chance than you will ever…"

"What is that?" Neil asked putting out his hand to the woman. From the tracks the strange squeaking sound had increased—a lot.

"Whoa," the blonde man said and now he hopped back. There were more of the rats and even by the low standards of sewer rats these were repulsive. Like the first they were mauled and chewed upon. Some were missing limbs, while others had necks that were near bitten through, or bellies that hung in shreds.

They stared up at the blonde with a look that spoke of hate or anger. It was a bizarre moment that was cut short by the rumble of the 1 train as it came into the station far down at the other end of the platform.

The woman looked pale and she began to walk away from the blonde man. "I don't want to share a car with him," she said, giving Neil a little sideways nod with her head. Eager to be further from both the blonde and the rats in the tracks, Neil began to go with her but by chance he turned to look back at the man who had so antagonized him.

The blonde was looking right past Neil at the oncoming train, which was growing louder with every second, and this was probably why he didn't hear the rats as they came from out of the tunnel behind him in a hideous grey wave.

Neil's mouth failed him; it dropped open but sound refused to come. So he pointed with one hand at the onrushing rats and slowly the blonde turned with a puzzled expression.

Now it was that many of these rats didn't appear injured and they ran with surprising speed so that they were on the blonde before he really understood what he was looking at. And then like small dogs, they leapt at him, latching on with their diseased teeth. He screamed and it was an inhuman sound that could be heard even above the approaching train. Neil ran, a move that was all instinct and panic and cowardice. Dozens of rats were all over the blonde and dozens more that couldn't get at him had turned toward the other two people on the platform.

Neil took off and almost as an afterthought he grabbed the woman and pulled her along, though he was quick to let go. Unlike in the movies where people sprinted hand in hand, in real life it only made them both slower and she wasn't very fast to begin with, not in her high stilettos.

"Don't leave me!" she screeched only seconds later.

He looked back and saw that he was already fifteen feet ahead of her and his lead was growing with every one of his strides. In a flash, he fought an internal battle as he judged the distances between her and the lead wave of rats, and the flash turned into a pause, and then the pause turned into a moment of *too late* as one of the least injured rats caught up to the woman in the tight skirt and the too tall heels. It sank its teeth into her ankle.

It didn't seem like much of a bite, however it was right at the tendon above her heel and the horrid beast severed it with a rip of its jaws. She went down and more of the rats rushed over her and her screams were added to that of the blonde who was still alive, kicking and flailing under a mantle of grey bodies.

And Neil ran. He ran grimacing and crying, staring over his shoulder at a nightmare come true.

Chapter 6

Sarah

Danville, Illinois

At eight in the morning, after an hour-long drive and an interminable wait going through security, Brittany Rivers boarded her flight to New York. Sarah watched the plane take off and stared without blinking until it was only a tiny spec in the sky and then, feeling empty, turned around and walked back to her car.

She was a mess. Sarah feared flying and she doubly feared it when Brittany flew, and she triply feared it when Brit flew alone, which happened from time to time. If she had heard about the ongoing rat attacks in the New York City subway system, her fear would've been enough for her to turn the car around right there on the highway. Unfortunately for her the rat attack story had been buried by worse news: Miami, Jacksonville, and New Orleans were under an actual quarantine. A situation that Sarah couldn't ever remember happening in her lifetime or even her mother's lifetime.

It was unreal. The army wasn't letting anyone in or out of those cities and that included journalists.

Because of this, the newspapers and the twenty-four hour cable shows were all over the place, reporting on hearsay and guesses as if they were actual facts. First they said it was Bubonic plague. People in the Gulf coast region went into a panic and shuttered their doors and windows as if a hurricane were approaching. And then it was suggested that it was influenza, but when that was explained as *only* the flu it wasn't deemed a creditable enough threat and the reporting on that only lasted a day.

The President had given a speech the night before telling the American public that it was an outbreak of

Legionnaire's disease, the same as was being reported in London and Cairo and along the Italian coasts. He went on in a calm voice to say that everything that could be done was being done. The speech was supposed to be reassuring, but Sarah hadn't been reassured in the least.

In her gut she knew a slow approaching anxiety, which had only been added to by the fact that her daughter's teenage rebellion couldn't have come at a worse time. Thankfully Sarah's ex-husband didn't live in the actual city. If he had, Sarah would've put her foot down for real; though in truth she didn't know how to put her foot down. Her discipline took the form of gentle and sometimes circuitous nagging, coupled with a light sprinkling of guilt.

Her ex, Stewart Rivers, lived on Long Island with his new and much younger wife. Sarah narrowed her mouth until her lips almost disappeared whenever she thought of the new wife and they did so again. Sarah had only been 17-years old and Stew twenty-two when they had married. Her daughter had been born five months later. Now, people often thought she and Brit were sisters: they both had long, blonde hair and were the same height. She knew she looked young and she had always had a good body, so it was hard for her to understand why Stew left her.

"I'm hungry," she said, deciding to push the thought of *Miss New Boobs* out of her mind. At that point Sarah was halfway back home to Danville and took an exit to somewhere called Waynetown. She had never heard of it, but McDonald's had and that was good enough for her.

Another thing that was good enough for her was the price of gas in the little burg. All over the country, prices had surged in the last week and a gallon of gas was now over six dollars on average, and so when she saw that it was just over the five-dollar mark there in Waynetown she slipped into the line behind a honking big SUV.

That was another thing the outbreak of whatever-it-was had caused: lines. Sarah really wasn't used to them. Waiting ten minutes to checkout at the Food Lion was about all she could handle. Anything more and she would grow impatient. Now the gas lines lengthened with each passing day. The last time she filled up, two days before, it was a twenty-five minute wait. And even here in Nowhereville, Indiana, she sat idling behind the Ford Expedition listening to song after song on the radio and turning the channel whenever the station went to news.

The people in the Expedition weren't just after gas. The driver, whom Sarah assumed was the father of the family, directed his two sons to a grocery store that sat just a few blocks away, while he walked away up the line of cars. When he came back laden down with bags, Sarah barely noticed, but when the two teenage boys arrived with a shopping cart full of canned goods, she watched them load the cans with an unsettling idea growing in her.

Should she be stocking up as well? She frowned at the idea. It almost seemed un-American. Sarah had never known a day of true want in her whole life. In her America, McDonald's could never run out of hamburgers; everyone knew they had an endless supply of them. And gas pumps couldn't possibly run dry—they hadn't ever before. And there would always be Stouffer's Pizzas in the freezer section of every grocery store, and every mall had a Macy's filled with clothes, and Hollywood was always releasing a new block-buster hit, filmed in ear-splitting surround sound. That was the America she was used to.

Still, as she watched the family piling their groceries into the SUV, she began to worry. When she finally got to the pumps she went into the convenience store as she fueled and was shocked at how empty the shelves were.

And what was left was being marked up in price even then by a frumpy looking lady in a housecoat and slippers. Sarah glanced at the new price tag on a bag of Cheetos and her eyes went wide.

"Eight dollars!" she gasped. "That's...that's gouging.

Isn't price gouging illegal?" It was a strange world she lived in: her daughter could throw a fit and fly half-way across the country and Sarah could barely muster the temerity to say more than a few dribbling words, but charge her eight dollars for a bag of chips and watch her outrage come out.

"And what about the morality of it? I should call the police!" she added.

"Be my guest," the lady in the housecoat said with a laugh. "I'm sure they're going to drop everything and rush right over."

The man behind the counter, though also looking tired, was at least in normal street clothes. He smiled somewhat embarrassed and said, "We're not gouging. Not really. First we charge only what the market bears and second, if we don't raise our prices we'll be out of business. Do you understand about replacement costs?"

"Of course she doesn't," the woman said. "If she did she wouldn't be all in a tizzy."

"What are replacement costs?" Sarah asked, trying to be civil and eyeing the Oreos that were next to be up-charged.

"Well, if I buy these chips for a dollar and sell them for two, I make a profit. But what happens if the next bag costs four dollars for me to buy? I wouldn't be able to afford them and so none would be available for you to buy at any price. It's why gas prices are so fluid. Sure the gas in the pumps cost me three-fifty a gallon, but the next truck in will cost me over five."

"I guess I see," Sarah said. "What about that grocery store? Are they raising their prices too?" She had a sudden desire to purchase as much food as she could afford before she couldn't afford any.

"Yes, though not as much," the man said with a shrug. "They have greater purchasing power than I do."

"Oh, ok. Thanks and sorry about getting so angry. I'm a little stressed out." Sarah left without buying anything except the gas and drove to the grocery store down the block and was amazed to see the parking lot was nearly full as if it were a Saturday and not a Wednesday morning. The crowd wasn't overwhelming; after all this was a part of the country where root cellars were still common and where some people still actually jarred their own preserves and canned peaches and other fruits.

Still the shelves could best be described as thin, especially in the Medicine/Pain Relief aisle, and barren in the fresh produce aisle. Sarah hurried to the canned goods and went among a dozen other women with the same idea and for once in her life she shopped like a man.

She looked beyond specials or prices, while the list of ingredients on the side might as well have been written in Greek for all she paid attention. The shelves were emptying fast and so she began filling her cart as quickly as she could without starting a panic.

This was a real worry. The women in the aisle were strained in appearance and had nervous quick eyes. One even said to another, "That's enough. Leave some for everyone else." This was ignored and a shoving match broke out.

Sarah, who had thirty or so cans of soup and stew and corn, left as quickly as she could. She went for rice, but the store was out and she settled for eight boxes of dried mashed potatoes, an item she would never have touched only the week before.

And then she moved onto the biggest shock yet. The store was out of toilet paper! For some reason this hit her nerves more than anything else, and feeling jittery, she grabbed the last three bundles of paper towel thinking she was crazy for doing so. Surely her Food Lion back in Danville would have more toilet paper and plenty of fresh produce, and everything else. Surely it would.

It had never run out of anything, before.

Chapter 7

Eric

Washington D.C.

As Sarah Rivers waited in another, even longer line at the Country Market in Waynestown, Indiana, Eric Reidy stood in the White House situation room, feeling sweat spreading from his armpits in an ever-widening circle while he touched his wiry brown hair frequently, patting it down. It tended to poof up if he wasn't careful. When he breathed it came out as a shaky sigh. He was normally good at public speaking, however he had never spoken before the Joint Chiefs of Staff or the Secretary of State, or the Secretary of Defense, or the Secretary of This or That. All these important people staring at him was bad enough, but when the President came storming into the room in a fury, Eric feared he would have a new stain to deal with.

"You've got ten minutes," the President said brusquely. "And let me be clear, I don't want your briefing done with any scientific mumbo-jumbo. The guy who was in here yesterday couldn't spit out a word unless it was twenty syllables long and all he did was confuse the issue."

The "Guy" had been the Director of the Center for Disease Control, Thomas Villar and his double PhD status hadn't impressed the President a lick. Eric, despite only possessing a master's degree in microbiology, had been chosen to do the follow up with the President because he was more in tune with public relations than actual laboratory work. The truth was, viruses gave him the heebie-jeebies, but the pay at the CDC was phenomenal and the expectations low. His kind of work, until now.

"Yes sir," Eric answered. How on earth was he supposed to cover everything in ten minutes? Quickly he turned on the projector showing the continental United

States. "Uh...first, the red shaded areas are where the known outbreaks of the uh..." Eric paused. He had been about to spit out the scientific name of the virus, which was a good thirty-two letters long, instead he swallowed audibly and said, "*The virus*. As you can see southern Florida and Louisiana are hardest hit, but we can now confirm that Mobile, Houston, Norfolk, New York and Providence, really all of Rhode Island has seen some activity."

"What about the orange circles?" the President asked, pointing, as behind him his Yes-Men all nodded sagely in agreement.

Their bobbing heads were a distraction and Eric had to force his eyes back to the projection. "The orange represents areas where we can't confirm the virus has traveled to, but we strongly suspect that it has. This is mainly due to reports of...yes, sir? Did you want to say something?"

The President sat glaring at Eric as if the map was his fault. "That's the entire eastern sea board and the gulf coast. And Denver? And Seattle? Are you sure?"

Eric shook his head. "I'm not in a position to confirm that any area in the orange zones has viral activity. However the Director has asked me to reiterate that if martial law is not called today it will be for certain that the virus will spread into those areas. Mathematical probabilities render it an absolute fact. I have a brief concerning the statistics behind the rendered..."

"Ahem," a general said clearing his throat and standing. The man's chest was so covered in commendations, medals and ribbons that it seemed almost to be a joke. He didn't wait for the President to acknowledge him. "This was suggested three days ago by the Joint Chiefs of Staff, and I want it on record that if you hesitate any longer, Mr. President, then containment will be flat out impossible."

"Will it?" the President asked, and it was a moment before Eric realized that he was being addressed.

Eric had to shrug. "I...uh, I don't know. I'm not sure

what your containment strategies are or how effective they'll be."

"Just give me your best guess, damn it!" the President thundered slamming his fist down onto the table. Behind him a dozen faces glared at Eric.

"A guess isn't really scientifically..." Eric bit his words off as the President's brown eyes bored into him. "Okay...if I had to guess, I would say that I'd agree with the general here. This virus has the capability to spread exponentially. How it began, and how it spreads we don't know, but it has a firm hold on the rat population in the major cities in the red zones. What we've found is that the rats have for the most part, been attacking the homeless and the indigent: prostitutes, runaways, or maybe just kids getting high and unable to protect themselves. From there the virus is spreading to the first responders. Police departments are reporting large numbers of their officers are complaining of flu-like symptoms..."

"Rats aren't the damned problem," a man in a blue suit said. "It's the zombies that are the damned problem." The word zombie had an odd effect on the men and women gathered: none so much as snickered, instead they glanced to the President who set his mouth in a hard line but said nothing.

Eric bobbed his head and stammered, "Yes, well, in a sense you're right, however as it pertains to containment, it is the rats that will be more of an issue than the, uh, *altered persons*. A wounded rat will crawl off to die, maybe in the back of a truck, or in the hold of a boat, or in a bag of potatoes destined for a grocery store five states away. And then when you think you have the, uh zombies contained that rodent will, uh re-animate for want of a better word and start the cycle up again hundreds of miles away."

"So if we can stop the rats, we can stop the spread of this *virus*?" the President asked making it clear with how he said virus that he wasn't going to put up with the term *zombie* any longer. He tried glaring some more but then sagged, looking haggard; his normally dark black hair seemed to have gone grey overnight.

"And the red zones will have to be contained," Eric said flipping back to the previous slide. "Completely contained. If that's even possible. Though it would help the CDC immensely if we knew the origin of the virus. There's been talk of terrorist attacks. If this is true we need to know the country of origin and..."

"We're looking into it," an advisor of the president mentioned.

Once again the general stood and his face was livid. "Save the political correctness for the media. We all know the Muslims are behind this. Every piece of Intel that's come across my desk says so in the very clearest terms. Hell, we even have the Iranians confirming this."

The President motioned for his general to sit before he said, "There may have been terrorist ties to this, but we don't know for certain and until we do I won't have Americans turning on one another. For now we will stick to the story that it's Legionnaires disease being spread by rats."

"And the country of origin?" Eric asked.

"Like he said, we're looking into it," the President answered vaguely. "In the mean time Mr. Reidy, I need an estimate on when we can expect a cure."

Eric cleared his throat. "There won't be one. Viruses don't have cures. What we are working on is a vaccine, which is a denatured version of the virus, meaning the pathogenicity is removed and thus the body's..."

"We know what a vaccine is," the President said coldly. "How long until one is available?"

"Months to years," Eric replied. "Maybe never. I can't tell you for certain at this early stage, though it would help if we knew where this came from, what family it's in. Right now we have scientists working blindly and any information could trim weeks off the initial work."

"When we have the information, you'll be the first to know," the President allowed. He then covered his face with his long brown hands and rubbed his eyes. "Alright...alright, as of now I am declaring martial law. General Chaky, I am putting you in charge of enforcing the quarantine for all the red zones. It has to be air tight, until we can set up safe zones in the rear to move people into."

"That won't be enough," Eric said. "Those orange areas can't be ignored. They have to be policed as well and the people in them can't be allowed to leave until it is known for an absolute certainty that they are clean. That means the airports and the harbours and the roads, all have to be shut down completely."

"See that it happens," the President said. The general did not wait for further orders and led his group of uniformed personnel out of the room.

The Secretary of Health and Human Services stood and said, "We have to create and distribute vaccines to three-hundred and thirty million people, before it's too late. I'm going to need every scientist from every university in America brought down to the CDC in Atlanta."

Eric sat down as the various cabinet members asked questions and made points, mostly concerning aspects under their purview. What escaped his notice, not until much later was that the Secretaries of Agriculture and Transportation were for the most part silent.

Unfortunately theirs were political positions, and each was usually concerned with renewable energies or climate solutions, or minority rights or the like.

All of which was fine under normal circumstances but the real issue facing America just then—besides a growing horde of zombies—was how they were going to feed three-hundred and thirty million people, none of who were allowed to travel legally, and those two men were utterly clueless.

Chapter 8

Ram

Los Angeles, California

Ram snuck a look around the edge of the building and gave a thumbs up to the two men behind him. The alley, a dirty stretch of weeds and trash behind the running warehouse was clear.

"Let's go," he whispered, taking point with gun drawn. Shelton moved to his left and the Fed, in truth they were all feds now, went to the right, each moving with all the stealth they could. Their target was a ratty mobile home that sat on a little square of a lot just past the warehouse. Ram prayed to God that it wasn't booby-trapped like the last one had been. There'd be no calling in a bomb squad, since as far as he knew everyone in the L.A. bomb squad was either dead or had been bitten.

Overnight, Los Angeles had officially gone from a clear zone to a red zone, though Ram had known for four days that it was red. Ever since they had interrogated the Iranian, it was known who they were after and what was happening. Sadly they hadn't been believed, until now that it was too late.

The terrorists were veteran killers and had taken out the bomb squad by the simplest method possible. They had put out a dummy bomb in an obvious location and had then set more bombs all around. These were far more cleverly hidden, and much more deadly because the virus had been added to the explosives.

The terrorist's aim was to cause as many injuries as possible, knowing what havoc would be caused when the men began to turn. This was their *modus operandi* all over the city. Their bombs were placed where people gathered: shopping centers, movie theaters, even police stations, and all the bombs were shrapnel bombs filled with nails, and needles, and roofing tacks, and of course, the virus.

Ram could honestly say that L.A. had turned. Zombies were everywhere, though nowhere were they worse than at the hospitals. With the blood and the wounds and the death, hospitals were natural breeding grounds for the creatures and Ram wouldn't be caught dead in one. Despite the zombies, he had a job to do and it was the reason he was presently crouched below the level of a waist-high chain-link fence and keeping an eye on a ramshackle mobile home. It was brightly lit and that was something. They had checked out several other homes; one dark house after another. Two had been booby-trapped and two others had been the home of living corpses. Fillmore had punched his ticket getting bitten on the shoulder in one of them.

No one had known what to do with him. They had tried the county hospital, but when they had rushed into the Emergency Room it was their first inkling that the city was lost. Zombies came at them from every door and some even jumped from windows trying to get at them. They had fled with poor Fillmore and in the end, when the fever was burning bright on his skin and no one wanted to get too close, he had shot himself in the head and they had left him there on some nameless side street.

That had been only the night before, though to Ram it felt like days ago. They had gone from lead to lead without rest and this was going to be the sixth house since Fillmore's death, and with each the team had shrunk.

"Who's going first?" Ram asked in a whisper.

"Man, I don't even know why we're bothering anymore," Shelton hissed back. "Look at this place! The city is fucking toast." To accentuate his point, or so it seemed, gunfire erupted on the next block causing each of them to crouch lower.

Gunfire had become almost as ubiquitous as the zombies and Ram had ceased getting worked up over it.

"You got a point. The city is toast, but what about the state? And what about the country? And what about Fillmore? I never even liked that guy and for some reason I'm pissed off that he died the way he did."

"I'll go first," the federal agent said. "It's my turn."

"Damn straight it's your turn," Shelton said angrily. Despite his talk he wasn't leaving his partner. "You've been hanging back all fucking..."

Ram put his hand out. "He said he's going first, so let it drop."

The Fed, a member of the weak Homeland Security force ignored Shelton and Ram both. He was too keyed up. His breath began to race in and out, and then he nodded and took off for the door with the other two agents right behind. There was no polite knock or even a 'hello', the agent went right at the door and slammed his bulk against it and immediately fell forward; the door hadn't been locked.

"Allah's will," rasped out a thick accented voice. "My work must be complete."

Ram stepped over the Fed and leveled his piece at a middle-eastern man who eyed him blackly. "Hands where I can see them," Ram ordered.

The man sat at a little table and before him were wires and a glass jar of nails and a little test tube filled with blood. "Or what?" the man asked. "Or you'll shoot me?" He laughed at this and Ram glared.

"Or I'll shoot you and then roll you in bacon before burying you with a dog. How does that sound?"

The man cursed in a foreign language and Ram stepped forward to let the Fed get up. Shelton stayed outside, watching their backs.

"Where are the others?" Ram asked. "We got Al-Fadl two hours ago and Amir last night. So?"

"The others? Denver, Chicago, Dallas, but it does not matter now. They can do no more harm. Allah has seen to it that only the most faithful will survive."

"How is he going to do that?"

"Thou bringest forth the living from the dead and thou bringest forth the dead from the living, and thou givest sustenance to whom thou pleasest without measure," the man said with a smile and hard black eyes.

He had turned slightly in his chair when the door had burst open and Ram had a clear shot with his Beretta. When it came to how prisoners were dealt with, things had changed considerably with the declaration of Martial Law, and without the least warning Ram pulled the trigger on his gun, sending a bullet speeding into the man's knee. And then he waited as the man rolled around on the floor of the trailer grunting and moaning in agony. While Ram waited he inspected what the terrorist had been working on, and, taking rubber gloves from his back pocket, the DEA agent very gingerly took the blood-filled test tube and held it up.

"You're going to tell me what I want to know or I'm going to pour this on your leg."

"Go ahead, pour it," the terrorist grunted and spittle flew. "I am Allah's servant and that blood can't hurt me."

It had been a bluff only. There was no way in hell that Ram was going to open a vile of *that* blood and risk catching the virus. Yet his threat hadn't been in vain. He was a good agent and this was primarily because he could spot lies in an instant and there was something about the man's attitude that struck him as odd.

"This blood can't hurt you? What about other blood? What about black as hell zombie blood?" The man answered Ram's question with the tiniest sneer, yet the agent read more into it than the terrorist wished. "What about pig's blood?"

Now the terrorist set his face in stone and Ram reeled with sudden knowledge. The Middle Easterner did not fear being turned into a zombie yet he was horrified at the idea of pig blood. There could only one reason for this.

"You've been inoculated, haven't you?" Ram demanded. The man looked away for the briefest second and said nothing, and Ram knew he was right. "Shelton! There's a cure. Did you hear that?"

The other DEA agent backed into the trailer, staring out. "I heard and so did everyone else. There's some zombies heading this way."

They all ducked down so they couldn't be seen and Shelton locked the door. It was a flimsy door.

It was tested a minute later as a number of the creatures pushed and pulled at it and then hammered and thumped at it, shaking the trailer. Shelton, his eyes huge in his brown face, had a firm grip on his gun with both hands. He had it pointed straight at the door and he wasn't the only one. Both the Fed and Ram had their guns at the ready as well.

Thankfully they weren't needed. The zombies gave up after a few minutes and went shuffling down the alley in search of easier prey.

"Oh shit, that was close," Shelton whispered, passing an arm across his brow. "I thought for sure..." he stopped staring past Ramirez.

The Middle Easterner was lying there, staring upwards and in his neck was a small screwdriver. He had killed himself.

"Damn," Ram whispered, staring in amazement. He then hurried forward.

"What are you doing?" Shelton asked. "Don't touch him."

"I have to. He's got the cure in him," Ram said pulling out a pocketknife.

Chapter 9

Neil

Montclair, New Jersey

Neil Martin saw his first zombie, his first human zombie, on the thirteenth of October. It wasn't much of a sighting. It was an old lady with a great deal of her left leg chewed off. She was grey-skinned and scabby with oozing wounds. Her hair sat limp and greasy, her clothes were torn and hanging off her, and her eyes were filled with a vicious, unnatural hate. As she wandered down the middle of Grove Street, people watched her from the safety of their homes. Neil clutched a broom to his chest until she was gone to who knew where.

On the fourteenth the army rolled through the neighborhoods and there was some sporadic shooting and Neil felt safe enough to make an attempt at his neighborhood Whole Foods. He was out of many of what he deemed were essentials and had a craving for smoked salmon and bagels. Climbing into his trusty Prius he drove the near-silent machine the two miles to the store and in that time he only saw three people.

They stared at him as if he was crazy and his friendly waves weren't returned.

He found the Whole Foods was not just closed, it was also boarded up. Hoping the one in East Orange was still operating he drove southeast, passing closed shop after closed shop, only to find this Whole Foods was boarded over as well. With nothing better to do, he drove on to Newark, but never did make it to that city.

The intersection at Bloomfield Avenue was blocked by four military Humvees that sported dreadfully large machine guns atop them. Along with the vehicles, thirty or so ragged and dirty soldiers stood guard or slept in the October sun, which was unseasonably warm. Though the soldiers on duty had their guns initially pointed away down the street, most turned and leveled them in Neil's direction when he drove up.

"Excuse me?" Neil said as one of the soldiers stepped in front of the Prius, forcing him slammed on the brakes. "Can I get by? I'm trying to get to the Whole Foods in Newark."

The soldier, a man with three little chevrons on his arm, gave a laugh of disbelief. "No, you can't. Don't you listen to the news? Everything from here east is quarantined."

"I don't, actually," Neil admitted. He tended to look down on people who watched TV, though this wasn't something that he would admit to a soldier. He tended to look down on them as well, but was smart enough not to do so when one was so near. He looked up and down Bloomfield and saw that there were soldiers all up its length. Neil wasn't the only one gawking, people on both sides of the street gazed fearfully out their windows.

"So those people who live in those houses over there can't come over here?" Neil asked, feeling his stomach begin to quiver in fear.

"Nope," the soldier answered. "And you can't go over there. That's how it works. Though why either of you would want to go in any direction is beyond me. There's really nothing west of here that's any safer. You should go back home, you're not supposed to be on the streets."

"And what if we need some stuff from the store?"

This was answered with a shrug. "I'm sure it's all being worked out. They'll let you know. Don't worry."

Easier said than done.

Neil drove home, spotting his second zombie as he did, a very large one, wearing only a single shoe. It's lower lip dangled from a shred of skin, yet still it managed a fierce glare as the Prius scooted by. The sighting sent Neil's heart banging in his chest and when he got home he rushed to his living room where upon he immediately turned on his dusty

TV. It showed nothing but static, which was an unpleasant shock. Like bagels and salmon, the TV was always supposed to be available when one wanted to watch it. It was like a law.

Shut in his house, as he had been, there was no way for Neil to know that only the day before, Navy Seal teams had been dispatched to destroy the broadcast studios of every news station in the quarantined zones.

The administration believed that the news coming from inside the Q-zones, as they were called, would only demoralize the rest of the nation if they understood the breadth of the issue. So, the Seals swooped down in their Blackhawks, planted a few hundred charges, shot some first amendment resistors and a number of zombies, and then zipped out again just as the charges detonated.

Neil smacked the top of his TV set in annoyance and then went to make a sandwich, which he ate on his screened in porch, keeping his only weapon, his trusty broom, near at hand.

That evening there was much more shooting in his neighborhood and he woke the following morning, to what sounded like a World War 2 battle being waged. Wearing nothing but striped pajamas and a green terrycloth robe he went to stand on his stoop, facing west.

"That isn't right," he said to himself, aligning his arms with the rising sun. The army should have been east of him not west. "Oh, no," he whispered. Had they expanded the quarantine zone? Was he now on the wrong side of the barriers and the guns? Without a working TV, he had no way of knowing, so Neil went across to his neighbors, completely forgetting his broom.

A zombie, not fifty yards away reminded him. It was rooting around in the ivy next to Mr. Park's house and Neil froze out in the open.

"Neil! What are you doing out there?" Mr. Krauthammer asked from his second floor window. This caused Neil to practically squeak in fright and he grabbed the only weapon he could find that was near at hand—a garden gnome. "Hey, that's my gnome," Mr. Krauthammer said angrily.

"Shh," Neil said with his finger to his lips. He then pointed at the zombie, only Mr. Krauthammer couldn't see it because of the angle.

"Is it one of them?" Krauthammer asked without changing the volume of his voice in the least.

The zombie looked up from the ivy and stared at Neil for all of a second before he went charging across the fading green of Mr. Park's lawn. Neil squawked and ran for his front door, which he had, fortuitously, left open.

"That's my gnome!" cried Mr. Krauthammer.

Neil wasn't about to reply, nor was he going to return the gnome anytime soon. He sped across the sidewalk, leapt his flower border and made it to his front door safely, slamming it shut behind him and then locking it. And then he waited, listening to the zombie sniff at the door, shake the handle, and bat at the heavy wood with its fists.

All the while Neil shook in fright.

Eventually the creature left and Neil tiptoed to his bathroom and urinated for over a minute with quivering hands. For once he didn't wash his hands. He didn't even flush. Instead he went to his own second floor window and called to Mr. Krauthammer.

"What do you want?" the old man asked. "You know you shouldn't yell so loud it attracts the undead."

"Are we in the quarantine zone? I only ask because my TV isn't picking up any channels and that's got me a little shook, I can tell you."

Mr. Krauthammer looked up the block and nodded with a grimace that was nearly a smile it was so twerked. "Yeah, they moved it sometime last night. It's now out to interstate 287 on the west and it goes north all the way to Nyack."

Neil didn't even know where Nyack was which made

him think it was far indeed. "So what do we do?"

"Stay indoors. Keep 'em locked and wait for all this to blow over. I'm sure the army is doing something. And the administration says that they don't expect the quarantine to last for more than two weeks. But then again they keep telling everyone it's Legionnaire's Disease. With all the rumors, I don't know what to believe anymore."

"Rumors?"

"Oh yeah. A lot of people are saying that Denver and St Louis have been overrun and Dallas, too. It's why we aren't leaving, who knows where it's really safe?" Krauthammer chewed his lip for a moment and then started to pull down his blind. "Well, it's been nice talking to you."

"Thanks," Neil muttered, his mind drifting over the rumors. Though he gave each its due he kept coming back to the idea, or rather the hope, of only having to gut it out for a couple of weeks. Did he have food enough for two weeks? If he cut back on his snacking and rationed what he had left, he probably had enough for three. "Well, thank you, Mr. Krauthammer. And don't worry about your gnome. He's in safe hands."

Neil shut his window and then decided to get some work done. If he had two weeks to kill, he figured he would put it to good use, after all his quarterly taxes would be due soon. He worked steadily until the sun began to set and then fixed himself a very small dinner. He cut his usual portion by a third, not realizing even then how significant food had become.

For both sides—the human and the zombie—food would mark the difference between containment and outright anarchy.

Chapter 10

Dade County, Florida

The men of the 504th of the 82nd Airborne Division were the "ready brigade" in October, meaning they had to be prepared to deploy anywhere in the world with eighteen hours notice. Who knew the deployment would be to Florida and who knew they'd be fighting their own countrymen?

Certainly not Private First Class Marshall Peters. He had enlisted with the express purpose of going overseas and fighting America's enemies, not figuring that the Iraq war would end so quickly. According to every news account the war was going horribly and then come 2009 it just ended and somehow we had won.

Quite the opposite was true in Afghanistan. It was the quiet war for so long, but then we made a promise to leave and it flared up—just not for PFC Peters. Somehow he just missed a deployment by the first Brigade Combat team and ended up sitting around Fort Bragg bored to tears.

But then they got the call.

"Miami?" he had groused. "What the hell's in Miami?"

No one knew, and though they all joked about fighting alligators and toothless hillbillies, it grew serious when they were given a full combat load. And when they waddled onto the C-17, as only paratroopers do when carting sixty extra pounds around and a chute on their backs, it got serious indeed.

PFC Peters' unit dropped along a twenty-mile stretch of Okeechobee Road and was told to form one continuous line and not to let anyone across it. The orders were of such a vague nature that on that first day they didn't know which way to face. By the third day they had things worked out and they faced east toward the lights of the city, and on the fourth evening, they began to turn back the first stragglers.

"You don't understand," a man said in a pleading voice.

[47]

"The dead have risen. They're walking around eating people!"

They shooed him away, but he was replaced by others who said the same sorts of things. Soon rumors went up and down the line like fire before the wind.

Peters had the second guard shift on the sixth night of their deployment and he had never been more afraid. In the dark things moved and whispered and rifle fire broke out occasionally. Mostly it was one sided with dug-in paratroopers firing blindly at imagined monsters however, fire was returned on two occasions, causing Peters to hunker and mumble the half-remembered words of a childhood prayer. Near the end of his shift, screaming began, running across the night air to freeze his bones and shiver his spine. It went on until there came more rifle fire--a long pop, pop, pop--and then silence.

Even after his shift, Peters didn't sleep a wink that night. Gradually it came to be that guards were needed more in the daytime than at night since very few could sleep when the sun sank and the night came alive and the guns flicked little flashes of light.

On the eighth day the line went through a major shift. Rumor had it that huge sections of the line south of the city had been overrun. Men were shifted southward and their lines were stretched thinly. On the tenth day it happened again. This time whole companies were yanked to fill gaps that had sprung up and the men around him were further away. That day Peters shot his first zombie.

It was near evening when the thing came stumbling right at his foxhole. Not knowing what it was exactly, Peters stood to show the woman that he had a gun. "Go back!" he yelled. "This is a restricted area. You can't come through here." The woman didn't listen and kept on coming and so Peters fired a warning shot.

"You're going to have to shoot her," a friend said from the next foxhole as the woman neared. "But don't worry. It won't matter much, since she's already dead."

"Shoot her quick!" a sergeant called from two foxholes down. "She's got the disease!"

This did it for Peters. He brought the M16 to his shoulder aimed for center mass and fired a single round. The grey-skinned woman went down and no one said a word, while Peters felt the immediate weight of guilt, which vanished in a flash as she got back up again.

"What the fuck?" Peters swore. "I hit her. I hit her square in the chest!" Quickly he brought the gun up, flicked the selector switch to 3-round burst and put three more into her. When she got up a second time at least ten of the soldiers in the foxholes around him fired on her, and this time she stayed down.

When the story of the woman made its way up and down the line, the fear among the soldiers grew to such a degree that gunfire became the norm that night. Anything that moved was shot at: leaves and birds sometimes, people at others and zombies when they came their way, but mostly bullets were fired at imaginary enemies. By the thirteenth day many soldiers were low on ammo and what was left had to be distributed among them.

"When are we going to be resupplied?" Peters asked his sergeant. This earned him a shrug. "And what about artillery? Shouldn't we have some mortars at least?"

"Nope," the buck sergeant answered. "Rules of engagement: no artillery, no air power. If you can't identify what you're shooting at then you can't shoot."

"But you can't tell what they are until they're right up on us!"

The sergeant spat in the dirt and said, "Yup. It's nothing new, Peters. Iraq was worse. We couldn't shoot at the terrorists until they shot at us first. That was messed up."

Peters slumped, depressed, thinking the situation couldn't get worse, and yet they hadn't really been put to an actual test.

That came the following night when a plague of zombies crossed the open field to their front. Now it was a battle, though thankfully it was one sided and rarely did the stiffs get within ten-feet of the lines and no one was injured. Despite that, the victory was costly. The unit had been resupplied earlier so that each man had two-hundred rounds, however since the soldiers clung to their training and fired center mass, riddling the bodies that came ever closer, they went through ammunition at a prodigious rate.

Peters had only eleven rounds left when a group of a hundred men, women and children came across the open flat the next day. They were a good sixty yards down the line, and his sergeant picked out a few men to bolster that section, Peters among them.

The people wouldn't stop, and they were real people, too. They came on, crying and begging for help and when they were not thirty-feet away the sergeant had to shoot the leader in the leg when he wouldn't listen to reason. The rest finally stopped and a long argument ensued, with both sides refusing to budge.

This led to a very strange situation. The people basically made camp right in front of the soldiers who could do nothing to stop them. They were still there the next morning. All day they sat huddled together or they went up and down the lines of soldiers begging for food or water. The men were under strict orders not to give them a thing, yet almost all of them did.

The people had lived all in one apartment building and had shared their food among themselves until the last scrap was gone—then they were forced out onto the streets where the zombies had been growing in number. The creatures came out of every nook and cranny after them and the people fled, leaving the old and the sick to be feasted on, and then turned.

For the most part the camped in front of the soldiers were weaponless, though a few carried rakes or hoes or large sticks. Each had a bag upon their back carrying little besides an extra change of clothes and maybe a photo album. It was dreadfully sad and Peters was among those who tossed them food.

The situation lasted only another two days. The line had been thinned again and Peters had a hole all to himself, something that would have unnerved him beyond belief except for the fact that he had his own family parked twenty feet in front of him. For the last day and a half he had given over most of his MREs and in return they were his early warning system.

Just before midnight the young girl with them whispered, "There's some right there."

Peters had been blinking trying to fight sleep when the words came and now he stood up, peering into the dark. A scream rent the night and then gunfire; this was off to the right, and everyone looked that way, even the girl. It was a mistake that would cost her. By the time she glanced back, zombies came lurching out of the dark. They were faster than they should've been and although the family got up and ran, the girl was clawed down and smothered beneath a pack of the foul beasts, yet despite that she screamed and screamed.

There were many screams just then. The family screamed and ran toward Peters and he tried to shoot around them, which only meant he wasted ammo. And then they were past him and a zombie was right there only a few feet away; he shot instinctively and holed the beast through the neck. And then another came with mouth wide to bite and this he shot through the forehead. To his right and left gunfire blazed.

He could only stare for a moment and then he had two more to deal with. As he was standing slightly higher than they were, he shot them both in the head at point blank range, yet this was unplanned. Another moved to his right and he aimed and pulled the trigger and nothing happened.

"I'm out of ammo!" he yelled to his friend Murphy in the next hole.

Murphy said nothing. In front of his hole was a gang of zombies going down one after another with gaping wounds, until a clawed hand grabbed the gun barrel and pulled Murphy forward. Peters ran to help, but he was snagged around the ankle and down he went. It was the zombie he had shot through the neck. Black blood dribbled from the hole; however the creature didn't seem fazed in the least by the huge wound. It reared its head and bit through Peters' camouflaged pants tearing a chunk out of his calf.

The pain was like fire and the soldier went wild kicking with his free leg until the zombie let go. And then he was up and hobbling away uncaring that he had left his gun, and his post, and his buddies to die. He ran until the fever brought him down and then later he rose again and turned back, remembering only one thing. He remembered where the humans were.

Chapter 11

Eric

Phillipsburg, New Jersey

After meeting the President and playing the part of personal servant to the Secretary of Health and Human Services, who had practically moved into the CDC, it should've been nothing for Eric to speak to a simple two-star general.

It wasn't.

Major General Fairchild wasn't an easy man for anyone one to speak to even under normal conditions. He kept Eric waiting half the morning on the hard wood benches outside his improvised headquarters. The 10th Mountain Division had its base of operations set up in the municipal building in the town of Phillipsburg, which sat right on the border of Pennsylvania and New Jersey. It would have made more strategic sense to have his base two miles further west across the Delaware River, but there was the morale factor to consider: it would've been difficult on the men to give up New Jersey completely after losing so much ground already.

It had certainly done a number on Eric's morale to learn where the lines had been pulled back to. "What happened to holding the Hudson?" he asked his driver. After a chopper ride from Atlanta to Camp David, he had been given a lift in a hard-topped Humvee to meet with the Commander of the 10th.

The soldier had only shrugged at the question.

Now as the hours slipped by Eric couldn't even get that much out of the officers whisking past. Finally he grabbed the first man to come out of the General's Staff office. "I have orders from the Secretary of Health and Human Services to see General Fairchild," he said to the man. "I demand to see him." Though his tone had been commanding, almost to the point of being imperious, the man, a full bird Colonel, only made a noise of dismissal and flicked his hand over his shoulder as he walked away.

"He's in there. Go on in."

"Does that mean I can just go in? Really?" Eric asked, however the colonel was already out of earshot.

Summoning his courage he pushed open a door and slipped into what had at one time been a courtroom. In a way it still was. Now General Fairchild, sitting in the judge's seat, presided—he glared at Eric as the officer who had been speaking faltered at the interruption.

"Who the hell are you?" Fairchild demanded.

Eric had been about to sit in the back row but now he straightened and introduced himself, "Eric Reidy of the CDC with orders from the Secretary of Health and Human Services."

"First, I don't take orders from that bitch. Second...what's with that get up?"

Over his three-piece suit, Eric wore a dun colored flak jacket and upon his head, sitting crooked, was a helmet— supposedly it was one-size-fits-all, however it made his skull feel like a clapper in a bell. "I was told this was regulation," he said defensively.

"I'm sure it is at the CDC," the general mocked. "Out here, if a stiff gets close enough to bite you on the head, you're a dead man anyways. But hey, if they start planting IEDs or tossing grenades you'll be the safest one of us all." This brought on a chuckle from the assembled officers. Red-faced and angry, Eric began to protest, but the general slammed his hand down growling, "Shut your damned mouth. I'll get to you when I get to you."

Eric dropped onto the bench and steamed in an angry silence, slipping the helmet off and undoing the heavy flak jacket as unobtrusively as possible. As he did he cursed his boss under his breath. Eric had asked for a gun and had been given the stupid heavy outfit instead.

With nothing better to do, he listened to brigade commander after brigade commander beg for more ammunition, more fuel, more food, more reinforcements, and really just more of everything.

The general seemed like a single mom trying to satisfy a dozen bickering children. "We can detach the 186th support battalion from the 3rd brigade..."

"With all due respect, Sir," the 4th Brigade commander said. "Is that the Vermont Guard unit you keep pushing on everyone? The one with the God damned rainbow patch? No, sorry. The 3rd can keep them. I can't supply my own men, and now you want to give me a bunch of guys who are just a waste ammo? Those guys can't fight a lick."

"Maybe if you tried a different strategy," 1st Brigade suggested. "The men I find doubtful I use in other ways: I have them run ammo or dig trenches. I even have them construct little forts out of logs or cars. They give the men a base to rally around. Sort of like redoubts back in the day. I'm just saying someone carted these guys from Vermont to Denver and then out here, we might as well use them."

4th Brigade blew out loudly. "Well you're lucky you can. You still have actual neighborhoods and actual houses to funnel the stiffs at you. Me? I got a hundred miles of open rolling land north of New York City to cover. If you can do the math I got 40 men per mile to guard the Q-zone. It's not nearly enough, especially when you realize we're fighting both zombies and civilians. A fort will just leave the men inside stranded when we pull back."

"I don't want them either," 2nd Brigade added. "They're as bad as those Air Force pukes you tried to give us. They eat up my supplies and half the time they run off at the first hint of trouble."

"Then how about this, we make another attempt to retake Fort Dix," 1st Brigade put out. "We can re-establish it as the forward supply point for the Northeastern Theater of Operations. Just think of all the stores we had to abandon, there's enough fuel and ammo to last us weeks. And there are actual tanks and Strykers there. I say fuck the rules of engagement. Give me five or six companies of infantry and I'll solve our logistics issue and gives us some fire power to boot."

4th Brigade threw down his pen and scoffed, "And lose the country in the process. We can't afford to give up even one man on the lines and you want six hundred? That's absurd. What we need more than supplies are real soldiers who can fight. And not more of these damned REMFs! The last reinforcements I received were laundry specialists. What am I going to do with a bunch of guys whose main training have been in laundry services? I tell you they weren't worth a shit. What we need are 11 bang-bangs."

"Bang-bangs?" Eric snorted. He thought he was whispering it in a mocking tone that no one would hear, however the room had quieted just at that moment and all eyes shifted his way. The general looked on him as if he were a previously undiscovered form of moron.

"11 Bang-bang is slang for the MOS designator 11 Bravo," he explained. "An infantry man. A man trained to fight. What did you say you do again?"

"I'm a scientist," Eric said, stretching the truth.

"Look, we have a scientist in our midst," the general declared. "Why don't we put aside the defense of our fine country and deal with you?" Fairchild was no fool. He had seen that his colonels had been on a verge of a brawl and had decided to use Eric's intrusion to diffuse the situation.

"Ok, good," Eric said, standing once again. "As I mentioned I have been sent by the Secretary of Health and Human Services..."

"Whom I don't answer to," Fairchild reminded Eric.

Eric could only shrug at this, not knowing where in the chain of command a cabinet level appointee ranked. "She has the full faith of the President, and on this I think she is speaking for him," he said. He came forward with a manila envelope and pulled from it a picture. "This is Yuri Petrovich. He was the managing supervisor of the Scientific and Technical Institute for Microbiology located in Stepnagorsk, Russia. According to new reports, it is believed that the virus might have come from there."

"And?" the general asked at Eric's pause.

"And the CIA has just found out that he took a leave of absence from the lab just four days before the first known outbreak of the virus. This may be coincidental, however he also showed up in New York three days before the Atlantic Princess docked in Miami with its deadly cargo." Eric paused again, for questions. The general only tapped his pencil angrily on the wood of his table. "And he may have been in contact with terrorists," Eric said in a rush. Silence seemed to fill the room at the end of each of his sentences and it made him distinctly uneasy. "Supposedly he came into a lot of money suddenly."

"That's it?" Fairchild asked, looking at his gathered colonels as if he had missed something. "A scientist leaves Russia and comes here? Why on earth should I care?"

"Yes...I mean there's more," Eric stammered. The general was so much more of a force than the President that Eric felt his mind scattering to the wind. "Yuri was in charge of the chemical and biological warfare component of the lab. It was a Biopreparat facility. You must know what that is. It's where they prepared for germ warfare, and really it doesn't take a genius to see that his sudden moves coupled with his new-found money, *and* the outbreak of this virus isn't coincidental."

The 4th Brigade commander seemed confused. "And therefore what? Are we supposed to find this guy and arrest him? Or shoot him?" When Eric began to nod, the colonel threw his hands in the air and cried, "We can't even find the Vice president!"

"It won't be like that, we know where he was staying," Eric replied. "He was at the Waldorf Astoria in Manhattan."

"In New York?" General Fairchild asked in surprise. He then barked out a derisive laugh as the colonels whispered among themselves, none too quietly, with the word *moron* being more clearly pronounced than any other.

Eric grew angry. "You don't seem too concerned with finding an opportunity that may help us develop a vaccine. The President might want to be made aware of this." Eric thought his implied threat would have some impact on the general, but he was wrong.

Fairchild glared under bushy brows and growled, "Do you think I give a rat's ass what this President thinks? Mister *Good war—Bad war*? Mister getting-a-damned-Peace-prize-for-just-showing up? Hell the fuck, no! If he had spent even a tenth of the time studying war as he did in protesting it, he would know that even asking about a mission into New York City is idiotic as all hell. Fuck, even a Harvard educated dipshit such as yourself knows that there isn't anyone left alive in New York."

"Maybe not," Eric said in a small voice; he was pale from the general's tirade. "Maybe Petrovich is dead...probably he is, but that doesn't matter; we still have to try. We might find a clue to his present whereabouts, or perhaps notes on the virus, however the main reason for this mission is that he may have had an actual vaccine on him! This is the why we have to go."

"We?" the general was quick to pounce. "Finally someone in the administration that's showing some balls. Good for you, Doc. Too bad I can't spare any men. Try the Navy. Them pukes aren't doing nothing but sitting out in the ocean wasting fuel. Don't worry, they have helicopters. They'll take you right in and out. You'll be safe and sound."

"No, Sir, you don't understand, I can't go with you," Eric said quickly. "I'm not authorized to go...and we tried the Navy. They said they were short fuel as well. With all the ports being in the Q-zones, they can't refit or refuel properly. At least that's what they say."

"They're a damned bunch of cowards is what they are," the general groused. He then sighed out the words: "Damn. Fine, we'll do the job just like we do everything else around here." He glanced to a colonel who had been relatively quiet. "Teddy, it's time for that aviation brigade of yours to finally do something besides taxiing politicians all over the damned country. Scare up a Blackhawk and see that the good Doc here gets a weapon."

"But..." Eric began, however a bushy eyebrow and a hard blue eye shut him up quick.

"You're going, Doc," the general ordered. "We could come across all sorts of crap, and so I'm thinking we need an expert on site. And that's you."

"I'm not. Not really." Eric wasn't an expert in any field, but there was no gainsaying the general when he had made up his mind. Though Eric did try, until the general took him by the scruff of the neck and pushed him out the door.

"Teddy, if he keeps up the whining," Fairchild said to his Combat Aviation Brigade commander. "You have my leave to toss him from the chopper when the mission is complete."

"With pleasure, Sir."

Chapter 12

Sarah

Danville, Illinois

For most of America food was fast becoming a problem. With travel restricted, stores sat empty, gas stations ran dry, and people's cabinets grew more barren with each passing day. The elderly and inner city residents ran out first and they took to begging at their neighbor's doors or at city hall, or fire stations. Thousands dared the zombie-infested streets because they were without a choice, and when begging proved useless, some moved on to stealing, and then to mugging and then to murder, but mostly they took to dying.

The undead feasted.

And when the dead came back as the undead, it created a ripple effect that turned into a wave, which then turned into a tidal wave. It wasn't a pebble tossed into a pond sending out its gentle little waves, it was like a boulder tossed into a puddle.

To combat this was the US military and they proved worse than useless. The quarantine zones kept otherwise healthy people caged up with monsters. Each zone inevitably became a breeding ground for vast zombie hordes. Yet what was worse was that the zones kept the soldiers pinned in one location, waiting. Sometimes doing nothing for days on end, sometimes killing civilians who tried to fight their way out, and sometimes, most of the time, the soldiers fought and died beneath the onrushing grey wave of undead.

Unexpectedly, at least to the morons in Washington, where the war was being fought by people with full bellies and who slept in warm safe beds, the Army's casualty rate was far greater than they could have dreamed, especially among the medics and hospital staff, which were decimated in the early days.

Fort Bliss on the Mexican border ceased to exist altogether.

At that poor facility, endless waves of zombies crossed the muddy Rio Grande and raged up against the wire emplacements, surrounding the base. A less politically motivated commanding officer probably would probably have ignored the irrational rules of engagement, however General Lewinski, being a stickler for rules, let the Abrams tanks and Stryker armored personnel carriers sit in their perfectly lined rows and tried to fight off the huge numbers of zombies with increasingly fewer and fewer soldiers.

The men were burdened with a sense of futility that was magnified by the psychological horror of fighting the undead, and over the course of a few wild nights nearly as many simply ran away as died fighting. Those who stayed fought until the last bullets were fired, and then died like heroes swinging their guns like clubs and roaring out battle cries.

With his army being destroyed, the President called up the Army Reserve and the National Guard. Tragically, what few men did answer the call to arms soon became more of a hindrance than a help, as most took up their M16s and as much ammo and food as they could carry and then left again at the first available opportunity. They had their own families to defend and it was clear that if they didn't do it no one would.

Thus the army was being bled from the inside as well as from the outside and everyday they were called upon to man ever-lengthening lines. Of course this meant that the quarantine zones failed to quarantine anything.

On the nineteenth of October, Santa Fe, New Mexico suddenly flared up with massive numbers of undead. This required thirty-thousand soldiers to man a two-hundred mile perimeter, which wasn't near enough. It broke down to one-hundred and fifty men per mile, standing watch day and night. On the twentieth, a horde of zombies estimated at twenty-thousand came surging down Route 77, which was being guarded by less than forty soldiers.

These men fired their weapons and then fled in the face of certain death, leaving their fellows alone in their foxholes as the zombies changed direction like a flight of swallows. To the zombies, the strung out lines of men seemed a buffet and they rolled up the army lines, curling around them where the burrowed men in their holes were nearly defenseless.

On the twentieth the Q-zone of Houston was overrun.

The remaining citizens in the city gathered together and, out of desperation, battled the soldiers in a bloody gunfight in order to free themselves. This left a glaring hole in the Q-zone and a horde estimated at quarter of a million broke free. This occurred just as the thin line of men trying to hold San Antonio disintegrated from lack of support. With their numbers swollen by zombies sweeping up out of Mexico this vast undead army moved east, trapping the soldiers of the 1st Cavalry Division between two great masses. By the twenty-second all communication had ceased.

Still the President stuck to his ill-thought-out plan, and the Joint Chiefs of Staff sent men back and forth across the country, wasting precious fuel and thinning lines that were already dangerously thin. And all the while tanks and planes and attack helicopters sat unused and rusting as their operators were handed rifles.

By the end of October, most communities in the interior began to consider looking to themselves for protection. Danville, Illinois was one of these. They knew of the zombies, however their main problem was other humans. Refugees from the nightmare that was Chicago came streaming south by the tens of thousands and they were like locusts: eating everything in their path.

When food and shelter wasn't freely given, it was taken.

On that morning, Sarah Rivers left through her kitchen door, making sure to lock it both inside and out. With her father's help, she had added a hasp and a padlock to her two doors. She walked north on Jackson Street heading for her parents' place. There were a number of people walking about and, like her, they carried weapons openly.

She had only a baseball bat and a kitchen knife in her back pocket. "Morning," she said and smiled to the other people of Danville. She didn't know everyone in the town of thirty-thousand, however it was safe to say she knew everyone once removed. A friend of a friend, or an acquaintance of a distant relative.

Mostly she knew people through her parents, who were social at their church and in the various clubs they belonged to. So it wasn't really a surprise to see they had visitors: older men toting shotguns and older ladies sipping her mother's tea. Denise Rivers loved her tea, while her pantry had always been stocked as though she expected to have to throw a dinner party for twenty at a moment's notice.

"Did you hear?" she asked her daughter as soon as Sarah set her bat beside the door. Sarah had 'heard' much though what was true and what wasn't she had no idea. She gave a shrug and her mother said in a whisper, "Rossville was burned to the ground last night. It was looters out of Chicago."

Sarah's anxiety, a thing she had lived with for the last couple of weeks, grew inside of her. Rossville was only twenty miles north of them. "Looters? As if we don't have enough problems. Have you heard anything from out east?"

Her main anxiety stemmed from the fact that her daughter was in the New York Q-zone and no one had heard thing one about it for days. Truly no one had heard much of anything for days. To keep panic in check the President had ordered the phone companies "Nationalized", meaning they were shut down until further notice. The same was true with the internet, newspapers, radio, and television stations. The people were in the dark, both figuratively and in most cases literally.

The power in Danville went out on the seventeenth—to preserve precious resources it was said and the people did not protest, because this was understandable and reasonable, and people in small towns were generally both.

"I've heard nothing, same as you," Denise replied. "Same as everybody."

"Not me," Mrs. Farnsworth said from her seat at the table. She had pudgy, wrinkled hands and these she had folded daintily on her lap. "My boy, Henry, told me that some refugees from Indianapolis came west yesterday. You know Henry volunteered to stand out at the Lynch Spur road, which is fast becoming dangerous work." Mrs. Farnsworth took a long breath; she liked to be the center of attention and frequently dragged out her stories if no one spoke over her. "Anyway, the refugees coming this way tells him that Indianapolis doesn't have a human left in it!"

"And the perimeter?" Sarah asked. She hated the idea of zombies wandering around the autumnal farmlands of Illinois. To the west of Danville was the North Fork River, and to the south was the Middle Fork Vermilion River, however to the east the land was wide-open farm country.

"Gone," Mrs. Farnsworth answered importantly. "No one knows what happened to the army there. Killed or run-off I suppose."

Denise raised her brows to her daughter, but Sarah ignored the look and asked, "What about south of the city? Why didn't the refugees head that way?"

"They didn't say. Why do you ask?"

Sarah only shrugged but her mother replied, "Because my daughter has a fool idea about going east to find Brittany."

The women traded looks and Mrs. Farnsworth said, "If she's in New York, you have to know what that means."

More than anybody, Sarah knew. "It doesn't mean anything. She's actually on Long Island and would it really matter where she is? What sort of mother would I be if I didn't do anything?"

"A smart mother!" Denise said, banging the table lightly. "If you go out there it'll be the same as if you killed yourse..." Denise bit back her words suddenly and licked her lips. One of the ladies in the room, Mrs. Allen, had lost her son to suicide a few days before—there had been a rash of them in town. "I mean it would be very dangerous," Denise finished, lamely.

The near mention of the word suicide, coupled with Sarah's apparent death wish, left a pall on the room and in the silence a bell could be heard. "Gary!" Denise yelled as she hurried to the doorway that lead to the hall. "It's the emergency bell. It's coming from the north." This she added to reassure Mrs. Farnsworth who had turned white at the news.

"Sweet Jesus," Gary muttered, heading out the door with the other men. They weren't the only ones. All over the neighborhood, men grabbed their hunting rifles or their shotguns and went quickly toward the sound of the incessant ringing.

The women sat around pensively, their ears perked, listening for gunfire. Sarah didn't. After a minute she was too anxious to sit still any longer and she got up and hurried after the men trying to ignore the derisive looks many of them gave her and her baseball bat. She knew it was practically useless, still it was all she had.

Before the crowd got to the cars that had been pushed across the road as a makeshift barrier the bell had ceased it's ringing, and yet the men hurried forward excitedly.

The army had finally come to Danville!

"Reinforcements!" a man cried, which had the crowd grinning happily. The last of the cars were pushed aside and through the gap poured a long train of Humvees and five-ton trucks all painted in swirled greens.

A colonel in the lead vehicle smiled sadly at the people and shook his head at the rumor going around. "I'm sorry, but we aren't reinforcements. We're here for supplies; food mostly, but also gasoline and medicine. It'll be temporary only, and I can assure you that the army will reimburse each of you fully."

"No reinforcements?" an older gentleman asked appearing befuddled at the idea.

"Can't spare them," the officer replied, looking down the street at Danville proper. "Besides, this town seems to be pretty well off compared to the rest of the country. There's not a stiff in sight."

"What about New York?" Sarah asked, shyly. "Have you heard anything?"

The officer was tall and tan; at his hip he wore a holstered Beretta and he rested his hand on it easily as he gave Sarah a long once over, taking in her trim figure and long, blonde hair. "I'm sorry; New York isn't such a great place to live these days. It had been classified as *Red*, but as of yesterday they've changed that to *Black*. Sorry to be the bearer of bad news Mrs..."

"It's Ms Rivers. And...and what do you mean by Black?"

The colonel sighed loudly before saying, "It means there's no sign of human activity. The Air Force has been sending recon planes over the different Red zones, and in New York there ain't any more people. It's only stiffs now. Again, I'm sorry."

Sarah's body went numb and her mind switched to *off* mode at the word "stiffs" and she was slow to catch up to what was going on around her. Here was the proof that her darling daughter was dead. She had failed as a mother. And as a wife. If she had somehow kept Stewart from cheating. Or maybe she could have learned to accept it. If she had, Brit would still be here in Danville and she would be safe and whole and...

Someone jostled her and she blinked stupidly. "Sorry," she said, though she had done nothing wrong. Only then did she realize that the crowd had grown angry around her.

"How can you ask that?" the colonel stormed. "Where have you been living for the last couple of weeks? My authority rests in executive order #7239. The United States has been placed under Martial Law! And as stated in the order, *all* US citizens must acknowledge the authority of military personnel and comply with *all* orders, whether you find them reasonable or not. Now my men will be going door to door commandeering any excess food."

"Then you've come to the wrong town," Gary Rivers said. "We don't have excess anything here."

The officer wore a tight smile. "Excess is a relative term. Now, if there is any resistance, arrests will be made. And if there's any hoarding, there will be punishments. So let's not have that happen, ok?"

No one answered. Instead they looked at each other, wondering what had happened to their country. When the Humvees and the trucks pushed forward, the crowd dispersed in a hurry, clearly going to do exactly what they weren't supposed to.

"Hide what you can," Sarah's father whispered and then left her to empty his root cellar.

Sarah Rivers, at thirty-five, with her honey-blonde hair and good figure, was still fine looking and this attracted every one of the service personnel as they drove past. Many whistled or made crude comments, which was annoying, however the pair of soldiers, slowly driving the last Humvee in the line was downright scary.

Her fear even drove out the pain in her heart over Brittney.

They followed her all the way home. As she fumbled with her locks they came up smiling pleasantly but with a lecherous leer just beneath.

"Hey why don't you just relax in your jeep-thing," Sarah said, cringing at her door. "I'll...I can bring the food to you. Or I can leave it on the step. I think I should do that, don't you?"

The soldier's cold response sent a spike through her chest, "Sounds like we have a resistor. That's too bad."

"You don't," Sarah said desperately, partially turning to the pair. One was black, he was canted away from the door, blocking the sight of her with his wide frame. The other was white and ginger-headed; he stood very, very close. The name Singer was stitched across his jacket pocket. "I'm not a resistor. I promise."

"We'll see."

His blue eyes were inches from hers and in her fear she choked on the air in her lungs. "Ok...ok," she opened the door to let them pass but the gingery man edged right up on her and pushed her inside. She hid partially behind the door and pointed. "The kitchen is right through there. That's where all the food is."

Singer stepped in and then the black soldier, Quinn, walked through and shut the door easily, despite the fact that she held the doorknob. He smiled at her futile attempt against his overwhelming strength.

"Now you don't have to be like that," he said, putting his hand lightly on her shoulder. "This could be a good time if you let it, or it can be very bad time if you go and scream or do anything else stupid."

Sarah quailed beneath his touch and slid across the wall away from him, knocking pictures down that had hung there undisturbed for years. "No, please. I have gold...rings and necklaces. And a diamond ring. It's a full carat."

"What is that stuff anymore?" Singer asked. "Money, gold, it's all worthless now. But there are still some things in life that I'll always want." He raised a little smile and looked her up and down, and all she could do was clutch herself.

"And that sweet thing you have is valuable to you, too," Quinn added. "You can get something out of this. We can mark this house as empty; your food won't be touched. Or..."

Singer took over where Quinn left off, "...Or we take a

little more than you'd want us to and come back in a few weeks and let you blow us for a ham sandwich."

"You can't..."

"Who's going to stop us?" Singer asked and again he moved so close that she could smell the stale sweat burning up from beneath his uniform. "All I saw out there were some shopkeepers. Ain't no fighters out there."

Her head went back and forth and her mouth came open as she tried to think of something to say that would stop this, however, when Singer reached out and undid her top button she clamped her mouth shut. The soldiers were too strong and too well armed and she could imagine herself later if she screamed and made a ruckus, she'd be standing over the fresh grave of her father or her neighbor, Charles Wiley, or maybe a dozen such graves and she'd be saying: "If only I had let them, they'd still be alive."

He undid the next button and asked her, "You gonna make this good?"

Unbelievably her head nodded, though her bottom lip quivered in fear.

Just then her front door opened and the colonel she had seen earlier walked in. His hand still rested on the butt of his gun, only now he had more of a grip to it. "How's the commandeering coming along?"

Singer gave Sarah a very pointed look and said, "We were just getting all civil with the civilian, Sir. Didn't want her to think we was stealing or something."

"I think public relations is more a job for an officer. Why don't you two go see about the neighbor across the way?" Though the words were softly spoken, there was a hardness to the colonel's brown eyes. The two left in a quiet rage. The colonel stood for a long time looking out of the window.

Sarah buttoned her buttons and said nothing. Could she trust this man any more than she could trust the last two?

"What a world we have now," the colonel said softly.

"You should start taking that into consideration. You and this whole Howdy-doody town. All of you walk around like this is still America."

"It's only been a month," Sarah whispered, barely daring to contradict the man. "Maybe the stiffs will die out. And America will be back to normal."

He blew out in a long breath. "No, it won't. New York's gone. Boston, Washington...did you know that? Oh yeah, Washington went last week and no one really cared. Florida, California, most of Texas are all gone. And Illinois, almost right down on your damned heads and you *still* have a friggin' malt shop going for God's sake! The writing is on the wall and you people in this pristine little town just can't see it. I give the country ten days."

"Ten days...what are we going to do then?" Sarah asked. Desperately she wanted someone to be able to answer that simple question. The colonel did.

"Survive or die. That's what I want you to think about before the next time we come through."

"The next time?" she asked breathlessly.

He smiled. "Of course. We have twenty thousand soldiers strung across the whole of the Kanakee River and we're trying to hold back a million or so stiffs. And we aren't getting much in the way of supplies. If you don't feed us, you don't live. It's as simple as that. Which brings me back to the question of survival. How does one tiny slip of a woman survive in these hard days? Can you shoot? Can you fight?"

She shook her head and looked down at the man's mud-stained boots.

He lifted her chin and looked into her eyes. "Whatever you were before, that's not who you're *going* to be. We don't need insurance salespeople or realtors or office administrators. What we need is something to fight for. Now that the country has up and died, the time for patriotism is done. We could fight for honor, but where is the honor in getting your face chewed off? Am I right? We could fight to defend our homes, our families, but they're all gone too. There's nothing left but the basics now. It's a truth that a soldier will still fight for his girl and you Ms Rivers are the finest girl I've laid my eyes on in a long time." His hand went from her chin to her shoulder and then caressed gently down her arm.

"You're no better than those others!" she cried backing away. Her anger only made him chuckle.

"Fine," he said heading for the door. "Good luck."

How he said this perplexed her and scared her at the same time; she asked, "Why do you say it like that?"

"Because until you realize that this world has become a world of *take*, then you're going to need all the luck you can get." He laughed and then laid his head on the door. "There'll be no more roses or boxes of candy for you. The men who survive this are going to be men who take what they want, not some hippy-dippy liberal, peace-assholes. So someone is going to *take* what you have, or you can make the smart choice and give it away. Just make sure you give it to the right man. A man who can protect you."

"Like a colonel of infantry?" she asked breathlessly, and again her hands stole to her chest covering herself in a pathetic attempt at protection.

"Is there anyone who could protect you better?" he asked, opening her front door. "Or feed you better? Or treat you better? All I'm asking is that you think about it. The choice is yours. I'm not a man who will take when there is a better option," he said and left her reeling.

Chapter 13

Ram

Devore, California

For the last who knew how many days, Ram had been DEA in name only. He wasn't even attached to Homeland Security or the US Army for that matter. He had been a man who stood shoulder-to-shoulder with other men trying to stop what had felt like an infinite number of undead.

They had failed. The Army just seemed to disintegrate as a cohesive force—uniformed men still fought with honor and died under the claws and rending teeth, or in a delirium of fever, however units had dissolved in the chaos, and logistics had broken down. Some places had a comfortable amount of ammunition while others were counting every bullet and waiting to fire until the stiffs were at point blank range.

Eventually, when Glendora, Walnut, and San Bernardino fell in successive days, the remaining men realized that Los Angeles was lost. Gradually some eight-thousand pulled back to Devore, which was the furthest edge of the furthest suburb of L.A. There I-215 joined I-15 in a valley that was less than half a mile wide.

So far the zombies weren't noted as mountain climbers; like running water, they followed the path of least resistance and so Ram and the men around him, despite their increasing exhaustion, dug in all across the face of the valley and beat off successive waves of undead. Sometimes the battles were enough to break a man and a number went screaming off into the night or cowered in their holes and refused to even look up at their oncoming death.

And still the rest fought on. Stinking bodies lay in huge rotting mounds before the men. The mounds were covered in an undulating black shimmer; these were millions of flies, eating the dead. They were the first inclination that another attack was coming. They'd rise up in huge buzzing cloud that couldn't be pierced by the sharpest eye.

Now, after days of fighting, Ram felt something give within him. It started small, like an internal, mental hiccup; just a little nothing that had him pausing like a statue, unthinking and unmoving. This grew until he felt himself grimacing for no reason or waking up from a staring contest with a distant rock. By sundown, when the zombies began to gather again, he found that his chest was aching and that breathing had started to be an effort.

"Hey...hey, I gotta take a dump," he announced suddenly to the men around him. Shaking uncontrollably, he got up in a hurry, and that was when one of them grabbed him.

"Leave your ammo," the man said. He was one of the older men and he had eyes that knew much.

Ram shook him off. "I'm just taking a dump," he lied. He had to go alright, very badly, but after he had squatted behind a car for a few minutes and cleaned himself up, he didn't go back to where he had been fighting. As the firing commenced all along the line, he went up into the steep hills. He just walked away in a sweat, and although he tried, he couldn't stop his own traitorous feet.

As he climbed he muttered excuses to himself which were pitiful even to his own ears. Atop the first ridge he turned to look back at the one-sided battle and almost screamed: "I can't do it anymore. I can't! I need a break. That's all I need. Just a little one and then I'll be good to go. Just a break and then I'll be back."

He wasn't coming back. He had snapped. Whether it was shell shock, or posttraumatic stress disorder he didn't know. He just knew that he couldn't stop his hands from shaking, while tears were on the verge for no reason.

Without really knowing where he was going he climbed one ridge and then another and was tromping down a long hill when he saw below him a rugged trail and upon it tens of thousands of zombies stumbled and shambled. Even in the dim light, he could see them stretching far into the distance and he stared at them with gritty eyes and a brain slowed by unbelievable stress and days on end of sleep deprivation.

The trail they were following hooked off to the left and gradually he came to realize that if it continued in that direction it would eventually cut across I-15—it would cut off the line of retreat of the men he had just left. That was a horrible thought, yet the idea of going back, of trudging over all those hills and facing all those zombies left him with a dark dread that he hadn't felt since all of this started.

Ram knew in his gut that if he went back he would die. There were just too many of the creatures and there were just too few men to stop them, and the men had too few bullets. It was a certainty in his broken mind.

Yet could he leave them to die? No answer came to him. He stood there with his hand on a pine tree, feeling the sharp bark and no answer came to him. His courage, which had been that of a lion for so long had left him completely, and now his sense of duty was unraveling as well, because what did any of it matter? They were all going to die eventually and that eventually was fast upon them.

"Everyone's going to die," he whispered, completely forgetting the vial of blood in his pocket, and the very existence of the CDC for that matter. His world had been narrowed: it was filled with immediacy of death and the big picture eluded him. Just then his mind could only comprehend: himself, the river of zombies and the men he had left to die—in that order.

A sudden spurt of gunfire to the northwest made him turn in that direction. "There," he said, relaxing and feeling ill at the same time. "They know now. They got their warning."

And just as his sense of duty died with that rationalization he saw a gap in the ragged lines of zombies.

Like a cat he slunk down the hill, hiding behind bush and tree, feeling crazy for approaching the things. "There— there's the gap," he muttered and then raced across the road and sprinted up the hill on the other side. His breath was a storm in his ears and he was sure a thousand of the beasts had heard him, but it was only a few—twenty or thirty that came after him.

Though he might not have been a sprinter, Ram could run for miles without let up, but, thankfully, the things turned aside when he cleared a hill and was out of sight.

That night was the first he spent alone since the sixth of October, when he found a note from his girlfriend. She had gone back to Mexico; a huge mistake in his eyes. It was smart to flee the city, but Mexico was suicide.

Ram walked in the dark until he realized that moving, stumbling about in his exhaustion, making a racket that could be heard for miles, was worse than just sitting still. He stopped immediately, lay down and covered himself with some branches and slept like he hadn't for days on end. Voices woke him when the sun was high overhead.

He sat up with his M16 in hand. It hadn't started out as his; he had picked up the assault rifle just as soon as the opportunity presented. It had been four days before, as they had taken a stand at Glendora. His unit had been holed up in an elementary school and had decided to use the fencing surrounding the building as a way to funnel the stiffs at them in an orderly manner. With the machine gun chattering away, cutting them down as they came through the gate, more zombies had spread out and covered the fence like a wall full of roaches. Someone had screamed "charge" and half the unit had rushed forward with knives and makeshift spears. They had stabbed through the chain-link fencing making a mess of the zombies and killing many.

A man came running up late. He had a spent M16 with a bayonet attached and just as he thrust it once the whole section of fencing came down pinning him. Ram and a few others next to him were trapped as well. The zombies rushed forward and it was the worst moments of Ram's life. Crushed beneath the metal and the monsters as they were, they couldn't defend themselves and the dead feasted. Ram was saved for a second when the zombie above him was bowled over by others pushing from the rear.

The man with the empty M16 wasn't so lucky. He was screaming in a high-pitched wail as his face was being eaten away and more zombies came to feast—and then a large one, one that used to be a muscle bound man, pushed aside the squirming mass and exposed Ram. The beast dropped to his knees with a strange gleeful hungry look on its grey face and opened its mouth revealing yellow teeth, from which blood dropped. It leaned down to bite Ram, but just then the M240 pivoted in their direction.

Blazing lead raced above Ram's face, missing him by inches, and struck the zombie atop him, tearing off chunks of flesh and bone and brain. The creature fell back and others came forward to be shredded just as the first had been. Ram squirmed and kicked himself free and then he was crawling for his life. Next to him was the man with the M16. Though he had only a single eye left to his face he was crying; the rest of him looked like bleeding hamburger.

Ram couldn't look in his direction except to shoot him once in the head. It was a mercy he told himself in that second when the blast echoed in his ears…and then he took the man's rifle.

Now, four days later, as he sighted down the length of the black weapon at six men walking far too casually, he couldn't remember where he'd got the gun. He remembered being trapped under the fence, but very little of what had happened before or since.

He did remember these men coming toward him, not specifically, just their type. Like Ram, they were Hispanic, but that was where any resemblance ended. They were six walking stereotypes: gangbangers with moronic neck tattoos, inked knuckles and even worse, they were still wearing their gang colors despite that their city had been overrun with the undead.

Regardless of this Ram hurried forward. He'd been alone for a little more than nine hours and already he missed being around people. With his weapon pointed to the sky, he came to them and immediately despised them, while they distrusted him. Still they accepted him, while he tolerated them.

The alternative was to be alone in a land of death.

In the past, in the *before*, Ram had contemplated the different forms death could take: bullets, fire, drowning, heart attack. Fire had always seemed the worst, but now after seeing what he'd seen, he knew he could embrace a death by fire. The trick, he thought, was to just accept it and breathe deeply, letting the flames and the heat destroy his lungs.

It was these thoughts and the nagging surety of his approaching death, which allowed him to tolerate the gang-bangers. They were ill mannered, unkempt, and completely undisciplined. They traveled northeast with little thought as to their destination and they argued amongst themselves to distraction.

Still, they were people and Ram felt his mind coalescing again into something that was vaguely familiar. He even laughed with them once or twice. It was strange to smile after such a long time of dealing only in death, and he touched his face and his teeth as if it were his first smile. Though he still wasn't close to being his old self and this was evidenced when the sun went down and a girl joined the group.

She was a hood-rat out of Compton and how she had managed to get as far as she had, he never found out. They could hear her out in the dark creeping close as if she couldn't tell which was the greater danger to her, the zombies or the gang-bangers.

"Hey? You got sumtin to eat?" she asked from the

supposed safety of a shrub.

One of the bangers grabbed his crotch and said, "Yeah right here. It's all you can eat, baby."

This should've been warning enough, but she came closer and asked, "What's that you got there?" The seven of them were sharing a large can of pumpkin pie filling. A few weeks earlier Ram would have laughed at the idea, now he made sure his spoon was heaping before he passed the can on to the next guy.

The girl was maybe eighteen. She came forward with her large brown eyes staring about nervously, reminding Ram of a doe stepping lightly through a forest. She had nothing but the clothes on her back, and when she came and knelt she was tense as if ready to flee, but it was too late for that and everyone knew it.

The bangers let her eat with them and as she did they began to paw at her and although she grew angry and pushed their hands away, she accepted what was happening. What choice did she have? They were all armed to the teeth and she had nowhere to go.

For the most part the girl was silent when they took their turns with her, only grunting if the man on top of her was particularly rough. She only spoke once, when the last guy had his turn and seemed to take too long. "What you waitin for?"

This caused the others to laugh and one of them turned to Ram. "What about you, Ese?" Since he hadn't volunteered a name, they called him Ese.

"I'm good," he replied. His hand had been on his M16 the entire time, yet he hadn't been anywhere near to firing it. Things were different now. Right and wrong had been turned on its head. What did he owe this girl? If zombies came he would kill them for her. And he'd share his food. But would he risk his life for her because she didn't have the sense to stay away? He knew, just as she did, what sort of men these gang-bangers had been in the old days, and still were.

"I'll go first next time," he lied. In a nest of her clothes, the girl laid on her back, shaking and looking up at the stars. "Why don't you give her a drink," Ram said to the man closest to her.

"Shit. She can get her own," the man said, then tipped a water bottle back and emptied it into his mouth.

The night passed and no one guarded the girl, or even much looked at her. She could've run away at any time. Instead she stuck close to the men who raped her and when one made a joke at Ram's expense she laughed harder than the rest. He was weak in her eyes. A real man, a man in this new world, would've done whatever he wanted with her.

On some level she understood the new fundamentals better than any of them. There were no laws anymore. Might made right and any man who was too weak to take what he wanted would be too weak to protect her. She despised him for his weakness.

He didn't really care, not just then; in fact he was hard pressed to find anything he did care about. At some point he found the last vial of blood he had taken from the terrorist and after looking at it he nearly tossed it away. To him the CDC was in another world and maybe even another time, though in the end he stuck it back where he'd found it.

They walked until nearly midday when the group found a pile of cars jumbled at the intersection of two country roads. One of the cars had a case of bottled water and a few bags of groceries in the trunk. Still without discipline, they gorged themselves and drank greedily, which sparked their libidos again. One grabbed the girl and rubbed up against her and she rolled her eyes as if they were asking her to sweep the kitchen the floor.

"How bout I just blow you guys? My puss hurts from last night," she said. They took their turns and Ram turned away.

"What are you some sort of fudge-packer?" one of the bangers asked.

"Naw," he said over his shoulder. "She didn't look so clean last night and in the light it hasn't gotten any better. And besides I was never into hood-rats."

"Don't like the sistas? You're missing out."

"Sure I am," he said to himself as he went to the other cars and checked them. One, a Subaru Outback, was still drivable, but it was out of gas, though this was nothing for someone as capable as he was. He yanked out a hose from one of the disabled cars and used it to siphon gas into a bucket he had scrounged.

When they were done with girl, they were too tired and full to go on. Ram nearly left them. He had a car and a gun, but he would be alone. That night the girl stuck close to the biggest of the gang-bangers and Ram slept in the Outback alone.

The next morning they crammed in the car and headed off, and still none of them knew where they were going. They were all just happy that there weren't many zombies about.

Almost mid-way between Los Angeles and Las Vegas along Interstate 15, sits the dusty little town of Baker, California. In the last census there were a little more than seven-hundred souls residing there but unlike everywhere else in America, that number had crept upward in the past few weeks.

It was a strange fact given that the town is bordered by the Mojave Desert to the south and Death Valley to the north, and that for the last ten days the sun had blistered down with average temperatures over ninety degrees, and that not a drop of rain had fallen in three weeks.

It hardly seemed like a place worth fighting for, yet for some insane reason the people of Baker clung to their slice of hell on earth with a tenacity that rimmed close to insanity.

Ram and his little group came across the first sign: "Baker Closed" twenty miles earlier and had thought little of it. And then: "Warning Baker Closed" a few miles later.

Finally, just before an exit for a place called Zzyzx they saw a number of bed-sheets arranged and spray-painted with the warning: Trespassers will be shot. Detour.

It was here that they had to deal with their first real traffic since leaving L.A. That dead city had been choked with cars and overrun with zombies, but after that the roads were clear, save, of course for more of the unending zombies. These Ram took a perverse pleasure in hitting with the Outback until the two bangers who were forced to ride on top because of the lack of room, began to complain.

Ram hadn't planned on taking the detour, however the highway had been purposefully blocked. Cars were stacked one on top of each other and behind them were men with guns.

One of them yelled, "Move on."

They were about forty yards away and Ram yelled, "Do you have any gas or water?"

"Depends on what you have to trade."

They had little beside their guns and no one was willing to give up their guns—that was the same as suicide. The bangers looked at each other and then to the girl. "No!" she cried. "You can't trade me for some fuckin water."

Her attitude shocked Ram. "You'd rather stay with us and get raped every night? You're messed in the head."

"What do you think they'll do to me in there?" she asked, getting loud. She then squinted at the cars and the men. "Sides, they ain't gonna last no how. Them zombies gonna roll right over all this."

It seemed patently true, but that didn't stop the bangers from turning to Ram. "See what they'll trade for her."

Chapter 14

Neil

Montclair New Jersey

For days on end Neil hoarded his food and kept his water jugs filled. He had six candles and he made them last by sleeping when the sun set and waking when it rose. Fearing the coming winter he pulled his mattress into the living room and broke apart his bed-frame for firewood, though as yet he was too afraid to use his fireplace, worried that it would attract more of the monsters.

He then barricaded his doors and shuttered his windows, and turned his broom into a spear, although afterwards he was perturbed because he had a made a mess and had nothing to clean it up with.

Zombies were a nuisance at first, coming along Grove Street in dribs and drabs, and he assumed that the Hudson River was holding back the millions in the city, and he was right. Those that went into the water off Manhattan usually came ashore in south Jersey where humans had mostly ceased to exist.

The great majority of the undead went north and crossed over the few remaining bridges at a rate of three-thousand-an-hour. In the prior two weeks more than a million had surged against the dug in army which was trying to hold the quarantine in place. Many turned aside, following the path of least resistance, looking for easier prey. They swept down New Jersey and their numbers proved too great for most.

Only the sturdiest doors and windows could keep out the voracious mob. Thankfully Neil possessed such heavy doors and windows. Out of fear of break-ins and the fact that he was against guns, he had long ago changed out his originals.

He had suggested to Randal Cattau, whose house was corner-on to his, that he do the same, but Randal hadn't taken Neil's advice and now his family was all dead. In dread fascination Neil had watched from his upstairs guest room as the zombies had swarmed all over the streets and lawns of his suburbia. They banged on doors and punched windows, until the Cattau's front bay window gave and then they poured in by the dozens. Then there was only screaming.

Mrs. Cattau and one of her three daughters became zombies. They had been horribly chewed upon and the girl could barely walk there was so little left to her. The others had been far too damaged to come back, or so Neil guessed.

The gathering had come for him as well, many, many times. When it happened, once or twice a day for the last week, he would retreat up to his attic and sit there clutching his stick, wondering about the possibility of suicide and wishing he had a gun. Tucked away as he was, there wasn't much chance the monsters would get at him, yet he knew that if they got in once he would never be safe and that had him also thinking about trying to make a run for the safety of the army.

Surely they would let him through the lines. After all if they weren't going to protect the American people then what the hell were they doing?

The one problem with the idea was that every day the sound of the guns firing seemed to come from further away and eventually they ceased altogether. This stopped his planning dead in its tracks and he gave up on the idea until two days later.

His guest bedroom afforded him the best view of Grove Street and he liked to take his meals there when the zombies weren't out in full force. That day his lunch consisted of cold New England clam chowder—it wasn't bad if he took tiny spoonfuls, anything more made him want to gag. As he ate he watched the littlest Cattau zombie trying to get at a cat who sat just out of its reach in a tree. Cats seemed to have multiplied since the zombie plague had descended on the world. They were everywhere and, unlike dogs, Neil had yet to see one zombiefied.

He had never cared for any animal in a pet sense, but just then he was lonely so he rooted for the cat to live. And this seemed very likely because the derelict zombie girl turned away and stared at something out of Neil's line of sight. Even standing didn't help. Whatever the zombie was seeing was on Neil's side of the street.

Then he heard a tapping on wood and a little voice whispering, "Hello? Can you let me in? There's zombies out here."

Neil ran to another room that had a better view, and there outside the Krauthammer's front door was a girl of maybe sixteen, knocking gently.

Neil raised his window and whispered to her, "There's a zombie right over there."

"I know! That's why I need in."

Neil pointed to the back of his house and then ran downstairs to let her in. He expected gratitude, but instead he got a pistol pointed square in his face when the girl stepped across his threshold.

"Thanks," she said without the least hint of nervousness. "Who you got in here with you? Wife? Kids? Gay lover?" This last she said after giving his neat attire a glance.

"I'm not gay," he said petulantly. "And there's no one here but me."

"Are you sure?"

For some reason the gun wasn't scaring him as much as he figured it would and he allowed his anger to show. "Don't you think I'd know if I was gay? Trust me, I like women. I like boobies and..."

"I meant are you sure you're here alone? I don't want any surprises. People get killed that way, or worse."

"Oh. No it's just me. And sorry about the boobie thing.

It's just when you're not the most masculine man around people make so many assumptions. And then..."

She raised the gun to his face and said, "Shut up and show me where your food is."

"You're robbing me?"

"Duh!" she answered. "Now, turn around and don't be stupid, because I swear I'll put a hole in you." She then dug in her pocket and pulled out a walkie-talkie. "Did you see which house I went in? It was the one with the green shutters."

Her radio squawked and a quiet voice said, "Yeah, but we got a few stiffs coming this way. Leave the back door unlocked and I'll be in soon. Over."

The girl, a Goth chick dressed all in black with short spiky hair, looked around, though her gun never wavered. She went through his cupboards while keeping one eye on him and didn't seem to care that he still had his sharpened broom handle in his hands. He held it tightly as though he thought the girl would take it from him.

A minute later a brutish man came through the back door, he had a shotgun and pointed it at Neil. "Is it just him? Did you check?"

She shook her head and pointed at the sink. "One cup. One dish. He's all alone and he's got some choice stuff. Look, hot cocoa."

The man unslung a large empty duffel bag from his back and started taking Neil's food, pulling down the neatly stacked cans in a rush. "What about his car?"

The girl shrugged. "He looks like a Prius-fag." When Neil dropped his eyes she laughed. "I can pick em. And no guns either. Don't worry, Mister we won't take your stick."

"Are you going to leave me any food?" Neil asked.

"This can of asparagus," the man said and tossed the can to Neil. "And this squash, blech."

In the end they left him four cans total and when they slunk back out into the dangerous jungle that Jersey had become, Neil cried. He didn't know how to live in the world anymore. With his food gone he didn't think he would make it for very long in his hermetically sealed house either. He cried because he was a fool and a coward, and he was lonely and so very depressed. Yet for all that, he cried for less than a minute and then, still sniffling and with damp eyes, he went back to his guest room and picking up his bowl, he watched as the pair worked their way down the street, looking for suckers to open their doors. The girl would go along acting all scared while the young man hung back in a big black truck that looked as though it could squish any zombie that got in its way.

They were out of sight before Neil asked a question that had been bothering him in the back of his mind: "Why wasn't the girl scared?" She was smaller even than Neil and her pistol wasn't some "Dirty Harry" piece of hand artillery, either. It was little enough to fit her small palm.

Then what was it that made her so fearless?

Why didn't the zombies scare her and how could she rob people so easily when she was little more than a kid? What made her so special? Was she special because she was so courageous? Or was she courageous because she was special?

Neil wiped his eyes and decided somewhat rashly to go outside, wondering if by acting bravely he would actually become brave. He stepped boldly from his back door. Then immediately hid behind his rhododendrons; there was a pack of zombies shuffling by, however they were going away from him and he fought the temptation to run back inside.

After a few minutes they were far enough away that he was able to come out of his hiding place. Looking up and down the street, he felt suddenly strong over his tiny victory—not running away *was* a victory, Neil assured himself. Proudly, he went along the side of his house breathing deeply the autumn air.

"Now what?" he asked aloud. A few zombies were out,

pecking about, and he felt stronger still when he decided to turn his back on them and walk across to his neighbors the Krauthammer's. He hadn't heard anything from them for a couple of days and now he knew why: their front door was open.

He glanced in, though when he heard something moving about he pulled back.

And then he heard a leaf crunch behind him and he spun and there was the little Cattau girl zombie. Neil made a noise and began to run for his back door, but then something gripped him around his heart.

There wasn't any future left in his house. His future had been stolen from him. Yet what kind of future had it been? One of slinking around in perpetual fear? That wasn't living! Neil Martin stopped running and turned, deciding to fight for the first time in his life.

It wasn't much of a heroic battle. As small as he was, he was still twice the size of the zombie-girl, yet he was shocked when he stabbed her in the chest with his makeshift spear and she kept coming, sliding herself up the smooth wood of the broom handle.

In desperation he swung his end of the broom handle and with her weight suddenly shifting outward she slid off the stick and fell into the street. Next Neil tried to knock her upside the head with the silly spear. He cracked her a good one and he felt bone give; unfortunately his spear also split in two.

Now he was defenseless and the girl was getting up again. Neil stared around him and even took a cowardly step back toward his house when he caught sight of one Mr. Krauthammer's garden gnomes. A strange fury overcame him just then. It was part anger over his situation and part sadness for poor Mr. Krauthammer. And then in a rage he rushed to the gnome and used it to dash the little zombie's brains in.

She went down like the dead thing she was and Neil

raised the gnome with a battle cry in his throat, only to choke on it. The zombies that had gone down the street earlier had turned around and now he saw there was a good chance that they would beat him in a race to his door if he dared to go back that way.

He didn't. Neil's daring had left him and he ran the other way, down Grove Street. He ran, keeping low, close to the hedges because there were other zombies out. Mostly they seemed oblivious of him and so he kept going, yet where he was going he didn't know, not until he saw the big black monster truck rumbling on the side of the road a block ahead.

As he watched he saw the same brute of a man who had robbed him only fifteen minutes earlier get out with an empty bag on his back and a shotgun in his hand. And then Neil had a wild idea.

He couldn't go back. Even if he could get into his house safely, what then? There was only going forward and that meant he was going to have to take some chances. Keeping even lower Neil scurried down the block until he heard the zombies behind him. He could hear their odd grunting and their slapping feet so, with his heart in his throat, he gave up any notion of sneaking and took off at a sprint, running straight for the truck, praying that the door would open.

It did! With a mad, cackling laugh he climbed up into the beast of a vehicle and set himself behind a wheel that was wider across than he was. Reverting momentarily to his former self, he adjusted the seat and checked the mirrors before driving off, bowling over a pair of zombies in his path and making a retching noise in his throat as he did so.

Chapter 15

Eric

New York City

The chopper banked over the Hudson River and Eric puked into the water rushing below. It was his second time. Some of the soldiers with him chuckled, though they were grey in the face themselves. For them it wasn't from airsickness.

Normal combat was a strain on the human psyche, fighting the undead, however took a toll that couldn't be measured. Hearing the thump of bullets striking a man and seeing him keep coming on and on had turned these soldiers old before their time. Still they were trained and experienced, and they handled their weapons with a sureness that Eric Reidy found comforting. His own ability was in such doubt that he wasn't allowed his ammunition until they landed. They were afraid he would set his pistol off by accident and kill the chopper.

The Blackhawk already seemed to have something wrong with it. It flared up and down, while at times it flew sideways and always Eric clung to the harness that barely kept him inside with a desperation that had his muscles vibrating.

Finally the lieutenant in charge of the operation, a tall black man with sad eyes, spoke into his headset, "Thunderbolt, cut the nap of the earth shit. No one's got missile lock on you. All you're doing is making the Doc queasy and it isn't pretty."

For Eric, queasy had been thirty minutes before at lift off...he was well past queasy. Thankfully the helicopter's flight path flattened and they made straight for mid-town Manhattan.

"One more time," Lieutenant Mathers yelled above the

noise of the wind and the engine. "We can't fast-rope or rappel down so we're going to land across the street from the hotel on another building. If for some reason we get turned around it's just to the east. East, you hear me? Across a two-lane road with, like hedges and shit running between. If you cross a street that doesn't have hedges you're on the wrong street and you're fucked, ok?"

The men nodded and one shook Eric's shoulder and said, "Thanks Doc. I hate rappelling. Getting from point A to point B by the quickest route is such a drag, right?"

Knowing he was being made fun of didn't help Eric's nausea. It wasn't his fault he had never learned to rappel out of a hovering Blackhawk. Still, as one of the boys, Eric gave the soldier a thin smile anyway.

"Zip it, Slim," the lieutenant warned. "The mission is what it is. We cross the street and go up to room 4312 and, yes, that's the 43rd floor."

"Shit," the M240 gunner swore. His was the heaviest weapon and everyone knew it would be a bitch to climb that many stairs toting a machine gun.

"We'll make sure the Doc helps you out, Smitty," Mathers said. "He's travelling pretty light, he can carry some ammo. So we hit the room, get whatever we can lay our hands on and get out. If there are stiffs we go down the east-side stairwell and if we have to loop around a couple of blocks, we do it. Remember that firing our weapons is the last thing we want to do."

Just then the chopper banked around the Empire State Building and the sight of it stopped all conversation. One full side of skyscraper was blackened and crumbling, while grey smoke drifted up out of it making it look like a spent birthday candle. Then they were past the horrible sight and flying over a city of the dead.

Too quickly for Eric's liking, the chopper slowed and the men tensed. Eric was beyond tense. He actually thought he might soil himself right there in the chopper. The feeling was close to becoming a reality when the nose of the craft flared up slightly, but then, with a gentle thump they landed.

"Go!" Slim ordered from behind Eric, who hadn't moved as had everyone else. With shaking hands he unbuckled his harness and then was out in the cold, as air pushed down at him from the churning blades above. They hustled to a roof access point and discovered it locked. A soldier with the name of Baer took a heavy sledge to the door and almost dashed in Eric's face as he brought it back: Slim grabbed Eric from behind and pulled him away just in time.

"Stand back, damn it," Mathers yelled, unnecessarily— Eric was now a dozen feet away with Slim holding his pack as though he were holding a dog's leash. Like everyone else, the lieutenant was keyed up; stress was on his brown face twisting it into angry lines.

The door took forever to come open and each strike was like ringing a dinner bell. "Hey, can I have my ammo?" Eric asked, suddenly, remembering that he was basically unarmed without his bullets.

Mathers paused, trying to think of a reason not to give up the ammo, but then as the door opened and the first of the zombies came hurrying forward ready to eat, the officer handed over three thin magazines for Eric's M9 Beretta.

Baer dispatched the first stiff using the sledgehammer, while the other men took out the remaining three zombies with fixed bayonets. That there were only four of the beasts seemed to bode well for their mission.

There were seven soldiers total—a number that did not include Eric of course—and they walked and fought as a team, talking among themselves in code or in plain English, depending. It didn't take long for Eric to realize that when they spoke of baggage they meant him. Baggage was exactly how they treated him, passing him from man-to-man, pushing or pulling as needed to get him out of the way. This wasn't bad in the dark of the stairs, because the flicking flashlights only added to his fright and he was happy to know the men were right there, however when they were still 20-stories up and they found the stairwell crammed with groaning bodies of the undead coming up to get them it was not at all good to be passed to the back of the line.

With their flashlights all pointed forward, the men ran back up the stairs, leaving Eric struggling to catch up in a panic. He could hear the beasts coming fast, letting out low groans that drew closer and closer in the dark.

The soldiers took the first door they came upon and when it opened there was a cry from above and then firing. Something fell into Eric, clawing at his suit. At first he thought it was Slim, hit by friendly fire, but then as a beam of light swept him, he saw it was a zombie; what once had been a bike messenger. The creature had been right next to him on the stairs with only the dark saving him! And there were more zombies just behind him.

Eric pointed his gun at the nearest grey-faced beast and clicked on an empty chamber—although he had sunk the clip into the butt of the weapon he hadn't known to chamber a round. Hands reached for him and he could feel them on his suit and then there were explosions of light and the closest zombies fell back, shedding blood and brain.

Slim had him by the pack once again and screamed something that didn't register on Eric who felt partially deaf and totally mentally paralyzed. He still couldn't get over the fact that there had been a zombie right next to him for two flights of stairs!

They passed through to the next floor and ran on while a redheaded soldier began barricading the door behind. "Leave it!" Mathers ordered. Eric didn't turn to see if the man had obeyed. He ran with everyone else. As unencumbered as he was, Eric gradually pulled ahead wondering why they weren't sprinting at top speed. In his mind they should've jettisoned all the bulky weapons and ammo, but he wasn't thinking straight. His thoughts were on the Blackhawk and not on the mission.

The men were more focused.

Their running was not a panicked sprint but a jog designed to eat up the distance between them and their objective without leaving them exhausted. They crossed all the way through the building, found the far staircase and began to descend once again with Eric in tow. This stairwell had but a single confused zombie trapped within it. They found it at the bottom and killed it quickly.

Exiting the stairs, the squad arrived in an open lobby where the floor was of crushed glass and the zombies wandered blankly not yet aware of them. They could see the Waldorf sitting just across the street.

"Looks like we just have to make a run for it," Mathers said. He took the sledgehammer to use both as a weapon and to open doors. Then he unslung a belt of ammunition that Baer had strung around his neck and put it on Eric's shoulders.

"That's better," Baer remarked.

Eric didn't think so. The bullets were heavy and swung awkwardly; they did remind him of something. Just as the men were about to take off in a sprint he said, "Wait! My gun doesn't work." He held it out and Slim took all of four seconds to see the problem.

"You gotta jack the slide, asshole," he said. Though he had cursed it was not out of contempt. All of them called each other such affectionate names. "Or when you run dry, stick a new mag in here and then press this gizmo on the side. You'll be good to go."

"Now, unless Doc needs help working his fucking zipper, it's time to go," Mathers announced. Without looking back, the squad ran onto the streets of New York where the stiffs woke to their presence before they got five feet. A Private First Class named Heddles, pointed wordlessly, straight ahead: the hotel seemed suddenly more like a theater letting out the 2pm matinee. Dozens of the undead were flooding down from the lobby.

"Side door!" Mathers yelled, though he only did so out of excitement. The city of the dead was eerily silent and his words echoed strangely in a way that was worse than the zombies.

As one, the squad turned and sped to the right. All along the block, out of every window and door, came zombies alerted in some unfathomable fashion to the presence of running meat. With their last resort upon them so soon the men in front cleared the sidewalk of the dead with a rattle of small arms fire that must have alerted half the city to their position.

And if that didn't do it, Slim yelled, "Grenade at our six!" A second later an explosion shook the very air and made Eric's lungs spasm. When he looked back he saw the city street littered with body parts and sprayed with blood. Yet still the mangled corpses crawled or dragged themselves on, only to be trampled by more of their brothers and sisters.

Mathers swung into a side entrance to the hotel, running past stiffs that were just becoming aware; these closed in fast and Eric shot his first. It was the strangest feeling. After all the gunfire and the explosion he thought that his gun would be equally loud and that its kick would tear the gun from his sweating hand. Instead he barely felt the thing jump beneath his finger, and if there was a noise he didn't hear it. He shot a second time, and then a third before Heddles grabbed him by the neck just as they gained the stairwell. "Aim for the fucking head! You're just wasting ammo."

"Right. Sorry," Eric said.

"Don't be sorry, Doc," Heddles replied. "Just aim for the head. You're doing good." The words cheered him for the briefest moment and then a second grenade went off behind them, the vibrations of it running along the railing beneath his hand. "A little fucking warning next time!" Heddles cried.

"Stop your bitchin," Mathers said. "Just watch our six

and don't let the Doc get killed. Not until we get to that room."

"Was that a joke?" Eric asked, breathlessly. He was a doughy man who had in the past used his position to dine out far too regularly; and now he was feeling the effects.

"Yeah, don't get your panties in a bunch," Slim said over his shoulder. "And keep up. We got another thirty-five stories to go."

Thankfully the zombies had been stymied by the shut door below so that the squad was free to toil upwards unmolested. At the thirtieth floor Eric thought he would black out and just sat rubbing his legs until the lieutenant called a general halt.

"This is stupid," another PFC said. "We shouldn't be resting. You know the stiffs aren't."

Baer punched him in the arm sharply, while Slim chucked a bottle cap at him. Even Mathers didn't agree. "We need to be fresh as we can be. Let's get those mags topped off while we rest."

They sat for ten minutes before they pushed on again. Up and up, all the way to the 43rd floor and then they rested again. With a deep breath, Mathers cracked the stairway door, only to shut it right away.

"We got stiffs. Smitty clear 'em out."

The 240 gunner went to the door and let his weapon do its horrendous work and while the butchery went on Eric sank back clutching his ears against the noise. He wasn't the only one; each bullet seemed like a pickaxe sinking into his ear canal. Then the firing ceased except as an echo in his head and the soldiers moved out, walking crouched with their bodies held tight and their guns facing outward, covering every door. Eric went in the middle of the pack and was glad for it.

"Here we are," Lieutenant Mathers said, gripping the sledge in both hands. "Get my back, Heddles." Two swings of the hammer and the door fell in. A zombie was right there and the ginger soldier shot it through the face.

"Is that your guy?" Slim asked. It was a joke that Eric didn't get until he saw the state of the man's face. There hadn't been much of it left even before the bullet had shattered it.

Still it wasn't Yuri. "No, this guy is too fat. My guy was a rail. Can I get one of the soldiers to check his pockets? We need to collect everything."

"What everything?" Mathers asked with an edge to his voice. He raised his hands at the empty room. It was beautifully appointed; plush in every way, but clearly empty save for one raw smelling corpse.

"Mother fucker," Heddles griped opening up the closets and the drawers and finding nothing. Not even a stray sock. "We came all this way for one worthless zombie? What a fucking waste of time. And now we got to fight our way out again. Damn it!"

"It's not a complete waste," Slim said, kneeling down in front of the mini-fridge. "We got a stocked bar. Warm beer is better than no beer. Can we, Sir?"

"Drink up," Mathers replied. "Two drinks maximum. Doc you can watch the fucking door."

A soldier tossed Eric a cell phone he had found and said, "It's as dead as this mission." He then held up a driver's license. "Barry Ciccereli from Jersey City. There ain't no luggage here; probably coming to get in a quickie before the apocalypse hit. What an idiot."

Eric took the license and went to the door to look out as the soldiers drank. He didn't want to drink. He wanted to go back to the CDC, put on his lab coat and look important until the real scientists found a cure, or a vaccine, or a way to kill the monsters from afar. What he didn't want to do is go back down into those streets.

The squad sat about and drank, though they weren't in the least as relaxed and composed as they tried to pass themselves off as. They knew that getting out was going to be far worse than coming in.

"We'll take the north exit onto 51st street," Mathers told them, sipping at a tiny bottle of Jack and making a face with each sip. "A left will lead us to Park Ave and right across the street is where we want to go. The only problem is I'm not sure how to get to that exit."

This didn't sit well with the men, however no one knew any better than the lieutenant so when they had finished their drinks, the squad stood, checked their weapons and went back into the hall. Mathers led them to the next corridor and tried the first staircase he came to. It was filled with stiffs. They went back to the one they had ascended and took it forty-one stories down to the second level.

"This should get us to the lobby," he explained, taking a moment to wipe the sweat from his face. "If anything happens, head north and find any way out. Remember, speed is our best defense."

The door did lead to a concourse that was open enough to suggest they could wind their way through restaurants and bars and little shops to the other side of the building. At first the way seemed promising, however their obvious humanity soon attracted the wrong attention. Stiffs, some still in a state of undress, as if they had been trying on new clothes, came at them. The squad sprinted away, which only drew more eyes. Within a minute the lieutenant had to fire his pistol twice to clear the way in front and then the day descended into mayhem and screams. Zombies came at a shambling run from every direction.

"Keep your three clear," Slim advised. "I've got your six."

"What three?" Eric cried. He shot at a zombie's head, missed and shot a second time. This one hit and the beast collapsed down onto a gilded French chaise as if it had just had a very long day at the office and wanted to take a load off.

"Yes. That's your three," Slim yelled over the sound of

the guns banging away. "You got your right. Smitty has your left, you see?"

"Keep my..." Eric shot another stiff, this one through the neck, though it seemed to do the trick. "...My three clear." If it were only so easy.

They came to a lounge spread across two levels and everywhere there were tables overturned and chairs knocked over, and, of course, the place was thick with zombies.

Heddles, just in front of Eric, went down under a mass of them when his weapon took the wrong moment to jam. Mad with fear, Heddles kicked and screamed at the stiffs. Eric shot two of them, but then his trigger bit on nothing. The scientist clawed at his pocket, desperate to get a new a magazine out, but the stiffs were all over Heddles before he found it. The man screamed for help in a terrified voice, however his squad mates were fighting six separate battles.

Eric only had the single pistol that he couldn't quite get working. His fumbling fingers did not possess the muscle memory of a real infantryman and he had to flee with the pistol in one hand and the magazine in the other while Heddles screamed in such a way as to nearly crack Eric's mind.

He wasn't the only one who fled; four others took to their heels with him and since Smitty and his 240 were nowhere to be seen, Eric threw off the bulky run of bullets that hung, chaffing from his neck. He did this while in a full sprint. There was no choice but to run. To stand and fight meant to stand and die.

Slim took the lead, running and shooting. Eric, in the back, struggled with his gun until he finally got the clip in place. When he pressed the little "gizmo" and the bolt slid in place, he felt the greatest relief.

"Grenade!" one of the men called and a mere second later an explosion blasted a gaping hole in the hordes to their right. Slim rushed through it only to have a grey arm reach out and grab the strap of his M16. The soldier yanked on it, desperately, but the zombie was too strong. A soldier behind him paused long enough to fire twice at the beast, only to be tackled from the side by another.

Eric ran by, shooting his weapon haphazardly in the direction of the soldier, hoping to hit enough of the converging horde to give the man a moment to get to his feet. It didn't work. It turned into a dog pile and there was no helping the man—Eric could see that he was already bitten in at least five places. Still, with Heddles' dead screams running through his mind, Eric didn't think he could run away a second time and leave a man down, but then there was a wumping explosion right before his eyes and pieces of human and zombie went everywhere.

The soldier had blown himself up and by that act caused a suspension of the horrible battle as the remaining zombies paused long enough to ascertain who was human and who wasn't. It gave Slim enough time to rush back and grab Eric. Of the other soldier there was nothing to be seen; it was just the two of them.

"Come on! Now!" Slim cried, as Eric looked around in a daze. "Make for the lobby."

They leapt the low hedges marking the middle of Park Avenue and then fought their way into the lobby with guns blazing. Eric found that a shot to the center of a zombie's chest would slow it considerably or even knock it down, and just then that was good enough for the moment. Their accuracy or their luck allowed them to gain the lobby and then the dark stairs beyond.

Then came a desperate fight to shut the door of the stairwell against the rushing zombies. It was a fight they began to slowly lose as scabby arms kept the door from shutting. Slim was the stronger of the two and he threw his back against the door, saying, "Go on. I'll hold them off."

Now Eric was torn between fears: death here with Slim, or death alone in the dark stairs as the stiffs caught up with him. "Like hell," he said, getting an idea. He grabbed a grenade from the soldier's belt, pulled the reluctant pin and tossed in through the crack of the door. Eric expected to be blown off his feet by the explosion, but he barely felt more than a vibration as dozens of zombies absorbed the brunt of the blast.

"Thanks," Slim said, once he cleared the door and shut it firmly. The soldier then began to shake and this turned into a crying fit that Eric pretended not to notice. He wanted to cry as well. The mission he had fought to arrange had done little besides add misery to the world.

Chapter 16

Major General Fairchild

Reading, Pennsylvania

A week later General Fairchild watched from the safety of his command vehicle as what was left of his men gave up the city of Reading. They were dusty men, ragged in both appearance and in mind, and the general wondered what exactly would happen if he got out of his armored Humvee.

Would they frag him? Blow his ass to hell where it belonged? Did they blame him for the endless days of fighting, or the constant retreats? Or the wasted lives? Did they think that the moronic rules of engagement were his idea?

"I'd deserve it if they did," he said to himself. None of this was his fault in the strictest sense, but it was clear that he had failed his men and his nation. Commonsense told him long ago to ignore the President's orders, only he had been a good little Nazi and had gone along with the buffoonery instead of doing the right thing.

His division had once been an almost perfect fighting force, trained and equipped with the world's most high-tech weapons, but the "Rules" said: no mortars, no artillery, no tanks, no LAVs, no jets, no helicopters, no nothing. Without questioning his leaders, he had set aside millions of dollars worth of equipment, giving up every advantage in the process, and fought the hordes man to beast.

He still had his guns, but they had the numbers. From the urban agglomeration that was the New York area, it was estimated that twelve million stiffs had come at them. Yes, he had guns, however he'd only been allocated fewer than three million bullets. It didn't take a genius to see the math wasn't going to add up.

Reluctantly, he took his eyes from the men and scanned

the blue skies. "Where the hell is he?" asked the general, again under his breath. His driver barely stirred, having grown used to the general mumbling to himself over the last two weeks as things had gone from bad to worse to hellacious.

Then came the wump, wump, wump of the choppers blades. "Here he comes. Inspection time." He said this louder, an invitation for his driver to respond.

"Gonna kiss his ass real good, Sir?" Sergeant Bower asked in his thick southern 'Bama drawl. "You need some lip balm? We may be all out of grenades and fifty cal ammo and such, but we got cases of lip balm and I think this would be a good, heroic use for 'em."

"Fuck you Bower," he said genially, stepping out of the Humvee, and checking his gig line—out of habit only. He didn't give a rat's ass what the Secretary of Defense thought of his uniform, or really what the useless son of a bitch thought of anything.

"Yes Sir," Bower replied. The whipping rotors sent a storm of dust their way and they squinted into it. The sergeant yelled over the noise, "What do you think it's gonna be this time? They gonna make us read them zombies their Miranda rights before we shoot em?"

The general smirked at the comment; sadly it wasn't so far-fetched with this administration. The smirk faded into a grimace when he heard the Secretary's actual request.

He wanted a hundred picked soldiers for a "secret" mission; this usually meant going to fetch a niece of the First Lady or some Hollywood starlet. This time was different. The men had been chosen already.

"What's so special about these men?" Fairchild asked, flipping through the hundred pages: each had a short bio of the soldier and a picture stapled to the top right. "I know some of these men are dead."

"Not according to the last casualty list you submitted," the Secretary responded in his flat mid-western accent.

"You may have noticed that I'm dealing with about ten million fucking zombies," Fairchild replied, intentionally leaving off any honorific. As a favor to himself he had given up on paperwork altogether, and who was there to say otherwise? His boss, Lieutenant General John Hickey, and everyone else in the command structure were: *no longer one of the living*, as it was being politely put—being *dead* had too many meanings these days. "Hey, Bower," he said. "They got you in here."

"That right?" Bower drawled. "They must want sumpin' mighty important done."

"Yeah, that's right," Fairchild remarked, his voice becoming fainter with each syllable. Bower was a good man, not an exceptional one. Why on earth had he been chosen for a secret mission? Something wasn't right about this, nor about the way the Secretary's politician's smile stayed fixed just so. After another glance down the names, he noticed the men had two things in common: every one of them was from the deep south and every one of them was...

"Mr. Secretary, this man is dead for certain," Fairchild said holding up one of the pictures at random. "But I have a good replacement; that man right there. Bower, what's that soldier's name?"

Bower squinted at the soldier, a man with skin the color of molasses. "That's Jackson. He a PFC, but he's a hell of a good guy, Sir. He's a shooter is what he is."

"No, not him," the Secretary said, quickly. "Just the men on the list."

"That's what I thought," Fairchild growled. "Bower go take a walk." When the sergeant left, Fairchild looked long at the politician and then asked, "What's going on?"

"It's need to know only," the Secretary replied with a warning for the general in his eyes.

"In that case, the men on this list...they're all dead. We don't have what you're looking for here. So sorry you had to come all the way up here for nothing." The general began walking away and the politician grabbed him and pulled him close.

"You of all people must see how bad it is from a military point of view. And you know we can't go on like this. Don't you think it's time for a change?" Their eyes met and a thousand words were conveyed with the look. The question had been a loaded gun, and the hundred white soldiers the bullets, and there was only one possible target.

"The President is touring the front...what's left of it," the Secretary said speaking in a conspiratorial whisper. "He's going to need a security force that's been around the zombies, that knows the score, that knows how things have been and how they should've been."

Fairchild took a step back and watched his soldiers go by—they were so tired from the constant fighting that they looked a little like zombies themselves. It could have been different. The war could've been winnable at the very start. Now it probably wasn't even survivable except by a lucky few.

"No. I'm not going to have you hang this on my men. And I don't want anyone thinking this is about race. I'll do it myself," he said, putting his hand on the butt of his gun and caressing it lightly.

The move wasn't lost on the Secretary. "Are you sure? He'll have a security detail."

"Will I be able to carry my gun?" When the Secretary nodded, Fairchild added, "Then it'll be no problem."

It wasn't.

Two days later, just behind the lines where soldiers lived and died, the secret service agents faced outward not seeing the danger that was so close. The President was twitchy and nervous at the proximity of so many zombies and was easily distracted. No one noticed as General Fairchild slid his pistol from his hip holster and used it to give his few remaining men a real fighting chance to at least save themselves.

Chapter 17

Sarah

Danville, Illinois

When the military left Danville the first time they left a town, which had once been thriving, on the brink of disaster. It wasn't just the food, it was the attitude the soldiers had displayed. It left no doubt that they saw the people of Danville as little more than servants in the best of cases and slaves in the worst.

Sarah's parents had their vast larder pared down to a week or two of food, and they were some of the lucky ones. A few people were arrested for resisting and had everything taken from them. And while an unknown number of women were rumored to have been raped, two other people were actually shot.

With all the killing in the world, those two deaths caused reverberations out of all proportion. Thousands of people panicked and fled the town thinking incorrectly, that they would find things better somewhere else. Among those who stayed a strong majority felt an overwhelming need to fortify the town. All remaining fuel was used to operate a bulldozer night and day, digging what was in essence a huge moat around Danville. They even redirected the waters of the North Fork River into it, making a tremendous muddy mess out of the eastern side of the city.

And then they sat around passively waiting. Nothing in their staid, dull lives had prepared them to do anything else. Within a few days the moat proved its worth when the first real wave of zombies came at the town. The alarm sounded and the men went off, while the women, save for a hearty few, watched from the eastern buildings.

The firing went on for a long time as the men were slow to catch on that only headshots were effective and hundreds of rounds were wasted in a time when every shot counted. Eventually the moat was breached in a number of spots and the farmers fled to their homes, where they proved far more effective. Firing down from second floor windows where they were safe allowed them to aim with far greater accuracy, and though a number of homes were broken into and some two-dozen townsmen were slain, the town lived to fight another day.

"Was everyone checked for bites last night?" Denise asked at breakfast the following morning. In order to pool their dwindling recourses, Gary and Denise Rivers, had moved into their daughter's much smaller house. It was easier to heat and had only two entrances to defend in case of an emergency and one of these was blocked with a now-useless refrigerator.

They were eating cold oatmeal with only a spoonful of sugar to sweeten it. Since the army had left, their meals had been dreadfully bland and Gary sighed with his spoon halfway to his mouth. "Yeah. Johansson and Cargrave went around after the fight. Found a couple."

"Who were they?" Denise asked taking a small nibble of the grey paste.

"Please," Sarah said, shaking her head. She didn't want to know who they were. The list of dead and missing in her life was beginning to grow in length and just then she'd rather believe her friends were alive someplace else; someplace nice.

"Well what did they do?" Denise demanded. "We can't have people turning into monsters smack dab in the middle of Danville!"

"Trust me, it was taken care of. In a respectful manner."

The room went silent as the two women pondered what a "respectful manner" entailed and in the silence the dreaded bell began to sound again. Denise's mouth started to quiver; she stared down at her bowl and said, "You better get going, dear."

He had only just opened the door when someone ran by and yelled, "The army's back. Hide what you can!" They didn't have much to hide, so it only took a few minutes, and that was all the time they had.

"What is that noise?" Denise asked hurrying to the window and peeking out. "Oh, my lord! They have tanks. Why would they have tanks?"

They found out moments later as orders began issuing from a loudspeaker: "Residents of Danville, remain indoors. Resisters will be shot. Remain indoors until further notice. Anyone on the street will be shot as a resister. All weapons must be placed just outside your front door. Anyone found with a weapon indoors will be shot."

This was repeated up and down the street.

Gary had gone upstairs to get a better look around and he came down in a sweat. "They've got four tanks and all sorts of armored Humvees. They..." A *tat-tat-tat* of machine gun fire began. It ended quickly and everyone stood frozen, listening for more. Gary swallowed hard and asked, "What do we do?"

"Put your gun outside!" Denise cried.

"But they'll take it," Gary said, clutching his shotgun with both hands, like a toddler with a toy. "We'll be defenseless."

Sarah felt her insides cave as she said, "They won't. I know the commander. Um, he uh...we have an understanding."

Her father seemed puzzled by this. "What sort of understanding?"

"Just put the gun outside," Sarah said, going to sit down at her kitchen table. She didn't think her legs would hold her up for long. "And hurry. They seem trigger happy and I couldn't stand for anything to happen to you."

He did and then the three sat at the kitchen table with their oatmeal hardening in front of them. The tanks systematically went down each street, stopping at every house where their presence made the good people of Danville feel small and vulnerable. When they finally came to Sarah's house, there was a knock at the door that caused each of the them to take a great fearful breath. "Come in," she said, her voice cracking.

Two soldiers came in pointing mean looking assault weapons at the three and right behind them came the colonel whose nametag was visible: Williams. He spoke pleasantly, "Good morning. Don't get up, enjoy your breakfast."

"Are you going to take my gun?" Gary asked quickly.

The colonel's eyes went to Sarah first and she found that she couldn't look him in the face. "That all depends," he said, slowly. He then raised his eyebrows to one of the soldiers who had come in with them.

The man read aloud from a piece of notebook paper: "By command of the military governor in compliance with Executive order 7249, Section one: In order to fairly and properly defend the people of Danville, all weapons and ammunition are to be turned over immediately. They will be redistributed as warranted by circumstance."

Sarah's father gasped and began, "That's outrageous. You can't take our guns! Our second amendment rights..."

Williams held up a hand and cut Gary's words off with the simple gesture. "I can actually. Forget the executive order, those tanks out there say I can."

"You'll leave us defenseless!"

Colonel Williams sighed and nodded. He pointed to the two soldiers. "Wait outside please," he ordered and when they had left he went on, "I wish it weren't so, but the cold reality is that many of you will die. Hell, all of us may die for that matter. It's a sad truth. Our lines were broken in four spots and most of my men are dead or have run off. The remainder, about two-thousand are on an island in the Illinois river, fortifying it as we speak."

"But how are *we* supposed to live?" Gary demanded. "Taking away our guns is the same as murdering us!"

"Right now I have to look out for the greater good," Williams replied. "Communications with my superiors have ceased, we're no longer supplied, and every major city is categorized as *Black*. That's the paradigm in which I have to base my decisions. America has fallen. That's the truth. And even if I let you keep your guns, you'll all die, very soon. This town is essentially defenseless and now that the army has failed, there's nothing between you and close on a million stiffs. From my point of view it makes no sense not to take what can be saved and leave the rest."

"What about honor and duty?" Gary asked in a raspy whisper.

The colonel made noise of disgust in the back of his throat. "I don't know what those words mean anymore. Is it really the duty of the strong to die so that sniveling weaklings may live? I don't think so. If mankind has any chance it's the strong who have to flourish, even if it is at the expense of the weak."

The room went quiet this, while from outside screams could be heard. Sarah listened to them and they sunk in, going right to her heart; they were the screams of Mrs. Hayes, one of her neighbors. The sound made her oatmeal want to come back up.

She swallowed hard, forcing the sensation of nausea from her mind and then stood. With a forced smile she went to the colonel and put her hand out and he took it. "Thankfully, the colonel and I have an understanding."

Her father had been ghost-white and staring blankly, now he came alive. "That's what you said before, and I ask again, what sort of understanding?"

Williams glanced down at Sarah and then put an arm around her. "Nothing nefarious I assure you. I am somewhat smitten with your daughter and I can't stand the idea of something happening to her. Somehow she was able to pick up on it."

"Somehow," Sarah agreed with a barely repressed

shiver. The colonel's hand had slid down her back and now he was gently massaging her ass. "And you'll bring my parents with us back to this island?"

"How could I say no?" he replied. "Though I have to warn you, I'll expect a lot out of you on a *daily* basis."

"You won't be disappointed," Sarah said, agreeing to become his whore.

Chapter 18

Ram

Baker, California

Slinging his M16 across his back and raising his hands, Ram moved toward the barricade of cars. As he went he was forced to step on rotting bodies. They carpeted the road two deep. To the side of the road was a sharp edged drainage ditch where bodies were piled in the hundreds. As gingerly as possible, Ram stepped on the ones in the road and still they shifted and squished beneath his feet, letting out horrid yawns of putrid gases that had his head feeling light.

"That's close enough," a voice from behind the cars said. Ram felt the world begin to spin and he stumbled forward gagging against the smell. The men behind the barricades made threats, and still he staggered on until he had his hands on the passenger side window of a four-runner.

Across the car from him, pointing a short-barreled shotgun was what he at first thought was a large chubby hispanic. When Ram's eyes began to focus, he saw it was a man who didn't seem to belong in the heat of that desert. He was sumo wrestler, right down to the odd ducked haircut.

"What, are you bit?" the wrestler asked in such a thick accent that it took a moment before Ram realized that it had been a form of English. He started to shake his head and the sumo was pushed aside by a much smaller man. He was white, but with such a deep and permanent tan that he was darker than Ram.

"You bit?" he asked.

Ram shook his head and said, "No, it's the smell. You know you gotta move these bodies or you're going to get some diseases."

"We ain't worried about no diseases much. It's the

fucking zombies that we worry on. So what you got to trade? We got all the guns we can use. It's the bullets we need. You got any? Or alcohol. Or some good food. Not just rice and beans, and that crap, something good, like some Pringles. But mostly we need bullets."

"Bullets? No, I got a girl."

The man tilted his head like a puzzled dog. "A girl? What do you mean? To trade? You wanna trade a girl?" he pulled back from his side of the car and yelled to his right. "He wants to trade us a girl."

Another man squinted from between two of the piled cars and said, "That's fucked up, mister. We don't buy and sell people. You can just take that shit somewhere else."

"No, you don't understand me," Ram said. "I want to get rid of this girl. She's, uh...she's getting passed around, if you know what I mean."

"I do," the man between the cars said. "And that's just as fucked up."

Ram couldn't agree more. "That's why I want to give her to you. But those assholes think I'm here to trade so I'm going to need something to bring back. Like some water, do you have any?"

The man with a tan made a face and shook his head. "Look we don't want the girl."

"Maybe she's cute," another voice put in. "Is she cute?"

She wasn't, not in Ram's eyes. He made a face and was about to put it as nicely as possible, but the tan man spoke over him, "We don't need no more girls here. We got too many and not a one of them can shoot for shit. Just waste bullets is all they ever do. So, no, we don't want the girl. But if you're good with that there rifle we can talk about bringing you on. Can you shoot?"

Standing among the bodies of the dead, Ram felt the cold, familiar dread that he had lived with for so long. He was sure, just as the black girl back in the car was, that this barricade wouldn't hold, and even if it did, would the other parts of the town? It looked wide open on the south with just a highway fence to keep the stiffs out.

"No I can't. I'm not the best. And I don't have a lot of rounds left."

The man shrugged. "You get some bullets and come on back, but leave the girl somewheres else, we don't want her. And don't give me that crap look. We got eight-hundred hungry mouths in this town and can barely feed them, so sorry. If you don't like how she's being treated you go and do something about it."

Ram started to argue, but the man's face made it clear that his decision had been made. Ram went back to the Subaru and said, "They don't want her. Though they don't seem like bad guys. I bet if we just leave her here they'd take her."

"That's dumb, Yo," one of the gang-bangers said. "I'm not going to just leave a piece of ass on the side of the road, not for nothing."

This was agreed to by the rest and then another had an idea that sent chills down Ram's spine. "Maybe we can pretend to do some trading and then when they think everything's cool, we can pop a few of them? How many were there?"

"I saw seven," Ram lied, quickly. "And I heard another dude. And that's just the guys here. There's a town just down the road and he said there's eight hundred people living there. We try anything and it'll end badly."

Thankfully common sense prevailed. They took the detour around the town and although it was only a mile or two out of their way it was enough to begin to knock some sense into them. As they passed car after car, each stranded without gas and the people begging for water, the eight of them began to talk about rationing what they had left.

This started with the girl. They refused to give her a drop and though she whined at first, she accepted her place eventually. Because there was so little room in the Subaru, two of the gang-bangers rode on top. Ram drove slowly along the desert highway, stopping at every broken-down car, searching for gas and water or really anything they could use.

For the most part this was a waste of time, and the sun went down before they found a thing. That night was cold and they had no shelter or blankets. They talked about starting a fire which thankfully they didn't do. Ram had argued against it and when the votes had gone against him at first, he had for the briefest moment, felt the desire to leave the pathetic group.

His new cowardice swept it away, but it had been there and it had him thinking that maybe, in a few days, he could leave this group behind. His old self wouldn't have put up with them for a minute, because the truth was that they were zombie magnets with all the ruckus they made, and had they been anywhere other than in one of the most desolate areas on earth, they would've been killed long before.

Just then, the idea of firing his gun or facing the smallest zombie made him go queer inside. He slept in the car, with the seat pushed way back and was better off than the others because he had on a woman's pink parka he had found in a car earlier that day. The gang-bangers had laughed, but now they shivered and pulled the hoods of their sweatshirts over their heads to hold in their body heat. With the seats folded down in the back, the Subaru held five of them; one in the front with Ram and three in back. The girl was in the back. She might have been thirsty, but she was snug, acting as an anti-gay buffer between two of the men who pressed in on her for warmth.

The three men outside, with their foolish machismo, kept their distance from each other, and at about two in the morning one of them was killed by a pack of undead dogs. They came out of the night in utter silence and just tore into the first man they came to. Ripping into the flesh of his face and hands and then when he was crawling around blind and crying blood, more of the pack came up and tore out his belly.

Ram couldn't watch and he was not alone. The others, in a state of near hysteria demanded that he drive away. He went on for another hour with all seven of them crammed in the car and the heat turned up high and that was how they slept, folded on each other like cats. By morning they were stiff and in a foul mood from lack of water. Ram still had a third of his bottle left, which he kept hidden from the others, figuring it was their fault that they couldn't ration properly. The group drove on and the lucky bangers got lucky again.

They found a minivan that not only had gas, but also a gallon of water in an unopened plastic jug. Unfortunately the van came complete with a pair of zombies who were trapped inside. The pair must have been there for days, baking in the closed van, and Ram had never seen anything more disgusting. The heat of the desert sun had bloated them and there were deep fissures in their shiny grey skin.

Ram's disgust turned to outright nausea when one of the bangers got up the nerve to open the van door. The smell hammered his senses and he reeled, but when one of the men shot the first zombie and it literally burst like an erupting zit, Ram hurled up the little he had eaten for breakfast.

He wasn't the only one. All the men were in various degrees of sickness, however the girl only made a face and said, "Oh that's nasty." When the second zombie had been killed, thankfully with a clean head shot, the girl braved the smell and came away with the prized water.

She drank until one of the bangers noticed and took it from her. Though Ram wanted to drain the van of its gas and use the Subaru because of its better gas mileage, the others wanted the extra room that the minivan afforded. He was over-ruled then and was again an hour later when he wanted to leave I-15. It led straight to Las Vegas and Ram didn't want to go anywhere near another big city, where the stiffs seemed to breed.

He was vindicated when a few miles later the road became impassable and not just with stalled cars, but also with zombies by the scores. They turned the minivan around and took the first main road that went east. A few hours of steady driving later, he was again vindicated: the van sputtered and ran out of gas.

The Subaru would've lasted another fifty or sixty miles.

They spent another night cramped beyond reason and in the morning, with no other recourse they began walking down the middle of the two-lane road. If zombies came at them in any numbers they'd be in deep trouble, but again the bangers were lucky; they saw few stiffs and those that they did were the slower type.

Ram had seen enough of them to be able to categorize them as either fast/strong or slow/weak.

The strength and speed of the zombie was mainly due to its size and its overall state of health—child zombies or those with missing limbs or injuries to major muscle groups were relatively weak. Another factor in their strength and speed was how they were feeding. The better fed they were the more dangerous they were. The heat of the desert seemed to sap the strength of the creatures and those that came at the group moved slowly in ones and twos. Still this was a drain on their resources.

By sundown, Ram was beginning to get nervous. The land was no longer as bitterly dry as it had been a hundred miles west, but it was still mainly scrub and there was no cover whatsoever. As always the bangers had another spurt of luck: just as the sun dropped below the horizon and twilight made an appearance they saw a brief light a few miles away. It had been manmade.

Excitedly the group hurried across the empty land and saw a house sitting along a dusty little road. It was a pretty, two-story home in the middle of nowhere Ram started to grow anxious when he saw the bangers began to check their weapons.

With his stomach suddenly going queasy, Ram hung back with the black girl. He had no taste for what was to come. Though he tried to tell himself that the bangers would just bluster and threaten to get what they wanted from the people in the house, in his heart, he knew differently. He knew their type: fatherless gangbangers raised on the streets where morality essentially boiled down to: if it feels good do it, and if someone gets hurt in the process of me getting mine, well that's just their too bad.

They had been killers before the zombies and now they were ten times worse. The five remaining bangers spread out as they approached the house and the girl next to Ram scoffed at him, "You is such a pussy. What do you think is all up in there? A house full of zombies? Shit, it's probably just a couple of crackers."

She was very likely right, still that didn't stop Ram's heart from beating any less thunderous. He didn't want to go near the house. It would mean too many questions that he couldn't answer: would he allow more innocent people to get hurt? Would he just stand there and watch, impotently, as he had when the black girl had been raped? Was he really a pussy now? Something was wrong with his brain. It was as if he couldn't get a handle on things. It was as if he had cracked.

Once, he had been the toughest of the tough. He had killed with a grim determination. He possessed a hardwired instinct to protect the weak, and a desire to do his duty. Now, he wiped his sweaty hands on the pink parka he was still wearing and wondered what had happened to him.

"Hey, pendejo!" one of the bangers hissed at Ram. "What you doing? Go around back."

He could do that. He could go to the rear of the house and wait there, though he was certain that if anyone came out that way he wouldn't be able to do anything. There wasn't a chance that he would do more than point his gun at them, and even that wasn't a guarantee.

Ram went around to the back and leaned against the white vinyl siding and tried to control his breathing. His lungs had begun to work like crazy as if he had just sprinted a mile. "What the hell?" he asked himself as sweat stung his eyes.

He wiped it away with his sleeve and then switched the berretta to his left hand just long enough to run his palm on his pant leg again. Inside someone was yelling. It was a woman's voice and she was threatening...and then there was a crash and gunshots.

Seconds later, the back door came open and a woman stepped out. She was redheaded and very thin and her hair obscured most of her tear-stained face. In her hand she held a shotgun, which she raised to point at Ram's chest.

"I won't hurt you," he said. This seemed strange to both of them since he hadn't budged in his position and his gun was pointing down at the dirt. More gunfire erupted in the house—three or four guns going off at once. "What's happening?" he asked.

"My mother, she's trapped upstairs."

Ram looked up at the house and said, "We should run. We should get away while they're preoccupied." His fear was obviously sincere and for some reason it bolstered the woman's courage and she shook her head in a tiny way.

"No, I can't leave her." She began to head back inside and Ram grabbed her. He wanted to say something to warn her of her danger, but he couldn't put it into words. "Let go," she said and jerked her arm away.

"No, get behind me," he ordered, though he did so with his mouth pulled back in a grimace. It had just sprung upon his face and he couldn't seem to relax his facial muscles to stop it. She didn't notice for her fear was nearly as great as his.

He opened the back door and went through a small mudroom to a hall in the rear of the house where back stairs led up to the second floor. Midway up them one of the bangers crept. He turned with a start at Ram's appearance and then when he recognized the man he started to relax.

Then his eyes went large and he pointed his gun and cried, "Behind you!"

Ram's heart was a hammer in his chest and his breath was ragged and on fire, and yet, as the gang-banger swiveled to point his gun at the woman behind him, his muscles reacted from years of training. Quick as a cat he tracked down the barrel of his pistol and fired. The man fell back on the stairs; he stared at the ceiling while his hands hooked into claws.

If he died just then Ram didn't know. Despite the thunderous explosion from his gun, his ears picked up the vibration of someone running. He dropped down into a crouch just as another of the bangers came down the hall. Ram didn't wait to explain himself; he sighted on center mass and shot a second time.

When the banger when down with a horrified look, as if he were choking on air instead of blood, Ram reached behind him and grabbed the woman. Together, they eased up the back steps as the house went suddenly quiet.

"Mama?" the woman whispered as they got to the second floor. When no one answered she wanted to press forward, but Ram held her back. He peeked around the corner and the wood next to his face seemed to come apart in a thousand splinters.

"Call to her, damn it!" he hissed, wiping shards of wood from the side of his head.

"Mama. It's me Julia, don't shoot." The woman looked around the corner and made an odd noise before leaving Ram and running with thumping steps.

Julia's mom was leaning against a wall and pointing her gun Ram's way; all around her, the floor and walls were wet with blood. From below came two quick shots and then orders yelled in Spanish. Almost below Ram someone began shooting.

He ducked down and saw two of the bangers, one firing up the stairs and the other rushing forward. They weren't bad as a tandem, but they weren't all that good either. The use of cover fire like this might have worked on the older woman, but Ram simply slipped back to a point that it would take a master marksman to sneak a bullet up at him.

Ignoring the lead flying his way, he waited with his gun at the ready and squeezed off his own shot as soon as one of the bangers broke from the cover of a side room. He went down with a gut shot and Ram decided to waste a bullet and finish him off.

Below, the last two bangers jabbered in Spanish, which Ram understood perfectly. They seemed to think that they were only dealing with a single person on the second floor and that the front stairs were clear. To mask what they were planning, one began to fire up at Ram. He fired back just for show and then he waved frantically to Julia, and pointed at the stairs her mother had been guarding. The older woman now was glassy eyed and vacant.

Julia nodded and hitched her shotgun, waiting. After a few seconds she fired twice, her thin body jerking back with each shot. And then there was the sound of running feet. Ram spun and there was a banger right on the stairs not four feet away; the two stared at each other and when the banger began to lower his weapon Ram brought his up.

When he pulled the trigger it had the feel of an execution.

"Hey, pendejo!" Ram called out to the last one. "Your boys are all dead. If you want to live then you better get to running."

"Manny? Dino?" the lone banger whispered with fear outweighing the hope in his voice.

"Dead," Ram told him as he came down the back stairs. "And you will be too if you're still there when I get to you. Go out the front door and start running. You have to the count of ten. One, two, three."

The front door opened and after the sound of the man's footsteps died away there was silence in the house until Julia said, "He's runnin' off." There was a pause before she added in a frightened voice, "Mister? Can you help my mother?"

"Just a second," Ram said. He had begun to shake so violently that he had to sit down. His breath started to hitch and he was afraid he would begin to cry, but the cold barrel of a gun pressing against his head from behind soon stopped that.

Chapter 19

Neil

Montclair, New Jersey

The truck beneath Neil was such a beast, was so tall, and rocked to such a degree as it bounced over the living dead, that it felt as though he were riding a giant bull. It was not a sensation that agreed with him and, so as soon as he could, he took a side street where the undead were fewer in numbers.

He made to sure to lose himself in the convoluted and squirreling streets of Montclair, feeling sure that the previous owner of the truck wouldn't find him. When he felt safe, he cut back on the gas and pulled over to take stock of the treasure he had stolen.

The back of the truck rattled with canned goods and weapons, while bullets of various sizes rolled about everywhere. As well there were six large plastic jerry cans filled with gasoline and many jugs of water. In the cab with him were two sleeping bags, some more food and enough alcohol to kill a man of Neil's size.

There was also a Sig Sauer 9MM on the seat next to him. It was black and deadly. Gingerly, Neil slid the pistol under a sleeping bag, making sure that it pointed away. For Neil the greater prize than a fully loaded pistol was a package of doughnuts, the kind one would find in gas station convenience store, the sort that Neil had routinely turned his nose up to all his life.

After weeks of rationing everything he consumed, he ate them greedily while clouds of white powdered sugar flew about. When he finished he blew at the powdered sugar in vain trying to get it off his clothes. He then fretted about having left his toothbrush back at his home. A pair of old and ratty toothbrushes jutted out of a beer can that sat in a cup holder. With his doughnuts feeling odd in his stomach at the sight, he took the time to pinch the can between two delicate fingers and throw it out the window.

The entirety of the cab was far too messy for his liking and so he tossed out all the trash he could find, feeling a quiet guilt as he did. It was bad enough to litter, however it was the fact that he wasn't recycling that bothered him most. From everything he could see, the planet was thoroughly trashed and he didn't like the idea of adding to the mess.

When he was done, he sat up in the cab, on a quiet, tree-lined street and felt tall and powerful so high off the ground. The big truck made him feel invincible until he remembered the gun. Cautiously he moved the sleeping bag, exposing the Sig Sauer, however he could barely summon the courage to even touch it, and when he did, he did so wearing a face twisted in disgust and fear.

Picking it up he looked it over and asked, "Is this even on?" By this he wondered if it was ready to fire. He honestly couldn't tell—there was a button on the side just behind the trigger as well as a couple little switch like levers. Nowhere were the words *Safe* or *Fire*. Neil pressed the little button.

"Oops," he said, as something black fell out of the bottom of the handgrip. He picked it up and saw that it was a chamber, which held a reservoir of bullets. "A clip," he said, snugging it back up where it belonged and feeling a slight taste of victory over his fear of the gun. Still he didn't like the thing and he glanced in the bed of the truck for a 'normal' gun.

He saw what his mind classified as a pistol and after a quick look around at the deserted street, he jumped down out of the cab and then climbed up into the bed. He felt relatively safe up there. The zombies seemed to lack either the mental capacity or the coordination to climb more than the simplest steps, and he was high up in the air.

Neil inspected the weapons making sure they were pointed away from him; he wasn't worried over much about injuring another person. Every house on the block had windows that were smashed or doors that hung crazily, attesting to a home invasion by the beasts. Still, he didn't purposely point the gun at the houses either, it seemed rude to him somehow.

He found a .357 Magnum and decided that it would be his gun of choice. In the movies it always seemed a powerful weapon and what was more, its double action trigger was simple. Feeling slightly silly, he stuck the gun in the waist of his jeans and then went to the next firearm—a very large shotgun.

With a heavy breath, he decided now was as good a time as any to learn how these things worked, and so grabbing up a box of shotgun shells—ignoring the possibility that they could be the wrong gauge—he hopped out of the back of the truck.

"Darn it," he exclaimed as the Magnum fell from his pants to clatter on the street. He stuck the gun back where it had been and then brought the shotgun up to his face and looked at the various slides and buttons. One of the levers had a little tick mark pointing to a green circle.

"So does green mean go? Like it's ready to fire?" he wondered aloud.

Neil set the butt of the gun in the pocket where his shoulder and chest met, sited down its long length at a mailbox across the street, closed his eyes, and pulled the trigger...or tried to. Nothing happened which had him squinching up his face in confusion. What did green mean if not *go*? He moved the lever to the red circle, which he had assumed before meant *stop*.

Now it was that Neil's total ignorance of shotgun shell "loads" was even more impressive than his ignorance of guns in general. The shell chambered in the gun was not designed to shoot a little dove out of the sky; it was a three-inch magnum firing double-ought buck shot, and it turned the gun into a piece of field artillery. When he pulled the trigger it seemed to explode with an ear-splitting roar, while flame and smoke shot out the front, and the recoil, possessing all the grace and brutality of a mule's kick, knocked him over. Neil found himself lying on his back, having tripped on the curb behind him.

"Holy cow," he said in what might have been a whisper, though he didn't know; he couldn't hear his own words. Thankful that there was no one around to see what had just happened, Neil got to his feet, groaning as he did, and then squared himself up and aimed again at the mailbox, which was disappointingly still intact.

He aimed, closed his eyes, while making a face that suggested the onset of pain, and pulled the trigger...and nothing happened. "It's empty!" he exclaimed; a port on the side sat open and vacant. He loaded a shell into it and that was simple enough, but when he tried to load a second one the gun balked. After much fiddling around he discovered to his amazement that the gun was a single shot affair.

"Well that's stupid," he said with some irony. "Who would design a gun that has to be reloaded after every time it's fired?" There had been a time not long before that he had argued that all weapons should be single shot. That had been at a dinner party where his greatest worry was if the wine had been allowed to breathe long enough or not.

With the shotgun loaded, and his body braced, Neil pulled the trigger, grimacing against the vicious impact of the gun. When he opened his eyes, he was at least still standing, however the mailbox remained untouched. On his third attempt, he forced himself to keep his eyes open and had the satisfaction of seeing the top of his target disintegrate.

"That's good enough for now," he said, working his shoulder in circles and growing nervous as zombies began to flock to the sound of the gun. Forgetting to reload it, Neil brought the shotgun into the cab with him and put it on the backbench, and then decided to put some more miles behind him.

He drove with a caution that made little sense with such a rugged truck at his disposal; his reasoning was that he knew less about cars and their upkeep than he did about guns. There didn't seem to be a need to hurry, after all he didn't know where he was going or where it would be safe.

The army hadn't provided safety. They couldn't even protect themselves. Among the many zombies that Neil had seen wandering around suburban New Jersey, were undead soldiers in uniform. This didn't seem right or even possible in his eyes, yet there they were shambling along with all the rest.

Another reason that Neil putted along at an average speed of six miles an hour was that Jersey roads were notoriously narrow and it didn't take more than a couple of stalled cars to block an intersection completely. By the time the sun dipped in the west, he had zigzagged his way barely seven miles west of his home.

That night he backed the truck into a cul-de-sac and slept fitfully when he slept at all. The dark was when the hordes tended to come out in force and between midnight and three there was a sea of stinking grey bodies all around his truck. He watched them, shaking in an all-consuming fright, until the windows fogged up. Then he slunk down, shaking in fear and wishing that he was at home, warm in his bed.

The next morning the thousands had moved on, leaving just the usual stragglers. These seemed more anchored to their neighborhoods or homes and Neil wondered if they had more mental acuity than the average zombie. If so it was to a very slight degree.

Ignoring them, Neil drove to a nearby high school and parked in the center of the football field where he could see all around. There, he went through the tedious chore of feeding three of the five-gallon Jerry cans into the gas tank of the monster truck, and as he did he fretted about fuel. It was one thing to fill up at the neighborhood gas station, especially when state law mandated that an attendant do the actual pumping, it was another thing altogether to get at that same gas when it was trapped underground.

Of course there was always the option of just choosing a different vehicle, however Neil was loathe to give up the truck. It was like a traveling fortress.

When the refueling was complete, he sat in the bed of the truck wearing a jacket that was two sizes too big and ate cold raviolis, not realizing what the little grey cans that read Sterno were. There were a number of them lying about and he assumed that they were a kind of stew or cat food when in fact they were 'Fire in a can' and he could have used them to heat his meal.

He ate and relaxed, and although it wasn't quite ten in the morning he wondered at the possibility of having a beer. Normally he only drank after five and when he did he was a Pinot Noir kind of guy. Perhaps it was the truck or the fact that he was now a gun owner, or that he was simply a survivor and that all the old rules seemed to have been jettisoned. Whatever the reason, just then he thought a beer sounded good. Neil was just in the process of reaching for one when a scream reached his ears. It was a woman's cry.

Standing, he picked up his shotgun and cocked his head, trying to fathom where the scream had come from. Another one broke the still morning and he oriented on the cry. It was coming from the neighborhood that bordered the south end of the football field. *Not* in a flash did he leap from the truck and race to save the day.

Instead he held the unloaded shotgun to his chest and wondered what to do. Should he go to the woman's aid? Or would it be better to see if someone else showed up to help?

A third cry decided it and Neil climbed down from the back of the truck. He didn't run across the field—that seemed like suicide to be so out in the open—he drove instead to a point where part of the fence had been torn down. Only then did he take his Magnum and his shotgun to see what sort of rescue he could arrange.

The street on the other side of the fence was barren of life…or death for that matter. He began to creep along when he heard a thump and a crash from a ranch style house to his right, and so with his cannon of a shotgun leading him in, he went through the open front door. The house was smallish and he stood in a dim living room. Off to the right was what looked like a dining room while straight ahead was the kitchen and it was from here that he heard the unmistakable sound of a zombie.

With his chest shaking, Neil went as far as the edge of the kitchen linoleum, peeked around the corner and saw the zombie. It had been a woman, probably a mother seeing as she still wore an apron. She had been clawing at a door, but turned when she heard his panicked breathing.

Neil raised the shotgun, clicked off the safety and, once again demonstrating horrible form, closed his eyes before pulling the trigger. Nothing happened. "What the…?" Before he could figure out what he had done wrong, the zombie was upon him and all he could do was scream and try to fend the thing away with the tip of the gun.

Suddenly, right next to his head, a black pistol appeared and when it went off, blasting a hole in the zombie's head, the pain in Neil's right ear was so intense that he actually cried out. "That hurt!"

"What a McGoo," a light voice said. Neil turned and there was the Goth-girl who had robbed him the day before. She pressed the muzzle of her pistol against his neck and it was hot.

"You!" Neil said, his face set in comic surprise.

She smiled easily and said, "Small world ain't it."

The door the zombie had been clawing at opened and from it the girl's partner emerged, hulking and smirking. "You were right, Sadie. He is a hero." The man came forward, jerked the shotgun from Neil's hands and said, "I thought you'd be too much of a chicken shit to risk that soft skin of yours. Too bad you picked the wrong time to grow a pair. Sadie, go wait in the truck."

The man turned the shotgun on his captive.

"Hey, no hey," Neil blabbered. "I...I...you can have the truck, I barely touched anything. Just don't shoot."

"You should leave him like he left us," Sadie said, flashing her dark eyes toward Neil and then to her partner. "The guy's harmless, John."

"He ain't all that harmless. Now go, unless you want to watch me splatter him all over this kitchen. I know you aren't into the blood."

Sadie nodded slowly, with a look of revulsion, and then said in a low voice, "I'll just get the keys."

They were still in the truck, but Neil wasn't in the mood to be helpful. The girl ran her hand over his pockets and when she felt the .357 Magnum tucked into his jeans under his jacket, her eyes narrowed, but she didn't say anything, she only gave Neil a very long look as she left. What she meant by the look he didn't know. Certainly she didn't expect him to pull the gun and shoot his way to freedom, not with the shotgun aimed at his face. It would be impossible.

The young man, John, waited until Sadie had cleared the house and then he gave Neil a shove with the end of the shotgun. "You fucked up, Bro. You don't take a man's truck and think he'll just let it go. Saying sorry don't mean shit to me." John took a step back and then pulled the trigger and Neil fell to the floor with a great rushing sound in his head as the world ended in black.

Chapter 20

Sarah

The Island

The Island as everyone referred to it, was little more that a series of rocky, tree- covered humps rising out of the Illinois River. The main island was over a thousand feet long and a few hundred feet across at its widest. Every inch of its long shore was covered in rolled concertina wire—a much more effective cousin to barbed wire—and behind that armed men sat in bunkers, ready to repel any invasion.

They crossed onto the island by way of a pontoon bridge, which was nothing more than floating barges that were linked together by chains. That they shifted beneath the weight of the Humvees had Sarah nervous. "Can't the zombies just cross over to the island the same as we are?"

She and her parents were riding in the lead Humvee with Colonel Williams. He laughed at her question. "Didn't you see those tanks?"

"I guess I didn't," she admitted. Her mind was in free fall. They had left Danville, taking with them a score of women, every gun and bullet the town possessed, and the last of the food. There had been a number of deaths, but nothing compared to what was to come for those poor people. The convoy drove west to another town that was about to be devastated by the army and as they did they went by a horde of zombies that seemed uncountable; it went on for miles.

They were heading straight to Danville.

"You see?" Colonel Williams had said gesturing. "You should be thanking me. Danville won't last the night."

No one had thanked him. Instead they were thinking about the friends they had left behind, and trying not to cry. Shows of emotion seemed to upset the colonel and since they were at his complete mercy they each tried their best to be good.

Now on the bridge, the colonel pointed at the chains on the far end. "If the zombies get past the tanks, we can always disconnect the bridge from this side. Sure it will be a pain to put back together but the alternative is far worse."

"That's smart," Sarah said, eager to please.

When they had crossed to the other side, they saw that the island was a beehive of activity. Trees were being felled and walls were being created out of their trunks. Trenches and postholes were being dug and firewood was being chopped. There was no machinery for any of this. Fuel was simply too precious, and so it was men who swung the axes, worked the heavy-bladed saws back and forth and hewed at the dirt with shovels and pick axes.

The Humvees went to the center of the island and there the colonel began issuing orders while Sarah and her parents stood with a gaggle of women and a few civilian men who appeared young and strong. They were separated into groups—the men were volunteers and were sent to be outfitted in uniforms—the women were volunteers in only the loosest sense of the word.

Gary and Denise Rivers were taken to the second island, which turned out to be far less secure than the first. It had only two banks of the coiled wiring and the few guards on it had to walk the perimeter instead of sitting safe in earthen bunkers.

"We're going to work on that island next," the colonel assured Sarah. "But we have to make at least one as secure as possible. If there's any trouble, your parents can always come over here. That's our plan. Now, this is where you are staying," he said pointing at a rectangular white tent. It seemed very large for just one person. "You are going to be my new executive assistant if anyone asks."

Sarah missed altogether the word *new*. She went to the tent with her one piece of luggage and eyed the six cots with unease. Two were clearly spoken for, with women's clothing draped here and there, and so she went to the furthest cot in the back. On it was an olive-drab sleeping bag, a pillow, and a little kit with soap and shampoo and toothpaste. She was just finishing up arranging her things when another woman came. She was tall and blonde and she too had just a single bag.

"Hi," Sarah said coming forward to introduce herself. "I'm Sarah Rivers. I'm from Danville."

"Roberta Clement, but everyone calls me Bobbi. I'm from Laurette, or what's left of it." Her blue eyes started to fill up with tears but she blinked them away and tried to smile. "I'm hoping things will change for the better. That's what I keep telling myself, and at least this island seems safe."

"That's true. It's safer than Danville ever was." Sarah replied. "I should be like you and look on the bright side of things. Things could be worse and besides, I'm going to be the colonel's new executive assistant."

Bobbi's eyes turned sharp. "No, I think you're wrong there. I'm going to be the colonel's new executive assistant."

"You both will be," a woman at the front of the tent said. "Just as we are." Another woman followed her in and they went to the two occupied cots. "I'm Cindy. I'm the colonel's favorite and this is Veronica."

"Favorite what?" Bobbi asked, crossing her arms.

"His favorite *executive assistant*," Cindy answered with a wink.

"What are you saying?" Bobbi asked. "Are you saying that you're…that we're…"

Veronica was the older of the two, being roughly the same age as Sarah. She was pretty and her brown eyes were kind, but also pitying. "We're executive assistants, dear."

"No," Sarah replied, dropping her chin to the canvas flooring of the tent. "We're whores. That's what we are."

This caused the little group to grow silent and each was

grim in the face until Veronica forced a smile on her lips. "Come here, honey." She took Sarah to the front flap of the tent and pointed out at all the men working, they seemed to be everywhere, each sweating from their labors. "There are two thousand men on this island. See all those big tents? Each holds twenty men and the colonel authorized only one woman per tent."

"Twenty?" Sarah asked, feeling sick. Bobbi looked as though she was about to throw up. "Twenty guys for every..."

"Yes, twenty," Veronica said. "Those poor women are the whores. We are executive assistants."

"Don't get her hopes up," Cindy said. Sarah looked back to her and watched, with her mouth hanging open, as the younger woman undressed quite unselfconsciously. She had the body of a stripper and the wicked gleam in her eye of a porn star. "Face it honey, unless you can suck dick with the best of them you'll be destined for platoon work, where you'll get all the practice you can stomach. You got a cute face, but your body is only ok."

"This is ridiculous," Sarah whispered as if she couldn't push out the air in her lungs. It was bad enough when she had thought she was going to be the colonel's "Girlfriend" but now that she had found out that she was part of some medieval harem it seemed worse somehow. "And it's unfair. This is the twenty-first century. We should be treated as equals."

She looked at Bobbi for agreement, but the woman had her make-up bag out and was busy trying to apply foundation to cover the worry lines that had sprung up across her forehead.

The two experienced women exchanged looks and Cindy rolled her eyes. "Look at me," she said pointing at herself, indicating her body. "I'm a hundred and eight pounds, and eight pounds of that is titty. I've never fired a gun before. I can't swing an axe more than five times without

[133]

getting exhausted and I can't mix and pour cement. I can't dig a trench or haul firewood or any of that. The truth that you can't seem to see is that there isn't a job on this island that I can do that a man isn't better at. Except for one and this may sound skanky, but I'm glad to do it."

Veronica agreed. "I was with the colonel almost from the beginning. What those soldiers did...how they fought with all those zombies everywhere and people dying and..." she paused to take a steadying breath. "I'm with Cindy on this. My entire job is to please one man and for that I get shelter, protection, and three meals a day. It's a fair trade. It's better than fair if you think about it."

"But twenty at a time," Bobbi asked. She held an eyeliner pencil in a hand that shook. "I can't do that."

Cindy struggled a halter-top over her breasts and said, "I could do it, no problem, if my only other choice was going out there with the zombies. I could do it easy. Just lube yourself up and let them go at it."

"And it's not that bad in the platoons, now," Veronica said. "The colonel instituted a new policy: each man gets a blowjob every three days and gets one *date* a month. I know twenty times a month seems like a lot, but when I was with my husband, back when he was still alive...when we first met I mean, we were doing it three times a day."

To Bobbi it seemed far more than she wanted to handle and she appeared almost to swoon, however it was then the colonel called from outside the tent, "Are you ladies decent?" She bounced up with a strained smile on her face. She was also quick to undo the top two buttons on her blouse.

Sarah couldn't stand. Her legs felt too weak to hold her up and her stomach wanted to rebel against the thought of what was being asked of her. The colonel beamed at his ladies, though his smile slipped when he took in Sarah.

"Just wanted to see how you're settling in," he said.

"Just fine, Sir," Bobbi said very quickly. "This tent is

going to be just great. And these two…uh women…were just telling us how lucky we are." Sarah nodded along, it was the best she could do.

"Great," Williams said. "Well that's all I wanted, except…" he paused and looked the women over. As he did, the two more experienced women straightened just the slightest. "Except, I was hoping that Cindy would like to have dinner with me tonight."

"I would love to," Cindy replied as Veronica's smile faltered. "That sounds super."

When the colonel left, Bobbi slumped back down. "He didn't pick me. Was I wrong somehow?"

Cindy snorted at this, letting them know who the favorite was, while Veronica shook her head and said, "You did the right thing, you just need to tone it down a notch. Be eager, but not too eager. And you…"

"My name is Sarah."

"Let's take a walk," Veronica said, heading out of the tent. When they were alone she asked. "Are you sure you want to be here? They'll let you go anytime. You can walk right over that bridge whenever you want."

"My parents are here. They're set up on that island over there. I can't go even if I wanted to. Who would watch out for them?"

"Then you need to change your attitude," Veronica said. "The colonel is…don't ever tell him I said this, the colonel is a big fake. He pretends that we are his girlfriends, and he wants us to act like we're in love with him."

"I don't know if I can," Sarah said, pleadingly.

Veronica could only shrug. "Then I wish you and your parents the best of luck out there. You see, here is a painful truth: the colonel doesn't need you…"

"But…"

"But, nothing! If you can't please him then you're gone. I've been with him for almost five weeks and I've already seen it happen. I saw one woman walk out of the lines and get torn apart before she went twenty-feet. And don't even think that you'll be able to sweet talk one of the men into protecting you. They fight and die for him. They love him…just as I do."

Sarah gazed at Veronica in wonder until the woman curled her lip and snarled, "You don't know thing one about what I've gone through! That man protected me when no one else would. He's like a father and a husband and a god all rolled into one. I know I said he was a fake, but maybe I am too. I don't know. But if you can't please him…"

"I can," Sarah said quickly, grabbing her hand. "I just don't know what to do."

"Just want him. He wants to be wanted. And don't just 'lube up' like Cindy suggests. That may work for someone with her body, but you and I have to try harder." Her face drooped suddenly as though the fact that she hadn't been picked for that night was an omen.

"And what happens if that doesn't work?" Sarah asked, dreading for the first time in her life that she wouldn't be good enough for a man. "What am I supposed to do? If I can't please one man how can I please twenty? And why would I even have to! There were plenty of women in Danville, why didn't he just get more?"

"I asked the colonel that already," Veronica replied. "Each extra person means they have to scrounge for more food, and more fuel to burn, and more medicine, and more of everything. You are very lucky that he agreed to take your parents on."

After seeing the zombies heading for Danville, Sarah knew that she was lucky. "That's why I'm suddenly scared I won't be good enough. I have to be good enough for their sakes."

"I get it…and you're not the only one who worries," Veronica said. "What happens if he gets tired of me? Or what happens if he finds another girl like Cindy, all tits and ass? Or another girl like you, only more adventurous? I think that's your problem. You're beautiful but..."

"You don't think I'm kinky?" Sarah asked. When Veronica nodded, Sarah slumped. "I'm not...I don't really know how to be, like I said. I can do all the normal stuff, it's everything else that I wouldn't know where to start."

"There's something you could do that could help us both out," Veronica replied, shifting her eyes away nervously. When Sarah only waited patiently for the girl to explain herself, she added, "It's what every guy wants..."

Sarah shook her head, not understanding. Guys seemed to want a lot and nothing in particular sprang to mind that is until Veronica reached out and touched her arm very softly. She then ran on her fingers higher until Sarah gasped. "Oh, that! I'm not...uh, I'm not into girls. You're very pretty, I'm just not..."

"I'm not either," Veronica said, quickly. "And I know it's...it's freaking crazy to even ask, but if you want to be picked, I think this would do it."

In truth Sarah didn't want to be picked at all, she wanted to go running and screaming back into the past and never leave it. The past was a happy place where she would never have considered faking a lesbian relationship in order to sexually satisfy a man she considered no better than a Nazi, in order to keep her and her family safe from zombies?

Her face went a light pink and she said, "I don't know how."

"Me neither. Though I suppose if I do to you, the things that I like and you...you know do the same to me, that ought to do it. I don't think there's anything more to it. Except..."

It felt like Sarah's ears were on fire as she asked, "Except what?" She was afraid of the answer and all sorts of crazy thoughts went through her head.

With her own face a glowing red, Veronica answered, "We'd have to practice. I mean if we're fumbling around like idiots, it's not going to be sexy. It'll just look stupid and we only have one shot at this."

"Oh...practice," Sarah said and it felt as though she would choke on nothing. It wasn't that Veronica wasn't appealing, she was very pretty, but the idea seemed to hang up within her, as if her soul rebelled against. She fought it back and nodded, though her head wobbled on the X axis when she did.

"We'll practice tonight, when Cindy is out. I'll send Bobbi on an errand and then..." Veronica finished by taking a deep breath and Sarah understood.

Veronica used her pull so that they were able to hold their practice session in private. Bobbi wanted to go find some friends that she had come in with anyways and then the two women were alone. They took one look at each other and giggled like teenagers.

"And that is why we have to practice," Veronica said. She then held out her right hand and said, "Look, I'm shaking. Isn't that stupid?"

"Me too," Sarah admitted. "Though for me it's all in my chest. Like it's my first time. I could use a drink."

"The colonel doesn't allow alcohol on the Island, which means we're just going to have to do it."

"Ok," Sarah said with a shake of her head. She began to peel off her shirt and Veronica stopped her.

"No. Wrong. You don't shake your head like it's a chore. The colonel would be turned off in a snap. And don't tug your clothes off. We undress each other, but slowly. Remember, this is a show. This is theater and we are performers. Even if you don't feel it, fake it."

Minutes later, after Veronica ran one of her hands beneath Sarah's hair and to the back of her neck, while the other slid up her thigh beneath her dress, Sarah was surprised that she wouldn't need to fake it. Veronica's lips were softer and more alluring than any man's had ever been, and her hands knew exactly what to do.

"You're so wet," Veronica purred and Sarah's eyes opened wide at the thrust of the small fingers within her. She grabbed the woman's wrist and didn't know if she wanted to pull the fingers out of her or grind them deeper. Veronica paused as well and they stared for a second into each other's eyes.

"This is when you should kiss me," she told Sarah. Veronica had lowered her onto one of the cots and now Sarah reached up and pulled the woman down to her; their tongues met and crossed. Veronica's was so soft and delicately warm that it sent a thrill down her back. Then the woman's fingers began pumping in and out of her and Sarah threw her head back and moaned.

The hand kept going and Sarah couldn't help herself; she thrust her pelvis with each move and her breath grew heated.

"Just like that?" Veronica asked, her lips brushing Sarah's.

"Yes," Sarah said, practically begging. "Yes..." and then she couldn't speak as the orgasm rocked her. Though the feeling was fantastic and completely surprising, Sarah knew she wasn't a lesbian because just then she wanted a cock in her badly. It wasn't the colonel that flashed into her mind, it was her ex-husband, Stewart. He had good thick cock that filled her and just then she craved it.

The thrum of her muscles went on and on and then her mind slipped from Stewart and went to Brit and the orgasm shut down like a switch had been thrown.

"Ok, that's good. I think it should be your turn," Sarah said, withdrawing, mentally.

Veronica eyed her and saw that the heat had gone. "Ok, but first I have to do this."

"Do what...oh that. Really? You don't."

"Yes," the woman said. She went to her knees so that she was at the level of the cot, and then with gentle pressure spread Sarah's legs. "Don't lie all the way back. Go to your elbows and lift your legs, like you're inviting me," Veronica instructed. "Yes, just like that."

Veronica kissed Sarah's inner thighs and took a playful nibble and then used her tongue—and immediately Sarah giggled despite the weirdness of it all. "Not so light," she laughed. "That tickles. That's better...that's..." That was too good for her liking, especially with her mind dwelling on her daughter. "Ok, you did good," she said breathing heavily after a few minutes, pushing Veronica gently away.

"All right, but tomorrow you just let me go. Now you do me." She sounded eager to Sarah, who had to remind herself that it was all for show, except Veronica didn't look like she wanted a practice session. Before Sarah really had an idea what she was going to do, her partner took her hand and brought it up her thigh and up and up until it wouldn't go any further.

And then she groaned as Sarah's hand explored, and again Sarah was surprised at her own level of excitement. Veronica wasn't much of an actress, she was hot and wet, and her muscles twitched and...

Just then voices came from outside the tent and the two girls jumped apart.

"And these are my tent-mates," Bobbi said, coming in. "Oh it's dark. Is there a light?"

"We try not to light the light...I mean waste light...I mean waste electricity," Veronica stammered as she straightened her clothes. Her jabbering seemed to suffice as an explanation and Bobbi waited outside the tent for them. "You could've used just a bit more practice," Veronica whispered to Sarah with a wink. "Another minute or so and you would've been an expert."

"I'll go first next time."

"Next time will be tomorrow night, I hope," Veronica said pensively. "I haven't been picked in three days and if this doesn't work, I'm afraid I'm going to be sent to one of the platoons."

"It'll work. It has to for both our sakes."

Chapter 21

Ram

Western Desert

"You is such a pussy," a cold voice spoke. It was the black girl they had been traveling with. She had picked up a gun from one of the dead bangers and had it pressed hard against his head. "And a back-stabbing son of a bitch. These were your friends!"

Ram shrugged and said, "They weren't my friends, and they certainly weren't yours either."

"Yeah but they kept us clear of the zombies, didn't they? Which is more than I can say for a gutless piece of shit like…"

"Drop the gun," Julia ordered. She had crept halfway down the stair and had her shotgun aimed steadily despite that her red hair hung in her face and her chin dripped with tears.

The black girl put up her hands and said, "It's all good, cracker bitch. Be cool. I'm putting the gun down. There it goes." She tossed it on the carpet and kept her hands up.

Picking up the gun, Ram nodded toward the door. "You still have one of your friends left and if you hurry you can catch him. You can take a gun with you."

"Naw," the girl replied. "You may be a pussy but I'll take my chances with Annie Oakley. She looks like she got some kick to her."

"That's enough," Julia said. "Mister, can you look at my mother? She's been shot." When Ram started for the stairs Julia added to the black girl. "Have you considered the fact that I may not want you around? I don't like your mouth or your cheek."

That she used the word 'cheek' had Ram giving her a closer look as he passed. She was older than he had first thought; about thirty, though her thin delicate features made her seem younger.

However old her mother was, she wasn't going to make it to her next birthday. The poor lady had been shot through the gut and the bullet had exited her body through her right kidney. Had there been an open and functioning hospital nearby, she might've had a chance. There wasn't one. Ram inspected the wounds and felt the woman's pulse; it grew quicker and lighter with each passing second. It was a sure sign that she was bleeding internally.

Ram took Julia into another room. "Your mom is not going to make it. The bullet took out one of her kidneys, and she has massive internal bleeding. I'm sorry."

"How long?"

He could only shrug. There were too many variables; one of the chief of these was a person's will to live. Julia left him and went to sit on the stairs next to her mother, uncaring that she was sitting in a warm puddle of blood.

"Julia, we're going to be right downstairs cleaning up," Ram said in a soft voice.

"I'm not cleaning up shit," the black girl announced.

Ram looked at her for a long time until she turned away and then he asked, "What's your name?"

"Cassie. It's short for Cassandra. An' I din't make none of that mess and I ain't gonna clean it up neither."

"My name is Ram. It's short for Ramirez. I know you didn't make the mess, but if you help clean it up. I'll make sure you get food and water. And if you don't, I'm going throw you out of here. I think that's fair, don't you?"

She gave a sullen shrug and then went about collecting the weapons and ammo from each of the bodies. She also checked their pockets for anything interesting. "This one was married. Ain't that something? He looks so young. He look younger than me. Can I keep his ring?"

"Stealing from the dead is bad luck," Ram said. He didn't know if this was true, but he found the idea repulsive.

She kept the ring, as well as any other odds and ends she found desirable. "I ain't never been lucky anyway," she explained. "Can I have some water now?"

"You're alive when most of the world isn't. I'd say that was pretty lucky." They went to get water, found that the taps in the house still ran and each drank until they were unpleasantly full. Ram took two glasses up to the second floor. "You thirsty?" he asked Julia.

"Why did you guys do this?" Julia asked as new tears ran down the tracks laid by previous tears. She touched her mother's shirt and then her white cheek. The woman didn't stir. "You killed her. You killed my mother. My only family left in this world. Why did you do it?"

Ram wanted to proclaim his innocence. After all he didn't kill the lady and he had risked himself to protect her daughter, but that wasn't the real truth.

"Because I'm weak," he said in a choked voice. "I used to be strong. I use to be very strong, but then something just broke inside of me. It was all the zombies. They never, ever stop. Every day they came more and more, and I just broke. I should have stopped those bangers. I should have stopped them, but I couldn't, not until it was too late." He dashed tears from his eyes with the palm of his hands.

"Because you pussed out is why," Cassie commented. "I watched you all this time. I can see you wanting to say this or that, but you never did. You just puss out all the time. Like when they did their thing on me. You shoulda done something but you up and pussed out instead."

He nodded because that was the truth as well.

Julia sat there and her face was empty, yet she heard everything. "Are you still weak?" she asked, staring blankly at the wall with its red splatters. "Because I don't want you around if you're still weak. My mama was the strong one. She held it together as all the men around here died and became zombies. Is that what they are?"

"It's a virus," Ram said, thinking about the terrorists for

the first time in weeks. Had it been only weeks and not months? If felt as though the nightmare had been going on and on, day after day, hour after hour for longer than was possible. It had been going on since the Iranian and Shelton and...

"Shelton. Whatever happened to Shelton?" he asked suddenly and his face slipped into its hated grimace, while his mind felt like a record needle that had hit a bad groove.

"Who is that?" Julia asked, looking around with a little more interest in the world. "Another one of your *friends*?" The word friends came out in disgust.

"No, a partner. My partner. My best friend, really, so yeah. We were in L.A. and there was a terrorist. He had the virus and we caught him but it was too late, but, but what happened to Shelton?" He looked at Julia, though his dark eyes were in another time and place. They stared at a world where there were still men fighting; real men. Once Ram had been one of those men. And so too had been Shelton.

"I don't know who that is," Julia answered, looking at him sharply; her eyes were reddened but also such a beautiful blue that Ram found that he couldn't think straight.

"Andre Shelton. He was with me before. He was there before Glendora. Before I got this," Ram said holding up the M16. Where had Shelton gone after that? He was there one minute and then he just wasn't. Ram's memory had all the consistency of smoke.

"So much for you being strong," Julia said, standing. Her face had been misery, but now it was stiff with anger as she looked down at her mother. "I have to shut up the house. Those zombie things come mostly at night." She left and Cassie went with her, pushing past Ram with a sneer.

"I was strong," Ram said to the corpse. Julia's mom was a redhead, like her daughter, but the older woman had been weathered by the sun; her skin had the leathery look of an old smoker and her hair was a fade ginger color.

"I was strong when I thought I could stop the virus and I

was strong when I thought we could win. When I thought if we could just hold out for another day people would come for us. We all thought that someone would come." Ram could hear his voice shaking. It was a weakness, like a vein of yellow butter that ran all the way to his core. "I am weak but somehow I lived when so many others didn't, like Shelton."

What the hell had happened to Shelton? His face kept popping up. Shelton had only his Smith & Wesson to fight with. "He didn't like it," Ram told Julia's mom, crouching down beside her. "He wasn't the best shot, you know. So he hung back, but that was ok, because when the stiffs would get close, he always was there. He'd hang back but he wouldn't run. He would step up and if there was a stiff coming at me that I didn't see, Ol' Shelton would get him. He was tough in his own way and he never ran."

"You ran," Julia's mother said, though her lips didn't appear to move. She was still slumped against the wall and now her blood was dry, looking black in the dark.

It was only then that Ram noticed the sun had long since gone down. "A lot of guys ran," he hissed, leaning close to the body. Then he realized he was too close.

The way her chin hung to her chest and how her hair fell forward made him nervous. Was she watching him? Had she turned? He brought his gun up with the growing certainty that she had.

"I'll shoot. I swear; I don't care whose fucking mother you are."

"Then shoot," the corpse whispered.

Ram pulled the trigger. The safety was on. The gun did nothing; it just sat there in his hands cold and useless and now Ram began to back away from the corpse, sliding on the hardwood, kicking with his feet, as his hands fumbled desperately to figure out how to get his gun to shoot before it was too late before…

"Are you alright?" Julia asked from lower down the

stairs. She shone a flashlight his way and for some reason he felt embarrassed and hugged his gun to his chest. He squinted around the light at her, making sure that she was still alive, making sure that her milky skin had not gone over to grey. She was fine, but her mother wasn't.

Mama was dead, dead, dead. But would she come back? Had she moved? Had she really spoken?

"I'm ok. I guess. We should move this thing. It's got to be burned. We can't trust it."

The light seared into his face again and he held up a hand. Julia kept the flashlight there regardless, studying him. She said, sharply, "That's my mother you're talking about, so show some damned respect. We'll bury her in the morning. She deserves a proper burial. However, those friends of yours? They'll go into the pit with the others just as soon as the as the sun rises."

"Is it nearly morning?" Ram asked. Time seemed a concept beyond him just then. Time was only the interval between killings. He would kill and eat and sleep and kill some more, but—and here Ram's very soul felt jittery—but everything he killed was *already dead*. Just then his psyche was on the verge of breaking into little pieces. His hands shook as he lifted them to his face and tears seeped between his fingers. Julia kept the light on him.

"You're not ok, are you?" she asked.

"No he ain't," Cassie said from further down the stairs. "He be talking to himself, sometimes. He never thinks none of us sees him do it, but I see. And his eyes are all crazy."

"I'll be alright," Ram said, trying to convince them and himself. "Just it's…it's worse than it had been, before. You know? It's worse than when I…" He stopped talking. He had almost admitted that he had run away, but that was his secret. His and Mama's. She knew. Somehow she knew that he had run from the killing, run off and left men to die.

Julia held out her hand to him. "Come here. Let's go get something for you to eat. Mama made a pie yesterday.

There's plenty left. And then maybe you should get some sleep."

"He talks in his sleep too..." Cassie began.

"Why don't you hush!" Julia snapped at her. Softer, she said, "It's a wonder we aren't all bat-shit crazy. I know I get closer to crazy every day, so I won't hold it against you Mister..."

"He calls hisself Ram though I think sheep be more like it," Cassie answered.

This earned her another hard look from Julia, who then turned softer again. "Some food and some fluids, that will do you well. Mama can rest here until morning."

Despite that her mother had just been killed, Julia pulled herself together remarkably. She fed two of the people who had been associated with her mother's murder and made up guest beds for them. She then went around and secured her home, drawing curtains of black velvet and locking the heavy doors that had kept her safe.

Ram didn't think he would be able to sleep with the corpses in the house for fear they might turn, but he dozed lightly until midnight when dreams came to him of them walking about the house like shadows. When a dark figure crept into his room, he went from sleeping to wide awake in a blink. Just as quickly his gun was drawn and pointing into the bare breast of Cassie before her mouth could even fall open.

"Can I sleep with you?" she asked in a whisper.

The words didn't jibe with his state of mind; in the dark he had been sure she was one of the undead and then a second later she was alive. Had that been a dream?

She didn't wait for an answer and climbed into the bed, naked. Her hands went to his body and he pulled back, confused. "What...what are you doing?" he asked, grabbing her hands.

"It's ok," she said. "You don't need to share me no more. I know how some boys don't like that. Come on, I'll take care of you." Her hands became insistent on him and he had to grab her roughly to make her stop. "What? Is you a racist?" she demanded. "Is that your problem? You'll stare all over that skinny, cracker bitch, but you won't give me the time of day? Well, fuck you."

"Cassie, that's not it," he said.

The truth was that he hadn't had an erection since he could remember. It used to be that he always had one part of his mind on a passing hottie or on some chick's ass or on his girlfriend's rack. Now he could barely remember what she looked like. And worse, his dick just sat there all day long, useless and numb, except for when he had to take a leak.

With everything that was going on he hadn't really thought about sex much. He had shoved his sexuality into a back corner of his mind and there it sat, gathering dust. He had shoved a lot of himself back there.

"What is it then?" she asked. Despite making all the motions of leaving she hadn't left and was still in the bed with him.

"Things aren't working right," he admitted, lowering his gaze to her body—and not feeling a thing. "It's all up in my head. Everything I've done. All the…look it's not you."

"I could help. You be surprised how many boys get a little thing worked up in they mind. I can straighten you out." Her hands went to him again and he began to tighten up, his face reforming into its hated grimace.

"No, thanks. Maybe in a few days. Right now it's in my head," he tried to laugh off the ball of stress that was a hard pit in his chest. "Why would you want to anyway? I'm a sheep. Remember you said that?"

"Cuz you a ram," she said with a little shrug. "I thought it was the white girl what kilt all those boys, but she says it was you. And then there's this." She held up something that was both familiar and ancient to his mind. It was his DEA badge. "You're a badass. A girl could do worse."

He took the badge from her hands and touched its

shining surface. How proud he'd been when he first earned it; he was still proud, he just wasn't proud of himself. He had run and left others to die, that certainly wasn't what he'd been taught. That wasn't the way a man behaved.

"You want it?" Ram didn't feel as though he deserved it anymore.

She smiled and her teeth were white in the darkness, like a Cheshire cat's. "Yeah. But I'm going to need a gun. You and that white bitch..."

"Her name is Julia," he said with a hint of warning.

"Julia, whatever. You guys don't think I should have a gun. No one thinks I should have a gun and that's just stupid. I gots to be able to defend myself."

"I'll show you how to use one in the morning. So..." he left the word up in the air; a hint for her to go, but she just smiled more and snuggled deeper into the covers. "Ok. I guess," he said to her. Just then he didn't think he had the capacity to fight even her.

She slept on him and snored loudly, and for some reason he found this reassuring. At daybreak he slipped out from her grasp and went down the stairs on tiptoe, wrapping the pink parka around himself warmth. He found Julia sitting at the table in the kitchen with a cigarette burning in front of her. She was pale and disheveled. Tears had dried upon her face and she seemed to be in a daze, but as he stood there, she began to blink as if her mind was just coming alive.

"I would've killed you if it wasn't for that stupid coat," she said with a sudden snort of laughter. "I thought you were a really ugly girl."

"Nope, just an ugly man."

This caused her to look at Ram in earnest. "You're not ugly."

He felt ugly, if not on the outside then he certainly did on the inside. "Are you going to smoke that?" he asked about the cigarette in order to change the subject. "Or just let it burn away?"

"I don't smoke," she said, turning to the grey wisps. "They were Mama's. From when I was a little kid that smell meant Mama was home. Oh, how I used to hate it, too. I was always on her about her damned cigarettes. *They're going to kill you some day*, I'd tell her. I guess I was wrong."

"I'm sorry," Ram said. He had apologized a dozen times already, and still he didn't think that he could ever apologize enough. "I didn't even know their names. I only just met them."

"Cassie told me everything. Maybe too much. She tends to mix wishful thinking in with reality. Like the fact that you two are an item." Ram's mouth dropped open and Julia smiled at it. "Oh yeah, she says you two are hot and heavy in one breath and in the next she admits she only just met you and didn't know your name until last night."

"She's been through a lot."

Julia turned suddenly bitter, "We all have. It's no excuse."

Besides his own miserable life, excuses were all that Ram had left to him. Julia saw that she had wounded him with her words and she made a small fist of frustration and said, "I don't blame you. I'm sure you didn't know what would happen."

Ram felt his face begin to pull back again and he turned away, saying, "That's what I keep telling myself, but it's a lie. I knew what kind of men they were, but I was weak. I'm sorry." He wanted to say it again and again. He wanted to say it to Cassie as well. He should've killed them when they were raping her.

"Yeah," Julia said in a breath. "Can you do me a favor? I need to bury Mama. Can you watch over me while I do it? It can be dangerous out there if you're attention's divided."

It was the least he could do. Ram wrapped the woman in the sheet Julia gave him and carried her out to the back of the house where three fresh graves sat looking very sad. When he had laid the stiffening body down in the grass, Julia went to give him her shotgun, but he refused it, handing over his own pistol instead.

"I'll dig. You can watch over me."

He dug deep until his hands were blistered and Julia said it was enough. Then he stood away from her as she cried some more. Eventually she waved him over and he filled the grave around the body and then she asked in a choked voice, "Can you dig another? Right there?" She pointed to a spot on the far left.

"Who's it for?"

"Me," she said simply, and then with a smile she put his pistol to her head. "I'm sorry too."

Chapter 22

Neil

Montclair, New Jersey

From the floor of the suburban kitchen Neil blinked up at a world that couldn't possibly exist. It was a world in which he was still alive. He had fainted briefly when the robber turned-would-be-murderer had shot him with the giant shotgun, only there hadn't been an explosion as there should have been.

Instead there was only a clicking sound.

"What the fuck?" John said, turning the shotgun on its side and seeing that the port was open and empty. "You charge in here with an empty gun? You come to save a girl from zombies and you don't even check to see if the fucking thing is loaded?" John broke down, laughing until he cried. "Oh what a fuckin' Rambo you are," he said, still chuckling as he tugged a pistol from his waistband. "I think I'm doing the world a favor by killing you. It's survival of the fittest out here and you're a genetic misfit that needs to be culled."

With this he lowered the gun to point at Neil, who was still lying on the floor, cringing and feeling stupid. But Neil was saved for a moment longer when outside the heavy revving sound of the monster truck could be heard: louder at first and then fainter. Sadie had driven away.

"What the fuck!" John cried and raced from the room. "She's stealing my fucking truck!"

Neil sat up as John ranted, and when he did the .357 slid out onto the floor. John didn't seem to notice it as he stormed back in and punched the refrigerator, sending gaily-colored magnets flying. Neil picked up the gun, and said. "Don't move. This one is loaded."

John's anger turned to surprise as he saw the gun, but he wasn't afraid of Neil. No one was afraid of Neil, not even when he held a gun in his hands. "You gonna shoot or what?" John asked. He was angled slightly away from Neil and his gun was pointed at the floor.

"I want you to drop your..." Neil began, but John turned swift and agile and squeezed off a shot. An angry bee zipped past Neil's ear.

In a panic, Neil flinched, pulling his own trigger more by accident than design. John fell, clutching his throat as a gout of bright red blood sprayed the refrigerator. "I'm sorry!" Neil cried, coming to kneel over the man. Even as he said it, John went limp and ceased to breathe. "Oh I killed him. I killed him! I didn't mean it, I swear."

He hugged himself feeling an urgent need to both vomit and evacuate his bowels and before he knew it, he was crying. What had just happened made no sense to him and really he didn't try to make sense of it. Crying seemed the only thing to do just then and so he went with it, until eventually his tears ceased and he was forced back to the reality of his unreality. In this strange, new world a man didn't cry after shooting another man; he went on with his life.

"I'm not a genetic misfit," Neil said, running a sleeve across his face and trying to be tough. "Who's alive and who's dead? Huh?"

He went through the pockets of the dead man, doing his best not to look him in the face, and came away with two clips for the gun that had fallen from John's dead hand.

Figuring he was going to need every bullet and every gun, Neil took them all. The shotgun, though it was still empty, he slung over his back and then he stood and stared around him, not knowing what he should do. The outside world was terrifying yet the little suburban home was no castle and offered scant protection.

Neil stood for a long time, pondering his next move. What he needed was a ride. With light steps he went to the garage and was disappointed to see only a little Toyota

Tercel parked there. After the monster truck, the Tercel looked like a toy car. Still it was better than hoofing it and so he scrounged around the house until he found some keys. Minutes later he had backed from the garage, ready for the open road...except the street was blocked with cars and zombies.

Neil performed a very delicate K turn and drove toward the hole in the fence where he had parked the monster truck. That thing had been too big to fit in the gap but the Tercel slipped through neatly and then Neil was off with a sudden idea.

Sadie had left John for a reason, and what's more she hadn't narked on Neil concerning the hidden .357. Maybe she wasn't so bad. She was resourceful and very brave, qualities that Neil seemed to be lacking. Maybe she would let him take up with her.

This was his hope as he tracked her throughout central Jersey. It was easier than he could've imagined. At the edge of the football field he saw fresh muddy tire tracks heading north on Garland Way. This street came to a four way stop and down the road to his right he saw a zombie that was near cut in half; it had been run over by something very large.

"He-he!" Neil giggled and took the right. The next clue took longer to find. So many of the roads were blocked that he had to go to each and inspect them before turning around to go to the next. After twenty minutes he found what he was looking for.

A Porsche that had been a part of a pile-up had its rear crushed inexplicably. Neil banked over a low hill and across someone's flower border and then paused to take in his choices: to the east and north, more houses. To the west a strip mall. He went west and found the monster truck. Sadie had used it to punch a hole in the wooden planks covering the front of a convenience store. Neil honked his horn, a light and friendly: *meep, meep*, and then parked behind the truck.

Before he could get out, however the truck coughed blue smoke all over the red Tercel and then began to back over him with a throaty roar. Neil screamed and dove out of the car just as the driver's side was flattened.

"Oh it's you," Sadie said, squinting down at him. He lay in a spatter of glass clutching himself and thanking God that his bladder hadn't let go. "I thought you were John."

"No. I'm me," he replied, feeling tiny next to the huge truck.

"Why didn't he kill you?" she asked. "That's all he talked about. *I'm going to kill that bastard!* It got dull I tell you. Hey, look out behind you. There's a stiff right there."

She seemed so relaxed that Neil was casual about turning and there was a zombie five feet away and rushing at him quickly. A scream ripped out of his throat as he pulled the .357 and fired at point blank range. It was a heavy-duty gun and the zombie fell to the ground with a gaping hole coming out of the back of him.

Immediately it started to get up again and Sadie snorted, "You have to shoot it in the head, dummy."

"Oh, I didn't know," Neil said, taking aim at the creature struggling to get up. He pulled the trigger, keeping his face turned partially away, yet still somehow managed to hit his target, sending grey-pink brains scattering across the parking lot. "That's gross," he said, feeling his stomach turn over.

"Yeah, but they're zombies so what do you expect?"

They just looked at each in a silence: Neil because he had shot her friend and he didn't know how to bring it up, and Sadie, because awkward silences didn't seem to faze her.

Finally Neil blurted out, "I killed your friend, John. It wasn't really my fault. He was going to kill me, too. Honestly, you could say he was hoist with his own petard...I just wanted to let you know."

Sadie looked skeptical. "Are you sure you killed him? You're not just saying that to impress me?"

"I'm sure," Neil said, a little defensively. "It was like an old fashioned duel: he shot and missed and then I shot and didn't. I don't know what's so hard to understand. His body is back at that house. You can go see for yourself."

She looked back the way she had come and then gave a half shrug. "For your sake I hope he's dead. That guy had a mean streak in him a mile wide. It's why I left. He was bad news. That and he kept trying to, you know. He was always like, *Come on Baby. We have to procreate for the sake of the species.* What an asshole. I think the species is better off with him dead."

"Well, he is dead," Neil said again.

"That's what you said." She gave him an expectant look and then asked, "So are you just going to stand there all day? We got incoming stiffs."

"I can come with you?" he asked, happily climbing into the truck. She refused to budge out of the driver's seat and he had to basically climb over her, but since they were both small and trim it wasn't so bad—except for the fact that she kept her pistol trained on him as he did.

"As long as we have an understanding," she said, indicating the gun. "Like I told John, the only gun I want anywhere near me is this one. So make sure you keep your hands to yourself."

Neil held his hands up to show how harmless he was. "I respect your lifestyle choices. I'm a very modern man."

"When you say lifestyle, are you suggesting I'm a lesbian?" Clearly his look made it obvious and she rolled her eyes. "I'm not a lesbian. Wow, some modern man you are. I just don't want to have to play *that* game. If I like a guy, I'll let him know."

"Sorry," Neil said, sheepishly. "I didn't mean to imply anything. And thanks for taking me on."

"It's ok. I don't like to be alone, which is strange because I used to be the ultimate loner in High School. I was a junior by the way and I was the most closeted person you'd ever see. It probably was because I was all Goth and everyone thinks Goths are all, like freaks. But here we are and I have all the chance in the world to be alone and now I can't stand it."

As she spoke she backed over the remains of the Tercel and tooled up a street, driving aimlessly. "So how old are you," she asked.

Neil got a twinge the way she said *old*. "I'm only thirty-four. Do you know where you're going? Do you have a plan?"

"You don't look thirty-four," she said, giving him a long look. "You have a baby face. Anyone ever tell you that?" Many people had, almost all of them perspective women he had his eye on. He nodded, not wanting to continue on the subject and she let it go. "And I don't know where I'm going. This way, I guess." She pointed down the road.

"I think we should go west," Neil said. "There are fewer people out there, which means fewer zombies. What do you think?"

She gave him a shrug and said, "Sure. West it is. What did you mean earlier when you said John was a *petard*? What's that? Is that like a retard?"

He had to laugh and she smiled back showing straight white teeth. "No, I said he was hoist with his own petard. It's from Hamlet."

A groan ran from between her lips. "Hamlet? That's Shakespeare isn't it? Well you can count me out. He puts me to sleep."

This put the conversation on hold for a while and Sadie drove the great beast of a truck until they came to I-80 which was dreadfully clogged both ways and littered with soldiers, both dead and undead. They had to settle for a zigzagging route that reminded Neil of a sailboat tacking into the wind. They'd go north till they found a good route west but when that clogged up they'd swing south until they found another. And so on.

Eventually gas became an issue. Neil emptied the last of

the jerry cans into the tank while Sadie watched, blowing tremendous bubbles with her gum. This lasted them a good thirty miles of back and forth, however by the time they found an open spot to gain access to I-80, they were getting low again.

Sadie pulled over at a tangle of cars and said, "I'll keep watch while you go check 'em for gas. The hose is in the back."

"The hose? To siphon with? I don't know how to siphon gas. Do you?"

"John always did it, but it can't be too hard. He was a petard remember?" She tried to be cute about it but Neil was nervous. When it came to direct hands on projects he was notorious for being mechanically inept.

Neil tossed down each of the jerry cans and then fished around beneath the mayhem in the back for the hose. With Sadie keeping watch, he went to each car and found a few with tanks that were nearly full. "Here goes nothing."

When it came to siphoning, he only knew that he had to suck at one end of the hose while keeping the other end within the fuel, but after that...

After that came vomiting. The fuel wasn't easy to bring up from the tank at first, and then, when it did come up he sucked it right into his lungs. It was horrible beyond the telling. He choked, and then began to vomit up the franks and beans he had for lunch. Sadie came over with a hunting rifle over one arm and a bottle of water.

"You're not very good at that," she commented, handing over the water.

"Maybe you want to try it?" Neil groused, between hacking coughs.

"You're the man here, not me."

"Yes, I guess I am. Sorry, but this tastes horrible," he said.

She gave her patented half-shrug, lifting only her right shoulder. "John used to put his thumb on the end between, you know, sucks. And then when it got close he'd put the end down into the plastic can."

Neil tried this approach, biting back a wave of crankiness over the fact that she had failed to mention this little helpful hint before. When the gas came gushing along the tube, he sat back on his heels feeling a touch of competence.

Sadie climbed up on the car and began rocking it. "John used to have me do this. I don't know why. So what did you do before? I'm betting you weren't a mechanic."

Why did it seem that she put him down with every sentence? And why did he care? She was a kid, who was exactly half his age. It shouldn't have mattered at all, but it still did.

"I was a corporate raider," he answered. "I was one of the most feared men on Wall Street." He had hoped that she would be somewhat impressed, but she set her lips and raised an eyebrow.

"I may not know what a petard is, but I know what a corporate raider is. I saw *Pretty Woman*. I know what Bane Capitol was. You destroyed companies for your own greed. You fired people just so you could make a buck."

The gas fumes were giving him a headache and he didn't think he could win with this girl—and again the question of *why* he would even want to came to mind. It certainly wasn't sexual. She was nothing but a kid.

"If that's what you think then you should probably try reading a book, maybe learning something instead of watching movies. *Corporate raider* is a fancy and not very descriptive name for what we really do. I was in mergers and acquisitions. And we not only saved jobs, but created them as well."

"That's not how it is in the movies, and before you get all high and mighty they told us about corporate raiders in school, too."

"Teachers never had to make a bottom line, do they?"

Neil replied and again attempted to boost his image in her eyes. "Let me explain as easily as I can. Let's say you had a bunch of grapes. If one got moldy it might spread to the rest and ruin all of them, so what do you do? You cut the one off to save all the rest. In essence that's what we do. Yes, we fire people, but when the rest of the company starts picking up and doing better they hire people back."

She raised an eyebrow and said, "Well it sounds awful boring either way. I bet you're glad that's over with."

"No, I'm not," Neil said, dropping his chin. "My life wasn't great. I mean on a personal level it sucked. I was lonely. But I was happy with my work. I made good money and I could point to many instances where I helped people. I figured the rest of my life would turn around eventually. You know, a girlfriend and maybe a family. But now, I think I'm built even less for this world than I was for the old one."

"I think you're doing fine," she said, with a little smile. "You're a survivor and there aren't that many people left who can say that. And look, you have this fine truck and all this food and you have me for a friend. What more could you need?"

"To find a way west," he answered. "And somewhere to bathe. I feel gross with all this gas on me." His needs were partially met; that evening he bathed in a clear lake in the middle of Pennsylvania. Afterwards, the two of them slept soundly high up in the monster truck—she in the front, he on the long bench in the back—and neither stirred as an army of zombies crested like a wave at the top of a hill and flowed around them.

Chapter 23

Sarah

The Island

At night the Island wasn't the calmest of places. Gunfire rang out frequently and a gunshot at one end of the island was only slightly muted at the other. Sarah's sleep was even worse compared to most. She dreamed first about her daughter, then of the colonel, and then of Veronica. This last wasn't a sexual dream and she was glad for that. If it had been it would have only added to her confusion.

Her one lesbian experience had been so good, yet she knew it would never likely be repeated. The circumstances she had been under: the pressure, and the fear, and the great mental taboo, and the girl, Veronica not being a lesbian either had helped tremendously, these all added up to a moment that could not be replicated.

Especially not that night. It was one thing to sneak into a dark tent and explore another woman and be explored by her, it was another thing entirely to do it under the watchful eyes of the colonel. It wasn't going to be a magical moment, it was going to be do or die. If Veronica was on the verge of being sent to the platoons, that meant Sarah would have only one or two chances to show the colonel what a good little whore she was or she would be sent packing.

No matter how the girls spun it, the idea of being a platoon whore was a terror for her. She would go crazy for certain, and then what would happen to her parents? They were only allowed to be on the second island as long as she played along.

The second island was rudely called The Island of Misfit Toys, because the people there were just that, misfits. Some were parents of soldiers or tag-along family members or friends, but mostly they were people who just had clung to the unit and refused to leave. They did odd jobs such as cleaning the latrines, cooking, or laundry work. The soldiers barely regarded them as people.

After breakfast, Sarah crossed over the rickety pontoon bridge that connected the two islands and visited her parents. Both put on painfully fake smiles.

"We have jobs," Denise said. "They're not such good ones, but I can't complain."

Gary Rivers nodded and smiled agreeably although he smelled overwhelmingly of chemicals. His eyes were bright red from them. "And what of you?" he asked looking at her sharply, seeing the clean dress she wore and the fact of her painted face—Veronica had helped her with her makeup. "Are you being treated fairly? There are rumors about the colonel."

What could she say to her father? That she was a whore, but a high-class whore so it was ok? "If there are, I haven't experienced them. So far he's been a perfect gentleman. Are you getting enough to eat? My tent has a little private stash. It's not much but I can bring some over."

Her mother's lips formed happy words but her head shook side to side. Her father was a better liar. "We have everything we need, but it does come with a price." He took his wife's hand. "Time for us to get to work."

Sarah watched them go, feeling low, and this Veronica picked up on quickly.

"Chin up, chin up," she said. "The colonel likes to make his plans early. He's all about schedules and perfect plans. Are you going to be ok?"

"Yes, I think so."

Veronica looked around and then stepped close with a look of determination and placed her hand on Sarah's right breast. "No, don't flinch. Act like you want me to do this. Press into my hand…good." She took her hand off and it shook.

"What about you?" Sarah asked trying to sound

nonchalant. "Are you going to say your hand is shaking out of excitement?"

"Yeah, maybe. I guess," she said, seeming more nervous even than the day before and Sarah gave her a look. "There's a new girl," Veronica explained. "Even Cindy is worried."

"That pretty?"

"Yes, and that slutty, too. When she heard what was to be expected of her, she didn't bat an eye. She says she likes to do everything and I mean everything. She went down a list and let's just say that what we are planning is just a warm up for her."

"How's Bobbi taking it?" Sarah asked.

"I can't worry about her," Veronica said, distractedly.

Sarah feared that if this experienced woman freaked out things would definitely fall apart. She wouldn't let that happen. She reached out with both hands and took the woman's face in her hands and pulled her in close.

"We'll start just like this," she said and then kissed Veronica deeply and felt a zing down below. "It'll work. He'll love us."

Her confidence was misplaced. When the colonel came in to "check on his girls," his eyes went to the new girl. She was tan, raven-haired and very pretty; what was more she was wearing a very high cut pair of denim shorts that had most of her tight ass hanging out. Sarah owned underwear that covered more than those shorts.

"Good, I'm glad to hear you're all getting along," he said easily, and then, just as the day before, he looked the girls up and down. Cindy stood as far from the new girl as she could, while Bobbi looked sick. Veronica and Sarah held hands, hoping the colonel would notice. Unfortunately the new girl sucked all the oxygen out of the room.

The colonel, eyeing the new girl's tan thighs, began, "I was hoping that…"

"Excuse me sir?" Veronica interrupted. "Sarah has a

question for you, but she's too shy to spit it out."

"What is it?" he asked. He saw that the girls were holding hands and then he saw Veronica's left hand was out of sight behind Sarah; there was movement to her dress and it was clearly captivating him.

"If you pick her, she wants to know if I can come too. I think it'll be fun." Veronica's smile was all vixen.

"That does sound like fun," Colonel Williams said, his eyes widening at the idea. "I'll see you two tonight at seven."

The plan did not go over well with the others. "You fucking bitch," Cindy seethed at Veronica. "Why didn't you choose me? I would have been much better than her."

Bobbi went to her cot and cried, repeating over and over: "That's so unfair." And then she sat up with an idea and turned to the new girl. "We could do that too. We can be a team."

The new girl made a dismissive noise and said, "I don't need a partner. I'm more than he can handle all by myself."

Then came the waiting. Sarah and Veronica went through a plan of action for that night, move by move. When they would jettison this article of clothing or that, when they would kiss and when they would move to the next position. They memorized the plan until each could repeat it by heart. Veronica grew more relaxed, but Sarah felt her insides tighten.

If all she had to do was make love to Veronica she would've been just fine—the woman was pretty, sweet, and had a kind heart; the problem was that the colonel would join them at some point and both women knew that he would be aiming most of his affections Sarah's way. That was something she dreaded.

Sarah knew him for what he was: a horrible man. He stole from the weak; he bartered the lives of innocents for personal gain; he abused women to a hellish degree, and perhaps worst of all he did these things wearing a false mantle of honor. He had turned honest, decent American soldiers into mercenaries, thieves, and assassins. Evil should be seen as such, but instead he had women begging for the chance to prostitute themselves, and thanking him when he consented to it.

How she could allow that sort of man to touch her she didn't know. Her whole body shuddered at the thought of it.

Thankfully the evening started well enough. It started to rain heavily and the colonel was late. Veronica passed the time giving Sarah a neck rub. It wasn't sexual, instead Sarah felt very much like a boxer before a fight. Veronica kept up a stream of talk about how pretty Sarah was and how the colonel would likely cream himself the second they started kissing.

This got them laughing, so it was easier to smile when he came in mid-way through. "What's so funny?" he asked, taking off his hat and heading for the already set table. Veronica actually told him the truth and he laughed as well. "Maybe. I hope it's that good."

"Oh it will be," Veronica assured him. "We've been practicing."

"Veronica!" Sarah cried, so embarrassed she blushed.

The colonel had them sit on either side of him and now it took a purposeful will to keep her smile pinned in place. Eating helped. The colonel had a private cook who had served up steak, which was a huge surprise.

"Oh, yes, quite a prize," Williams said around a mouthful. "One of our scrounge crews found thirteen head of cattle, untouched by the stiffs. Man, this rain is coming down hard." It beat upon the roof of the tent and they had to practically shout to be heard over it.

Sarah ate greedily, and when she was almost done she said, "You know what this needs? Some red wine. Tell me you have some?" As the dinner had progressed she had stiffened up more and more and she worried that she would be dry as a desert when the time came.

"I don't," the colonel answered. "Alcohol and soldiers

are a deadly combination, though I suppose that I will have to lighten up on that rule eventually, but...first...is that thunder?"

Even as he asked there came another heavy, crunching noise that shook the air. "Crap! What are the tanks firing at?"

He left in a hurry and the two women sat there growing more and more nervous as gunfire could be heard all along the upriver edge of The Island. It then began to slip down the banks of the island on both sides. A few minutes later a soldier burst into the tent.

"Where's the colonel?"

"Why? What's going on?" Sarah pleaded. She had a terrific fright going and felt vulnerable in her summer dress and high-heels.

"The second island is being overrun. Now where's the damned colonel?"

Veronica said something, but Sarah didn't hear; she was busy running. Out into the night and the rain she ran, but did not get far before her heels sunk three inches deep into the new mud. She stepped out of them and ran toward the south end of the island where the firing was picking up.

The scene around her was nearly beyond her ability to comprehend. The river on both sides was clogged with zombies. Thousands had entered up-stream and now they were being swept along. At the sight of so many humans they were doing an odd swim; they basically clawed at the water. It would have been ineffective except that there were so many of them that the ones in the rear pushed the others forward.

Many hundreds were hung up in the concertina wire, while others were climbing slowly up the pontoon bridge that connected the two islands. Guns were firing at a rapid rate, shredding the creatures, but more came on and on.

And then the colonel came up in a Humvee. He took one look at the situation and ordered: "Cut the bridge! Let it go! Don't waste any more ammo unless they actually come onto this island."

A second later he was shocked as Sarah grabbed him and screamed over the gunfire and the rain, "No! My parents are over there."

He shoved her roughly away and she went down in the mud. "My orders stand. In every war there is collateral damage. It's for the greater good."

The colonel was lucky she wasn't armed or she would have killed him on the spot. In that moment she realized her parents were defenseless—not a single one of the misfits was allowed a gun.

A soldier in front of the bridge put down his M16 and began working on one of the pins that held the pontoons in place. In a flash Sarah ran forward, picked up the gun and sped out onto the heaving bridge. A grey hand reached out from the water and tripped her. She almost lost the gun. She tried to get up, but, by then, the bridge was swinging crazily as the first of the chains let go.

Someone yelled over the din, "There's a civilian on the bridge! Don't cut the chain."

"No!" yelled the colonel, staring right into Sarah's eyes. "Cut it." The chain let go and Sarah, who had just regained her feet, fell into the water where thousands of zombies waited.

Chapter 24

Sarah

The Island

That afternoon, as Sarah and Veronica had talked nervously about how they were going to fake orgasms—not too loudly Veronica advised, because the colonel would see right through it if they sounded like a low budget porno movie—the river that parted around the Island was slate grey in color and home only to a few catfish and a million minnows. That night it was a different story.

It had literally become a river of zombies.

Thousands of them were swept along, fighting the current to get at the Island in their greed to devour human flesh. While just above them, on the now loose pontoon bridge, cold rain lashed at Sarah as she leapt from one wood section to another. The mostly unsupported pontoons were slick, heaving up and down as the zombies struggled to get at her. With her feet slipping about and the pontoons yawing and bucking it was an inevitability that Sarah would go into the water. Mid-way across, the pontoon she was on began to tip on its side. Her feet slid to the edge and she knew that her options had all disappeared and so, with her heart in her throat, she was forced to dive in over the arms of the nearest zombies.

Even when the sun had been out and the day had been agreeable in its fall warmth, the water had been icy cold. Now, as Sarah splashed down into it, she didn't even notice; her panic was too great to feel warmth or chill, or the inch-long splinters in her feet, or even the weight of the M16 in her hand. All she knew was a wild, mindless terror and she was determined to get out of the river before the zombies could tear her apart.

When she came up for air, she saw that the bridge had

been taken completely by the current and had swung down the river at a gaining speed and as it did it pulled the creatures along, creating a V-shaped lane where the water was clear of the beasts. Immediately she swung the M16 across her shoulder and began to swim.

Her stroke was dreadfully inefficient and ugly. She had been taught to swim in the proper fashion: face down, body aligned to cut the water, toes pointed, and arms spinning like twin waterwheels. In that river, the river of zombies, form gave way to survival. Out of fear, she swam with her head held high out of the water and to keep the rifle in place she felt the need to swing her arms wide. She churned the water like a drowning victim, which could not fail to draw the wrong kind of attention. Zombies came at her in a rush, clawing the water, raking it back to get at her.

They had her thirty feet from shore. Every zombie within sight ringed her and churned the river white in their mindless desire. Sarah screamed and tried to fight the gun from her shoulder, but it wouldn't come and the waste of effort only had her sinking lower in the water as the monsters came just within reach, and then a wave swept over her, and her panic became hysteria.

But it was only for a second.

Above the water the air was filled with soul tearing screams, and machine gun fire and the hateful hungry moans of the zombies, but below the water there was utter calm.

Sarah took a big breath and ducked beneath the water, this time on purpose. She went deep, before angling to the second island where her parents were. In the dark she swam blind, kicking like a frog until her hand hit slime, and then a submerged log, and then sand. Only then did she dare raise her head up out of the water. The sight reinvigorated her panic. The second island teemed with zombies. More were all around the island in the water, and hundreds were clawing their way through the coiled razor sharp concertina wire.

Three of the beasts were just in front of her but their focus was ahead and so she slunk back down in the river and kicked off the bottom, moving to her left where the bridge had at one time been connected. The current had pushed her away from it, however now, as she yanked the M16 from her back, she slogged along keeping as low as she could, trying not to draw attention to herself.

It was easy to do. The second island was utter chaos. Not even a tiny fraction of the zombies from the river had made it through the wire yet the people were practically defenseless. What few soldiers who had been assigned to guard the perimeter were burning through their ammo even though they knew there would be no more to replace it. Where there weren't any soldiers, the zombies came on unchecked and the non-essentials fought back with anything at hand: axes, shovels, even rakes.

It was clear to Sarah that the island would be overwhelmed in a matter of minutes, if not sooner. She also knew that for her to keep going was tantamount to suicide, but after failing to do anything about rescuing her daughter she couldn't just leave her parents to die this way. With a glance down at the gun in her hand to check that the *safe* had been switched to *fire* she slipped out of the water, stepped carefully on through a section of flattened wire, and ran up the bank onto the island.

Her parents had been staying in a little green tent at the far end of the island so she went that way, ducking behind trees to avoid fleeing workers and hiding from zombies. Once she almost shot a human. It was man so covered in blood that she was sure it was one of the living corpses and her gun came up to his face before he screamed at her in what sounded like a foreign language. He tried to grab the gun, but fortunately his hand was slick and red, so that with a mighty tug she remained in control of it. The gun was her only chance.

She ran, bent over and low until she came to where the

tents were; thankfully her parents weren't there. The people hiding in the tents were fools, trusting to a shell of thin nylon to save them. They were "safe" at the moment, however in a short time they would become easy meals.

A shout that sounded more like an order than a panicked scream brought her head around and there, sixty feet away, was a group of nonessentials trying to form a perimeter wall out of picnic benches. Her father was with the group, straining to keep one of the benches on its side as zombies tried to pull it down. Sarah charged the beasts from behind and at point blank range fired into the back of their heads sending brain and gore sheeting across the tabletop.

"Sarah!" Gary Rivers cried at seeing her. "Get in here."

She ducked around the bench and breathed a sigh of relief at seeing her mom a few feet away in the middle of the perilously upended tables. The relief could not last; Sarah had seen their danger from the outside and it was far worse than they knew. "We can't stay here," she yelled over the din, before rushing to grab her mother's arm. "Come on, this whole island is about to be overrun."

Denise pulled back against her daughter. Her face was white and the skin of it so drawn in fear that she hardly looked like herself. "There's nowhere to go! They've cut the bridge and the river is full of zombies."

This was true, and yet when Sarah looked around and saw the undead trampling over their brothers struggling in the wire, using them to bridge the emplacements she knew the little perimeter would not hold for more than a few minutes. She wasn't the only who saw all of this. Already the people closest to the river were beginning to run and this began a general stampede of the non-essentials.

The picnic benches were allowed to fall one after another and the people took off north. When her parents saw this they gave up on the perimeter they were just fighting for, and wanted to run along with everyone else.

Sarah pulled them back. Having just come from the

north side of the island she knew that it was going to be even worse than where they were, and yet the zombies were coming so thick that they couldn't stay. An idea came to her and she yanked her parents around and pulled them to where the tents sat. There had been only a few zombies sniffing around minutes before and she hoped that would still be the case.

Even before she got there she saw it wasn't. The easy meals were screaming as they were being eaten alive and this only drew more of the monsters on.

"Sarah! Behind your mother," her father yelled. A stiff had come up out of nowhere to grab Denise. Sarah shot it from inches away.

"To the river," Sarah said. "It's our only chance." Hoping they would follow, she ran to the river, shot more of the undead and then stopped just as the land sloped down to the wire and the river beyond. There was no going that way—it had become a wall of zombies. There was no going in any direction. People screamed and ran about mindlessly going from one danger to the next.

"The trees!" Gary cried. "Help me get your mother up."

It was a slim hope. Most of the trees on the little slab of an island were thin pines and those that could bear some weight weren't easy to climb as their branches started so high up. One that could be used by her mother was close to a steep edge of the island—they pushed her up into the tree and she scrambled as best she could.

"You next, Sarah," her father ordered.

"Don't wait for me," she said slinging the rifle. "Get in that tree over there." He went to climb it and she leapt for the lowest branch of the pine. It bent under her grip and she clung to the trunk with her bare thighs, feeling the bark burn. Had she been in another time or place she would've dropped with a scream but the zombies had caught sight of the little group off on their own and were rushing at them.

"Hurry!" Denise screamed. "They're right behind you."

Sarah reached for another branch and pulled and shimmied her way higher, while her mother went on screaming in horror. It was a moment before Sarah realized the screams weren't for her. Her father was only seven or eight feet off the ground, just within reach of the tallest of the zombies. One of them had a hold of his ankle and would not let go, while Gary's grip grew weaker with every passing second.

Now her mother was grabbing Sarah by the shirt and yanking and screaming for her to help her father, however stuck in a tree like that it took too long to get the rifle off her back, and in a position to shoot. By the time she did, Gary had been pulled down. He fought with a rage and a strength that surprised Sarah. He had been carrying a hoe, which he had laid aside to climb the tree, but now as he dropped he grabbed it up and swung it around with great vigor.

Yet it was not a sword and he was not a knight in armor. It struck dead the beast in front and a second, but it was a clumsy weapon and fouled momentarily in the next zombie. Before Sarah could untangle her weapon and find a way to hold on to her precarious perch and shoot at the same time, a horrid creature with most of its face missing launched itself upon her father. In a second Gary was down, lost from sight under a pile of zombies.

"Shoot...Shoot!" Denise screamed, pointing at the mesh of bodies.

Sarah sighted at the best target she had, the side of her father's head. Shooting the monsters would be a waste of ammo. Dozens were converging on the helpless man and the fact that he was already bitten, meant his time was up—the fever would destroy him even if she managed to shoot every single zombie on the island. She aimed and fired.

True to the teaching of the man she shot, she didn't blink or pull away. She didn't yank on the trigger or try to breathe through the shot.

She caressed the trigger and sent a bullet smashing

through his head and then nearly dropped the gun as her hands went numb.

"You missed," Denise said in a little voice. "Oh, God! Don't look." She turned away, while Sarah never had any intention of looking. Nor would she look at any part of the island. Instead she stared at the hateful sky, letting the rain beat into her face, letting it wash away the tears and what was left of her soul. After a long time, many, many hours, she thought she was done with the pain.

Chapter 25

Ram

Western Desert

"Don't shoot," Ram pleaded. Julia had the gun twisting into her hair, digging it in, and her breathing was picking up. Sure signs that she was seconds from pulling the trigger.

"You can have the house, Ram. And all the food and the trucks, just bury me. I don't want to be eaten."

He threw down the shovel and said, "I won't do it. I won't bury you. And...and it's a sin to kill yourself."

Julia laughed and then cried. "Is that all you have? That it's a sin? Do you think I care about hell anymore? I'm in hell already! That grave there," she said pointing to the one on the left. "That's my husband, Jack. The next one is Taylor's grave, my little brother. And that's Papa, and that last one you know is for Mama. That's all the love I have. Have you ever experienced that? All the love you have is buried in front of you. My love is just sitting under the dirt, rotting."

"No it's not all your love," Ram said. "There's more love out there for you. You just have to live, and you will find it."

She shook her head and the gun dropped to her side. "Who am I going to love? You? Or maybe some other stranger who doesn't know the first thing about me?"

"No. That's...that's not what I meant, I..." he flailed for words and she gave him a cheerless smile.

"See? There isn't any real reason to live. We just keep eating and breathing but there isn't any reason to it. We only go through the motions waiting until it's our turn to die."

"That was true before as well," Ram said. "Nothing has changed except scale. The problems are basically the same: disease and hunger and war. Life has always been hard. That's why we look for happiness in it. That hasn't changed either; we look for love and friendship, and we look for those things that make us smile or laugh. None of that has changed."

"But...it has," Julia said through new tears. She pointed at the low mounds of dirt. "Look at them! They were everything to me. I wouldn't want to replace them even if I could."

"You're right, you shouldn't," Ram agreed staring down at the graves and wondering if anyone would bury him when he died. Probably not; he'd be left to be eaten. He sighed and it was for himself. For just a few minutes there, as he had spoken, he had felt confident and strong, like his old self. Julia was weak and needed someone strong and he had been...but now the feeling, like a snuffed match, just went out at the idea of being left alone to be eaten. "I don't know why I'm trying to talk you out of this. It's your choice, really, just like before. I'll bury you, I promise."

"Thanks, I appreciate that." She didn't sound thankful; her words were hollow, devoid of thought or feeling. The gun went back up and Ram turned away, not wanting to watch.

When there was the briefest pause he said, "I think I was lucky. My parents died a few years ago. I didn't think I was lucky at the time, but now, I think I am. My father had a heart attack and my mom had cancer. I never had any brothers or sisters."

"What about a wife?"

"I had a girlfriend, but I never did consider marrying her. Now I'm pretty certain she's dead. She went to Mexico when all this started and every report I heard made it seem that places like Mexico or India or China are nightmares."

"Nightmares?" she scoffed. "They would have to be bad compared to here."

Ram turned around and shook his head at her, and said, "I had this professor and he couldn't say a sentence without sticking the word *relative* in it. Everything's relative. My misery? I thought I was doing bad, but compared to you, I guess I'm doing all right. And your pain? I don't want to diminish it at all, but I bet there are people out there in worse shape. I guess it's just how we deal with it."

"I'm not going to love again," she declared in little clipped words. It was though she bit off the very end of each. "I can't."

Ram smiled suddenly, remembering. "I had this other teacher who said: In each of us is an infinite capacity to love, but only a finite capacity to hate. When he said it, the class all nodded along and I could see that they were thinking *Dude, that's deep.* When I was a kid I had this friend. His family was very catholic, and every time his mom got pregnant, he would moan and groan and swear that he was just going to hate this next kid. He was the oldest of eight and each new brother or sister meant more work and a little less at Christmas or at the dinner table. But he always loved each one. He always found room in his heart."

"I can't get pregnant," Julia said suddenly, perhaps looking for reasons to keep up the high tempo of her pain. "It's why Jack left me, or that's what he said. He only came back to sign the papers and then the airport in Vegas got closed and then he got bit and then he died." She took a long shaking breath and added, "He said I was broken. Do you think that was the real reason he left me?"

"Maybe," Ram replied. He had never given much thought to having a child; he figured when the day came that would be that. "You never know with men. Some guys really want children; some would use your situation as an excuse. I don't know. Can I have the gun? It makes my stomach hurt to see you holding it."

"I could kill myself without it," she said. "I thought about it a lot this last week. I thought about all the different ways. But I had my mother to think about. Now she's gone, I kind of feel like a boat that's lost its anchor, you know? I'm just drifting away."

He came to her and put out his hand and said, "That

hasn't changed either. I think grief will always be like that."
She looked at the gun and shrugged at it before putting it
into his hand.

"For now," she said, yet Ram guessed that her crisis had
peaked. It was likely that her pain would diminish with each
day until it became manageable. And if not? If she really
wanted to kill herself, then she would and there really wasn't
much he could do about it. "Here comes your *friend*." Cassie
came strolling out of the house with a pistol in one hand and
Ram's M16 in the other.

"I told her that I would teach her how to shoot."

"Maybe you should hold off using guns for a while,"
Julia suggested, forgetting her tears. "You're exhibiting all
the classic signs of Post Traumatic Stress Disorder."

"I don't think life without guns is possible anymore. I
just need some rest." Even as he said this, the broken feeling
inside him became stronger and he had to force the grimace
off his face. "Want to stay and watch?"

This struck Julia as funny for some reason and she
laughed with tears still in her eyes. "Are you trying to get me
killed? No. No I shouldn't. She's probably looking to have
you all to herself."

This turned out to be true. Ram wanted to set up targets,
however Cassie had the idea that it was a waste of
ammunition, when there were so many stiffs still walking
about—a few, no more than twenty or so—meandered here
and there on the dusty land. They started walking to the
nearest one and as they did he explained the features of the
Beretta 9MM.

He had to wonder if she was listening when she asked,
"Were you guys talking about me?" When he told her, no,
she followed up with, "You know she was getting divorced?
Her man didn't want her. Must have been sucky in bed or
whiney or something."

Ram coughed into his hand and said, "I don't know the
truth. Ok, why don't you forget about her for a while and

concentrate on that stiff." He showed her the right stance and then had her dry fire the gun until the zombie was twenty feet away. At fifteen feet, when Ram was beginning to feel his heart begin to skip in his chest, she shot and holed the thing through the neck.

It still moved feebly, though it shouldn't have been able to. "You got its spinal cord but it still moves," he mentioned. "That's weird. You'd think it would be paralyzed." She went to finish it off, but he held her back. "Don't the waste the ammo." There was a heavy rock nearby and he crushed its head with it. Again he felt strange through the chest, like he was on the verge of a heart attack.

"Why you gots your face like that?"

He touched himself and felt the grimace. "I don't know. Maybe the stress?"

This made her laugh. "You don't need to stress, baby. You see that shot? I kilt that bad boy no problem. Let's do another."

They went on to the next.

"Was that where you were aiming?" he asked after she had plowed a red furrow through a zombie's cheek. "Or were you aiming at center mass like I said? I didn't think so. You're jerking the trigger back. Make it gentle and steady. When you get good you can try for headshots, until then go with your best chance of slowing them down."

She was better with the next and Ram was as well. It was easier to deal with the stiffs when he saw them as targets only and not as people. Shooting people was something the soul rebelled against.

The two of them made their way through one zombie after another until Julia's house was small in the distance, and then Cassie turned on Ram suddenly.

She was very close and somewhere in the last minute she had undone the buttons on her top. "You ready to take a walk on the wild side?" she asked, moving her shoulders so that her breast swayed. "Where the colored girls say doo, do, doo, do? Huh? What do you say? No one's around. No one will know." Before he could say anything she went on with her dance, singing, "Doo, do, doo, do..."

Ram wanted to tell her no, but just then he felt a twitch down below. Just a twitch but it was something and it likely would have grown into something considerably more, but Cassie said, "That white stick ain't got nothing on me. I know how to rock your world. I do things to you that she ain't never done."

It was her *need* that Ram discovered bothered him so. It wasn't a sexual need, it was a personal one. It was a need to be wanted, and a need to be loved and it was so over-powering that he feared she would drown him in it. Just then he could barely keep afloat himself and he shook his head.

"Not yet."

Her smile left and her full lips went tight against her teeth. "A hug?"

"I can do that."

She grabbed him and crushed herself to him and it wasn't enough. It would never be enough for her—nothing would be. She was a taker and he had nothing to give. When he stiffened, turning cool, she shoved him back and he went down on his butt. "I'd not waste no more time if I was you or I'm gonna take it somewheres else."

He was sure that she would anyway. There'd always be another man, smarter, better looking, perhaps even mentally stable; and then she'd leave him. He shrugged slightly and she stomped away, buttoning her shirt as she went, ignoring the zombies who ambled her way. One was particularly aggressive and quick.

From the prone position, lying in the spare grass of the desert hill, Ram took up his M16, flicked off the safety and sighted on the man....no, not a man, a zombie, or better yet, the *target*. At a hundred yards a head shot shouldn't have been a problem. He knocked the right ear off the zombie, leaving an ugly grey hunk of flesh dangling.

Cassie turned and raised her gun, but Ram was quicker. This shot sent the target flopping face down. "Serviceable," he whispered to himself, feeling the butterflies in his gut calm.

He felt more himself that afternoon and he was happy to see Julia no longer had the lost look in her eyes. Cassie acted as though she hadn't been turned down, yet again, and constantly put herself between Ram and Julia, much to their hidden amusement. Her actions only brought them closer together since they shared a secret laugh every time the girl would accidentally pin Ram against a wall, or make an overt suggestion.

It wasn't funny however when she came to Ram's bed in the middle of the night once again stripped down to nothing. This time Ram felt more than a twitch, and so did she.

"That's more like it," she said, gripping him, showing that her need wasn't just mental and emotional.

"No," he said taking her hand off him. A part of him rebelled—the part that just wanted a good fuck and be done with her. The thinking part of him knew that if he gave in to a night's pleasure, she would be like a leach. "I'm sorry, but you were right before, about Julia. I think I like her."

"Oh fuck this!" she screamed loud enough to get Julia out of bed and loud enough to alert the zombies outside. Cassie didn't care. She was in a full steam: "She just put her man in a hole and you think you're going to move in here and take over? You so dumb! She just using you, boy."

Actually it was the other way around, Ram was using Julia as a buffer to keep Cassie away. Also, he used Julia to help keep himself sane. Her problems were so much easier to deal with than his own, and whenever she was around it was like a vacation from the stress that ate him up inside. It wasn't that he didn't like Julia he did. She was smart and pretty, however he didn't think it would go anywhere, she had seen him weak.

Just then she came padding down the hall in a hurry.

"You need to calm down," she hissed at Cassie. "There are zombies all over the place outside and our doors will only hold them back for so long."

"Why don't you shut the fuck up. Telling me what to do, shit!"

Julia looked taken aback at the girl's rudeness. "This has got to end," she said to Ram. "Why don't you just take care of *business* so we can all get some sleep." By business she indicated the naked girl. Cassie seemed completely at ease with her nudity and in fact she was far more striking than either Ram or Julia who both wore baggy grey warm ups.

"He won't," Cassie answered for Ram. "He's all Julia this and Julia that. Maybe *you* should take care of business and then he'll see that there ain't nothing there but..."

A heavy thud struck something downstairs, and this was followed by more blows. "Get to the attic," Ram whispered—they had made an emergency shelter out of the attic, with food and gallon jugs of water. It would keep them alive for a few days if it came down to it.

They didn't need it that night. Ram went about and checked the doors and windows with his Beretta at the ready. The larger windows had been boarded over with plywood, while the doors were heavy and of good quality. Yet these measures hadn't proven strong enough in most homes; what had kept this home intact for so long were the rigorous light and sound restrictions at night.

Normally the home seemed so dead that the undead walked right on by, but now voices had been raised and the undead turned toward the house. They began an assault, which petered out after a while when nothing was heard. The three humans had retreated upstairs to the attic where the silence was strained to say the least. Cassie steamed in anger, while Julia looked uncomfortable. Ram couldn't think of anything to say that would make the situation better.

The strain continued the next day. Julia felt the need to cook for everyone at every meal, however at breakfast

Cassie took her waffles and went outside rather than be in the same room with the other two.

"Cassie was right," Julia said at one point. "My husband is right out there. How can you think that I'd..."

Ram held up a hand. "I lied to her. She was all over me and I figured if she thought that she didn't have a chance, she would tone it down."

Julia looked at him and her blue eyes were narrowed to slits as if she couldn't quite figure him out. "If you don't like me then why don't you just show her some affection? She has needs like we all do."

"*Some* affection wouldn't be enough for her."

"You're a guy," Julia said with a shrug. "It shouldn't be a problem."

"And if we were back in the old world it wouldn't be," Ram admitted. "Now it's different. I just can't screw her and then toss her away. I'm responsible for her and for you."

"Not me," she insisted quickly. "I'm a big girl. And if you're worried, I wouldn't look down on you if you took one for the team, if you know what I mean. Cassie is in a delicate state right now, she told me that she's lost everyone. She feel empty inside." Her blue eyes went vacant and Ram stared into them and she didn't even seem to notice.

"When you put it like that, you're talking about all of us," he said. "Wasn't it just yesterday that you put a gun to your own head?"

"I'm tougher than I look," Julia said, though just then she seemed delicate like a porcelain doll. "But I don't think Cassie is."

At this Ram snorted. He remembered how she had accepted her gang rape with a stoicism that he still couldn't believe. "She's a tough one," he insisted, but in this he was only partially right.

That night Ram did not wait for Cassie to climb into his bed as she had for the previous two nights, instead he went to the bedroom down the hall. "What's wrong?" Julia asked.

She had clearly been awake.

Her eyes went wide as Ram took his clothes off and slid in next to her. "What are you doing? I told you to go to Cassie," she whispered.

"You told me that we all need affection. I don't like Cassie; not like this."

"And you like me?" she asked. Her words were nervous and hopeful in equal parts.

When he nodded she seemed to hesitate and he said words that he didn't think that he would ever say, "We don't have to do anything. I can just hold you."

"Ok," she said and cautiously slid toward him. "You just want to cuddle? Is it because of your *issue*? Cassie told me about what was going on with your, you-know-what. Girls don't keep many secrets between them. It's nothing to be ashamed of."

She ran a trembling hand over his body and then suddenly pressed herself to him, wrapping her arms around his chest, as if she wanted to seal him to her, to fuse him to her skin. At first she held him tight and did nothing but cry, but then he kissed her bleary face and she smiled, and reached out to check the condition of his *issue*. Her beauty and her soft body and her gentle need had fixed the issue, and now she gripped him with a more urgent need.

In the morning Ram slipped out of bed and went to face the music. He heard Cassie banging around the house, knocking into things seemingly on purpose to get him to wake up. "Cassie, I wanted to let you know that..." his words dried up in his mouth.

It wasn't Cassie knocking into things. The kitchen was full of zombies. They charged at him, while behind he heard more coming down the hall.

Chapter 26

Neil

Columbus, Ohio

Sadie's choice in music was nearly enough to make Neil find his own ride westward. Every song seemed to consist solely of grinding guitars, and if there was a singer, if they could be called such, it sounded as though they were part demon. He couldn't understand a word of their lyrics, but judging by the song titles it didn't seem worth trying to fathom them out.

She complained of his music as well: said it all bored her and put her to sleep. This was true enough. When it was his turn to drive she curled up next to him and slept with her mouth open. She was much prettier when she slept. There was an innocence to her that only came out then. Normally it was hidden beneath the heavy mascara and the black lipstick.

"You should try a lighter color of lipstick," he suggested one afternoon. "I'm just saying I think you would look better. Don't get me wrong you're very pretty right now, I just don't understand why you wouldn't want to be prettier."

"Prettier for who? For the zombies?"

"I don't know, maybe we will meet some young men...now don't give me that look." She had raised her eyebrows at the word *men*. "You know what I mean. I keep up my appearance for the ladies." He did too. Every day since he had seen the first zombie rat he had shaved and dressed as he always had, very neatly.

Theatrically she grabbed the wheel and said, "Then you better turn around. I just saw a cute zombie-mama for you. She was barely chewed on. It was some prime zombie ass."

He exhaled wearily over her coarseness. "You never know where you'll meet someone is all I'm saying. There could be a boy right around the corner."

There wasn't.

The army in the east had died fighting, trying to hold lines that were flanked and pierced in dozens of places by zombies that numbered in the millions. Bodies were everywhere attesting to the bitter struggle.

They saw very few live people along the back roads of Pennsylvania, none of whom wanted the least thing to do with anyone driving such a farfetched beast as the monster truck. Yet they did run into a couple of people eventually, while looking for a pair of scissors for Neil. He hadn't had a haircut in a month and thought he looked no better than a hippie.

"You should grow it out," Sadie suggested. They were in the remains of a CVS pharmacy just east of Columbus, Ohio. The pickings in the store were slim. "Women like a man with long hair. You know like that guy from *Braveheart*, that old dude."

"I don't look anything like Mel Gibson and no amount of hair extensions will change that," Neil said. "Here we go, finally. Can you cut hair? I mean really cut like a stylist or have you only practiced on Barbie dolls...get down!" he hissed suddenly, ducking behind a counter. "There are a couple of guys near the truck."

She gave them a glance and then looked at Neil. "What do you want me to do about them? You're the man, remember. And you have a gun. You'll be fine." She began to push him to the door. He went out reluctantly, slightly panic-stricken. What would happen if they were mean?

"Hey there," Neil said, striving for a relaxed and easy going note, but hitting a combination psycho-killer and TV clown instead. The gun felt weird in his hands. Was he supposed to be pointing it at them? He didn't think that was very polite, so instead he just sort of played with it, twirling the heavy thing on his finger as if he was always doing creepy things like that.

The man was older and grey, maybe fifty. He was gritty looking with a long, greasy ponytail and wearing a dirty biker jacket over dirtier jeans. He too had a gun, but his was in a holster at his hip. "This your truck? She's a beauty," he said with a yellowed smile. Clearly he was a smoker and the acid breath that he spewed covered the distance between him and Neil in a second.

"Oh yeah. It's mine, or really it's my friend's. My name is Neil," he said holding out his hand and grinning in a sick sort of way because of the man's rancid breath.

"Chuck," the biker said crushing Neil's hand in a hard grip. "And this is my boy, Charlie."

The boy was a full head taller than Neil and seemed to have something to prove in the handshaking department as he tried to outdo his father in the creation of hairline fractures in Neil's hand. "Nice to meet you both," Neil said, struggling not to massage his hand when he stepped back.

"You too," Chuck said, turning from Neil and looking at the truck with interest. He glanced up at an angle to see the inner workings of the thing. "What you got in there?" he asked.

After considering the question, Neil had to shrug. "You mean other than the engine? I'm not sure. Just the usual stuff I think."

The father and son shared a look along with a smile. "I meant what size engine? Forget it. Would you mind if I popped the hood? It's ok, I'm a mechanic." Without waiting for permission Chuck climbed up into the cab and triggered the latch.

"I guess it's ok then," Neil said, staring about for Sadie. He felt oddly vulnerable without the girl near. Above him, the man touched here and there, giving hoses and belts a sturdy shake, while he squinted at all of the mechanical workings. As he did, he mentioned strange sounding words to his son, such as nitrous, coil over and leaf spring. The boy seemed to understand and he gave Neil a wink. In return,

Neil nodded as though he knew what they were talking about.

Chuck eventually shut the hood and climbed back down. "So what do you want for her? I'm willing to trade quite a bit, though I won't go all out seeing as there is some damage to the springs. This isn't a true monster truck, but it's clear someone has been acting as though it is."

"It seems pretty big to me," Neil replied, getting defensive.

"Yeah, she's big, but she's only a custom job. Four-hundred CCs, and a premium suspension don't make her a monster truck. She ain't built to run all over every car that gets in her way. Now, as for a trade, I got some guns and ammo, and tons of gas, and more water than I really need. I even have a smaller truck that would be more your speed. I'll throw that in as well. It's a Ford Ranger. A good truck."

"I don't think I want to trade," Neil said, feeling the gun again in his hands. He didn't like the look in the man's eyes; it was how all mechanics looked. As if they knew damned well that you didn't have a clue what they were talking about and that they knew they could rook you just like an oil-stained gypsy.

"Yeah I get that," Chuck said, easily clapping Neil on the back as if they were old buddies. "It's understandable, but here's why you should: you got a leaking manifold. It could be just the gasket is bad, but the way the undercarriage is all dinged up I'm betting you got a dent in the manifold itself and that's going to spell trouble down the road."

Neil had no clue what a manifold was or what it did. For all he knew it was a made up word—though it did sound familiar. "What sort of trouble are you talking about?"

"The kind that'll leave you stranded in the middle of nowhere. And it ain't like you can call Triple-A now, can you? So, I say let's work a trade while you still got something to trade with. What do you say?"

Just then Sadie appeared behind the truck; Neil only

saw her head and it was shaking vehemently. "No, I don't think so," he said. "You're nice to ask, but we don't plan on traveling forever. We're going west. Maybe find a mountain town without too many zombies. I'm sure the truck will make it that far, especially if we're a little more careful." This last he said for Sadie's sake; she enjoyed smashing over things way too much. He had warned her but like every other teenager in the world she thought she knew more than her elders.

Chuck shrugged a: what-can-you-do kind of shrug. "West? Maybe that isn't a bad idea. We just came south from Toledo and I can tell you, that's one direction you don't want to go. You can't swing a dead zombie cat without hitting another zombie. Here's a plan, me and my boy will team up with you and your partner for a while. You don't think he'll mind, do you?"

"I don't mind," Sadie said, coming out from behind the truck with the heavy shotgun looking like a bazooka compared to her thin frame. "As long as we come to an agreement beforehand. What's ours is ours and what's yours is yours, and whatever we find from here on out we split down the middle. Kind of like a pre-nup."

Chuck smiled at her and if she were closer he likely would've patted her on the head. "This is your partner?" he asked Neil. "This is her truck? I find that really hard to believe. She steal it?"

"No, *she* didn't steal it," Sadie answered for Neil who hadn't known how to reply to the question. "You can't steal from a zombie. They give up all rights when they start eating people. But what's it to you where I got it from?"

"Feisty," Chuck commented, earning him a giggle from his boy.

Neil went to Sadie's side and declared, "She is feisty and brave, and very smart. Look, I don't think it's a good idea for you to come along with us if you can't be civil."

Chuck blew out a long breath. "Hey, don't get your

panties in a bunch. I meant nothing. Hell, it's good she's feisty. It should be a compliment these days. I was just wanting to know what sorts of people me and my boy are thinking of taking up with. Trust is going to be hard to come by, you know."

"Oh, we know," Sadie replied, eyeing Chuck as if he were a very large cockroach."

"Ok then," Chuck said and then paused to glance at his son. "I think this pre-nup idea is a good one. Though we should make allowances for services rendered. What would happen if your truck broke down? You wouldn't expect me to work on it for free, would you?"

"No, I guess not," Neil said, scratching his neck absently with the .357. He looked to Sadie for agreement, but she made a face.

"I'm glad you aren't one of those mechanics who take advantage of women and noobs," Sadie said with something close to a sneer. "But we won't need your mechanical expertise either way. If something just 'happens' to go wrong with the truck, I'm going to put her out of her misery. Lighting up a gallon of gasoline in the engine compartment should do it."

Chuck stared at her in amazement and then he burst into a huge smile. "Woo-wee, you got a wild one, Neil! How did you manage to land her? I bet she's just crazy in bed."

"What?" Neil asked, feeling the metal of the gun in his hand. It suddenly felt very heavy as though it wanted its presence known. "Sadie is not my girlfriend. We're traveling together as companions only, and I have to ask that you respect her. She is a very capable young lady."

The mechanic stuck out his lower lip and bowed his head acknowledging his chastisement. "I'm sorry. I'm a kidder. Ask Charlie here. I like to joke around...and I can take a joke, too. So if you want to razz me I won't take it personal. Listen Sadie, it's your truck. I won't try to take it I promise."

This was a promise that didn't last.

They agreed to travel together, though they didn't get very far that day. It was late afternoon by the time Neil found and siphoned enough gas to fill both the truck as well as all the jerry cans. Then Chuck and his son wanted to pull over just before six. They were driving the Ford Ranger and said that they didn't sleep in it.

"We can't sleep in it, really," Charlie told them as his father went to check out a little farmhouse off the highway. "The stiffs come and bang on the windows all night long. I hate it. You ever go to Red Lobster? I feel like I'm one of the lobsters that they have out front in the fish tank. I feel like the stiffs are pointing at me and saying: *I want that one.*"

"It's why I'm not giving up my truck," Sadie said, squinting from the glare of the setting sun off its chrome. "We're so high up the zombies pass right below us and don't even know."

Chuck came hurrying back. Behind him came a parade of dead bodies. "Not this one," he said with a high laugh. The next was better, and after Chuck shot a couple of the former occupants who were shuffling around in house slippers and staring vacantly with dead eyes, the father and son moved in and locked the doors behind them. They had asked Sadie and Neil to join them, but the two demurred as politely as possible.

"Did you see that pervert looking at me?" Sadie exclaimed, locking the doors of the truck one after another. "Man, he wouldn't stop. All through dinner. That's why I had to move."

Neil had seen the looks. They weren't as bad as Sadie made them out to be, though he could understand that it might be a little upsetting to a seventeen year old who had never had that sort of focus on her before.

"And you want me to go and pretty myself up?" Sadie went on, taking a look at herself in the truck's useless rear view mirror; it was so high up that the only traffic it could effectively show would be low flying airplanes. "No way. Just think how much they'd stare if I did."

"They? Was the son staring as well? He's a bit young for that." The boy was fourteen and almost six feet tall.

Her right shoulder did its little bob and she said, "He looked some. He was a little bit more circumcised about it."

A grin tried to creep across his face, but Neil fought it back. "I think you mean circumspect. Circumcised is a whole other word."

"Oh yeah? I thought it sounded weird when I said it. What is circumcised? It sounds familiar...what? What's wrong? You look all weird."

"I do?" Neil asked, touching his face. "I guess it's because I never figured that I'd be explaining circumcision to a girl, I mean a young woman. It, uh, it has to do with the removal of the, uh, membranous foreskin of the male genitalia. It..."

At this Sadie burst into a barking laugh. "You should see your face!" she said, hitting the steering wheel with her fist as she laughed. "Oh, my stomach! Oh crap that hurts." She continued to laugh until tears came and she fell over onto the seat.

"You know what circumcision means then?" Neil asked, feeling relieved despite that he had clearly been the butt of a joke.

"Of course, you dolt!" she said as her laughter petered into a wheeze. "I'm seventeen, not seven. My friends and I used to put words like that into sentences to see if anyone would even notice. Though it never worked so good as it did on you."

Neil didn't know what to think about that, but at least he wasn't stuck explaining the birds and the bees, something that had him in a sweat. "I thought I was about to have to give you *The Talk*."

She snorted again. "I am good, thank you. But when you do, don't use words like membranous or genitalia, it's either a wiener or a ding-dong. At least it is for normal kids. I can see your kids being all nerdy, walking around saying: I have to urinate through my genitalia..." Sadie stopped talking as she saw Neil's mouth turn down. She bit her lip before saying, "Hey I was joking around about the whole nerd thing. I think you're a real nice guy."

"I am," Neil admitted. "That's what all the girls tell me." Sadie missed the bile in his words. In her mind being nice was a good thing—and it wasn't just her. Every girl he had ever met had labeled him a "nice guy", which essentially meant he was harmless, like a neutered dog or a toothless shark. For Neil it was the kiss of death. Whenever a woman called him "nice", he might as well have died in her eyes, unless of course they needed a favor: a ride to the airport or moving her furniture, or dog sitting while she was off to Vegas with some other guy.

Not that Neil looked at Sadie that way. To him she was little more than a child. What bothered him was that even in the infancy of her womanhood she saw him as a eunuch to be used and abused.

"What's wrong? Really?" she asked, her eyes and her mind disconcertingly sharp.

"Nothing. Nothing." Nice guys don't make waves. Instead they take the crumbs that life gives them and pretend they are good enough. "I'm just getting sleepy." The twilight had turned into true night at some point and now the stars and the zombies were beginning to show.

Out of the blue, Sadie mentioned, "You snore...but I guess you knew that."

"Is it bad?" At her look he added, "How am I supposed to know if I snore? I'm asleep when it happens."

After her half-shrug she said, "You're right, how could you know. It's not that bad. It's like you just breathe loud is all.

That night Neil snored again and Sadie just sighed at the sound.

Chapter 27

Neil

The Island

The four of them left just after daybreak with the general idea of "west" as their destination, though this was not always the direction they traveled. They made a conscious decision to avoid anything that resembled a city and so they snaked their way north of Indianapolis and far south of Chicago.

Along the dusty back roads they found little hamlets which they stopped at to scrounge anything they figured would be of some use. At one point they found toothbrushes. Immediately Neil and Sadie set to brushing their teeth, moaning in pleasure since it had been a few days, while Chuck looked on with a disgusted look and puffing on a cigarette.

Despite the constant stopping and the round-about route, they cut through all of Indiana and half of Illinois before they saw another live human. They had entered a little nothing of a town from the east when a group of three military Humvees came in from the west. The two groups eyed each other in an odd moment.

"We should leave," Sadie advised.

Chuck made a face and pulled out yet another cigarette. "No, we should be cautious," he countered. "I want to know what's going on. Who knows, maybe they have a cure. You ever think of that?"

"They don't have a cure. Look," Sadie pointed at the men who began to go door to door. "They're scrounging just like us." As was frequently the case she was right. The men went into homes with empty duffel bags and came out with them bulging. As the four of them watched an officer with two black bars on his helmet came down the street to greet them.

"Where you folks headed?" He had a twang to his voice and quick blue eyes—they caressed Sadie before moving on to their belongings.

"West," Neil answered. Chuck only watched the officer from behind a shadow of smoke. "We're thinking of maybe going up into the mountains to find a little town to hole up in until this whatever it is blows over."

"Oh yeah?" the officer said as he went around the monster truck. He even climbed up on the fender and glanced at all the food, weapons and fuel they had accumulated. When he hopped down he added, "I wouldn't do that if I was you. Everyone I meet is thinking the same as you and come winter they're all going to starve. There's no food up in the mountains. No cities, no stores, and no farms."

"What about the Army?" Chuck asked. "Do you have any food? Or the government? Don't they have stock piles of everything in secret underground bunkers?"

The officer barely glanced Chuck's way and then he headed for the Ranger to see what was in it. As he walked he said over his shoulder, "If there are secret bunkers full of food they were kept secret from you and me both. And as for the government, all I can say is what government? We haven't heard shit from anyone in nine days and before that they were even more clueless as to what was going on than anyone else. They actually thought that they could win this. Bunch of fucking morons."

Neil held up a finger, but when the officer ignored him, he tapped the uniformed man on the shoulder. "But they're the government. They have to be somewhere. Have you tried looking for them, or calling?"

"My guess is they're all dead like everyone else." The officer gave them a second once over and sighed. "Except for *The Island*, there isn't all that many of us left."

This was of course an obvious truth. The only soldiers any of them had seen had been dead ones, still the news coming from a man in uniform seemed to gain the weight of fact like it hadn't before and the four of them stood looking at each other with faces that had grown pale. They realized the real truth of the situation which was the government was no more and the army was now in the looting business.

Sadie finally spoke, "What's The Island? You said it like there's people there. Could we go?"

The officer gave her an even closer look, as if judging her as he would a suspect horse. He turned to them all and looked them up and down. "The Island is the last bastion of humanity that's left in America, at least as far as we're aware of. If I was you I'd go and see what the colonel thinks of you. If he likes you and thinks you have what it takes, then you can stay. We're always looking for good men. And women of course."

"And, if the colonel doesn't like what he sees?" Neil asked. When the officer had looked at him it had been with a bit of a smirk and Neil was fairly certain this colonel wouldn't think much better of him.

"Then you'll have to find your own way in this world," he answered, and then went on to explain about The Island in very general terms. After that he wished them the best of luck, jumped in his Humvee and signaled his men that it was time to go.

Chuck was enthusiastic: "We should definitely go. They have two thousand soldiers there!"

Sadie was definitely less happy at the idea. "We shouldn't go. They have two thousand soldiers and if they're anything like that guy, then no way. Could he be more inappropriate with all his staring?"

"Oh please!" Chuck wheezed. "All you women do is complain. When men look too much you complain. When men look too little you complain more. And if the guy is ugly then if he even looks a little, he's creepy, and if a guy's handsome then every look means he's in love."

"What are you saying?" Sadie asked, spitting the words

out in her anger. "That my opinion doesn't count because I'm a girl?"

"No, I'm saying let's check out this Island," Chuck said, pausing to hawk up something grayish yellow. "That one soldier was a little odd—yes, I thought he was weird too, all high and mighty acting, but that doesn't mean they'll all be that way. Let's check out the Island and if it doesn't work for us then we scoot on down the road. There's no harm in just taking a look."

Though Sadie still seethed over Chuck's attitude, she agreed to the plan and Neil did as well, although he did so only for her sake only. He knew in his heart that no military man would see much value in him, but Sadie with her bravery and her street smarts would likely fit in just fine. They would be lucky to have her.

With a heavy heart he drove the monster truck west, following the directions the officer had given them. The Island was only some forty miles distant, however they did not make it that day. An immense wave of zombies, inexplicable as ever, came down out of the farmlands of Southern Illinois and the group was forced to pull over. Their only other choice was to mow them down by the hundreds, which was just too sickening for both Sadie and Neil to consider. They didn't mind the wait, as they were high up and safe in the monster truck.

Chuck and his son, on the other hand, had to sit under blankets, afraid to move or make the slightest sound. It was a long evening for them, but eventually the swarm moved on and was replaced by a hellacious storm. It was loud and violent, yet it could not drown out the sound of a battle raging a few miles away to the west.

"That's The Island, I bet," Sadie said. "They're being attacked by that swarm. Do you think they'll make it?"

Neil shrugged in the dark. "I don't know. If that's the last bastion then I really hope so, but from what I've seen, fighting the zombies doesn't seem to work very well.

Remember in Passaic? There were more zombies in uniform than normal zombies."

"Yeah," Sadie breathed. They sat in the dark and watched lightning and artillery light up the sky and each wondered what they would find left on The Island in the morning. Would it be overrun? Would they find only corpses and walking corpses?

"Do you mind if I go up there with you?" Sadie asked in a little voice. "I'm cold."

She wasn't cold, she was afraid.

She was a teenaged girl on the verge of being a woman—a girl with a tight little body, with nipples that always seemed to defy anything she wore—but to Neil she was a girl who was afraid of the world. They fell asleep snuggled together, but only after Neil kissed her once on the forehead and only after she smiled at him.

At first light of day, the two vehicles approached the island from the south and Neil's worst fears were realized. All they saw was death. Bodies were everywhere—some hundreds were hung up in bright coils of concertina wire. These bodies were grey and foul. More bodies littered the island; some were dead humans, some dead zombies. Nothing moved that was alive. Only the dead went here and there in that dazed way of theirs.

"Shit," Sadie whispered, and for once Neil didn't correct her. That he didn't think he would be chosen to live on the island didn't mean he wanted to see the lucky few who did get killed. They drove on, staring glumly, but then another island came into view.

All along this one the dead were stacked like rotting pancakes, but this was only on its outer edge where the concertina wire had held. On the interior of the island not a zombie could be seen. Instead, the land between the rivers bristled with uniformed men, going here and there with purpose.

Neil and Sadie smiled at each other and then she asked,

"Can I drive?"

He understood. The soldiers all seemed young men in great shape and Sadie didn't want to be seen as 'just' a girl. "Sure, it's your truck," he said, knowing that although she would be elevated in their eyes, he would suffer a corresponding lowering in their estimation. After all 'real' men drove, they didn't sit back and let their women do it.

In the end it didn't really matter.

They were stopped before what looked like a very strange bridge and questioned by an officer. This one with a single silver bar on his collar. He introduced himself, "Hey there. I'm Lieutenant Turner and I must say that is one perdy truck."

"Thank you," Sadie said, as she climbed down. Although she had complained about the soldier from the day before, she didn't seem to mind that the men on this side of the bridge all stopped what they were doing to watch her. "I'm Sadie and this is Neil and Chuck and that's Charles."

"Charlie," the boy was quick to interject. Just as Sadie, he didn't want to appear weak or young in the eyes of these men. "It looks like you guys had a real fight last night."

"That we did. Them stiffs were insistent upon eating us." Turner looked around, his smile fading a bit. "So, what brings you to The Island?"

"We were looking to find us some shelter from the storm, so to speak," Chuck answered. "We ran into a group of soldiers who suggested we come here. They said, uh that you'd take us on."

"Of course we would pull our own weight," Neil added quickly. "We're not afraid of hard work."

Just as the soldier from the day before Lieutenant Turner gave them each a look and said, skeptically, "Not afraid of hard work? What did you do before?"

"I was on Wall Street," Neil said and when the lieutenant's smile became merely polite, he added: "And Chuck here is a top notch mechanic. He can fix anything and

I'm sure he taught his boy quite a bit. And Sadie..." he paused looking at the girl. She seemed suddenly very nervous, and had every right to be. The position of 'Loner Goth-girl' didn't seem to be in high demand on the Island. Neil cleared his throat and said, "She's a zombie killing machine. I've never seen anything like it. She walked the streets of Jersey as if she didn't even know the meaning of the word fear."

"Sometimes I was a little nervous," she admitted, keeping her face an easy neutral. Out of sight of the lieutenant she squeezed Neil's hand in gratitude for his words.

"You're from New Jersey, interesting," Turner said. "And you're a mechanic? I think Colonel Williams would be interested in meeting you. He's in charge here. Put any weapons you have in your vehicles and we'll go see if he has a few minutes for you."

This sounded very promising and so the four hurried to obey. Even Neil allowed himself to feel cautiously hopeful. The Island couldn't help bring it out of him. The soldiers were hearty-looking men, their weapons frightful in appearance and, most importantly, the fact that they had survived the zombie swarm of the night before made Neil wish even more he could stay.

They were brought to a tent and then left to themselves, however this was for minutes only and then a soldier came in and said, "The colonel will see you now." The soldier led them to another tent where a tall man sat eating steak and eggs. Unbelievably, there were four plates set out and he waved them to sit down as he chewed.

"Sorry, I shouldn't have started without you, but I've got a zillion things to take care of this morning. I'm Colonel Williams."

They introduced themselves and then sat. Charlie didn't wait on any formality and began to eat with gusto, while Sadie tried to be more discreet, however it was clear that after weeks of eating out of cans, the food was too much to resist.

"It's good to see young ones with such appetites, though sadly this isn't our usual fare," the colonel commented. "We had the largest attack yet occur last night and our refrigeration units on the second island were damaged. We either eat or let the food spoil."

"Did you have many fatalities?" Neil asked, and then politely took a bite.

Chuck seemed to have forgotten his manners about the same time he stopped brushing his teeth, i.e. long ago. Around a bite that was better suited to a gorilla's mouth he commented, "Yeah, there's all sorts of bodies out there. It was hard to tell which was a zombie and which was a person."

The colonel took a drink of water before saying, "At one time they were all people. Though I understand your question and your concerns. Our losses were negligible. Zero here on the main island, which speaks well for our defensive measures."

"What about the second island?" Sadie asked. "I ask because it was clearly not as prepared. Here you have foxholes every twenty feet and big machine guns and three layers of that wire stuff. Over there it looked like you just had the wire."

"I don't discuss casualties, ever," the colonel replied lightly. "It's bad for morale."

"The truth never hurt nobody," Sadie replied, showing her courage by not backing down under the colonel's sudden glare.

"Sadie!" Chuck growled in warning. "We ain't gonna ingratiate ourselves none if you act like this."

"Maybe Sadie has a point," Neil said. "If she's going to be staying here then I want to know she's going to be safe. What I see is that this island is as well protected as it can be and that the people who live here all just happen to be male soldiers. Where are the women and children? Where are all the older people? Did you keep them on that second island, Colonel? Were their deaths negligible because they weren't your soldiers?"

The colonel ate slowly, saying nothing. As he did he eyed Neil like wolf might. Neil did his best not to quail under the stare, in fact he rallied with the realization that he wasn't going to be chosen to stay anyways.

Remaining polite, Neil went on eating his meal with an air of expectation until finally Williams snarled, "There's no saying we're taking any of you, first off. Second, when I say negligible I mean negligible. We don't take many women for the same reason we don't take any children. This is a military base and right now our main concern is surviving. And in case you haven't goddamned noticed we haven't been doing that good a job of it. For weeks, while you've been probably hiding under your damned bed, we've been fighting and dying and this Island is the first bit of luck we've had."

Neil dabbed the corners of his mouth with his napkin and said, "I didn't mean to be offensive, Colonel. It's just your initial answer didn't do anything but worry us more that we already were."

"I wasn't worried in the least," Chuck remarked, sucking his teeth. "I'm sure the colonel runs his base as he sees fit. Like how a man should run his own home, with a firm hand."

This had the colonel agreeing. "You must be the mechanic I was told about. A good mechanic is worth his weight in gold these days."

Unexpectedly Chuck shook his head. "That's where you're wrong. Gold ain't worth dick just now."

This had Williams laughing. "You just may be right about that. And this is your son? He looks like a good strong lad. But, you two," he said taking in Neil and Sadie. "A Wall Street guy and chick zombie hunter." He blew out a long breath as he stared at them, drumming his fingers on the table. "I can't say I need any investment advice just at the moment and as for a girl who hunts zombies...I don't think so. I have a thousand men who are infinitely more qualified."

Neil and Sadie flicked their eyes to each other and both saw the disappointment in the other. Again Chuck surprised them by saying, "If you want me, you have to take them as well and, of course, Charlie--that goes without saying. We'll call it a package deal."

The colonel's smile widened a touch, however it didn't look completely genuine. He cleared his throat and said, "Ok, How about I give them a once-over first. Can you two please stand up and take off your jackets...and your extra shirt, Miss."

He didn't need to look for very long. "Stop hugging yourself, Miss. Put your hands down to your sides. Yes, just like that...Sorry, no deal. You can have your son, on the condition that he works."

"You'd just put us out there?" Neil asked with an uncharacteristic glare. "At least take Sadie. She is smart and quick. You won't be disappointed."

Williams shook his head and then Chuck surprised them for the third and final time. "Then I want the monster truck out there. I may have to scrounge for parts and it's an ideal vehicle to get around in. Great vision, perfect hydraulics, what do you say?"

"Who are you talking to?" Sadie asked, yanking her jacket back on in such a fury that she got caught up in it. "That's my truck. You can't bargain with something you don't even own!"

"Actually you can," the colonel said. "As long as you can get away with it. And in this case he can."

"You can have the ranger," Chuck insisted, trying to placate Sadie. "It's a great truck. Gets good gas mileage."

The colonel grimaced as though he were about to impart bad news, which he was. "About the Ranger, that you can have, but you'll have to leave the gas. And your weapons."

Neil's mouth fell open and Sadie looked about to faint. Williams went on, "And any food or water. I have to think of the greater good in this and the welfare of two thousand men comes before that of just two people."

"Wait..." Chuck started to say, but the colonel stared hard, shutting him up.

He then stood and stretched, though with a hand on the butt of the pistol at his hip. "Before you start in, let me be clear: I've heard it all. Yes, life is not fair—you're just going to have to deal with it. Turner, get in here!"

The man leapt in as if waiting for those exact words. "Sir, we have two packs ready as ordered. Two sleeping bags, two sets of clothes and assorted toiletries. A lighter, a can opener, etcetera."

"Just like that?" Sadie asked, with her mouth hanging open. "We don't get a gun or anything? And no car?"

"Should be no problem for a zombie hunter such as yourself," the colonel said as a parting comment.

Within seconds the two were escorted out of the tent and across the pontoon bridge. On the other side a number of tanks were parked and new rolls of concertina wiring were being strung. Turner handed them the packs and then gave them a light push toward the nearby forest and said in an undertone, "Don't hang around. Put as much distance between us as you can. Some of the soldiers can't be trusted around a young woman such as this. Do you understand me?"

Neil did and thanked him for the warning, but Sadie began to argue, and he was forced to drag her away. "There's no use trying," he told her as they began to quick march through the forest. "They won't listen to reason...oh, this is my fault. Why did I say all that crap about you being a zombie hunter? They probably thought we were both idiots!"

"I don't think that was it," she replied. "They wanted Chuck and all our stuff. Unless you were a doctor I doubt we had any chance from the get go. I mean they had these packs ready so quickly."

She was likely right, yet that did little to help Neil who was nearly overcome with guilt. All of his supposed help had only got them stranded in a zombie-infested forest, with horny soldiers looking for an excuse to leave the island so they could get at her.

Though just then it was zombies that were more of a problem. They had been walking southeast, not by any design, it was only in an effort to evade the many undead that were wandering down from the north. Thankfully the forest was thicker close to the river and they used its foliage to hide in as a glomp of nearly a hundred of the beasts came slowly on, moaning like a dread wind.

Huddling down and practically wetting themselves they let the zombies drift right past them. And then the pair was up and running, looking to put some distance between them. Unfortunately the foliage worked both ways and they ran smack into a second wave of undead.

One grabbed Sadie's pack.

Quick and agile she swung about, letting the backpack slide off her shoulders, flinging the beast off of her in the process. She was so impressively calm that Neil would've cheered if this was Little League Football, instead he stooped, picked up a heavy rock and dashed in the brains of another that had come too close.

Then they were running for their lives, and the glomp that had passed them by came up to trap them. Neil grabbed a new rock and Sadie a stick. Like cavemen against a pack of wolves they prepared to defend themselves tooth and nail.

Chapter 28

Sarah

The Island

Sarah was all cried out and her insides felt hollow. She clung to the tree, hardly able to keep her head up. Below, the zombies ate their fill of what used to be her father. When they finished, most went back to the river to be washed on to their next slaughter, but seventy or eighty remained, hanging about, mindlessly milling. They were too many for Sarah to consider taking on with her limited ammunition.

"I know what you did," Denise said in a choked voice. For hours on end they had sat on dreadful thin perches, which threatened to give way at any moment as the wind swung the tree back and forth with a fearful creaking. During all that time her mother had been silent.

"I had to," Sarah replied, unable to look at her. She hadn't once glanced Denise's way. Not once in all the long night. Now with the sun threatening to reveal the scene of Gary Rivers' murder, Sarah chose to shut her eyes.

Denise let out a hacking cough and said through rattling lungs, "You were right to do what you did. You kept him from pain. You kept him from becoming one of them. And I know you'll do the same for me."

Sarah's eyes were red and they burned and she wished for tears to relieve them but they did not come. "I will if I have too," she finally spat out.

"It's time, now."

"No. We're not going to just give up," Sarah said with anger and harshness in her words. "I didn't give up on you before, despite what they wanted me to do and I'm not..."

Her mother interrupted in a tired voice, "I'm not giving up. It's time. The fever has run its course." With a start, Sarah now looked up to see her mother's face alive with the heat that baked her from the inside out. "One of them got me," she whispered. "Just a scratch, I barely even felt it with all the excitement."

"No," Sarah said, breathlessly. "Maybe it's something else. Maybe it's tetanus, or a normal flu. We've been up here all night. It's only a cold."

"It burns like fire. It's the virus, I know the symptoms. Harry Jenkins got bit, remember? It's the same, and now it's coming on worse. Please don't let me go through this just so you won't have to feel bad about killing me. It's what I want."

"Mom..."

"I love you," Denise Rivers said. "Now come up above me. And please don't make me beg. It hurts too much."

Sarah climbed with numb hands and without care. If she fell she didn't think she would mind a bit, in fact it would be an act of mercy. She climbed and couldn't look at her mother as she passed, and Denise wouldn't look at her. The older woman stared at the bark of the tree with a look of dread and fear on her face.

"I love you so much," she said again with more life. Her wrinkled hands gripped the trunk with all her might so that little chips of it fell away. "Make it fast, please. It's in my head and it hurts so bad. Hurry."

"Love you, Mom," Sarah said and then took a deep breath and then another, and tears dropped where she was aiming, right at the top of her mother's head. Sarah's hands began to shake so badly that she had hug the tree with her other arm to hold herself steady and still she couldn't pull the trigger.

Below, zombies began to gather, looking up, as if hungry for their prize, like dogs would after treeing a cat. Denise started to look up at her too and Sarah screamed with rage and pulled the trigger, and then she screamed and screamed to drown out the awful sound of her mother falling from the tree, smacking against branch after branch before thumping to ground. Sarah screamed hate and shook the tree because the zombies ate loudly. The wet sounds of her mother's flesh being pulled apart and the snap of her bones and the sucking of her marrow had Sarah rocking against the tree as her vocal cords began to tear in her misery.

She went on so long that as the first light of day came, the tree itself took up the cadence of her misery and swayed back and forth. Soon the swaying became somewhat dangerous and Sarah didn't care. What was left for her? Her parents were dead and her life was ruined...even her life as a whore on The Island was out the window. She had seen the sharp anger in the colonel's eyes when she had disobeyed his orders. No one disobeyed him.

Not that she would consider sleeping with him even for a second now.

It was he who had stolen their food and weapons. It was he who had turned her into a whore just so she could save her parents. And it was he who had allowed them to die by cutting the bridge. Her hatred for him twisted her face and she felt a need to kill that would have shamed the zombies below. It fueled the swinging and now the tree tipped so far over at the end of each of its inverted pendulum-like swings that she unexpectedly saw how she could get off the island with her life.

At the end of each swing the tree hung out further and further over the river, which was now empty of the living corpses that had choked it the night before. Sarah swung harder and then as the tree reached out beyond the wires, she let go, dropping with a light splash.

The water was beyond cold, yet the air was worse and so she felt somewhat relieved as she let the current drift her along. She went for a few miles in this way, lazing, barely doing enough to keep afloat, letting the cold match the numbness she felt inside. Unfortunately her reality came jolting back to her as she saw zombies along the western shoreline ahead.

Keeping low, she paddled to the other edge of the river and was surprised to see more of the creatures. They stood beneath the trees as though they didn't care for the sun that was only then crawling into the sky and even as she watched they began to drift deeper into the forest.

The air began to warm up bringing a reminder of Indian Summer. Sarah left the water and crept along the bank of the river, leaving her small prints in the mud. She heard a sudden cry followed by the skitter of running feet. Sounds, Sarah realized, that only real people made.

Using the brush for cover, Sarah came closer to the sound, following behind a group of zombies who were hurrying forward in anticipation of a meal. She hoped they would feast. It was a hope boiled up from a place of hate. It was rancid within her that sick feeling. She hoped it was soldiers who were being attacked, but she soon saw that it wasn't.

It was a man and a woman...or rather what looked like a man and his daughter, or so Sarah hoped. The girl was Brit's age and the idea that she might be sleeping with the man, made Sarah want to run away and leave them to their fate. Then she saw the man, who was rather short and thin, brain a zombie with a rock he held in one hand, as he pushed the girl behind him with the other.

He was protecting her, like Sarah should've been doing for Brit all along.

"But Brit is dead," Sarah whispered aloud in an attempt to wrest her heart from the quick guilt that had infested her. Brit had to be dead. She was one of eight million zombies in New York City. That was a sad fact that Sarah had tried to pretend wasn't, only now, after the death of her parents she couldn't pretend any longer. The real truth was that Brittany was like all the rest. She had been eaten and turned into a soulless thing weeks ago. Just like all the rest.

Just like this girl would be if Sarah didn't do something.

The thought sent a spark through the cringing woman

and before she knew it, she charged the zombies from behind. At close range she plugged two of them with shots that were like explosions in the quiet morning forest. The sound had the creatures turning and Sarah shot another, making a hole for the trapped pair to dash through.

And then they were all running, humans and zombies alike.

"To the river," Sarah said, pelting barefoot and free with only the rifle to slow her down. "The stiffs can't swim."

The slope of the river came up fast and the young girl flashed ahead and leapt far into the water with her momentum, coming down feet first. In complete contrast, the man actually stopped at the riverbank to take off his shoes. Sarah took him by the pack and pulled him backwards while he gasped at the cold and spluttered something about not being able to swim very well.

"You can swim better than them," the girl said, making an easy time of the river. She turned on her back and did a gentle backstroke and introduced herself. "Hi, I'm Sadie."

The man cleared his throat and said in little more than a whisper, "And what do you say?"

Sadie smirked at him before adding, "Thanks for saving us. This is Neil. He thinks he's going to turn me into a lady one of these days."

"Manners don't go out of style just because of a zombie apocalypse," Neil replied. He then stuck out a small hand and said, "We really do appreciate the help..."

"I'm Sarah." For some reason the two words had been difficult for her to speak. Just then she didn't really know who she was. Everything that had made her Sarah Rivers before, was now gone.

Chapter 29

Ram

Western Desert

Standing in the doorway of the kitchen, Ram stared at the onrushing zombies and could not seem to connect them with reality. Where was Cassie? Had they eaten her in her sleep? Why hadn't he heard her scream or cry out?

Maybe it was because she didn't scream. Maybe she let the zombies in. Maybe you far underestimated what a woman scorned would do.

These thoughts smote his consciousness and, just like that, he felt the electric flash of adrenaline all along his skin; goose bumps materialized an instant later. Then he was running back down the hall, but zombies were there as well. He was trapped and empty handed, with just the dining room as shelter and, since the room was only fortified by a swinging door, it wouldn't be much in the way of shelter.

"There's stiffs in the house!" he yelled to Julia. The problem with a door that swung both ways was that there wasn't any way to lock it, or even to barricade it. All Ram could do was stand there waiting for the onslaught which wasn't slow in coming. In seconds the zombies pushed against the door and at first Ram held it closed with a minimal amount of effort, but then the creatures began to pile up against it and their combined weight and strength pushed him back inch-by-inch. When it was clear to him that it would only be seconds before they were fully into the room, he saw the futility of resisting any longer and jumped away suddenly so that half a dozen bodies piled into heap at his feet.

With no other weapon at hand, Ram picked up an old Ethan Allen dining room chair. It was solid workmanship that proved itself when he bashed it three straight times with considerable into the incoherent pile of undead, before it came apart in his hands. Left with just a sturdy leg—a better weapon than the chair since it wasn't nearly as clumsy—he plied the hunk of wood with gusto, feeling it bite into skin with each strike.

Beneath the wood he could feel skulls cave. Brains and black blood decorated the room. He was just thinking that he and the chair leg could go on all day like that when one of the zombies turned out to have a head like cement and the wood snapped square in two. Luckily the huge zombie dropped at Ram's feet at the same time.

"Shit!" Ram swore. Even as he said it he heard a scream from the second floor and then a door slammed above him.

Trapped as he was, Ram had been well past the point of fear; he was on the way to outright panic when he heard the scream. In the instant that followed, he forgot himself and his fears and the stress of the last few weeks and days unnumbered. He only knew that Julia was in trouble.

In a quick move, he snatched up another of the chairs and this he used as a battering ram to clear the doorway of the creatures. The clumsy things fell back and then he was in the hall where more zombies stood confused. They seemed to be wondering which way to turn; toward the scream from above, or to the man just a few yards away. Ram didn't give them a choice. He charged with his chair held out in front of him, bowling them over, before he paused at the front door.

"Hey you sons of bitches!" he roared at the zombies. This got their attention and the ones on the hardwood floors scrambled to their feet while the ones on the stairs turned to come down for him. "That's it. Come on. Come on." He waited until the closest one was just out of reach before backing onto the porch.

"This is what you want," he crooned to them, checking his six to make sure he wasn't backing right into any others. Like the Pied Piper he jogged away from the house with about thirteen of them following. Then when he felt he was at a safe enough distance he ran in an arc around them and sprinted back to the house.

"Julia? Cassie?" he called out as soon as he entered.

Wearing nothing but a grimace, and carting a honking big .44 caliber pistol, Julia came down from the second floor on tiptoe. "Are they all gone?"

Ram locked the door behind him before replying, "I don't know. Here let me take that. I'll secure the house." Even as he said the words the zombies that had taken part in his parade came banging at the front door. "Get dressed," he whispered and then crept down the hall looking for strays.

There were three lifeless corpses in the doorway to the dining room and one that was nearly so. Ram had broken its collarbone in the melee a few minutes before and it was now trapped beneath the enormous zombie that had broken the table leg. He left it for the moment and went to clear the kitchen and the downstairs study.

These were empty. On his way back to the hall, Ram grabbed a claw hammer from the kitchen junk drawer and seconds later left it sitting in the skull of the zombie. Killing the zombie had been easier than he expected, but the wet, nauseating *chunch* sound of the hammer sinking in made the idea of pulling it out too much for him.

"There are other hammers," he reasoned.

Julia met him at the bottom of the stairs. She had graduated from naked to wearing only a pair of panties. In her hand was his Beretta. "It's empty!" she hissed. "Cassie took a pistol and your M16 and all the ammo!" He began to check the .44 in his hands, but she stopped him. "That was in my room, but the rest of the ammo was in Papa's dresser and it's gone too."

She was getting loud and the zombies began to go at the door again harder than before. Ram took her by the hand and led her back upstairs and then sat on her bed thinking. "That bitch tried to kill us."

"Maybe," was all Julia said. She avoided Ram's eyes,

only staring down at her pale knees.

Ram exhaled angrily. "There's no maybe. She stole all our ammo and then let a bunch of zombies in the house. That's Murder One in my book. It's premeditated all the way."

The blonde went to her dresser and pulled on a pair of jeans; stepping into them easily. "Leaving a door open doesn't mean murder. If there were any zombies around, they would've gone after her. Maybe that's what happened."

"And the stolen ammo?" he asked, though in a less heated tone of voice. He couldn't stay angry while watching this fine woman get dressed. Julia had found an *Arizona Cardinals* sweatshirt and pulled it over a lacy bra. When he first met her he had thought her skinny but then, just the night before, he had felt the smooth play of her toned muscles. She was fit and trim, but not skinny.

She saw his eyes on her and she gritted her teeth. "This is my fault. I shouldn't have let you last night. It was wrong."

"Let me?" Ram asked, his eyes narrowing. "You didn't let me. *We* allowed ourselves to make love. It wasn't wrong. How can you call it wrong?"

"Don't be mad," Julia said, alarmed at his sudden anger. "I mean we should've been more discreet. We both know how Cassie feels about you. It was mean of us." Glass broke somewhere below. Ram began to get up, but Julia held him back, saying, "That's the little window in the front door. They can't get in through it."

He went to the bedroom door and then turned. "You don't know how Cassie really feels and neither do I. And I don't know what you mean about being discreet. She wasn't going to let go of me until she had claimed me for herself. She's a scary one and worse, she's unpredictable."

He began to walk away and she caught up quickly. "What are you going to do?"

"Get our ammo back," he said. There was a creak of wood splitting below which they both recognized as plywood being torn from one of the windows. Glass breaking came next. "I'll deal with them first, don't you worry."

After facing the infinite hordes in L.A., dealing with thirteen zombies was not all that difficult, especially when he had a Ford Bronco parked out front and the keys in his hand. He charged out the back door where there was but a single zombie and ran around to the front. Starting the Bronco was all it took for them to swarm the 4x4. He then backed down the road slowly, once again enticing them away from the house.

When he was a good two-hundred yards away he simply plowed straight into them and backed over any that still moved. He drove back to the little house in the desert, though when he did it wasn't with the same casualness. Something was attracting the undead to them. Ram could see them all over the desert heading their way.

He jogged inside, calling to Julia. "I'm afraid this house has outlived its usefulness. There are all sorts of stiffs coming right at us. I need you to pack."

When she saw the numbers, she didn't argue. Together they loaded up what supplies they had: food, water, tools, medicine, clothing, even old camping gear. The zombies were coming on so quickly that he sent Julia out in the other truck, a beat up F-150, to distract them. She turned circles in the dun colored scrub and secretly Ram thought it was a waste of diesel—she could've been running them over.

When he had the Bronco packed, he left the front door open with the keys on the porch rocking chair. It made no sense to lock the place. Zombies were far less destructive just shambling around, and if some stranger wanted in, they'd find a way.

A minute later, Julia joined him in the Bronco, watching the house grow little in the distance and crying as it did. He took her hand, worried that she would pull away after what she had said earlier, but she gripped him tightly.

"Cassie must have gone on foot, which doesn't make any sense," Ram said, squinting through the desert heat.

"It does if she wanted us to find her," Julia said. "Think about it. If she just left with a single gun and a few bullets you would probably say good riddance. She's basically made it so you have to come for her. It would not be out of the realm of possibility that she'll even set herself up in some way so that you'll have to rescue her. It's a cry for help."

A snort of disbelief escaped Ram. "I keep telling you, this girl isn't normal. The first night I met her, she let all six of those gang-bangers rape her. Didn't say a word, except to chastise one of them for being too slow." Julia's grip loosened suddenly and she gave him a look, which he interpreted correctly. "I didn't join in. I could've if I wanted to, only that's not my thing, in fact I wanted to stop them but she practically invited them..."

Now her hand slipped from his completely. "Are you seriously blaming the victim? She was raped! No one wants to be raped. That's the most insensitive fucking thing I've ever heard."

"Then I'm telling it wrong," Ram replied, growing louder as well. "Ok, she wasn't raped. She traded sex for protection. I could see it when she came up; the cold calculation: let these guys do me or get zombiefied."

Julia watched the desert go by and Cassie could've been right there for all she saw of it. "You should've stopped it."

"No shit," Ram said, bitterly.

The ride became awkwardly quiet and what was worse it was a slow ride. He drove at just over twenty miles per hour and they had a lot of time to sit in silence. Eventually Julia cleared her throat and said, "I'm sorry for speaking to you that way. I was wrong. I wasn't there so I shouldn't judge."

Ram grunted.

"That's all you have to say?" Julia asked. "It was six against one. I'm trying to apologize. I was wrong to imply you were a coward in any way."

He grunted again and then his anger spewed out, "I don't know if I would've stopped it if it had been just one guy. Cassie knew what was going to be demanded as payment for protection and even though she didn't like it, she paid the price. It wasn't just one time either, the next day she blew each of them, and at any time she could've walked away anytime. That's the kind of girl she is. She doesn't like me, she might even hate me, but that won't stop her from sinking her hooks into me anyway she can because she thinks being with me will help her survive."

"All of that was a cry for help too," Julia replied. "That's not normal behavior, that's crisis behavior. It has affected all of us. I've done things I normally..." She stopped in mid-sentence and shot her eyes to him. He could only grit his teeth. After a deep breath she admitted, "Yes...ok, last night was something I wouldn't normally have done. I barely know you. But I'm glad I did it. I needed that. I needed to be near someone."

"I understand," he said, giving her a smile to show that he wasn't mad. "I needed it even more. I don't mean sexually. I mean I've felt dislocated. Is that the right word? I've felt apart from people, like they aren't real. Before...before Cassie and the gang-bangers there was this group of guys...and uh, never mind," he said with a guilty laugh. "I shouldn't be going on."

"No, you have to," she said urgently. "It'll eat you up if you don't. And you could relapse." His chin turned down slightly and his lips pulled back at this. She touched his arm and went on, "It was pretty obvious that you were on the verge of something, a break down, I mean. When that sort of thing happens, it can be a while before a person can deal with even the smallest stress. You need to talk. You have to. So, you were saying that you thought people weren't real. Who?"

Ram had heard this before, but only in the movies. For a

tough guy like himself it was only a joke; he had always been too strong to need therapy. He had always considered his mind to be granite, but now he knew better. He had actually felt himself coming apart, melting under the strain.

"Cassie. She wasn't real," he said in a quiet voice. "The bangers, I never even learned their names. I didn't want to...and there were some of the men back there, in the line. I, uh, left them a few days ago and I haven't thought about them since because I know they're all dead. They stopped being real to me when I finally admitted that they were all going to die."

"What about me?" Julia asked. She took his hand and placed it on her chest, just beside her breast so that he could feel her heart. It was surprisingly strong. "Am I real?"

Ram stopped the truck in a cloud of dust and went to Julia and kissed her deeply, breathing her in and grabbing her arms almost to the point of pain. "I think you're real."

"I'm pretty sure you're real, too." She pulled him close again and they kissed a second time and then she said, "I—oh," while looking over his shoulder.

"What is it?"

It was Cassie, sixty feet away, sitting in the lee side of a gully where the shade hid her. In her hands was something blacker than the shadows: Ram's M16.

Chapter 30

Neil

Illinois River

Neil floated down the river in something of a dream. It started with a woman; blonde with strange, blue eyes. They weren't the blue eyes of a stereotypical Barbie doll or cheerleader. Instead they were the color of soft denim. They were the kind of eyes that had you curious, so that you wanted to investigate or puzzle them out. This meant staring, only you knew that staring would be impolite, so you looked hard and searchingly when you could, in those brief moments when decorum allowed.

Decorum being fickle, Neil decided to abuse the word and stared whenever possible.

"So Sarah, you were a pharmacy rep?" he asked. He had asked a number of questions already, unfortunately her replies were terse ; her mind was clearly somewhere else.

"She already told you that," Sadie mentioned. The girl was floating lazily on her back, kicking only enough to keep her chin above water. "Anyone know where this river goes? I don't want to end up in Mexico or Montana or any such dreadful place."

This was an opportunity and Neil turned to Sarah and stared some more. "Yes?" she asked at his look. "Oh, the river. Right." She pursed her lips and looked downstream, considering. "I think this sort of comes together with some others and goes on to St Louis, but I'm not sure. Here wait a moment."

She began to swim to the eastern edge of the river where the land was flat and unbelievably she climbed up on the bank to take in the view. Neil did the same. Over a clinging sundress she wore a white blouse and had nothing on beneath. Decorum be damned, he stared unabashedly and then had to adjust himself, his pants also clung and now there was simply no room.

"Your eyes are popping out. What's that about?" Sadie asked in a whisper. "You see something strange?"

"Not at all, I'm just interested in what she's looking at. It could be important."

"Really? But she was looking way over there and you were looking closer to right at her. I'm just saying."

"I'm also keeping an eye on her," Neil replied, kicking closer to the shore so that his feet could touch. He wasn't a strong swimmer or even an average swimmer, but the backpack helped. He used it as a flotation device. "I wouldn't want any zombies sneaking up on her."

"Mighty brave of you," Sadie commented with a sly smile and eyes that seemed to know too much. "Maybe you should go up there instead. Get closer so you can see better. See the monsters I mean."

That wasn't going to happen. With the water and the jutting nipples and the...everything, Neil was sporting an erection that could've been spotted from outer space. "No, I can see just fine from here. Why don't you go swim somewhere else? You're being a pain."

"I would but...look at that. She's waving us over. Come on." Sadie started to pull at Neil's sleeve.

"I'll be right there," he whispered, and then louder he called out, "I've lost my shoe. I'll be right up."

Sarah walked down to them, stopping just at the water's edge, and of course she slung the rifle so that the strap went between her breasts, accenting them even more. "There's a farm not too far away. Get your shoe and come on."

"Yeah, get your shoe, Neil," Sadie said impishly.

"I'm working on it," he groused, reaching down and pretending to search. "You two go on without me. I'll catch up. It's got to be here somewhere."

Though Sadie was chuckling at how foolish Neil was being, Sarah barely noticed. She peered in all directions, her face set. After a minute she looked down at Neil and was surprised to see that he hadn't budged. "Do you need some help?"

"I'm ok, I think," Neil replied, slogging forward, nearly losing one of his shoes for real. He had stood in one place for so long that the river mud had a good suction going on both of his feet and when he pulled his right foot up he could feel his loafer wanting to remain behind.

"Do you want me to take the backpack?" Sadie asked, doing her best to be a pain as he came out of the water. He was currently holding it in front of himself like a shield. "You've been carrying it all this time."

He gave her a quick glance and said, "I'm good, now let's get onto this farm, I'm practically freezing."

Sadie snorted laughter and whispered, "Yeah you're almost frozen stiff. What?" she asked at his glare. "I'm just playing. Besides, I don't think any of our conversations are being picked up by *outside* sources." When she said this she raised her eyebrows in Sarah's direction.

The girl was probably right. Sarah was there, walking along, yet at the same time she wasn't. Her eyes saw nothing and her mind seemed detached from the world around them. They were out in the open and the wind blew hard, which had Sadie shivering and Neil clutching himself, but Sarah made no move to wrap her arms around herself or to even wring the water out of her hair or clothes. She simply walked barefoot through the once farm fields, as though in a dawning trance.

"How about I take the gun, Sarah," Neil suggested. The walk, and the cold, and his concern for her had dampened his erection and now he swung the pack onto his back. Before he could snug it into place she rounded on him and now the black muzzle pointed straight into his face.

"Hell no!" she snarled. "The gun is mine."

Neil had his hands up next to his chest instead of up in the air. He shook his head back and forth on a quick little arc, saying, "Of course. I wouldn't think of taking it."

"Good," she said. "Now back off." She pushed the barrel at him forcing him to take two large steps backwards. As he did, he saw Sadie eyeing the older woman, judging the distance between them, looking for an opening. Her eyes had lost their easy humor and were now calculating.

"It's ok," Neil said, calmly, putting a hand up to both women. "I wasn't trying to steal it. I was just going to go, you know, inspect the house for zombies."

With her lip curled in distaste, Sarah looked him up and down, and then said, "I'd better do it."

She put the gun to her shoulder, slipped between rows of tall conifers, and then stalked carefully up to the little ranch-style house. Neil and Sadie hung back. Without weapons they were nearly useless, or rather Neil was. Sadie had been watching their backs and now she saw a line of dust advancing in a straight line toward them.

"There's a car coming," she said urgently. "It could be some of those guys from The Island."

"Quick," Neil said and reached out to take her hand, but Sadie blazed past him, leaving him to huff up to the house.

"Sarah! There's some people coming," she cried in a low voice. "Maybe soldiers…but not good ones. If they're from the Island, they can't catch me here."

A face appeared at the kitchen window. It was Sarah, but a Sarah who was altogether pale and shaking. In a second she was out the door and the two women were booking for the river with Neil left to straggle behind with the pack swinging this way and that on his back, making him run even more slowly than normal.

He had only just made it down the steep slope that cut away to the water, when the car could be heard crunching gravel as it pulled up. The vehicle held three men—all were armed with black rifles. Now Neil was nervous for the two women and scared for himself, while it was clear that Sadie was frightened near to a panic. Sarah, on the other hand, looked ready to kill.

Even as he watched she thumbed the safety on the rifle to fire.

"Don't do it, Sarah," he whispered. "There are too many of them and Sadie and I are unarmed."

She didn't respond; she only tracked the men until they went into the house. They were in it for less than a minute and then they were jogging to the barn, making sure to keep distance between them. Again they did a quick inspection before walking back to their vehicle.

When they were safely on their way, Sarah eyed her traveling partners. "You two were at The Island?" she asked in evident disbelief. "You're no soldier," she said to Neil, and to Sadie she remarked, "And you're just a girl."

Sadie riled at what she took for contempt. "Neil is better than any of those idiots! And if you want to call me 'just a girl' again, try doing it without a gun in your hands, bitch."

Sarah shook her head wearily. "That's not what I meant. I didn't mean to put you down. The truth is that I just came from The Island and I know that all the soldiers there are men and all the women are...are...they're older and not at all like you." When Sadie's eyes flared again, Sarah added, "They're all cowards. They're all gutless chickens and I was one of them, and maybe I was the worst of them."

Just as quickly as Sadie's anger flared, it was gone again. Being called brave did that for a person. Neil didn't have a warm compliment to sooth his anger. Instead it was just implied that he wasn't quite a man. "I'm cold," he said. Without looking at either of the two women he trudged across the still green lawn of the farmhouse and went inside.

The place had been home to an older couple, and the decorations and the furnishing reflected just that: everything was antique and not in a good way. Neil went first to the refrigerator, perhaps out of habit. The smell was atrocious and he quickly shut it. He then went through the cabinets.

"Anything?" Sadie asked hopefully.

"Just this." Neil plunked down a nearly full bottle of

rum, which featured a grinning pirate on its label. He unscrewed the top and gave it a sniff, which had him coughing gently. Sadie wanted to give it a smell too, and her eyes went wide when she did.

"Three glasses barkeep," she said and slapped her hand down on the mustard-colored countertop. "I'm buying!"

"I don't think so," Neil said, pulling the bottle back before Sadie had a chance to chug from its lip. "You're way too young." He pulled it too far back and Sarah, who had come around the counter, snatched it from him.

She also sniffed at the amber liquid, and before taking a long pull, she asked, "Are you two father and daughter?" Sadie laughed at that while Sarah screwed up her face over the bite of the rum.

"Naw," the girl said. "I don't really even know my dad and now he's probably dead. Neil is my apocalypse dad. Pass the bottle." Sarah took a mug and filled it half way before handing over the bottle to Sadie—despite Neil's protestations. "So were you two neighbors or something? You act like you've known each other for a long time."

Thankfully Sadie was coughing after taking a swig from the bottle and couldn't answer the question. Neil didn't want to go into how they had met, because he knew it would make him look even more like a wimp than usual. "We just met on the road. I'd say slow down on the rum, the both of you, but you won't listen to me so, whatever."

In a wrath, he stalked away and went to the back of the ranch house where the bedrooms were and then sighed at what he found. The farmer had been a big man and though there was plenty of dry clothing to choose from, nothing fit. Yet since he was freezing in his wet clothes he changed into a pair of white long johns, an old, green, John Deere T-shirt and a ridiculous pair of overalls.

He felt like a little boy who was playing dress up with his father's wardrobe. And he also felt a headache coming on. The two women would poke fun of him. It was a given and it would be mean, and what could he do but take it?

There was one thing he could do; he locked the door and sat on the farmer's bed. He could hear the two women going through the house and it became clear that Sarah was drinking herself into a stupor. She grew louder and more clumsy, banging into things. What's more, they began to laugh at anything and everything. Neil didn't need that

After a while, Sadie asked through the door: "You ok in there?"

"Yep, just trying some clothes on and looking for...supplies." Someone had gone through the room already; every drawer had been pulled open and ransacked. With a sigh, he poked around if only to kill time and discovered only two things that had been overlooked: a secret stash of old man porn—three Victoria Secrets advertisements and a Playboy from 1986—-and a stockpile of Jolly Ranchers.

He kept his hands well away from the porn, and filled one of his overall pockets with the candy. Next he went into the master bathroom and in the medicine cabinet he found a new bar of soap and in a little cubby next to the toilet, three rolls of paper. In the new paradigm, these were treasures that had been foolishly overlooked.

"Hey Neil?" Sadie called from outside the door. "You've been in there a long time. Are you sure you're ok?"

"I'm just fine."

"Did I do something wrong?"

He went to the door and unlocked it, expecting to have her laugh at him and his stupid clothes. And she did too, but he laughed at her just as much. It was totally unexpected, but the Goth girl had traded out her soaking wet black attire for a flowered muumuu the size of a tent and a pair of tube socks.

After they had stopped their laughing and only breathed out occasional little giggles, they stared at each other fondly. She was glassy-eyed, but not yet stumbling drunk and thus still retained some of her perceptive abilities. "Ok what did I do?" she asked. "There's something wrong, I know it."

"Where's Sarah?" Neil asked instead of answering.

"Passed out on the couch. She says she spent the night in a tree. That's messed up. So? What's wrong? Are you mad that I had a drink or two?"

"No, I don't care about that. It's nothing really, or rather it's everything. I guess I just miss my old life. Everything was better. Everything was easier."

"I doubt you mean that," Sadie said, walking past Neil to sit on the farmer's bed. "What would you be doing now if nothing had changed? Paperwork? Doing your taxes like a good little boy? Sitting home alone? Watching TV until your brain oozed out of your ears?" She laughed suddenly and fell back onto the bed. "You want to hear something funny? I bet half the zombies out there are doing more with their lives now than when they were alive."

"Maybe that was me, I don't know," he said, He sat down next to her and thought of the untold number of nights he had come home alone from work. He would read, or work some more, and then in the morning he would go back to the office, because that was his life.

"It was you," she said rolling over on her side, completely unaware that she had exposed her left leg all the way to her hip. She was naked beneath the muumuu. The sight was intoxicating to his lonely brain and he glanced away. "Remember, I've been in your place. You were boring before all of this."

"And now?" he asked turning back to her and gasping when he saw she had rolled even more and now her buttock was showing. As casually as possible he tried to flick the muumuu to cover her again—and was unsuccessful.

"What are you doing?" she asked, quickly.

Neil's eyes and mouth came open wide and he spluttered, "You...your...backside was open...I mean it was uncovered. I was only trying to cover you up. I wasn't trying to do anything."

Her eyes were narrow slits. "Anything? Like what? What would you do?"

"Like get frisky? Really I wasn't..."

She interrupted him, laughing herself breathless. "Frisky! You said frisky. Who the hell says fri...frisky?" She couldn't go on for many minutes and there were tears in her eyes when she finally stopped. "I know you wouldn't do anything. You're too nice of a guy."

There it was once again. "That's me." He stood and fished out a handful of Jolly Ranchers. "Look what I found us for lunch."

"Maybe later," she said with a big yawn big enough to show him her back teeth. "I think I'm going to take a nap. Would you mind staying in here with me?"

"I guess, but only until you fall asleep. Then I want to look around." She was out in minutes, but since she had forced him to lie down and then settled into the pocket of his shoulder, complaining that the pillow smelled of old people, it was some time before she rolled over and freed him to go snoop about.

He did so, taking Sarah's rifle and a pair of rubber boots he found by the garage. The garage itself was another treasure trove: Fishing poles, tackle boxes, an axe, and a sledgehammer and best of all, a small two-person tent that could fit three in a pinch, especially if they snuggled. His mind blinked rapidly between Sarah in the river and Sadie on the bed.

"Maybe I'm not as nice as everyone thinks. Maybe I'm just a dirty old man," he whispered, heading to the barn, wanting to clear his mind. There wasn't much to the red barn. Other than a hayloft, that was far too high up with only what appeared a very rickety ladder to service it, the only things of real note were a dusty tractor and dozens of bales of long, dry grasses that he assumed was hay or in the hay family. There really wasn't much more to the barn, save for a pitchfork, which he immediately leaned on, sticking a length of straw between his teeth.

He had just decided to show Sadie the new addition to his ridiculous outfit which he was sure would garner another of her snort-filled laughs, when he noted that the day had turned suddenly gloomy, and there was a nip to the wind, and there was a zombie shuffling toward the front door of the house, and that the front door stood open with only a flimsy screen door as protection to the women sleeping inside.

Lastly he noted that the zombie was well over six feet in height and was wearing an outfit similar to the one Neil had on. "Damn," he whispered to himself. "Farmer Jones has come to get his clothes back."

Now came the question of what to do about it. He had checked the status of the M16 when he had first picked it up—it had five rounds left. Too few to be wasting on a single zombie...but this was no ordinary zombie. It was practically a giant of its kind and the only zombie that Neil had proved himself against so far had been a skinny little child-zombie.

But what would Sarah and Sadie think if he managed to kill this fearful thing? He pictured himself tossing the huge head on the ground in front of them while they cast adoring looks his way. He liked the idea and it bolstered the gossamer courage that flickered within him. Peeking around the corner of the barn he called out a provocative: "Yoo-hoo."

Immediately, he wanted to smack himself. What sort of zombie hunter said things like *yoo-hoo*? He tried again and, at the upper limits of his vulgarity, he yelled, "Hey turd face!" This was better, although it wasn't needed since the zombie was already hurrying towards him at a quick trot that was much faster than Neil had expected.

Setting the gun down, Neil took up the pitchfork as a weapon and ran to hide behind a stack of hay. There he waited with a Jolly rancher in one hand and the pitchfork in the other, and when the zombie came in snuffling and grunting, Neil threw the candy at the tractor.

His primitive plan worked like a charm, only to be ruined by the civilized planner. The zombie wandered to the tractor, turning his back on Neil long enough for the man to come up from behind and crack it over the skull with the pitchfork. He used plenty of strength; enough, he thought, to render a man of that size unconscious. The problem arose in that he still considered this creature a man, not taking into account the fact that Zombies do not need an actual consciousness to kill.

Instead of falling to the ground, it spun and advanced on an utterly shocked Neil. He let out a noise that would have been more appropriate for a turkey to have made and stabbed the zombie in the chest with even worse results. The beast ripped the makeshift weapon from Neil's small hands and rushed forward to kill.

He could do nothing but flee for his life losing both of his over-sized boots in the process. Now the farmer zombie was well fed and healthy for its kind and since it could not grow tired, it would have run down Neil eventually. Luckily for him, there was a little feeder creek that ran along a narrow, but sharp-edged gulley, just off the first of the farmer's fields.

Neil leapt it, but the zombie went and became stuck in the mud. Upon seeing this, Neil knew what he had to do, though he wasn't happy about it. Gathering the largest rocks he could carry, he commenced to stone the zombie until the thing ceased to move.

Rain had begun to fall heavily during this battle so that Neil hadn't heard the approach of more zombies. By the time he looked up he saw a wave of them advancing just a few hundred yards away. Still bootless, Neil ran for the house where the locks on the doors had been driven in long ago and the bay window sat as an enticement for some hungry undead beast.

Chapter 31

Ram

The Western Desert

With the M16 pointed at them from a mere thirty yards, Ram couldn't chance heroics of any sort. Slowly he raised his hands and asked Julia, "What makes you think she's the one in need of help? She's got the gun."

"I studied to be a psychologist," she said, looking more pale than normal. "Got a degree and everything. Though at the moment I wish I had gotten bullet proof glass instead of a degree."

"Yep." There wasn't much more to say as Cassie came up to the car with the gun still pointed. The girl stared with hard, black eyes and gritted white teeth. "Would you like a lift?" Ram said with a bit of smile.

"Why did you come for me?" she asked as the gun dropped from beneath her chin just a fraction of an inch.

Julia leaned close to Ram so that she could see Cassie's face and said, "So we could be together in this. Ram and I made a mistake in not including you last night." Cassie and Ram looked at each other, both with raised eyebrows. Just then Julia realized her choice of words was poor so she added, "I should say we didn't include you in our plans and in our thoughts. It was a spur of the moment thing, but that does not excuse us from ignoring how it might have affected you."

"Oh," Ram said.

"Oh," Cassie agreed, dropping the gun a few more inches lower. "But what good would it have done? You wants him. He wants you. Where do I fit in? Nowhere, that's where."

Cassie took a step back and Julia leaned even closer saying, "You can be with us in a platonic manner as a friend, or an ally. You need people you can depend on and so do we. Otherwise none of us is going to make it."

"Well that's just it," Cassie said, raising a finger. "You gots him already. You can depend on him now, but I can't. What if he gotsta chose between you and me in a life or death situation? He gonna chose you. You see? It ain't fair or equal or none of that shit."

"And if we cease having a physical relationship?" Julia asked.

Ram raised his hands to his ears as if the words pained him. He then climbed out of the car, ignoring Cassie as she threatened him with his own M16, and walked away, looking out at the nothing of the southwestern desert.

"And when do I get a say so in all of this?" he asked, still turned away. "Shouldn't I get to decide who I save, or not save or sleep with, or any of it?"

Julia got out of the car on her side and answered him, "Of course. We're just talking right now."

"Then I'll tell you straight, Cassie. I won't be saving your ass, not because we are or aren't sleeping together, it's because you're immature. This is the second time you brought zombies down on us because you can't control yourself. And you," he said to Julia, shaking his head. Wasn't this the same girl that he was just kissing so passionately a minute before? "I guess I was a bigger mistake than you counted on."

"I don't look at it as a mistake, but I do see that my pleasure was at someone else's expense. Don't you see? Right now we are all vulnerable and hurting. I don't want to be the cause of any more pain. I hope you can understand that, Ram. And I'm not saying we can't renew our relationship later. We don't know what the future holds or who we will meet on our road. Who knows, you might find someone you like more than me."

Ram felt in his bones that it was a mistake to bring Cassie back in.

He knew her type better than some psychology book ever could, just as he knew that Julia wouldn't be dissuaded from this path. She had decided that this wasn't necessarily the best course of action, however in her mind it fell firmly on the "good" side of the moral equation. This was how her type usually went about deciding things.

He knew this about them because he was of the streets and yet not of them as well. He was a crossover, a bridge between America and the underbelly of America. His father had been a doctor, while his mother had been a migrant worker for most of her life until marriage. Ram could play poker in the basement of a brothel, where an inadvertent look could mean drawing a gun, or he could discuss theology or political structure over brandy at The Hamilton near his alma mater Georgetown University.

His life had been spent in both worlds and it was why he had chosen the Drug Enforcement Agency after college. Despite that he had been educated to believe that all cultures were equal, he knew better. To him moral equivalency was for pussies. Anyone with any sense or who had spent any time in the barrios of East L.A. could not equate it to middle America. In truth, life in the barrios could not even be equated to the Mexico of fifty years ago, where manners and a sense of right and wrong were the order of the day.

This was why he looked hard at Cassie, trying to delve into her motivations and her mind. Julia's motivations were all too clear: letting Cassie come back, even though she was a danger to everyone, was what a good person would do.

"Cassie is right," Ram said finally. "If I had to make a choice, I would save you, Julia. That's not likely going to change."

"That's cuz you trying to be all white," Cassie stated. "It's true so don't try denying it. You might have fooled them bangers but you ain't never fooled me. That's what I like about you, Ram: all men are dogs, but white boys are like them Labradors, all loyal and shit."

"Thanks," Ram said. He meant it sarcastically, but Cassie missed it. "So what are we going to do? Take a vote?" The three looked from one to the other until Ram added, "I think it's a mistake to include her. I vote no about her coming along, however I will abide if it's two to one."

Cassie smirked and said, "That's funny since I gots this…" She was about to threaten them with the M16 again, but she had let it slip so that it was pointing at the ground. Ram pulled the .44 magnum before she could finish her sentence and he had the hammer half way back. "Damn, boy," she said in admiration. "You is fast."

She let the gun drop to the desert floor and Ram huffed angrily—it wasn't how you treated a weapon. Before he could gripe anymore, Julia spoke, "I vote she stays. Three people have better odds of surviving than two, though you would be wise to listen to Ram concerning certain matters of security."

"Oh you think that wise?" Cassie asked with a bitterness that had Julia blinking and looking to Ram. Cassie dropped her eyes a moment later and said, "Sorry. I left without getting no water and now my head is pounding. I just need to know if I'm going to be treated as an equal before I say yes. Before it was all *Cassie do this, Cassie do that*."

Ram didn't remember it quite like that, but Julia was quick to apologize for any unintended slight.

"And, before I say yes, I wanna know where we going?" Cassie added.

"We're going to Atlanta," Ram replied immediately, patting the inner pocket of his jacket where a glass vacutainer filled with blood sat in a plastic tube that had once held a fat cigar. "There's a lab called the CDC; the Center for Disease Control. Hopefully they either have a cure for the virus or they're working on one as we speak." He certainly hoped they were. Ram had taken three vials of blood from the dead terrorist and had forwarded two to his supervisor. A nagging doubt had made him hold back the last one, just in case.

"I could do that," Cassie said agreeing.

Julia beamed at both the suggestion and Cassie's acceptance and then went out of her way to give in to every little demand that Cassie made. Cassie rode in the front seat for the rest of the day. Cassie got the largest portions of food and extra water. And Cassie made sure to put herself between Ram and Julia at every opportunity.

"It'll die down." Julia said in a whisper when they were exploring a motel in the dusty burg of Peach Springs, population three. At some point someone had tried to hold out there against the zombies. Every door and window was boarded up and there were bodies here and there shot through the head. The person had made a final stand in the far back of the kitchen where there was a walk-in freezer. The bodies were piled high and the stink so atrocious that Cassie had to leave.

In the freezer itself was a single body, dead of asphyxia, which was sad, but also several large cans of tomato paste, olives, and anchovies, which wasn't great but would do.

Sadly there were no springs in Peach Springs and they had to settle for using boiled water they hauled from a little place called Mud Creek. The same kitchen provided ten-gallon pots that they used over an open fire. These took forever to boil and as they waited, Julia slept in the shade while Ram stood guard.

It wasn't long before Cassie came up. "You aren't going to start in again," Ram said with a groan. "Didn't we just go through this?"

"I just want to talk some sense into you is all," she said. "We can talk without being overheard." He just stared until she went on, "You think she ever been with a latino dude before? Cuz I don't."

"What's your point?" he demanded.

"Birds of a feather is my point," she replied. "I betcha there ain't too many people look like us left. Black folks and you Mexicans lived in the city, and where's the first place this all break out in? The city. Where were all the Q-zones? The city. All the white folk in the middle of the country gots to go here and there, but not us."

"Again, what's your point? Are you suggesting that Julia is going to dump me for the first white guy that we come across? I very much doubt it."

"*I very much doubt it*," Cassie mocked. "Then you don't know shit about history. And you don't know shit about the human mind or white people at all."

"Then teach me," Ram said. "Show me the terrible racism in Julia. She's the one who wanted you to stay, when I wanted you gone. What have you to say about that?"

"Easy, there. You a self-hater. You kilt all those bangers no problem cuz you hate your own race. The whites got you brain-washed. Julia kept me around only cuz of her guilt. It wasn't anything for me. It was cuz she felt bad that I was upset. You saw me workin' her guilt today, right? Everything I asked for I got, because she feelin' guilty cuz she know whites don't treat us right."

Ram couldn't believe what he was hearing. "You're real messed up in the head. You better straighten yourself out."

"And you better get to learnin' how they like it: Yes, Suh. No, Suh. Can I kiss your ass, Suh?"

He thought she was the one in need of learning a lesson but he was wrong. She would be the one teaching instead.

Chapter 32

Eric

Atlantic Ocean

After his adventure into New York City, it was clear that helicopters and Eric Reidy did not mix. Barf bags did however, and he had become well acquainted with them on the chopper ride from the CDC in Atlanta, Georgia to the deck of the USS Harry S Truman, a Nimitz class aircraft carrier.

The Truman was normally based out of Norfolk, Virginia, however Norfolk had gone black early, as had Jacksonville and every other major Naval facility. Basically the carrier was without a port and was turning circles in the middle of the ocean, waiting to find out what was going on, and where it would be safe to dock.

Eric didn't have a clue, which meant that his trip was a waste of his time and his breakfast. They were on short rations at the CDC already and he was sad to see his eggs and toast go into the brown bags. When they landed, Eric went on deck and just breathed in the salt air for a minute, ignoring the officer who pulled at his sleeve and called him by the wrong title.

"Dr Reidy, the admiral is waiting and he hates to be kept waiting," the lieutenant said nervously. "It'll be better for both of us if we hurry."

It didn't matter if they hurried or not, not in the long run. However to placate the man, Eric stepped lively and went through the maze that was a nuclear powered carrier with all the speed he could manage.

"Any good news back at the CDC?" the officer asked.

There wasn't any, however as the man seemed so hopeful, Eric said, "The rat problem seems to have cleared itself up. We discovered that infected mammals die after a few weeks on their own. That's just the carnivores: dogs and wolves and foxes, that sort of thing. What's even better is that herbivores don't turn when they catch the virus; they just die."

"Oh, that's good, I suppose." This clearly wasn't the sort of news the man had been hoping for.

To change the subject, Eric asked, "Is it always like this? So crowded?" He had never been on an aircraft carrier and was surprised at how crammed with people it was. Every step of the way they had to squeeze past people, most of whom were doing nothing at all.

"No. We airlifted in as many families as we could, and now..." the officer's smile faltered and he only shrugged to add to Eric's confusion.

"And now, what?" Eric asked.

"Sorry that's need to know. Here you are," he gestured for Eric to head into the carrier's situation room. Eric would have rather gone in after the lieutenant, hiding in his shadow so to speak, but now he was stuck. The room was low-ceilinged like everywhere else on the ship, and cramped, yet it was also plush and bright, with the feel of an executive suite. "Dr Eric Reidy," the young officer announced.

"Where are we on the cure?" Rear Admiral Kurt Stevenson asked without waiting for Eric to open his brief case, and turning a lip down at the man's disheveled appearance. Dry cleaning had become a luxury only officers on board an air craft carrier could afford.

Stevenson was "The" admiral, but there were two more on either side of him looking stiff with starch and ribbons. Beyond them were a phalanx of captains and commanders uncounted and barely seen by Eric, who had trouble taking his eyes from the admiral's stern countenance. He did however, sigh at the word cure, but didn't bother to correct the man, thinking it would be a waste of time. "Ten, maybe twenty years," Reidy said and then waited on the inevitable explosion. It came as expected and he weathered it as best as he could.

"You have every scientist in the country!" Stevenson roared. "We spent valuable recourses flying all of you egg heads to Georgia and now you tell me twenty years? What more do you need from us, a fucking telethon?"

"You actually did too good of a job," Eric explained. "We have ten scientists for every microscope. They're climbing all over each other to get work done and it's only adding to our problems. The simple truth is that in even perfect conditions most vaccines take an average of seven years to complete."

"No one will be left in seven months," the admiral said, rubbing his eyes. He did this until the room became strained waiting on him. Eventually he asked, "What about the stiffs? Anything new you can tell us? Anything at all that'll help us fight these things."

Just as before any presentation, Eric cleared his throat loudly, he liked how the significant pause made sure he had people's attention, though in this case it was out of habit only. He had a multitude of eyes boring into him and none were the least bit friendly.

"We believe we have discovered the country of origin of the virus, Russia. There were signs leading up to our own…"

A marine interrupted. He was the only officer not in a starched white uniform. He wore mottled green as if he were about to go man a machine gun. "We have it as fact that muslim terrorists were behind this. We have videotaped confessions, flight logs, taped cell phone conversations, even hotel receipts. The evidence cannot be disputed."

Eric agreed, "Yes, they may have caused it, however I said the country of origin. We believe that the virus is either an offshoot of or the actual *Super Soldier* virus that Stalin caused to be created for himself in the fifties; something that was thought to be more of a hoax than a reality. For those of you who don't know, the program was designed to make the

Russian Army invincible. Stalin wanted soldiers who wouldn't feel pain; who could subsist on limited rations, or on little sleep and who could continue to fight even when wounded."

From his briefcase he took out a copy of the brief concerning the *Super Soldier* virus and gave it to the ranking admiral. "This is what they created instead: a virus that attacks the higher functioning centers of the brain: the cerebral cortex, the hippocampus, the amygdala. In short, it destroys the brain's ability to process memory, time awareness, motivating behaviors, emotion, personality, and language comprehension. At the same time it stimulates the very lowest functions, so that these altered persons are indeed super soldiers."

Now Reidy took out scans of brains, both normal and altered. "Here you can see the areas of the brain that controls aggression. It's highly active in the altered subject. It has a desire to kill. It fact it could be its only desire. All the other needs of a normal person are secondary. If we were to take Maslow's Hierarchy of Needs as a visual—I'm sure you have all seen it: a pyramid with the basics of survival at the bottom: food, shelter, sleep; and the lesser needs such as creativity or self-esteem at the top.

"In an altered person, that pyramid would have two levels only. The lowest and most pressing is the need to kill. The second being food and air; and even these are of minimal importance. We have a number of altered persons under examination and the information we are getting is phenomenal. They sleep less than two hours a day. They can maintain homeostasis on as little as three hundred calories and two cups of water a day.

"What they eat is also of interest. It's been assumed that they eat their victims, and on occasion it's true, however it's been discovered that the biting is actually an outgrowth of their hyper-aggression. In reality they are omnivores. For the most part they subsist on grains and grasses..."

"That's crap!" thundered the marine. "I have many hundreds of documented reports that the stiffs eat their victims."

"I wish to God that were true," Eric replied. "If it was, their numbers would be a tenth of what they are now. Instead it shows the genius of the Super Soldier virus; it can't replicate itself if it kills too many intended hosts. I have seen video on this. The altered person will cease eating a human as soon as he or she dies, even if the altered person hasn't been fed in days. It is a way to keep the next host as whole as possible, since it can heal far more rapidly when..."

"They heal themselves?" someone blurted out.

"Yes, they do indeed," Eric said, pointing at his brief as if the paper was the final authority. "Thankfully, this is a stunted ability. They cannot re-grow limbs, nor can they heal connective or even bone tissue, which is good for us, however on the negative side, they synthesize epinephrine at ten times the rate we do."

"And that would do what?" Stevenson asked.

Explaining simple science to non-scientists was Eric's forte and he began to relax, pacing in front of the gathered officers as though he were a professor. "Most people refer to epinephrine under the term 'adrenaline'. What we as humans use in our fight or flight response. In the altered person, we believe that epinephrine is what is keeping them alive against the will of nature."

"So we need to find a way to neutralize their adrenaline," the marine stated as though it were fact. "Can we count on the scientists at the CDC to make this happen?"

"There are ongoing studies determining the feasibility of doing just that," Eric said. "However, there is little hope of finding a method that wouldn't also jeopardize the remaining human population. A better idea and one which is possible right now is dispersing the aerosol form of hydrogen cyanide, though our biggest hang up is the fact that the Air Force has not been cooperative. They barely...what is it?"

To a man the admirals had exchanged dark looks over this. Stevenson sighed for the tenth time and said, "There is no Air Force left. The planes are all there but most, well, all of the bases except for two have been overrun."

Stunned, Eric shook his head. "That's not possible."

"Oh it is," the admiral replied. "The administration thought it to be the best policy not to panic people with the truth. The Air Force is gone. Their security had always been considered a joke among the other services. They had huge bases guarded by a tiny fraction of their manpower. They've always been wide open to attack."

Eric couldn't believe what he was hearing. "You guys are floating around out here doing nothing, and the Air Force is gone. What about the Army? Do we still have an Army?"

The admiral shook his head. "Not really. In Alaska, there's a mishmash of Army, National Guard troops, and citizens trying to protect Anchorage. We have great hope that they'll be able to hold out. There are about ten thousand or so troops retreating into the mountains of Colorado but early snows are causing more casualties than the zombies. And south of Chicago there were twenty thousand troops, but we haven't heard anything from them in a week. Added to this are pockets of soldiers here and there around the country, like little islands in an ocean of zombies...and of course what you have at the CDC."

There had been something of a question to the admiral's last statement, but it was lost on Eric, who felt his head spinning. "This is impossible."

"It's not," Stevenson said firmly. "So far this entire episode has been a cluster-fuck from top to bottom. If we have any hope of changing that we need to revolutionize our thinking. We can start with you at the CDC. What can we do to help?"

Eric was at a loss as to how they thought they could help. "I don't know. America almost seems lost, but what about other countries?" he asked. "Great Britain, or the United Nations? Can't they help? With troops?"

One of the officers in white laughed hysterically and was glared at by the rest. Stevenson turned from the man, with an angry look and answered, "There are no other countries. No Great Britain, no Europe no China or any of it. They're all gone. Except for maybe pockets in Switzerland and Norway, but most countries, hell, every country got it worse than we did. Europe was just too packed in. China and India was a fucking stiff heaven."

"There's still Iceland!" someone joked.

This brought a chuckle from the admiral. "Iceland might just survive. They lost about seventy percent of their people, but from reports they have managed to gain the upper hand."

"What about Russia?" Eric asked as a sudden thought occurred. The admiral gave him a sour look and shook his head to say that it too was gone. "Excellent!" Eric exclaimed happily to everyone's surprise. "When this first started they refused to speak about the virus, but now since the government has fallen we might be able to get some answers."

Admiral Stevenson shuffled the papers in front of him, looking at Eric steadily, as a poker player might. "What do you have in mind?"

"The old soviets had seventeen Biopreparat facilities, or at least seventeen that we knew of. One of these holds the key to the virus. We need to send teams to search each of them. Although the most important one is located near Rostov-on-Don."

An officer just to Stevenson's right gave Eric an incredulous look. "Some of those facilities are hundreds if not thousands of miles apart. And I know of at least two of them that are in the radiation belt east of the Urals."

"Someone used nukes?" Eric asked. "How come we didn't know?"

"Because you didn't need to know," the admiral said. "It wasn't us, in case you're wondering. The ruskies nuked their own land when fifty million Chinese zombies poured over the border. Someone panicked. It happens," he said this with all the compassion of a stone. "About those Bio sites, we don't have the capabilities that we once had, so I'll see what we can stir up." He looked at Eric with a stern expression. "I had asked you earlier about the CDC. How is your security detachment holding up?"

"They've had their casualties, a thousand or so. Thankfully the wall hasn't been breached in three days."

At the outset of the event, the CDC's small security detail had been augmented by a full brigade of infantry from Fort Stewart. The brigade's commander had been quick to react to the deteriorating situation by reinforcing the existing fencing with concrete emplacements and extra concertina wire. This had barely held in the first few days and, when the zombie numbers had swelled beyond belief, he took the extraordinary step of appropriating every car and truck within reach and these he stacked to make a second wall within the first.

Still this hadn't been enough and had it not been for the Stryker armored personnel carriers with their heavy machine guns, the facility would've been doomed.

"I was told we needed reinforcements and that I was to do anything I could to beg for ammo," Eric said, trying to smile pleasantly. His exact instructions had been to kiss ass until he smelled of shit and not to come back without at least a promise that they would be re-supplied. "We need..." he pulled out a piece of paper and read aloud, "5.56 rounds. Fifty cal and 7.62 rounds. Those are bullets I'm guessing. We also need supplies of all types, especially food. We have six thousand men, women and children to feed. What we have won't last."

"More mismanagement," the marine said to the admiral. Then to Eric he smiled like a lizard and held up a picture of a strange tank like vehicle with missiles hanging off of it. "Have you seen any of these on the grounds? No? What about these?"

The second picture showed a soldier holding a shoulder-fired missile. Eric shook his head. "No. I don't think missiles that shoot down planes work too well against altered persons."

"You're the expert," the marine said, easily. "What about artillery? You know what that is?"

"Yes, of course," Eric answered with a frown. "They have some big guns, but they haven't been used; something about rules that don't make any sense to me. Why? What's this about?"

"Just making sure that they are following protocol," the Marine officer lied. Eric knew the man was lying but why was a mystery. The colonel went on, "Do they man the artillery pieces when a crisis occurs or do they go straight to the perimeter?"

"The men just go to the perimeter. All the men are angry about not being able to use the guns. Are you suggesting that they should use them? Is that what you want me to tell them?"

"No sir," the admiral said, suddenly sweet. "You tell them that we'll have their ammo in a week. Maybe ten days. We'll chopper it in, but we're going to need some help from you. On this diagram of the CDC grounds can you show us where we could land a few choppers?"

Eric felt his stomach drop. "We use the baseball field at Emory University. It's right across the train tracks to the southwest."

"He meant within the perimeter," the Marine officer said, still with his reptilian smile.

"There's single helicopter pad on one of the buildings. You can't miss it since there's a big red cross on it. Just fly them in one by one in intervals."

The smile turned nasty on the Marine's face and he

squinted at Eric. "Are you telling the admiral how to do his job? Because from what I understand you and the other poindexters can't even do your own fucking job. That's why we're in this mess."

"I want to know what's going on," Eric said. He was unconsciously backing up trying to put distance between himself and the angry marine, but had to stop when he hit the wall behind him. "Why do you want to know where to land helicopters? Are you thinking about attacking the CDC? Why? That makes no sense at all. We're on the same side."

Another admiral with bands of gold on his arms cleared his throat and looked pointedly at Stevenson, who said, "Tell me, Dr Reidy, has the President tried to contact the Secretary of Health and Human Services, lately?"

"No, sir," Eric said quietly. "It's been days since we've had contact from anyone in the administration." This quieted the assembled officers considerably. The last time anyone had heard from the President had been two weeks ago. The Secretary of the Defense had spoken on his behalf a few times and then nothing. Rumors flew everywhere about assassinations and mass arrests, but who knew what the truth was?

After Eric's response, eyes began to shift around the room, waiting for the admiral to say something. There was a long pause and then he said, "I do not take pleasure in what I'm about to say but, as ranking officer, I hereby assume the duties as acting Commander in Chief until it can be ascertained that the President is capable of performing his duties or a new President is appointed by the people."

There was complete silence in the room though it was clear that the declaration was not unexpected.

"But, sir, you're not in the line of succession," Eric blurted, breaking the cold silence of the room. "The Secretary is. She's number thirteen if I'm not mistaken."

"The Secretary is a moron," Admiral Stevenson said. His words were clear and distinct so that no one could ever deny hearing them. "She was chosen for the position only to throw a few crumbs to the feminists and maybe to buy a few votes out in Kansas. Is this what the resume of the leader of the free world looks like?"

"And she hasn't even claimed the position," the marine cried, throwing his hands in the air. "She's derelict in her duty. It is her responsibility to assume the office when her time comes. What is she waiting for? It's been days and days, and we all sit around waiting for her to do something, while she hides in the CDC hoping you scientists can save her from making the hard choices. What we need now is not another politician, what we need is a true leader."

Standing in front of these hard men, Eric felt the desire to wet himself. Instead he folded his arms across his chest trying to appear defiant. "Then maybe you should arrest her or something, but attacking your own people is ludicrous."

"I agree," Admiral Stevenson said. "Unfortunately the Army brigade at the CDC has a zealot for a commander. I've known him for some time and he's always been a stickler for the Constitution. He'll fight for that bitch even though everyone knows she's worse than useless."

"We have a chain of command for a reason," Eric said obstinately. "To keep us from plunging into a civil war! Which sounds exactly what you plan to do."

"Yes," the admiral said. "Sadly, yes. I wish it weren't so, but that's the way it's got to be. The chain of command has snapped. You are evidence of this as you come begging for supplies. The truth is the Secretary can't even run the CDC properly. How can she possibly run a scattered people?"

Eric was quiet. He didn't have an answer to the admiral's question.

"Exactly," the admiral said as if Eric's silence was a tacit agreement. "Now there's still an answer that I need from you Dr Reidy, will you help us?" Eric started to splutter out a quick denial, but Stevenson spoke over it. "If you do not help more lives will be lost and the end result will be the same. We can crush the CDC with overwhelming force, but I'd rather do it neatly."

Eric was in shock. His country was dying and worse he was being asked to pound the final nail into the coffin.

Chapter 33

Sarah

Illinois River

Sarah came blearily awake as the small man dashed into the living room. "Neil?" she asked. Partially it was a question because she wasn't quite certain if that was his name and partially because she wondered why he was so flustered and shoeless. He stood there with mud up to his calves, panting and pointing.

"Zombies," he said. Louder he called, "Sadie, there's zombies coming. A lot of them."

And then he was rushing around grabbing his drying clothes and a damp sleeping bag and anything else he could clutch to his slim chest. Sarah stood and then wobbled in place, still under the effect of half a bottle of rum on an empty stomach. She looked down at the side of the couch, and even on the wrong side of tipsy she knew that she had set her gun right there. "Where's my gun?"

If anything the question turned the pale man whiter still and he looked back the way he came. "I left it in the barn," he said with large eyes. "I'll...I'll just go get it."

Sadie came into the living room then. She still wore her muumuu and nothing else, not even her black Converse sneakers which she carried in her hand. "You're not going out there, Neil. Look I can see ten of the things already."

"Yeah, we have to lock the doors," Sarah said. She went to the front door but Sadie pushed past with odd look on her face.

"Have both of you gone bonkers? Damn it's gotten cold," she said, stepping out onto the porch where the rain ran sideways with a heavy wind. "We could be in trouble. We'll freeze in the river."

"That's why you should be coming in," Sarah insisted.

Were these two idiots? They had to get in quick before the zombies came.

"There's a hayloft in the barn with a ladder you can pull up," Neil said. "I'll draw them away and you two..."

Sadie laughed at this. "I'll draw them off. You're too much of a slow poke. See ya!" And then she was skipping across the lawn, singing, "Tra-la-la-la, come get me monsters. Time for lunch."

Of course they oriented on her in heartbeat and she continued to skip. "She's crazy," Sarah said in a whisper. "We have to get her inside."

"Inside here? No way, not when they know we're here. They'll tear this place apart. Quick grab that green bag, it's a tent. And grab that afghan. With everything wet it's going to be a little cold. Oh, and there she goes."

Sarah grabbed the tent and the blanket in a hurry. Turning back to the front door she said, "I guess you aren't worried that they'll get her."

The teenage girl wasn't just nimble and quick, she could fly. The nearest zombies were coming after her skipping body with obvious hunger in their eyes and just when they got within a few steps the girl turned on the jets and raced away. After running half the length of a football field she stopped and huffed out volumes of grey breath as she waited for them to get close again.

"No wonder she isn't really scared," Sarah said with awe in her voice. "I wouldn't be either if I could run like that."

"We should hurry either way," Neil said. He was clearly worried for the girl. "One little slip and they'll be on her." They jogged to the barn and after a quick check to make sure it was empty, Neil pointed Sarah up the ladder. Then he ran for the M16 and waved for the young girl to come in from the rain and the monster play.

When she came in she was drenched and smiling, while Neil was mumbling, red-faced and vaguely pointing to the loft, instead of looking at the girl. Sarah understood if Sadie didn't; soaking wet the old muumuu was sheer and see-through.

"Come here," Sarah said to the girl as she came up the ladder. The woman held out the afghan and wrapped her in it, saying, "That was very brave."

She shrugged off the compliment, though her cheeks were a little pink. "I used to run track. It's not so brave if they can't catch you."

"It was still impressive to us," Neil said. "I bet you used to win a lot." He came up, bringing the ladder with him, and though the girls cuddled and he was as wet as Sadie, he sat a little off to himself.

"No, not really," Sadie said. "There's a ton of competition. There were even girls on roids. They might have been growing little penises but they sure could run." They chuckled at this and then Sarah's eyes went to Neil.

"What are you dressed for?" she asked, just then noticing that he had traded in his khakis. "Halloween?"

Neil looked down at himself and belatedly began rolling up one of his cuffs—it hung down past his foot and it made him look comically small. "All my stuff was wet so I borrowed farmer Jones' clothes." He got up and began to inspect the twenty-by-twenty loft. It was warmer in the loft than it had been down below, but it wouldn't stay that way for long and so Neil began to flatten out an area for the tent. When he did he discovered another stash: A jar of peanut butter, a box of saltines…and more Playboys.

He held them up and Sadie grew confused. "Do those three go together in a way that I'm too young to understand?"

Neil and Sarah locked eyes and then burst out laughing. "I'm far too innocent a creature to know, I'm sure," Sarah said. This was actually quite true. Counting her moment with Veronica, Sarah had been with a total of five people.

"Me too," Neil agreed. "All I have to say is yuck." He tossed the Playboys down to the zombies who were congregating below.

"Don't listen to him," Sadie said. "He was the stud of Montclair. I'm sure he knew all sorts of kinky stuff; he just hides it under his shy demeanor."

"Sadie," he said to the girl as if warning her. "I'm not like that at all, really. Or I wasn't before, back in Montclair, and Sadie knows it."

Sarah believed Neil. After all real studly types rarely blushed when they were called a stud. They usually only puffed up more like a rooster than normal. "How does she know it?" she asked. "If you met on the road then you could have told her anything. Like being the stud of Montclair."

"I never said that to anyone," Neil pleaded.

Sadie, who had begun to shiver, snuggled closer and said, "I've been to his house. We met when I was robbing him. That's how I know he was all studly. He had a big ol' house with lots of choice stuff and a fine car. It was a veritable babe trap. Any girl he got back there would have her panties off in no time…"

"Sadie!" Neil said, glaring. "The only true part of that was the fact that she robbed me at gun point." At Sarah's insistence he told the story and Sadie was quick to add to it.

"You don't know this guy Neil took on. He was a bad ass. John was like this savage; no one messed with him. Even I was scared of him. He was the reason why I started stealing. He thought other people were like sheep. And he was right. You know how many people are out there hiding in their homes, waiting to die? They'll eat through their food and then just starve to death, or they'll come out when they are weak and become easy pickings. John said we only speeded up the process."

"It was still wrong," Neil said gently.

"Yeah, I know, and besides what did it get us?" Sadie asked. "I stole from you, you stole from us, and then I stole from you again, and then it was all stolen from us by that bastard the colonel."

A shiver went up Sarah's spine and she gave herself a shake. "Maybe we should break out the peanut butter and crackers and try not to think about the porn. I'm getting kind of hungry."

"You two go ahead and eat," Neil said, standing up. "I want to get the tent set up before it gets too cold."

As he went about setting up the little tent, cursing the Chinese under his breath for having such bizarre instructions, Sarah and Sadie munched through the crackers. "You're lucky you found him," Sarah whispered. "Nice guys are a dying breed these days. I was from a whole town of nice guys and nice girls and I'm probably the only one left alive. In fact, I'm sure of it."

"You're lucky, too," Sadie replied with her little impish smile that seemed to impart more than her words. "Maybe you don't realize it yet."

Sarah's mouth came open but just then Neil said, "The tent's done. It's kind of small. I could probably make do sleeping in some of this hay. Cat's live in this sort of thing, right? That's what I hear..."

Sadie grabbed him and pulled him into the tent after her. Sarah, who had gone first, had to keep from laughing when she saw that Sadie had squished far to the right leaving him with only the option of the middle. He took a deep breath before settling himself down between them and in a very unstudly manner clasped his hands to his chest as if they couldn't be trusted.

That didn't sit well with Sadie who flung one of his arms wide and snugged in close. "I wonder what time it is?" she asked. "It's probably not even two and I'm exhausted."

"That's why you don't drink at ten in the morning," Neil reprimanded. "It ruins you for the rest of the day. That goes for you too," he added turning to Sarah with a smile that quickly disappeared.

"I had just shot my mother," Sarah said, wondering if the words had come out of her mouth. The idea, the fact, the concept, the truth had circled her head all during her bout with the rum—*I just shot my mother. I just killed my mother. I just murdered my mother. I just executed my mother.* She was sure that she had said it a number of times, but couldn't remember if anyone had been in the room when she had. "She was going to turn...she had the fever. I think I was entitled to a drink."

"I'm so sorry," Neil said. Sadie only gave her the smallest glance and then clung again to the man she had adopted as her father.

Just then, Sarah wished she had someone to hold her. Instead all she had was the feeling of being dead inside. She had mustered a bit of rage at seeing the soldiers earlier and she had smiled at Sadie running because it was such a pretty thing, but that was all the feeling she had.

Though in this she was wrong.

When the tent became unbearably quiet, Neil asked where she was from. "Danville," came her reply, and just to be polite she asked, "And you're from Montclair? Where is that?"

"It's right outside Manhattan."

"New York," she breathed out the words, and now she had feelings again. Her insides weren't dead after all. She only wished they were. "And is everyone...is anyone alive there?"

"I don't think so. Not in the city," Neil answered with concern in his light blue eyes. "Why? What's wrong?"

"Nothing," Sarah whispered. And then in a move that wasn't at all like her, she pushed closer and lifted Neil's other arm. "May I?" she asked and then didn't wait for his reply and placed her head upon his chest. She knew what his answer would be. A nice guy would never turn down an invitation to cuddle.

Even if they wanted so much more.

Chapter 34

Neil

Illinois River

Neil couldn't remember a better night since the entire apocalypse began. He laid there with two women huddled into him for warmth and was surprised to find himself enjoying the aromas of both. In his old life something either smelled good or bad too him—they had never intrigued him. This was a first.

With Sarah there was the particular odor that rum presented, though it was very light; and there was the grey, neutral smell of the river water, while beneath both she still possessed a hint of perfume in her hair and it was this that he concentrated on and he breathed her in longingly. On the other hand Sadie smelled like a kid—a touch of shampoo over the lightest scent of sweat, and above these an earthy, natural smell. It was the way a kid smelled when she came in after dark after a two-hour game of kick the can.

Since they had gone to bed so early, Neil woke while it was still deep dark and this gave him a lot of time to enjoy the different scents. He had never known such contentment in so little a thing before.

On the bad side, he was absolutely positive that he stank to all hell. It could not be any other way in his mind. He was a man and even the smallest man accumulated stink like a bee gathered pollen, he just had to walk around. There in the dark he vowed to bath in the river the following day no matter how cold it was, and if the weather could be judged by the wailing wind, it was going to be cold indeed.

He wasn't the only one who couldn't sleep for eighteen hours straight. At some point before dawn Sadie whispered urgently, "We need to talk real bad."

"Your talk can't wait until morning?" he asked. Her

dark eyes looked huge in the dim tent; she shook her head and he sighed.

Sarah stirred next to him and spoke with a sharp edge to her voice, "Your talk can wait. There were zombies down there a little while ago."

"I don't care," Sadie said, getting up and unzipping the tent. "It has to be now or else." Sarah began to argue some more and Neil tried to pat her on the shoulder but ended up patting her on the breast instead and to make matters worse because what he was touching was round like a shoulder but was so very soft he grew confused at what it was, which had his hand exploring until Sarah smacked it away.

"Sorry," he said quickly. "That was, um. I'll explain later."

Simply put Sadie and Neil were both rather gun shy when it came to using the relieving themselves in public, and since someone had to stand guard while the other went, they had developed codes rather than blurt out that nature was calling. They had come up with the idea in the short time that they had been with Chuck and his son.

There were two codes: *We need to talk* and *We need to have a long talk*. Thankfully it was only a *talk* that had Sadie so insistent just then.

When Neil backed out of the tent, Sadie was dancing the *I Gotta Tinkle Two-step* with her hand pointing in alarm. Below them something shuffled about, which ruled out a whole lot of privacy. Looking around, he grabbed her and tiptoed to the farthest corner of the hayloft and quickly made a pile out of the stiff straw to about three feet, giving her the tiniest bit of privacy. He would've made it higher but she was already heading in.

Walking away he made a great point of looking for the zombie below until he could hear her crunching softly up to him. "Thanks, that was close," she said in a breathy whisper. She held up the hem of her muumuu, which she had ripped. "Got plenty more if you need to have a *long talk*."

"I'm good."

Climbing in the tent they saw Sarah sitting cross-legged, she shook her head at them and said in a low voice, "That was one tough code to crack. You guys should work for the CIA." Sadie snorted at this, but Neil only smiled, noting that the blonde had shifted away from him. *Stupid!* He swore inwardly at himself. It had been the free feel that had scared her off.

In the morning, after the women took turns playing with each other's hair for two straight hours waiting for the sun to rise, they crept out of the tent and were happy to see that the zombies had all moved on, though some hadn't gone too far. A few stood about idly in the next field in that strange way of theirs. Just in case, Neil, armed with the M16, checked all around the barn, creeping around in the new frost, barefoot, pretending he was tough when his feet were really on fire with the cold. Next he made sure the house was empty and when it passed his inspection he waved the two women over.

Both were as barefoot as he and they came, limping and cursing, holding onto each other, until they got into the house and there they huddled under blankets that Neil had scrounged from the hall closet.

"It was warmer back in the tent," Sadie said, unhappily.

"Yeah but my back was killing me," Sarah put in. "And the snoring? Yikes."

Neil sagged, "I snored?"

Sadie nodded. "And farted. But don't worry it was a big manly fart, *ROOMP!*" She cackled lively at his look of embarrassment. "I'm just kidding. You didn't fart."

"And what about the free feels? What was that about?" Sarah asked with an eyebrow cocked.

"Who got a free feel? Neil did? You dog! You're a stinking dog. Especially with me right there. I'm a minor! There are laws against such filth, you know. I do declare I must speak to the church elders about you and your wicked, wicked ways."

He could feel his cheeks begin to burn and so he threw the blanket over his head. "I thought it was her shoulder," he tried to explain.

This had Sadie cracking up and it got worse when Sarah asked, "Has it been that long that you can't tell the difference." Neil pulled his head out to argue his case, but caught Sarah smiling at him in such an open manner that he forgot entirely what he was about to say.

"Maybe it was an honest mistake," Sadie said. "Once when John was about to kill Neil, I felt in his pockets for the keys to my truck and my hand came on something rock hard and bulging. I was all like: Is that a gun in your pocket or are you just happy to see me?"

"Sadie!" Neil said grimacing at how Sarah's smile went crooked. "It was a gun, honest. I had it right here in my pants."

"Relax Neil, I believe you," Sarah said, laughing again. "You two seem to have had your share of adventures, while I...I was like those sheep-people you were talking about, Sadie. Our little town wasn't hit hard at all by the zombies and we just sort of waited to see what was going to happen without doing much to preserve our future. It was stupid...I was stupid. I wish I had gone right away to New York. Maybe I could've saved my daughter."

"And maybe you could've met me and Neil in New Jersey," Sadie said. She had been smiles and now she slumped. "I miss my truck. None of this would be an issue if we had the truck. We could just light on out of here, running over any zombie that got in our way."

"Your choice of words reminds me," Neil said. "Where are we, and where are we going? The closest that I can put us is somewhere between Chicago and St. Louis. Aren't you from around here? Do you happen to know?"

Sarah stuck out her lower lip as she nodded. "Danville is a hundred miles east of here, but even if I lived closer, one farm looks a lot like another, so I don't know for certain. I don't even know exactly where on the Illinois River that Island was or how long we floated down the river yesterday. Two hours, maybe longer?"

"So you're saying you agree with Neil?" Sadie asked. "That we're lost."

She shrugged to say: yes. Neil blew out his breath in a gust. "Alright, we're somewhere between here, there and nowhere, but I wouldn't say we're lost. The Island is to the north—we don't want to go that way. We were warned against going west like we originally planned, so that leaves south...or south east toward Tennessee or one of those states."

"I like the way you say one of *those* states," Sarah said. "What you mean is one of those less important states."

It was true: Neil had always looked down his nose at what he saw as the backwardness of the southern states, and the endless farm emptiness of the mid-western states, and the dry isolation of the Rocky Mountain states. He shrugged as an answer.

"What about Southwest?" Sadie asked. "I could use some heat right now."

"Same reason we don't go up into the mountains: no food," Neil replied. "Not to mention water would be a difficulty as well. I think the southeast is our best bet. The winter will be warmer."

Sadie was up for the idea, while Sarah was noncommittal. She stared out at the cold, miserable day and didn't say anything except, "How are we going to get there. I don't have any shoes."

"I'll get you some, don't worry," Neil answered quickly. He knew the farmhouse could not provide for her since Farmer Jones' wife must have had feet twice the size of Neil's and wore something close to a twelve.

Because shoes weren't the only thing missing in their lives, Neil decided to go explore downriver, hoping to find a car or some food, or anything, really. They were without most of the essentials of life.

"I should go with you," Sadie said. "You need me to protect you."

"Hardly," Neil replied and then he added in a whisper, "I need you to protect Sarah. She seems out of it. Keep an eye out for the zombies and an ear out for the soldiers. Hide in the loft if anything happens."

After a few crackers layered with an inch of peanut butter, Neil took the M16 and the axe, and set out. He wore his now dry penny loafers and his khakis, and beneath he had on the long johns, which he had trimmed at the ankle with a pair of scissors, though they stuck out from beneath his pants. A heavy leather jacket borrowed from Farmer Jones and an orange hunting backpack completed his outfit. Neil smiled to himself--he would not have been caught dead in a crazy outfit like this before the apocalypse.

At some point during the night, Indian summer had turned into early winter and Neil's teeth chattered as he walked. He feared the cold more than the zombies; mainly because he knew that he could escape them by plunging into the river. It was the last thing he wanted to do. The river hung with tendrils of grey fog that seemed to suggest a deadly cold beneath.

Still he kept close to it as he trudged, and he kept a sharp eye out for the undead, of which he killed two before he came to the first house. Thankfully, both were smallish, women zombies, who came at him one at a time.

"Sorry," he said around a grimacing face as he hewed the first with the axe—the M16 with its scant ammo was for emergencies only. He split her head and then took the time to clean the axe in the river and that is where the second came sloshing toward him. She was having a rough time walking in the sucking mud of the river and he might have been able to simply walk away from her however he feared her following along after him and surprising him while he was in the middle of taking a leak or even just resting.

The axe was a good weapon. It had good reach and Farmer Jones had kept it sharp. After he killed the second zombie, Neil slung it on his shoulder and marched on to the distant farmhouse. This one was off the river a ways and so he approached it very carefully making sure to keep low.

A score of zombies prowled around a squat, rectangular outbuilding. Neil made sure to keep the house between him and it, knowing that if even one caught sight of him it would mean a wild chase back to the river. The backyard of the house was dirt and henpecked. Chickens had lived there, but had died in their wire cages, their bones all that were left of them. Whether it was the chickens or something more, the house had a rancid odor emanating from it, which had Neil's teeth chattering from more than the cold.

He tried the back door, turning the knob slowly, hoping that whatever was creating the smell was truly dead and not just zombie dead. The door opened onto a back hall that was dim to the point of dark and though the door had opened without sound, Neil's first step sent an empty soda can skidding away in a fuss.

"Darn it!" he whispered.

It was as good a test as any to alert him to the presence of zombies and with quick light breaths panting in and out, he hoisted the axe, ready to swing it at the first thing that moved. Nothing did. After a minute, Neil forced himself to take another step—this one came down on what he thought was glass, but what turned out to be broken china. He bent to squint down at the floor and saw it strewn with plates and cups, and this comforted him just the slightest.

When zombies made a mess it was incidental to their feeding. This mess had been done by humans, likely the soldiers from the Island, meaning there weren't going to be any 'live' zombies in the house. Still Neil was cautious and the smell had him nervous, though as he went room-to-room he grew somewhat used to it.

He found the source of the smell searing up from a

couple of bloated bodies in the garage. The stench was so overwhelming that he gagged and went dizzy. Quickly, he shut the door. Taking deep breaths to keep from vomiting, he went back into the house and stood in a hall until his stomach settled down. Wiping cold sweat from his forehead, he took a towel down off a shower curtain rod where it had been left to dry ages ago and, wrapping it around his face, went back to the garage to search for anything useful, Among the bikes and the sleds and the boxes filled with odd junk he found something that had been overlooked: a compound bow and six arrows.

The arrows had him whistling. The tips were sharp as razors. That they were deadly Neil had no doubt, but against zombies he didn't know if they would be all that effective. Could an arrow pierce bone? It was a question that he didn't have an answer to. He had whistled at the arrows, but to the compound bow he grunted as he strained at the cable that circled about two pulleys—one at the top and one at the bottom of the bow—until his fingers ached.

"What the hell?" he whispered. What kind of bow was it that you couldn't draw back? Wondering if it had a safety, like a gun, he studied it closely, but there was nothing to indicate a safety. He tried again, only this time he tucked his hand up into his sleeve so that the cable wouldn't bite as it had.

"Yes!" he said in a happy whisper as the cable came back. Strangely, the further he pulled the easier it became, so that when it was fully drawn it was nothing to hold steady. He decided to keep the bow, hoping that with a little practice it would come in handy.

Though the house had been long lived in, there wasn't more to it that Neil considered worth taking. He left, leaving the out-building to be explored by someone else. With the axe sticking out of his backpack, Neil continued his trek, flexing the bow at intervals, looking for an opportunity to use it.

Not a half-hour later another girl zombie came shambling down to the river, ignoring Neil who had frozen in place near a bush. He watched amazed as the creature actually drank from the water on all fours like a dog. This was a new phenomenon to him. Thus far he had only looked upon the zombies as something out of comic books that were created only to eat brains and frighten women into his arms. That it drank seemed absurdly unnatural to Neil Martin. In disgust he fitted an arrow into his bow, heaved back on the cable and let it loose with a satisfactory *ffft*. The arrow went into the river three feet from the zombie and Neil kicked at nothing in frustration.

The zombie didn't know where the arrow had come from. It only looked at the water, which had splashed a little in front of it. Neil got another arrow ready. "Hey," he said, remembering not say yoo-hoo. "Hey you."

This had the zombie's attention and Neil waited a couple of seconds as the thing got to its feet and presented him with a much better target. Neil even moved to his right so that in case of another miss he wouldn't lose a second arrow—which was very smart since the arrow whizzed past the beast harmlessly.

"Crap!" he said and grabbed a third arrow, but before he could fit it onto the cable he thought better of taking another shot and tugged out his axe instead. Only just in time. The zombie had been picking up speed as the ground beneath its feet had gone from mud to sand to hard-packed earth.

In fact she was so fast that Neil didn't get the axe around in time and only hit the zombie on its arm with the side of the handle. Before he knew it, the creature was on him like a rabid dog, biting and tearing, as maggots sloughed off its head to drop onto Neil's face and into his screaming mouth.

Chapter 35

Ram

Western Desert

Despite the death of her loved ones, and the pain in her life, and despite the endless zombies that had them hiding or fighting with guns that burned to the touch, Julia saw the world as she hoped it would be instead of how it really was. She saw Cassie as just a wayward child who would come around eventually if given enough love. In Ram she saw a man who could sit on his growing feelings without acting on them.

Indefinitely.

He tried to in all honesty, while Cassie tried in all dishonesty.

To Julia's face, Cassie had changed from a petulant demanding child to a girl aiming to please. Behind her back, Cassie was vindictive and undermining. She made it clear to Ram in word and deed that she would take over where Julia had left off when it came to sex, anytime he was ready. Once she had simply knelt in front of Ram with an invitingly open mouth.

"It'll pass," Julia explained when he told her about it. "She has a need to act out."

"Ok, so those are her needs, what about my needs?" Ram asked, feeling distinctly odd about saying it. He wasn't used to expressing his feelings beyond a grunt.

"Those are your wants, and I want them too," she said, touching his arm. "We will have each other again, I promise. We just have to give it time."

This mollified Ram—her words and the way she touched him so lightly. "It sure feels like a need to me, and a big one," he joked, stepping closer so that he was almost, but not quite pressing against her.

"You are currently fulfilling your most basic need," she said, becoming clinical. She did this at times, retreating into the world of science, hiding behind five dollar words to avoid being seen as vulnerable. That's how he saw it at least. She went on, pulling away emotionally and physically, "You have a hero complex. You don't value yourself unless you are protecting another. I saw it when I had the gun to my head, you changed right in front of my eyes. One second you were twitchy and your eyes were sort of lifeless and then in the next second you had pulled yourself together."

"No, I don't think I have any complex," Ram said. "You were in trouble. That's all. And why didn't I do anything to protect Cassie when she was being raped? And why did I leave those men back...back before? A hero would've stayed."

She looked at him closely before saying, "Those men were men, and not just any men, they were warriors. Warriors don't need saving. And we both know how you think of Cassie, that she's tougher than she looks. Maybe I'm wrong. Unless there was someone you were protecting before me. Someone who died?"

Shelton

"No one," Ram said, looking away as if keeping an eye out for stiffs. "So what is my prognosis if I had this complex?"

"I don't know," she said with a laugh, becoming herself again. "In the real world it could lead to neurosis or worse, but this isn't the real world any longer. Now it just may lead to you saving me. So don't look for me to cure you!"

Although it went against their mutual promise to "behave", Ram leaned in for a quick kiss, then backed slowly away, holding her hand until distance parted their fingers. That was how their relationship grew. Secret looks, little touches when Cassie wasn't around, and knowing smiles when she was. Despite the lack of sex between them Ram had never felt closer to a woman than he did to Julia.

They traveled in this way throughout the American southwest going from one tiny town to the next, eating into their food reserves and always finding just enough gas to make it one more day. Of weapons and ammo they were well stocked, having come upon a strange eight-wheeled military vehicle parked in the desert south of Albuquerque.

A soldier in dun colored battle fatigues stood outside it, while more sat within. Ram, sick with relief, hurried to them exclaiming, "Thank God! Am I glad to see you guys. We haven't seen another human so close..."

The standing soldier turned and his helmet wiggled oddly on his head. It had little flesh left on his face and so much of his scalp had been torn away that white skull was clearly visible. Ram's eyes went buggy at the sight and he froze in confusion as the zombie came at him. He would have died right there since he had left his M16 in the Bronco, but for Julia. Cool as the underside of the pillow, she marched up quick and shot the creature in the face from five feet, making a hell of a mess.

Two more of the soldier zombies had to be destroyed as well. When the smoke cleared they found the vehicle contained crates packed with thousands of rounds of M16 ammunition. Better than that, in Ram's eyes was the SAW that had been strapped uselessly to one of the zombies.

"A machine gun?" Julia asked as Ram came out of the Stryker with it on his thick shoulder. "Let's hope it doesn't come to that."

"If it does, hope won't save us, but a Squad Automatic Weapon just might." He went to the Bronco and studied it for a while saying, "Hmmm," and, "Maybe."

"What you gonna do?" Cassie asked, sweat running down her face as she lugged the heavy ammo boxes to the back of the truck.

"I want to mount this on top, but I'm afraid I don't have either the tools or the skill. Well, what I really want, if I had my way, is for us to ditch the Bronco and take the Stryker," he said this with a sigh, wondering how on earth zombies had killed three fully armed men in an armored personnel carrier.

"It didn't seem to help them," Julia said as if reading his thoughts. "And, gas is already hard to come by."

Ram knew she was right to worry. Like most military vehicles, Strykers were gas hogs and would leave them even more at the whim of fate. Fuel and clean water were the most valuable commodities in the desert. Even food was found here and there, though never in great amounts.

Because of the zombie menace in the larger cities the three avoided these, however, by their third day on the road they sipped the last of their water and they decided to chance Amarillo, in northern Texas. At one point it had been home to a quarter of a million people; not exactly a crammed to the hilt metropolis, yet still way too large when the zombie threat was assessed. Not willing to risk driving straight through the heart of the city they decided to slip by its northern suburbs first, only to find every Wal-Mart, Target, grocery, and convenience store had been looted long before.

Still, they had to try. For the first time since they had met, the three worked as a team. Cassie would watch the street, while Julia and Ram searched from room to room. Singular zombies were dispatched by Ram, usually with a thrust of his wickedly sharp bayonet that he had affixed to the muzzle of his M16.

If there was a herd, their plan was to run or hide, and this worked for the most part. They would scamper low around empty shelves and counters or sit in closets, waiting until the dead moved on, however twice the stiffs came too fast and the pair had to resort to firing their weapons. On both of these occasions the gunfire caused a swarm of undead to coalesce around them that had to be seen to be believed.

The stiffs came out of nowhere and everywhere like roaches and Ram and Julia were hard pressed to make it back to the Bronco on both occasions. Sweating, and wild-eyed they would speed away only to slow after a few blocks and again creep along. The slower the car went the less the zombies seemed to care about its existence.

"This isn't working," Ram said, discouraged. So far, after two hours of searching and hiding and running, they had discovered a very stale box of triscuits and two cans of Mr Pib. Just then they were slumped down in the vehicle outside an office park where the streets were relatively empty.

"Why don't we try in there?" Cassie said, pointing at the three-story high brick office building.

"For what? Staplers?" Ram replied.

"I could use a desk lamp," Julia said. "Or a computer to use as a paper weight."

"Oh, yeah. I guess all theys got is junk," Cassie said with a shrug. "It was a stupid idea."

"It wasn't stupid at all," Julia said, as always quick to prop the girl up. "Maybe they have something in there we could use."

Cassie rolled her eyes. "Like what?"

Julia couldn't think of anything, but just then Ram imagined what the building would be like if there were actual people in it. What they'd be doing. What sort of work. What they'd be jawing over standing around the water cooler. Or where...he laughed all of a sudden.

"Water coolers!" he said excitedly. "How many offices have them? A lot I'm thinking."

"And snack machines," Julia said. She turned to Cassie. "See, it was a smart idea."

Cassie gave one of her fake smiles that Julia bought into every time, but didn't say anything. Since they knew their roles, nothing needed to be said. Ram left the car first, hurrying to the door followed by Julia and Cassie.

The door was locked, which was both good and bad. It meant that the likelihood that looters had been inside was negligible, while at the same time it meant making noise. A heavy rock that had probably been used to prop the door open for the smokers sat near to them and Ram sent it crashing into the bottom half of the glass. He kicked in the remaining shards and then all three scurried through the low opening.

Just as in the other buildings Cassie stayed at the door to keep watch on the street, as Ram and Julia crept along, glancing into each office, They were on the lookout for zombies, but their luck was good and the place was locked up tight.

"This could be it," Ram said, relaxing. "I don't want night to catch us here so I think we should split up. Since this floor is empty, start here. Do a once over for anything obvious and if you don't see anything go through the drawers. You never know what people stash in their cubbies. I'm heading upstairs."

He kissed her once, before she could pull away and then went into the stairwell where black night descended on him as soon as the door shut. The deep dark actually had him unnerved. Tripping over the first step didn't help. He was glad he was only going to the second floor. One of the first things he saw was a water cooler—he drank greedily in spite of the fact that it was warm and stale tasting. He then hoisted the big clear drum off its base, turning it before he could lose more than a cup.

"Look what I found!" he gushed to Julia as soon as he came to the first floor. She was just exiting one of the offices straining under a cardboard box that was filled with all sorts of yummy goodies, none of which was nutritional in the least.

"Thank goodness. I found a six pack of warm Pepsi that I wasn't looking forward to brushing my teeth with." They went to the door and Cassie's eyes were big for everything they had found so far. Julia brushed her with the box in a friendly way and said, "This is all thanks to you." She and

Ram hurried to the Bronco with their treasures and were back at the office building in less than half a minute though they still managed to draw some attention to themselves from the local stiffs.

They were pretty far away so Ram did not worry over much. "Keep an eye on them," he advised Cassie and then went after Julia. "Find me some deodorant," he said to her.

"If you find me a bathtub filled with clean water."

He goosed her before heading into the dark stairwell. The second floor had been used as a call center for an insurance company and as such the pickings were slim. Mostly, more junk food, still he took as much of this as he could carry in a waste paper basket he had upended. One person, who was apparently a little more health-conscious, had three cans of tuna, which Ram pocketed.

The nicest offices were along the west side where the windows allowed the workers a better view than just more workers or the grey side of a cubicle. "Well, look at these." The owner of that first office was a bit of drinker. He had five little bottles of vodka, the tiny shot-sized variety found on airplanes or in the desks of alcoholics.

"Waste not want not," Ram said with a smile, placing them carefully in his pocket. As he did so, he happened to glance at the view outside the window and felt his heart flutter in his chest. A stream of zombies was charging toward the building, to the very door that Ram had broken into.

The wastepaper basket of goodies was forgotten and falling to the floor unheeded as Ram sprinted through the maze of cubicles, heading for the stairs. He did not make it before he heard the first shots fired.

"Shiiit," he moaned. He could tell by where the blasts were coming from that Julia was the one firing and she was alone. It was only the single gun.

Where was Cassie? Why wasn't she helping?

Ram hit the dark of the stairs and stumbled down the

first flight before he righted himself and swung his M16 off his back and into the ready position—and then he was in the light again and stiffs were pushing through the same doorway he had goosed Julia in only ten minutes before.

Holding back the fearful bile in his throat, Ram resisted the overarching desire to charge the stiffs. There were too many crowding the hall, dozens and dozens, with more pushing in from outside. Instead he sighted the M16 and began firing with single well-aimed shots.

How many had flooded into the large office Julia was in he didn't know, but his shooting caught the attention of the ones still in the hall and all ninety of them came rushing at him. He kept firing and they fell over their dead brothers in their eagerness to get at the man and rend and eat him.

He fired until his bolt sucked on nothing but air and then he ran into the next office and threw himself against the door. Immediately the beasts were on it pounding and slamming their weight in an all out effort to bash it down. It wouldn't last above a minute, while in the room next to his he could hear the desperate clatter of the lone M16 rattling away.

Julia was burning through ammo too fast. Just as he did, she carried three thirty- round magazines and there had already been two significant pauses in her shooting, suggesting she was down to her last mag. He slapped a fresh one in place and sank the bolt home just as silence came from next door—silence and then screams.

Desperation swelled in his soul and his fear for her caused actual pain in his chest. He couldn't go back in the hall; there were simply more of the stiffs than he had rounds, which left only one way to get to Julia.

Now he set the rifle to three-round burst, and running at the glass of the far wall he fired, pulling the trigger three times, and before him the window seemed to turn into frozen water and this rained down upon him as he jumped through. Thankful that he was on the ground floor he turned the gun to the window of the next office and again fired three times.

This one he didn't jump through. There really wasn't a need to. A crowd of zombies were in a literal pile seven or eight feet high, tearing at something beneath them. Ram should've run away. He should've saved his ammo and not called any more attention to himself however his anger and grief coalesced into a force that overrode any common sense. Gritting his teeth, he fired into the pile, not worried that he would hit Julia because he knew that for her it would be a blessing to catch an errant bullet in the brain.

He fired, knocking the stiffs back from the pile; laying them out with gaping holes in their nauseating heads. In apparent confusion at the new attack, the stiffs turned slowly from their meal, giving Ram time to mow them down one by one, until his bolt went back a second time on an empty magazine. With calm deliberate motions he pulled his final mag as the stiffs came up to the low wall that marked the border between inside and out. They began to climb through in their clumsy way and he only stood there sneering in hatred as his hands worked, and then behind him, just as he sent the bolt flashing forward, chambering a round, he could hear the door to the office he had just left come crashing in.

Things are about to get interesting, he thought. And yet they grew far more interesting than he could have ever dreamed as his eyes lit upon the area where he had seen the pile of zombies. Julia was still alive!

She had hidden under a desk and had pulled a swivel chair in front of her and had held on with all her strength while the beasts had crushed in around her. There were still two of them almost right on top of her, each pulling at the chair, but in opposite directions. Ram fired at the one with his back to him and it was only then that he noticed the odd way his gun vibrated—he was still on three round burst!

With his ammunition situation so desperate, he flicked the weapon to single shot, brought the gun back up to his cheek and paused. There was Julia running at an angle for the broken window. Beyond her the second zombie had fallen backward when the tug of war over the chair had ended so unexpectedly, while behind more zombies flooded the room.

Julia leapt past the zombies struggling among the jagged shards of the window and then the two of them were running for their lives.

"Keep the gun!" Ram said. Julia had been trying to pull the strap over her head as they booked around the back of the office building. "We'll make it and I don't want to have to try to go back for it." Now that they were in the open, he was confident of their chances. Though a zombie could practically run forever they were generally slow and all Ram had to do was get around one more wing of the building and then they'd be able to make it to the Bronco.

Except when they cleared the back of the building, the Bronco was gone. Only zombies, numbering in the hundreds remained. The sight was beyond terrifying but what was worse was Julia's leg.

"I'm bleeding," she said breathlessly and shaking. "I'm going to become one of them."

Chapter 36

Neil

Illinois River

The zombie straddling Neil Martin once had a name: Miss Kennedy, and she once had an occupation: pre-school teacher. Now she opened her mouth wide and bit down into his neck.

That he would scream was no wonder; that he would live for a while longer was, however. The zombie pre-school teacher ripped her head back and forth while Neil yelled himself hoarse and then with a shearing noise, she pulled back, chewing on a mouthful of flesh.

Beneath her, Neil coughed and sputtered and spat out the maggots and all the while watched in fascination as Miss Kennedy chewed and chewed on the flesh—it was skin actually. And it was the skin of a long dead cow. She had torn off the collar of his leather coat.

For a long time she worked her jaws on that leather and all the while Neil only laid there hoping she would either go away or choke on it. She did neither. She only chewed and stared at nothing beyond the river. Finally, when Neil couldn't stand it any longer, he threw the preschool teacher off of him with heroic strength, and grabbed up his axe. Now she came alive, in the sense that she wanted to kill, but Neil was ready for her this time and dashed in her skull, and she went back to being dead.

After this battle, he went to the river and shook with adrenaline, while he vomited. Later he picked a maggot out of his teeth and vomited again, though in truth he mostly just dry heaved and belched loudly.

"Thank God no one saw that," he whispered, picking up his bow and pulling the stray arrow from a hillock of river grass. He then looked down at the dead woman and said, "I think when I tell that story, you'll be an iron worker instead, with big muscles...and a black beard."

The woman continued to just lie there with her face in the wet sand. Neil left her and continued down river, wishing he was done with zombies for the day. It was a silly thing to wish for. The next house had them like a dog has fleas. And then he came to a loop in the river and found at least a hundred lined up at the water's edge as if waiting for a bus. This forced him to skirt far around and yet the detour had its benefits.

First he found an entire field of broccoli sitting there ready to be harvested. He filled his backpack with the greenest of the lot and then walked away eating and burping—broccoli always made him gassy. He then came upon a row of trees next to a dirt road and laughed when he saw they were apple trees.

"It is apple picking weather," he said as he dumped out half the broccoli from the backpack. "I bet Sadie would love this, and Sarah as well." He was so busy thing of the two women that he overstuffed the pack and had to dumps some out.

A while later, as he angled west over open fields, he found the river again and after a few miles of solid walking, he found a boat. It was a dinky little tin thing, or so it appeared, with its metal hull, rusting and grey. The nose of the boat had caught on a little sand bar seventy feet out into the wide river and Neil didn't hesitate. He stripped down to his shivering flesh, fearing that the water would grow deep at points, and waded in.

The water did indeed go deep and he swam nervously as the current swept him away from the boat, though he did manage to find the bottom with his feet at the far end of the sand bar. This allowed him to struggle up onto the little island and once upon it he rushed bent over and holding himself against the cold until the boat was laying there at his feet.

It had a motor and everything. Excitedly he pulled it further onto shore so that it wouldn't try to get away, and then he hunkered down, peering at the motor. Gleefully he saw that a key wouldn't be needed—there was a toggle that said: *On* and *Off*, and a handle like a lawnmower. Without hesitation he flicked the switch and pulled the cord.

It made a sad little noise, like a burp from a cow, and would not catch. Neil checked the gas and saw that it was mostly full. So what was the problem? The choke! There was a little knob on the engine low down. This he twisted full over and pulled again on the cord.

Now the engine caught and rumbled nicely. Neil turned the choke down and got in the metal boat after giving it a shove into the river. This was better! He chugged the boat back to shore where he quickly put on his clothes.

"Oh the girls will be so happy," he said, shivering in the back of the boat as he continued on his way. A boat by itself didn't mean all that much. He still needed gas for it and supplies in general. These were quick in coming, now that he could travel faster.

The very next house was zombie-free, though he didn't take chances and snuck up on it ninja-like going from bush to tree in short bursts. Like so many others it had been gone over by someone very thoroughly, but even the best searchers could overlook things. The car in the garage had been drained of gas, however the riding mower sitting right next to it was full.

Using a garden hose he siphoned out almost four gallons of gas that he put in an orange bucket. Next he dared the awful smell of the refrigerator and discovered a jar of jelly that hadn't been opened, and in the laundry room he found candles and flashlights. Though it was in a girl's bedroom that he found the best items: shoes, clothing, and pop tarts.

The girl who had once lived there had worn a size six shoe, which seemed about right. Neil compared the shoes to his feet and thinking that Sarah's were a little smaller than his own he decided to keep the ones that seemed the most practical. He then made a quick run through of the closet and picked out the most conservative clothing, while he took almost all of the panties and socks.

He had no idea if the bras would work for either of the two women under his care—this is how he viewed them, despite that Sadie was very capable and Sarah had already saved him once—so he took the bras as well, and that was when he saw the silver glint of the pop tarts at the bottom of the drawer. Six packages all told.

"Oh, Sadie will love this," he said, carefully wrapping the prize in a towel. "Though I don't know about Sarah, she seems a little too sophisticated for pop tarts. Still, beggars can't be choosers."

Like many of the homes in the area, this one had an outbuilding nearby.

Neil found this one was a storage unit for farm equipment with a chicken coop attached. Not knowing what chickens ate, and hoping it was sunflower seeds are something palatable like that, Neil went to the low storage bins next to the coop.

There were two and the first had its lock knocked off. Inside was chicken feed, the smell of which turned his stomach. Fully expecting the second to be more of the same, he took a stone that had been holding down a loose section of the chicken wiring and smashed at the lock. It held, however the hasp did not and with some twisting he was able to open the bin.

"Winner, winner, chicken dinner," Neil breathed at the sight of eleven plastic five gallon water containers. One was already open and after giving it a sniff, he drank, feeling the water run down his insides. It was glorious.

With this find, he decided he had enough supplies to justify going back to what, in his mind, he called home. Lugging everything to the boat was a matter of some minutes, nearly an hour , which was less than the time it took to chug gently back up-stream. He didn't hurry. The faster he made the boat go the more sound it made and he didn't want to alert the entire zombie population of southern Illinois and have them follow him back.

He figured he was in for a hero's welcome and he grinned confidently as he shouldered the first of his back packs—he had three of them--took a five gallon water container in one hand and the axe in the other. Then, remembering the fiasco in the barn, he put everything down again and strapped the rifle across his shoulder...Sarah didn't know him very well and probably worried more over the fate of her M16 than over Neil.

Hoisting his burdens once again he went up the incline to the house and stepping through the open front door said, "Ta-dah!"

There was no one there to see his big entrance. Feeling let down and a little arm weary, he put the water by the door and called, "Sadie? Sarah?"

"I'm in here," Sarah said from the back room. Neil happily turned in that direction and spoke just as someone came down the hall.

"You have to see..." Neil began.

It wasn't Sarah at all. It was a zombie with hair curlers and a muumuu that matched the one Sadie had been wearing. It was a big zombie as well and Neil squawked in fright and ran back the way he had come. He had left the axe and the M16 lying on the living room couch and it was a heated mental struggle for Neil to pick up the axe and not the gun...the zombie woman, though alone, was that big.

Still she was a waddler and a slow one at that, giving Neil ample time to swing his axe. Horribly, it got stuck in the woman's immense pumpkin head and was wrenched out of his hands as she crashed to the floor.

"Oh, that's gross," he moaned, feeling his stomach turn flops as he worked the axe-head back and forth. Suddenly

Sarah was there, looking dainty in a summer dress.

"Did you get both of them?"

Neil froze. "Both?"

The second one came out of the garage just then and Sarah pointed behind Neil. They ran—Sarah back to the bedroom and Neil, because the axe was still stuck in old pumpkin head, meant to run into the living room, but instead found himself playing a game of tag with the zombie around the long, polished table in the dining room. Finally Neil knocked over a chair and when the zombie went down he grabbed another and bashed the thing repeatedly until it stopped moving.

"Oh my, that was close," he said, shaking for the second time that day. "It's dead, Sarah. I killed it." Again he was hoping for a better reaction than the one he received. She scampered into the hall, looked around and then went to the living room where she took up the M16 and pointed it straight at his chest.

"Huh?" Neil said.

"Put the chair down and get your hands up," Sarah ordered.

Neil did, more confused than afraid. "I say again, huh? Why are you doing this?"

She stared at him for a few seconds and then let the gun sag. "Sadie tried to kill me. She sicced those stiffs on me. I swear she did. A little while ago, she was out in the rain and then she came in and said something about checking the garage. She went in there and the next thing I know these two stiffs come walking in. She led them in here!"

"It had to be an accident," Neil said. He went to the big, muumuu-wearing zombie, worked the axe out of its head and went to the garage, again more worried for Sadie than afraid of Sarah who had resumed pointing the gun at him. "Sadie?" he said in a low voice. The garage was dark and silent. "Hello? Sadie?"

When no one answered he went to the side door, a stiff

aluminum piece and opened it, flooding the room with grey light. Sadie wasn't in sight. "You see?" Sarah said. "She came in. Led the stiffs right to me and walked out that door."

"Then where is she? And why would she do this? Did you two have a fight?"

"No. We were just talking and poking around. She went back out to the barn and the next thing I know she walks these two in here and leaves me stranded."

It was impossible for Neil to believe that Sadie would do this. In a growing heat, he marched out to the barn and nearly walked right into two more stiffs. One was right around the corner of the red building. With accuracy born of long practice, Neil hewed it down with a single stroke. The other was staring up at the loft with its mouth open, as if hoping that a human would just fall into it. Neil konked that one as well.

"Sadie! What are you doing?" he demanded. He knew she was up there because the ladder had been drawn up. "Sarah seems to think that you tried to kill her."

"I don't want to talk about it," she said. "Not right now."

"No, that won't do at all," Neil said. "Aren't you even worried about her? She could be dead for all you know and you're acting like this. Like a child!"

"I'm not. I can see her right through the cracks. And I heard you two talking, before. So I knew she was alright and I knew she would be alright in the house. We talked about how heavy the master bedroom door was."

"So, you did plan this!" Sarah yelled. She had followed Neil to the barn and now stood with her hands on her hips. "Come down here right now young lady."

"No," Sadie whispered. "Maybe you two should go on without me."

"That's not going to happen either," Neil said. Sarah made a noise that suggested she thought it was very likely going to happen. He ignored her. "Come on down or I'll build a pyramid of these bales to come up there."

"They're too heavy for you," Sarah said. "I know from experience, hay bales weigh a ton."

Suddenly Sadie appeared looking down with her bangs swaying from her forehead. "If Neil says he can do it then he can. He's stronger than he looks."

"Then let him," Sarah replied. "Go ahead Neil."

Sadie glared once and then disappeared again, leaving Neil even more bewildered. "What is this about, Sadie? I thought you liked Sarah."

"I do, it's just she's practically blind!"

Sarah's anger softened a little. "What am I blind to?"

When Sadie hesitated, Neil spoke, "If we're missing something, you have to tell us. You just can't lash out. Now, come on down and we'll talk about it. I got a boat, with a motor and gas and everything. We could take it right down the Mississippi if we wanted to. I just want you to be there when we go. What do you say?"

"Can I talk to Sarah alone?" Sadie asked. "This is between us, Neil. So if you could wait back in the house..."

"No, that's not how we're going to do this," Neil replied stepping back so he could see the teen better. "We three need to be a team." He turned to Sarah. "That is if you want to?" It wasn't really something they had talked about and he didn't want to make assumptions.

"Before I say yes, we need to hear what she has to say. And I want the full truth. Half-truths will breaks up apart just as sure as outright lies will. Can you be truthful with me, Sadie?"

"Yes," Sadie said in a low voice. "You don't see Neil like I do. You don't see his good qualities." Sarah looked at Neil, who only shrugged, not knowing what good qualities he possessed that they hadn't already seen.

"I'm looking at him right now," Sarah said, looking his way. "And I do see his good qualities. He's a nice guy. And he's..."

Sadie interrupted, "No, he's not a nice guy. He hates

being called that. Neil is smart and brave, and he's loyal to those people he cares for. He did everything he could to get those soldiers to let me stay on that Island, even though he knew they'd never take him."

"It was a mistake to even try," Sarah said. Her words were harsh, but that only set Sadie off some more.

"You see, Neil? She won't understand. I'm trying but she's got her own shit to worry about. She'll never understand you, like I do."

Neil grabbed his hair and pulled at it in frustration. "Are you saying you like me, Sadie? I'm sorry, but that wouldn't be right..."

"Don't be silly Neil. I don't like you like that. I just want Sarah to."

A thick silence followed this statement and as it went on Sarah and Neil only stared at each other not knowing what to say. After a bit, Sadie spoke again, "I let those zombies into the house so that you could save her. So that she could see your brave side. So that she could see you're a good man and not just a nice guy. She only thinks you're sort of goofy and I hate that."

"I don't think that at all," Sarah said, looking stricken over the accusation, yet at the same time Neil could see her searching for something nice to say about him. "Really, you're a..."

Neil shook his head. "Don't. Just don't." He went to the door of the barn and looked out at the cold day. The rain had picked up again which made him realize that his precious gas was only covered by a ratty shirt he had found in the bottom of the boat. "I got work to do," he said and left.

"Neil, please," Sarah called, hurrying after him, her feet still bare despite the cold. "We have to talk."

He kept walking, his anger large in his mind as a way to compensate for his mortal embarrassment. Of course as a "Nice Guy" he did his best to hide his true feeling because that's what nice guys did. "Sadie is just mixed up," he said.

"It's not her fault so please don't take it out on her. We should just do our best to keep an eye on her."

"Yes I agree, but I wanted to talk about us," Sarah said, stepping around the rocks and larger puddles. "It's not a good time for me. I just lost my parents and you know..."

"Why are you telling me this?" he asked cutting right across her, his anger now growing so great that even his vaunted niceness wasn't covering it any longer. "There is no us. I'm sorry if you think I'm pining away for you, but I'm not. And I don't have a crush on you and I definitely am not doodling your name on my damned notebook in 5th period, so don't give me that crap about it not being a good time for you, because we both know it would never be a good time for you!"

"I know. I'm sorry. I shouldn't have said that, but Sadie put me on the spot and I just wanted to be clear."

Neil had marched angrily back to the boat and now he climbed in and stood there looking at everything, seething as the rain pelted him, but as always, his inherent niceness pushed its way forward and kept him from exploding on her in his rage. Yet he did sneer, "You were clear alright. Is this how you were back in the old days? Did you walk around telling men not to bother before they even knew your last name? I have to say, cutting a man off preemptively when he wasn't even going to ask you out is kind of rude, if you must know. Especially as the thought never even crossed my mind. Which it didn't."

Sarah hung her head and the rain dripped from her nose and even as mad as he was, Neil had to resist wiping the drops away, or giving her his coat. "Sorry," she said again. "I guess that wasn't very nice of me."

"It happens, right? We all have our moments," Neil replied, regretting having made her upset, turning back into the Mr. Nice Guy just like that. He gave her a smile to show there weren't any hard feelings. "We have to make sure Sadie is clear on all of this: You don't like me in that way and I don't like you in that way. Not at all. Here, this is for you." He reached into the bottom of the boat and handed her one of the backpacks. "It's just some shoes and some clothes and some grape jelly I thought you would like...and some more of that perfume you were wearing. It's nothing really."

Chapter 37

Ram

Amarillo, Texas

Hundreds of zombies, 27 rounds left, and a girl who had his heart in a tight grip, bleeding with a virus fighting to get into her system. Ram had zero choices. Running wasn't an option and fighting would have to wait. In his pocket was Julia's only hope, and he didn't so much as hand her his rifle, as he threw it into her arms and dug out the first bottle of vodka that he had hoped would ease them back into a more intimate relationship.

Instead she screamed as he poured it into the jagged wound that the broken glass had slashed into her flesh. "Shoot, damn it!" he yelled and then grabbed her leg and squeezed so that the blood and alcohol blended and came out pink. Another bottle joined the first and then the M16 started ripping the air with its thin thunder. He then spread the gash as far as it would go and poured a third bottle into the wound. Julia gasped, but kept on firing.

It would have to do for now.

"Come on," he said without waiting even a second for her to figure out what he meant by that, he yanked the gun from her grip and threw her over his shoulder. Whether she could run or not he didn't know or care. Some primal part of him had taken over. Now he was Tarzan and she was Jane, and this was no longer a PC world—there were zombies to worry over, many, many hundreds of them.

Julia had laid out those who had gotten close, some with headshots and some with hits that were just good enough. It gave him a lane that he pelted through with Julia bouncing against him. Across the street was another low brick building sitting ignored by the empty world. He was happy to notice that glass doors were in vogue for front entrances in this part of town, and made straight for it.

Upon reaching them, Ram dumped Julia unceremoniously her on her butt and dropping his gun in her lap. He said simply, "Cover me."

Julia might have been a psychologist by training with a woman's soft heart, but just then she was a Spartan in her soul. With the horde closing, she put aside her fear and shot with nerves as cold as ice. She aimed low, at knee height and a miss of a stiff in front still meant that the one behind stumbled and fell. The result was an obstacle course for the undead.

While she was buying time with the few remaining bullets, Ram was looking around in a growing panic; this time there wasn't a handy stone for him to use to break the glass and he feared to waste even a single bullet. With no other good choice, he threw himself against the glass door and all that happened was a shock went through him from shoulder-to-shoulder. He didn't try a second time, knowing it would do little beside bruise him. Instead he lashed out with a grunting front kick that set the power of his two hundred and twenty pounds in a three-inch area across the ball of his right foot straight into the glass. The door shattered and so did something within him. A searing pain raced up the tibia in his lower leg and right through to his knee, making his teeth clench.

He was operating in fight or flight mode and he hardly noticed the pain. However when he went to kick out the jagged glass remaining in the doorframe so that he and Julia could get through, his knee buckled and he went down. He knew that he injured himself badly, yet just then it didn't matter a hill of beans to him. His mind had set itself a goal and the punishment his body took in gaining that goal was secondary and of trivial importance. With his elbow he cleared the glass and then he reached for Julia who was already kicking backwards with her good leg, firing all the while. By the back of the shirt, he took her and dragged her through the low opening, pushing her head down to keep her scalp from being sliced open on the way through.

"I'm empty," she said, showing him the open port on the side of the M16, and not at all upset with her rough treatment. With the danger, she hadn't even seem to notice how he had manhandled her and in truth neither did he.

Ram stared at the gun for a second and with his mind still in its *Fire bad / Girl Pretty* mode, he could not quite make the connection between her words and the actual fact that they were out of ammo. All he knew was what he said aloud: "We shouldn't stay here," he said.

The gun went across his shoulder while she slung an arm over him for support. Together they hobbled on through an unknown building where one set of cubicles looked like another and their only saving grace was that the zombies, in their zeal to get at their victims, had plugged the hole behind them with three of their wriggling bodies. Ram didn't know this and he pressed on as fast as he could, heading down a central corridor with no particular destination in mind.

"Where are they?" Julia asked, glancing over her shoulder with every other step. He was about to say he didn't know, but there came a bang and a shattering of glass. Instead of answering he opened the first door on his left—the one on the opposite side of the building from which they had entered. He touched a finger to his lips to suggest she be quiet. She gave him a look that said: *No duh.*

The two spread out, each hobbling; Julia went to the back wall, while Ram looked up at the noise dampening ceiling panels, wondering if he could get her up there and if they would hold even her slight weight. It didn't seem likely except where the walls ran together and so he limped to what looked like a break room; as he did so there came a thumping and a rush of feet from the hall. The stiffs were hunting them.

Julia glanced at him, more pale than he had ever seen her and then went back to searching the desks and rooms, looking for something, anything, that would save them. Ram was beginning to think that being saved wasn't possible. He felt that putting off death for another minute, or another hour, or a single day was the best they could hope for. So he looked again at the ceiling, seeing in it a moment's refuge.

He just had to get up there. With a near silent grunt he placed a chair on the desk nearest to the break room and was just wondering how he was going to get his gimpy bulk up on it when he heard a short, urgent whistle from Julia. She had one hand pointing out the window, while the other waived him over with frantic motions. There was no hurrying Ram, impaired as he was by his bad leg and limited by the fact that any noise would alert the beasts that had descended upon the hall just beyond the doors. Still she tried.

"Come on!" Julia hissed. "She's leaving."

Finally Ram came up to the window and saw the Bronco, slowly drifting down the street. Their salvation was right there and what was more, there wasn't a stiff in sight.

Reaching for a tall, four-legged stool, Ram warned, "It's going to be loud. We may not make it."

"I don't want to die here," she said, nodding and pointing at the window. "Do it. Break the glass."

It was easier said than done. His bad leg kept him from putting his full power into the swing and so the first attempt saw the chair rebounding off the window and nearly coming out of his grip. It made a noise like a stunted gong, though in its effect it might as well have been a dinner bell. The zombies went into an instantaneous frenzy. The door shook as they attacked it, but worse, in a visceral way, was that the walls began to vibrate as the beasts tore at the paneling and the thin sheetrock beneath in order to get at them.

"Again!" Julia cried, slapping a desk with the flat of her palm repeatedly. A second time he swung and this time the glass flashed into a spider's web of cracks. Behind them was a splintering cracking noise—the zombies were breaking through the door!

Ram didn't need Julia's urging; he began to hammer at the glass faster and faster as a small hole widened slowly. When it was just big enough he grabbed Julia by the arm and pushed her to it.

"It's not big enough for you," she said pulling back. The first zombie began to slither through the hole in the door, unmindful of the sharp angles of wood. "We both go!"

Ram had fully intended on going, he had only wanted her to get to safety first. With a growl at even this tiny delay he went berserk on the glass, making the hole large enough with three tremendous swings of the mangled chair.

"Go," he said, breathing great gusts of air. He couldn't wait to help her through as he had planned instead he had the undead to deal with. Like horrible snakes the stiffs slithered through the opening they had made; already there were four of them in the room. In the first second he knocked one sprawling with the chair and in the next he over turned the desk at his feet and pushed it in the path of another.

"Ram! I'm through," Julia called. She then went limping out into the street calling Cassie back, as well as calling every zombie in the vicinity to her. There weren't any on the street, however there were plenty still trying to get into the building and these came charging around the far end. "Shit, shit, shit. Ram! Come on," she cried.

In the art of zombie warfare subtlety was wasted and Ram had learned this lesson well. There was only attack, attack, attack until the beasts were all dead. Unless, that is, one was winded and weakened through injury; and unless there was a way to escape. Ram smashed the third zombie with the awkward weapon, but it took three tries to bring it down and then the fourth was on him, arms and taloned hands reaching. Defense was normally useless since a single scratch could doom a person, but now Ram brought up the stool to chest height and when the zombie reached through the metal it effectively handcuffed itself. With its arms extended and trapped, Ram simply pivoted the creature back the way it came and shoved it at the next beast coming at him.

He didn't wait to see how much this was going to slow any of them down, instead he launched himself in an ugly one-legged dive through the window.

Julia was screaming for Cassie to stop, but the Bronco's brake lights didn't go on until Ram joined her on the street, waving his arms and screaming. Only then did Cassie put the car in reverse and back toward them as fast as her limited ability would allow. Few people practiced driving in reverse at top speed, and by the way Cassie fishtailed the Bronco all over the road, it was clear she wasn't one of those few. Ram had to pull Julia back to keep her from being hit.

"I thought you were dead," Cassie said as soon as they climbed in. She didn't need to be told to floor it when the doors were slammed shut and locked because the undead were all over the car scraping at the glass and the paint.

The sudden acceleration pinned them to the leather seats. Julia grabbing the *Oh Shit* bar above the door to hang on, however Ram was left to sway back and forth in a growing nausea as he pulled out the final two bottles of vodka.

"Let me see that leg," he said to Julia. To Cassie he barked, "Slow down! Nothing's chasing you." Julia scooted close, her face pulled by fear, afraid to even look at the wound. The cut was on her inner thigh and in order to get a better look, Ram took her blood soaked jeans where they were torn, and with a quick violent motion, ripped them wide, exposing the soft pale skin from knee to pelvis and then some.

On impulse from such a move she tried to close her splayed legs, but Ram, intent on sterilizing the wound, laid her thighs wide open with his large hands. For him it was an act that was non-sexual in nature and he was too absorbed, to mixed in his emotions to notice how dominant his mannerisms and position were, or how pink in the cheeks Julia had become, or how she put her shaking hands out to him as if to ward him off, or how big Cassie's eyes had grown in her dark face as she turned to look.

He didn't notice any of this because he was sick, not only with fear for Julia, but also sick because of Cassie's erratic driving. She was weaving left and right as she kept her chin half-turned from the road, trying to see what was happening in back. He was also nervous for himself. There was a cut on his left forearm that he hadn't noticed before and it, coupled with his stomach's strong reaction, had him wondering if he were infected as well.

"Face the road, damn it," he seethed.

"I'm just trying to see what the hell you doin' back there," Cassie replied, pointing her chin at Julia's spread legs and prone position. Only then did Ram see what the women saw and he grabbed a shirt from one of the packs and covered her.

"She bit?" Cassie asked in the same tone of voice as if she were asking if Julia had only stubbed her toe. "Cuz if so she needs to get the fuck out."

"It's her damned car," Ram snarled. Uncapping the fourth bottle he began working the alcohol into the wound, which begun to bleed afresh.

Julia grimaced as he did so, grabbing the bar tighter. "I got scratched is all...on glass," she said in a high voice. "This is just a precaution. Ram, you're bleeding as well. Do you know that? You need to save some for yourself."

"I have one more," he said, handing it to her. "Could you do it? I don't know if I can reach well enough." She sat up, covering herself with her shirt, and then with soft hands explored his wound, cleaning it thoroughly as Cassie watched and drove all at once.

"Will that work?" she asked. "Cuz if it don't you know what I gots to do."

"It might," Julia said. "Especially for me. I wasn't

bitten. But what about you, Ram? Were you bitten?"

"I don't know...or I know I wasn't bit, but I don't know if I was scratched by one of them. I can't tell from this angle. Does that look like glass made it?"

"I can't tell," Julia answered with fearful eyes and shaking hands. "What we should do is flush the wound properly with something better than vodka."

"And maybe you should put up them guns in case you two turn," Cassie cautioned.

Instead Ram dug for more ammo. "What the hell happened back there?" he asked, glaring, watching as Cassie quickly turned her attention back to the road.

"I don't know, alright. There must've been another door open somewhere in the back cuz I was just sittin' there and suddenly they be right there in the hall behind me. I would have warned you but I was too scared because they were right close up on me."

"They came in from the back?" he asked, trying to picture the layout of the building they had just escaped from. "I saw them out front."

Julia pointed for Cassie to take a right, toward a main street. After the turn Cassie explained, "They was out front, too. After I saw the ones in back I went to the front and made a run for the car. It was my only chance."

"But they were coming in. Why didn't they go after..."

Julia interrupted him. "Stop. Look, there's a dentist's office. They should have everything we need to clean these wounds properly."

At the idea of getting his wound cleaned, Ram was pulled away from the puzzle that had been bothering him: why had the undead come into the building instead of following Cassie in the Bronco as they normally would have?

"What's a dentist have that we could possibly want?" he asked with a touch of hope. He had an unspoken dread of contracting the virus. This fear had been with him since day one and it had never been closer to going from fear to reality than just then.

It turned out plenty. Dental offices were generally better equipped with medical supplies than most people knew, which was likely why this one hadn't been looted. They rushed in with barely a thought to security, although this time Ram kept the keys to the truck. He didn't trust Cassie's story. She was either lying about something big, or had run at the first sign of a zombie. That she hadn't run far suggested cowardice, however her eyes suggested much more.

Now in the offices of William Hargrove DDS, deceased, they found rubbing alcohol as well as gobs of medical supplies: novocain, zylocain , #4 suture kit. "Should I try to stitch you up?" Julia asked.

"Would it help?"

She bobbed her head a little. "Only with infection and scarring, but not with the virus."

"Infection? Shouldn't we be taking some antibiotics against the virus? Something strong?" he asked.

She was busy going through the cabinets, squinting at the tiny writing on the tiny bottles. "No," she said somewhat absently. "Antibiotics won't work."

"You don't know that," Cassie put in, her breath smelling of mint. On the receptionist's desk had been a bowl of candy—the girl was partial to *Peppermint Patties*. "Maybe it ain't been tried yet, not early like this. Shit, if you don't want to try you should at least let Ram."

Julia gave her a smile and patted her hand. "You don't understand. Antibiotics can't treat a virus. They only work on bacteria. Only a vaccine or the human body can combat a virus. It's a common mistake."

Cassie made a noise of dismissal as she picked through the candy bowl. "Ain't nothing on me. I ain't the one bit."

This set the mood for the rest of the evening—a mood of anxious waiting. Ram had seen the virus take anywhere from as little as five hours to as long as fourteen hours to kick in, but once the fever hit, that was all she wrote.

As the clock ticked over past midnight, he checked his temperature and then touched his throat. So far he was normal. Cassie was normal as well; she lay in the outer room snoring loudly as usual, sleeping easily and without care despite that her two companions could turn at any moment.

The thought stirred anger within Ram—not that Cassie was so relaxed about the events, but that this could be his last evening alive and he was spending it alone on a cold leather couch. He glanced over and saw that Julia was laying there with her eyes pinned to the ceiling and with her lips pulled back in fear.

He went to her and she saw what he wanted. "No," she whispered. "Cassie's right there. We promised ourselves we wouldn't."

Ram went to the door to the office and closed it gently. "No," Julia repeated louder.

"Listen, one or both of us might be dead in a few hours. Do you want your last moments on earth to be in lived in fear or in love?"

"We can't," she insisted, but Ram didn't listen and kissed her deeply. To keep pressure off of her wound she had changed into a light skirt and as they kissed his hand crept under it and her legs parted. With that one simple motion he knew that she wanted him as much as he wanted her. He hiked the skirt upwards and very gently entered her.

Too late she said, "But we shouldn't. Cassie is..." He stopped her words with a stronger thrust and then all she could do was moan.

Chapter 38

Sarah

Illinois River

Did Neil think he was being subtle in his affections Sarah wondered as she watched the man scurrying about collecting long grass to place under the sleeping bags for warmth and extra padding. Or was he blissfully unaware that he wore his emotions so openly? He was polite and reserved in his interactions with her. He seemed to be striving for *coolly cordial*, however when he let his guard down he couldn't seem to help but give her preferential treatment: he gave her the largest portion of their limited food, the choicest place to sleep, the first option at everything, while he took the last.

He always put himself last because, along with his obvious affection for Sarah, it was clear that he had fatherly feelings towards Sadie. As well he had a father's temper when she went too far in her joking, which was frequent. The girl could never seem to let anything pass without a comment or a look or a seemingly innocent quip that wasn't so innocent. In her way Sadie was just as obvious as Neil and just as optimistic.

The two were strangely happy and content. To be sure they had their moments, but on the whole, they acted as though the zombie apocalypse had been a benefit to their lives. Perhaps it had been, at that. From what Sarah could piece together, Neil had been somewhat of a hermit—a lonely man whose life revolved around work and keeping his vegetable garden from being pilfered by the neighborhood squirrels. While Sadie had apparently been virtually ignored by her single mom and had never known her father save for the yearly birthday and Christmas cards he'd send.

For them this was a new beginning and a grand

adventure. For Sarah it was one miserable day after the next with little to look forward to and only pain to look back on.

She knew Neil and Sadie tried their level best to make her happy and she allowed them to even though in her heart she knew it was wrong of her. They gave and gave and she had nothing to give in return. Yes, she helped with meals, and she stood watch, and she fetched and carried and did all the other chores of this new life, but she could never return their emotions.

She had already failed at being a mother and wife; it wasn't something that she could force herself to do again. So she tried instead to simply be a companion and, unbeknownst to her, in this she also failed.

Their third night on the river was as cold as the others had been and snow seemed to be threatening. "I wish we could build a fire," Sadie said through chattering teeth. "I'm fricken freezing here."

"When Neil finally puts the tent up we'll get the candles lit," Sarah said. "You'll see what a difference they'll make; I guarantee you'll be taking clothes off before too long." The three of them had camped out in the boiler room of an elementary school the night before and, despite being out of the wind and the light snow, they had shivered and snuggled to stay warm. Neil had forgotten entirely that he had found candles. When he had pulled them out of the bottom of his pack that morning with a laugh, saying: *Hey look at these. I forgot all about them*, Sarah could've smacked him.

"Taking off clothes, sounds sexy," Sadie said with her smirk. "Maybe I'll get my own tent. Or better yet, my own barn." They were in another barn for the night. This one had stairs that Neil pried away. Height or solid brick walls seemed to be the only real guarantee of safety against zombies. However, against the soldiers, who prowled constantly in search of supplies or women, only being sly and lucky proved of any use.

The day before, the rain had stopped for a few hours

around noon and allowed the dirt roads in that part of Southern Illinois just enough time to dry out so that Sadie, in the prow of the boat, was able to see a dust ribbon in the air just over the crest of a hill. Frantically, Neil had killed the engine and they drifted into a run of tall riverweeds as four Humvees came into view down river.

Luck had kept them from blundering right into the patrol. Sarah didn't want to think what would have happened if they had been caught. Neil would've been killed for certain. The little she knew of him made it clear he probably would have chosen that moment to make a stand for her honor, not knowing she had very little honor left. Every time she thought about the colonel and what she had been willing to do to save her parents and herself, a shiver racked her.

Being turned away from the Island without food and weapons had, in a way, been lucky for Neil and Sadie. They at least had been able to preserve their honor.

Their barn for the night was just south of a little burg called, Naples Illinois, where earlier they had been able to scrounge another ten gallons of gas and some more canned vegetables, which Sadie ignored; this wasn't out of place for her. The girl had turned up her nose at the fresh broccoli and after two apples refused any more. As she and Sarah watched Neil putting up the little tent, she nibbled on Jolly Ranchers and Pop Tarts contentedly.

Finally, Sarah felt she had to say something. "All that sugar is going to rot your teeth. There's nothing nutritious about any of it. And it'll stunt your growth." Sarah had just thrown that last in although she was certain it wasn't in any way true.

"I can't eat broccoli even when it's cooked," Sadie had replied. "And apples aren't all that healthy. Do they have riboflavin? Or six other essential nutrients? Because Pop Tarts do. It says so right on the box. And these are blueberry. That's a fruit." As emphasis she pointed to the blue filling that was likely ninety-nine percent sugar.

Sarah shot Neil a look that said: *Are you just going to stand there? Or are you going to say something?* He cleared his throat and announced: "Sarah's right."

"About what?" Sadie asked, taking another dainty bite at the edge of her pastry. "Am I really going to have my growth stunted? Is that what happened to you two?" Neil stiffened at this; he never liked his height mentioned.

"We're both taller than you," Sarah replied, and seeing his discomfort added, "I'm five foot, four and Neil is probably five foot, six."

This was such a clear lie—he stood, maybe, quarter of an inch taller than Sarah—that it had him mumbling, "I'm...I'm not that tall, really. But the point is, I guess, um, that you would do well to eat better. Even at your age, people still grow."

"I'll take my chances with the Pop Tarts," Sadie replied. "My parents were shorties, and you can't cure genetics, right?"

Sarah heaved out a big sigh and set her jaw as she would have when talking to her own daughter, but before she could say anything, Neil said, "Maybe you're right."

"Neil!" Sarah said, putting her hands on her hips.

"I'm just saying that maybe a break from broccoli would be good for all of us and since we share and share alike, I would like a Pop Tart tonight to go along with my apple. And I think you should vary your diet as well, Sarah." Her brows came down—she had made it clear to Neil that she thought Pop Tarts were gross—but then he tipped her a little wink.

"I guess I can have a couple," she said, not understanding Neil's play, but trusting that he knew what he was doing.

"But there'll be none left," Sadie said, leaping forward to grab the bag with the food in it and holding it back from Neil. "That's not fair. You two like broccoli and apples and corn. I don't. I would eat good stuff if you could find it; other stuff I mean. A cheeseburger. Something hot. I'm dying for hot food."

"We may like some things you don't but it doesn't mean we like them every single day," Neil replied, holding out his hand. "Come on, hand it over or maybe next time I'll just happen to 'over look' some Pop Tarts."

This was a real threat since it fell to Neil to do most of the exploring. Cramped places gave the fleet-footed Sadie the heebie-jeebies and Sarah wasn't strong enough for hand-to-hand combat with most of the zombies that would come storming out of their bizarre hiding places.

"If that were to happen then you'd either starve or learn to like other foods," Neil said.

"Then maybe I'll starve," Sadie replied, glaring.

"I could give you my Pop Tarts for breakfast," Sarah suggested. "If you'll eat an apple now. Or some corn? What do you think? The Pop Tarts won't last anyways as fast as you eat them. This way you can have what you like and we can sleep knowing that your bones won't turn brittle with malnutrition."

Neil was quick to agree, "I'll save mine for the next day and before you complain, yes this is extortion. It's what my parents did to me."

Sadie sulked. "I doubt it, Neil. You were probably the dream child. Did your homework, ate your veggies. My parents didn't even know I existed." She suddenly turned to Sarah and asked, "Can you cook? I mean like good food, like pizza? If we found the right ingredients could you make that from scratch?"

Sarah put on a brave smile and said, "I had never thought of myself as much of a cook, but I can try. We can do it together."

"And I'm a wiz at homemade bread," Neil put in. "I could make the crust for you. I'll do it as soon as we find some flour. Yeast will be easy. No one seems to have given it much thought. In fact we should be able to get some tomorrow."

The thought of what tomorrow held dampened their mood. They hoped to get through St Louis by running down the Illinois River until it joined with the Mississippi. This ran smack dab through one of the largest cities in the country and they all knew the stiffs would number in the tens of thousands, if not more.

Unfortunately tomorrow came very quickly. The candles and the extra blankets made the neat little tent a cozy nest and the night passed in a blur for Neil and Sarah, but not for Sadie. At the best of times she was a wild sleeper. She frequently talked or thrashed around, or seemed to think it nothing to throw a leg over either Sarah or Neil.

By unspoken agreement Neil no longer slept in the middle—it was always Sadie who acted as a buffer between the two adults.

That night she went through near continuous nightmares, though the two adults barely even stirred as they had gotten used to her unstable sleeping patterns. In the morning, as was usual for Neil, he got up before the rest and left the tent, making no more noise that a whisper. His routine was to kill any stray zombie left over from the night before, using his trusty axe if they weren't too big, or the bow from afar if they were particularly large or aggressive.

When Sadie first laid eyes on the bow she had practically squealed in delight—which turned into near instantaneous disappointment when she found out that she was too weak to draw back on the cable. Even Sarah couldn't budge it, and from that point on it became Neil's official weapon, despite that he wasn't very good with it...or so Sarah thought.

The morning they began their assault on St Louis, Neil demonstrated that he had progressed as an archer. The two women woke to a sizzle and the smell of cooking meat.

"What is that?" Sadie asked, her breath a grey plume in the morning chill air. "Is that meat? Is that a fire?"

Neil, looking more pale than usual, smiled up at them as proud as can be. "It's a rabbit. I shot a big one this morning."

"Aren't you worried about stiffs?" Sarah asked, looking out into the distance. "Or the army? We're only seventy or so miles from the Island. This is well within range of their patrols."

He shrugged and waived a hand. "I say *pish-posh* on the army. The fire isn't all that smoky and besides we should be gone in twenty minutes. I figured you two deserved a treat."

"I have been a good girl," Sadie said and then quickly amended the statement at Sarah's look. "I was a good girl yesterday. I didn't sic any monsters on nobody."

"*On anybody*," Sarah corrected, staring at the spread Neil had made for them. Along with the rabbit he had a can of corn frying in the oil they had found the day before. Glasses of clean water were set out next to plates and silverware. These sat around the fire at three spots where blankets and couch cushions had been hauled down from the house.

"Why don't you two go *have a talk* and I'll breakdown the tent. The food should be done by then." Work of any sort never fazed the man. He would do dishes, roll sleeping bags, haul water, carry all the baggage, without ever a word of complaint, and by the time the two women came back—one holding the axe and the other the M16—Neil had things ready to go at a moment's notice.

Sadie moaned and groaned her way through the meal and when she was done she rubbed her slightly swollen belly and belched loudly. Sarah and Neil glanced at each other, wondering which of them would correct her. They were both full for once and a little sleepy and only smiled at each other.

"What's up?" Sadie asked. "Aren't you going to say anything? I just burped like a pig and all you two are doing is smiling. Have you given up on raising me so soon? What happened to: *A girl needs structure*? And all that crap you two spun the other day?"

"Eh, you know what you did wrong," Neil said. "Now you're just looking for attention."

"I can't win with you two can I?" Sadie replied though she smiled as she did. She tried to belch again, but it was a tiny thing that only made her laugh. "I vote Neil cooks every morning."

Sarah shook her head at this. "My father always insisted that if he went out hunting, then mother would have to do the cooking. I think it's a good rule. Have you ever hunted before, Neil?"

This brought a snort from Sadie. "Yeah, right. He's from Jersey. Men there don't hunt. I mean really, anyone who says *pish-posh* probably cried when he had to kill poor thumper here."

Neil's eyes stole to Sarah before he admitted, "I didn't cry, but gutting it wasn't exactly fun. Now, Sadie, since you seem to be energized enough to run your mouth so much you can help me lug this stuff down to the boat."

Every day before sundown, when the zombies really seemed to go active, they did their level best to camouflage the boat on the off chance that someone would come by and notice what a treasure it was. The night before they had pulled it far up a muddy little tributary and now they freaked when they saw it was gone.

"It was right here," Neil said pointing. "See the weeds, how short they are? I pulled them up, remember?"

Sarah remembered. She could even see their footprints on the bank where they had gone up. "Do you think it was the army?" Her greatest fear was to be found by the colonel's men. It was even greater than her fear of the zombies, because the zombies would only kill her. The colonel would have her degrade herself first, would turn her into something less than a person and when he had used her, he would then set her out to die.

Sadie, who had loped off downstream, came back breathing easily. "It floated away. I can see it further on. We should get an anchor don't you think? Come on! Last one there has to sit by Neil." She took off in sprint that was slowed by her giggling. Despite that the adults were separated at night, Sadie made sure they kept close all day long.

Thankfully the propellers of the boat had got caught up in the submerged roots of a naked willow or they would've lost the boat for sure. After a bit of tugging they got the boat loose and set out for St Louis thinking it would be bad, but not understanding the true nature of what awaited them.

Like a few other unfortunate places in the world, St Louis sat in a convergence zone where waves of the undead migrated from all parts of the country, only to rebound once they got there. Generally they headed back the way they came, however some were more determined to get to where they were going and tried hard to cross the Mississippi from one direction or another. Very few made it—the rest turned the mighty river into a death trap.

Unaware of all this, Neil piloted the boat, moving at a good clip until the Illinois met the Mississippi and then he only slowed out of fear of attracting unwanted attention from the many stiffs walking the banks of the river on both sides.

These numbers grew as they approached the first of the suburbs north of the city and the three hunkered down low in the boat, hoping not to draw attention to themselves and to remain unobserved. This hope grew dim as they drew closer and closer to the center of the city.

They passed under bridges where it would rain zombies and then when Neil kicked the boat faster, the beasts on the banks noticed them and waded out into the wide river to get at them. Still the three were only unnerved and not yet afraid, because the zombies were dreadful swimmers. It wasn't until they began to knock into floating corpses ahead that they really knew fear.

The river was clogged with them.

"We have to fend them off or they'll get caught up in the

props," Neil said in a whisper. "Sarah, you steer." He and Sadie went to the narrow front and started the grizzly job of pushing the bodies away. Nothing could be more disgusting than touching the bloated corpses, even with a paddle…except, perhaps touching a bloated zombie corpse.

Sadie yelped and jumped back, nearly falling into the water. "It took my paddle! They're alive." The things in the water were slow and ponderous, but still very much alive in their vile ways and in moments they were clawing at the hull of the boat. "We're going to sink!" the girl cried in a panic. "We have to turn back."

Sarah was thinking the same thing, only she noticed that behind them the river was congealed with bodies, some coming up from the black depths, covered in sticks and mud. "I don't think we can."

"Turn the boat! Turn the boat!" cried Sadie, retreating to the center of the tiny vessel and drawing her hands in from the sides as if that would save her.

"Don't do it…" began Neil, but Sarah was already throttling up the engine and turning the boat sideways to the current. It was a mistake. The boat yawed to port and the zombies on that side gained more of a purchase and now the tipping became pronounced—allowing even more grey hands to grab hold of the edge of the little fishing boat.

Sadie screamed and Sarah froze not knowing what to do as Mississippi water poured into the boat. They were going to capsize.

Neil jumped to his feet and leapt to the high side of the boat where his weight was just enough to keep it from flipping. In his hand was the M16 with its pathetic five bullets—he used four of them to clear the stiffs fighting their way on board. With their weight removed the boat plunged back down.

As most small men are, he was nimble and danced among the baggage without falling in. "Downstream! Point us that way," he ordered. "Sadie, use the hatchet."

In the front, Neil used the axe, hacking at the hands that gripped the grey metal, while the girl in the middle wacked here and there, taking off fingers which began to litter the inside of the boat. Sarah turned the boat sharply feeling bodies bump along beneath, making her want to puke.

"Is it clear in front?" she asked, desperate to gun the engine and run free of the horrible city.

"There's a channel," Neil said pointing to the left. "There's less of em'."

She could see what he was talking about, a long narrow channel where the water was clear of the bodies and strangely lighter in color as well. She opened up the throttle as far as it would go and the boat sped forward.

Too late, Neil cried, "Turn!"

Sarah saw it as well; there was a capsized boat just beneath the surface. It was a barge of some sort and the little fishing boat ran up on it with a jolt, and a scream of metal. She felt and heard a hard clang beneath her hand. Their momentum added to that of the barge so that the pair of boats began to swing sideways. Once again the zombies came at them, clawing their way onto the barge where it was more stable.

"Get us off!" Neil ordered in a high voice.

Sarah tried. She stoked the gas and, though it made more noise and kicked out plumes of grey-blue smoke, it didn't do anything more. "There's something wrong with the engine. I don't know what."

"Dang it!" Neil cried in desperation as he jumped out of the boat and onto the barge where the zombies were scrambling to get at them. Almost immediately the boat tipped upwards in front. "Sadie, get to the back with Sarah. Please," he begged.

The beasts, though slipping and falling with every other step were getting closer, moaning louder in anticipation. When Sadie moved, the boat tipped even more and Neil, using all of his strength was just able to push it off the barge and leap back aboard at the same time.

"Are we alright?" Neil asked, shaking like a leaf and grabbing his axe again with white knuckles.

"We're not alright," Sarah said in a whisper, staring down into water. "The propeller is gone."

The engine was now useless, except to draw the creatures to them and so she cut it and they drifted among the bodies. The sudden silence seemed to confuse the zombies.

"What are we going to..." Sadie began, but both Neil and Sarah shushed her. Neil put his finger to his lips and then motioned them to get low in the boat, just as another grey hand reached over the metal edge. He found a knife and pried the hand away, trying to be as quiet as possible about it. They drifted down river in a fearful silence that was broken only by the zombie groans as the bumped into the boat or tried to climb aboard and each time Neil pried away the fingers or sawed at them with the sharp blade.

They laid in the boat, and as long as they didn't move or say a word, the zombies forgot they were there. The boat drifted among the corpses and the water moaned in a dreadful way and each wore an expression of fear. After a few hours of this the rain came, drenching them until Neil covered the women with layers of blankets. The two women cuddled together for warmth while he sat in the rain, cold and shivering.

Their hope was that the river would open up and the zombies would grow fewer on the banks and in the water, so that they would be able to get ashore somewhere.

Instead things only grew worse. The number of zombies grew so that their pace slowed and although they went past St Louis they were still stuck in the middle of the wide river. Eventually, they came to a bridge that had collapsed. The river beneath was clogged with sunken barges and overturned day yachts and frothed with the bodies of thousands of zombies.

The little fishing boat bounced off something beneath them and spun sideways, coming up against a long, white, bay liner, whose captain was grey and putrefying and hungry.

The creature launched itself at Neil and he shot it in the head with his last bullet. Throwing down the gun, he grabbed his axe and hacked away as more zombies appeared on the pile of stranded boats. Now there was no more hiding. Sadie sprang up with her hatchet and fought like a demon.

Sarah grabbed the M16. Turning it around she clubbed first one zombie, then another and was able to spare a moment to look around and get a fix on their situation. To her horror she saw that no matter how bravely they fought, they were buying themselves seconds only. Not only were they surrounded by dozens of zombies, the zombies themselves were surrounded by hundreds more.

Chapter 39

Ram

Amarillo and East

"So much for all your promises," Cassie said, barging into the dentist's personal office the next morning. "Gotta take a dump. I'd leave if I was you since there ain't no runnin' water." The dentist's bathroom was right there and she breezed into it as if she hadn't been the least bit offensive.

Julia sighed and placed a hand across her face. "Damn."

"*I'm happy to see that you lived, Ram. Me too Julia,*" Ram remarked in falsetto. He tried to get up, only his right knee was swollen and wouldn't bear his weight. "I think I messed my knee up pretty bad. How's your leg?"

"Fine, I'm sure. And, yes, I'm glad we both lived. It's just…" She nodded to the bathroom door. "We did make a promise."

"I was under duress when I made the promise," Ram replied. "It wouldn't stand up in court. Now let's see that wound."

She peeled back the dressing and took a close look, saying, "It was only a flesh wound, nothing serious. Though I should change the bandage every day and it would be smart to take an antibiotic as a precautionary measure."

Despite her words about it just being a flesh wound, she hobbled about as she, collected her supplies in a cardboard box. Ram worked his knee back and forth. When it felt warmed up enough he tried his weight again and swore like a sailor as he stood.

"Are you going to help with the supplies?" he asked Cassie as she left the bathroom.

"I am. Look, toilet paper. This stuff is gold, baby. Let me have the keys." She held out a hand and he shook his head. "Come on. What am I going to do? Drive off with all the toilet paper? Fine. Julia, let me have that box. Ram thinks I should be helping the woman who went behind my back."

"It was my fault," Ram said, quickly.

"I don't want to hear it," Cassie said holding up the flat of her hand to his face. "You two wanna team up and leave me out in the cold. Fine. Just so ya know, I can break promises too."

"Yeah?" Ram asked. "What promises have you ever made?"

"Here's some: I promise to always be here for you. I promise to have your back. I promise I won't run off with the first pretty face that comes along. I could go on, but what does it matter? You two knew how I felt but you didn't care."

"I'm sorry," Julia said. "I was...uh, I was weak and scared. I shouldn't have let him."

Ram shook his head at this. "A minute ago I wasn't sorry in the least, but now I am. Julia, stop trying to act like you aren't a part of this, because you are. We both know you could have stopped me last night at any point, and we both know that you didn't want me to stop. You wanted me right where I was. So, why the act? Are you having morning regret?"

"I just don't want to hurt anyone," she said, quietly.

"You're hurting me," Ram replied, his face stony.

Cassie rolled her eyes. "Whatever. Give me the fuckin' keys while she strings you along."

"Put the stuff by the car," Ram said without looking her way. "And don't forget to take a gun with you. We don't know what's out there." When she left, he and Julia stared at each other until she dropped her eyes. "Really, are you regretting sleeping with me?" he asked.

"Sort of," she answered, looking at the floor. "I dream of my husband every night, now. I made so many mistakes with him and now that he's dead I realize I should've done more...done something different to make him stay. And then

I wake up and I see you." Julia started to twist her hands together. "And I'm so afraid of driving you away just like I did him and I don't know what I'm supposed to do, or how I'm supposed to feel. I guess I do regret it, but at the same time, I don't. And then there's Cassie. She's looking for a reason to trust us and we keep disappointing her."

"I can't worry about Cassie," Ram said. "And if I had known about how you were feeling about your husband, I would have let you be. That's a far better reason to take things slow. That being said, I want you to know I will take it slow, but I'm not giving up. You see as well as I do that we have a connection between us, something that time and distance and zombies couldn't stop."

"I see it," she replied, moving closer and touching his chest with the flat of her hand. "I see there is a future for us. We just have to deal with the now, with Cassie, and with my past, my husband. Inside of me is this great guilt and fear." Her eyes misted with tears. "But I also feel you. I think we should get around more people. Let's go the CDC and find other survivors and see if what happens."

They had seen exactly three people on their trip, and none had been the least bit accommodating. Two had scurried away into hiding, while the third had aimed a rifle at the passing Bronco. There were far more unseen people. They had come across a number of smoldering fire pits and even more numerous were messages left to loved ones spray-painted on houses or barns. These were usually accompanied by a date, and some of these had been only days old when Ram read them.

Julia's plan to take their personal relationship slow seemed a good one but somehow it crossed over into their travels as well. They departed the vastness of the American west and their pace was slower than they had expected. A journey to the CDC would have taken only a day of hard driving before the zombies, now as they avoided cities and hunted for gas and water, the trip was much longer. That first day out of Amarillo they made it just beyond Tulsa, after following an extremely circuitous path.

They had thought to avoid Oklahoma City by cutting south, but ended up running smack into a legion of zombies which dotted the plain like herds of buffalo. The trio hightailed it back and went around the city northward and then was forced north again to bypass Tulsa.

The next day they crossed over into Missouri and from then on water wasn't a problem and gas was more plentiful, however the zombies were thick as flies. They came to the armed town of Mountain Grove, where a most inhospitable group of suspicious people had them again detouring north. So they were a tired and cranky threesome when they came upon the last barrier to the east, the Mississippi River, in the late afternoon.

"How the fuck are we going to cross that?" Cassie asked. The black water was a thousand feet wide at its narrowest. Cassie had tried to be surly after Amarillo, only it seemed to take a lot of effort on her part and she gave it up on her own after a few hours—something Julia had foreseen. Not that she was any more pleasant to be around, but she wasn't worse.

"I'm sure there are bridges," Julia answered.

A person would think so, however Ram went south on the western bank for miles and though he saw plenty of signs for ferry crossings, it was an hour of slow driving before Ram saw a sign for a bridge. They all cheered but were quickly disappointed when they rounded a bend and saw that the bridge had been demolished. A part of the span had fallen into the river and there was a great clogging of boats and debris beneath what was left—not to mention zombies.

Even a quarter mile away he could see them swarming. He made to turn around, but the road was narrow with abandoned cars and so he went closer, hoping to find a good spot.

"There are people down there," Julia said. She pointed

beneath the bridge where the debris had melded into a shifting island of sorts.

"They is good as dead," Cassie put in, her face looking a little disgusted. "I don't want to watch that."

A single shot split the air causing Ram to hope the people would be able to fight their way to freedom, however that one shot was all that came and now he could see the three people fighting with strange weapons.

"What are you doing?" Julia asked. At first he didn't know what she meant, but then he realized he had floored the Bronco and was speeding to the near end of the bridge.

He hadn't given it any thought, but the answer didn't seem to require any. "We're going to help. I'll work the SAW. Julia, you keep the stiffs off of me and Cassie, you keep me supplied with ammo."

"Why do I have to..." Cassie started, but he spoke over her.

"Because Julia's a better shot and because she's hurt and can't run back and forth. Now get me the gun," he said this slamming on the brakes and literally hopping out of the car. His knee still bothered him and a one-legged hop was his quickest mode of ambulation. "Hurry!" he ordered. The three were still alive only because the makeshift island was not easy for the zombies to cross however, more were coming up out of the water right at their feet.

Cassie came huffing up with the SAW in one hand and the first ammo can in the other. "Thanks. I'll need two more." In the time it took him to say that he had laid bare the feed tray, slapped down the links, thinking to himself: *Brass to the grass* as he he'd been trained and then smacked down the cover.

In a second, tracer rounds, like zipping glow bugs showed him exactly where to fire.

Chapter 40

Neil

Mississippi River

When the machine gun opened up with a sound like a thundering jackhammer, Neil didn't even notice. His senses were already on overload as he fought like he would never have believed himself capable of.

This was partly because he had managed to get his feet wedged in between his boat and that of another. This sturdy platform gave him a great advantage over the zombies who moved in a drunken lurch under the best of situations. Still, his arms were tired after just a minute of swinging the axe. He knew that in another minute his breath would be ragged and reactions slow, while the zombies would never tire.

Suddenly, Neil saw that right next to him, part of the Bayliner seemed to be coming apart in little fist-sized explosions, and as he watched, dumbfounded, he saw the same thing happened to the zombies on that side. What was going on? He swung the axe again, feeling his attacks already growing less crisp than they had been, yet he still managed to knock a stiff into the water.

Just then something yellow blazed past his face and he heard a cracking noise very close. It was then he noticed the gunner on the hill above the destroyed bridge firing down at them—he felt an instant panic as he saw the tracers zipping by almost within arm's reach.

"Is he shooting at us?" Sadie asked, cringing low. The answer came a second later as the tracers ripped the air in front of them, laying out the zombies, sending chunks of rotting flash flying and turning the confused island slick with their black blood.

"He's clearing a path," Sarah said, however when Neil and Sadie scrambled up onto the boat island, she didn't budge. "I won't go with the army. I'll take my chances here."

Neil clubbed down a stiff that had an arm shot away, before he cried, "You can't stay here. I won't let you."

He began to slide back down to her when Sadie said, "He's not army. He's just a guy and he's got two women with him. Can you see them? See they're on either side of him. It'll be alright, Sarah. Please come on." She was nervous because the firing had ceased and the zombies were coming up at her, alone as she was at the top of the pile.

"I'll protect you," Neil said to Sarah, holding his hand out to her. It hurt to see that she didn't believe he could. He read it clearly in her eyes and so he added. "I'll try my best."

This brought a twitch to her face that he took for a smile and she grabbed his hand just as the machine gun began chattering again. As bullets tore the air all around her, Sadie squeaked and froze with her arms pulled to her chest.

"That guy's good," Neil said in awe as he pulled Sarah along. When they gained the top he had to stop and hack away at the zombies coming up the leeside of the mound where the machine gun's bullets couldn't reach. "Go on. Go on," he ordered, backing up slowly, waiting until his footing was secure before taking his swings.

From an outside perspective he seemed cool and deliberate. Up close he was breathing so heavily he couldn't tell if he was close to exhaustion or near to panicking. A little of both he decided.

Someone up the hill suddenly yelled, "Get down!"

Bullets began to pass so close they warmed his face, but Neil ignored them, because just then the island took that moment to shift beneath his feet as something in its "foundation" broke free and spun down the river. A gap, that was more like a chasm in his mind, opened up between him and safety, and instead of getting down, he actually leapt. When he thudded into the other side, he lost his grip on the axe and it slid down the flat face of a barge to slip forever out of his reach into the black water below. Even worse he couldn't find a toehold for his feet. Everything was slick with blood and water.

As he teetered on the brink of following that axe into the black water, the undulating island came together again for just the briefest moment and he was able to heave himself up. Now there was a straight shot to get to the western bank of the river, which he took as quickly as he could, wobbling with his hands out for balance. The gunner saw Neil moving and so decided to turn his attention to closer problems; the near bank swarmed with the dead, closing in on him and the people he had just saved.

Neil saw that the gunner wasn't the only one armed. A woman, pale and slim with short, red hair, shot an M16, working it like she was on assembly line. Bam—Bam! Turn and aim, Bam—Bam! Turn and aim. Her targeting wasn't near as good as the gunner's, but still the zombies were generally easy to hit and she kept a lane open as Neil came running up.

"Get in!" the girl...the woman, said. Up close her actual age, somewhere in her late twenties, became more apparent. "You can drive, right?" she asked Neil indicating the Ford Bronco.

What kind of question was that? "Yes. Of course," he replied, hurrying to the driver's seat. Sarah climbed in and Sadie squeezed into the far back where a mess of baggage was piled; she looked as uncomfortable as a caged cat. Neil darted the Bronco forward between a dented Ford and an already crushed bicycle, turning it at an angle so that the gunner and the other girl who was with him could get in easily. Beside him, the redhead slammed the passenger door and yelled across Neil for them to hurry.

The man, limping badly came last, shoving the machine gun in the back where Sadie crouched. "Mother, that's hot!" she said, sucking her fingers after trying to push it aside.

"Sorry, I should've warned you not to touch that for a while. My name is Ram. This is Cassie and Julia."

Since Neil, with his queasiness unmistakably written on his paleface, was busy clipping zombies, or bouncing over them as he turned the Bronco around, Sarah introduced their group in small voice and added, "That was some fancy shooting, Ram." Her voice cracked when she added, "Are you with the military?"

"No, I was DEA, but I learned to run a SAW back in California fighting the stiffs. There were plenty of practice dummies to work on, if you know what I mean and everyone rotated carrying the SAW."

Neil straightened the car, gave a glance back at Sarah, thinking he would give her a reassuring look, only to feel his own spirits slip at the way she looked at the handsome man across from her. "Thanks," he said instead. "I just wanted to say thanks for saving us. I know you didn't have to."

The woman sitting next to him smiled at this and said, "Actually he did have to. It's in his nature. Tie a woman to a train track and he'll be the first to come swooping in to save the day."

To this Neil gave a watery smile and turned back to the road. He was thinking: *First this lady doubts I can drive and now she's suggesting I'm only fit to be on the girl's team and need to be rescued.* It made him feel a touch smaller than usual.

"You can save me anytime you want," Sadie put in. "That was too fuckin' close. They…"

"Sadie!" Sarah and Neil warned in unison. "A lady doesn't curse," Sarah added.

Julia laughed at this and asked, "Are you a family? I see the resemblance between you two in the full lips and the high cheekbones. You're both very pretty."

The two women glanced at each other and Neil saw that Sadie's color had risen at the compliment. "They are very pretty," Neil agreed. "But we aren't a family except that I'm Sadie's Apocalypse Dad." He was hoping Sarah would add her motherly role but the woman remained silent. "It's sort of an honorary title."

"No it's a real title," Sadie said. "I'm a problem child, you know. One in need of direction and constant supervision, because it wouldn't be good if I was to have an independent thought. Right?" She said, with a smirk and she nudged Cassie in front of her.

"Whatever you fucking say," Cassie said, looking out the window.

Sadie cleared her throat at this and caught Neil's eye. "How come she can curse and I have to be all prim and proper?"

Neil couldn't answer this without sounding completely mushy and even less like a man than normal. What would big, tough Ram say if he heard that Neil looked on Sadie as if she was his own child to raise and nurture and protect? And what would he do besides snort in amusement if he knew how Neil felt about Sarah—a woman so far out of his league that even with an apocalypse occurring she wouldn't give him the time of day. In fact she gave truth to the old adage: *Not even if you were the last man on earth.*

"Cuz I ain't no fuckin' lady," Cassie remarked, saying what everyone was thinking. Though what she said next certainly wasn't. "There's enough white people in the world without me sticking my pinkie up in the air and trying to act all white."

This made for an uncomfortable few minutes for everyone but Sadie. The youngest of the group seemed to thrive in uncomfortable settings. "I don't think there are enough white people," Sadie replied serenely. "I don't think there are enough people in general, but clearly there is one too many racists left."

"What'd you just call me?" Cassie barked, turning to glare at Sadie. "You just called me a racist? Is that what you just done?"

Sadie met the glare with an innocent and slightly puzzled look. "I think so. I did. Yes, now I'm sure of it."

Neil glanced in the rearview mirror, worried that Sadie's behavior would jeopardize their already very precarious situation—they had no shelter, no car, no weapons, no food and no water. They were completely dependent on these people.

"Sadie, please, we are their guests," he said with a nod and a disarming smile to Julia, next to him. In the back Sadie started to open her mouth to protest her unfair treatment—and he saw that it was unfair. Simply because she was the youngest she was being told what to do, something that would be considered rude if she was a year or two older like Cassie.

"So where am I going?" he asked, trying to change the subject and lighten the mood.

"*We're* going to Atlanta," Cassie said, making it clear that she didn't want the new people tagging along. "Who knows where you be going."

Right behind him Ram sighed in evident frustration. "The Center for Disease Control is based in Atlanta," he said. "We're hoping that they have a cure, or are very close to finding one. You're welcome to join us if you want to."

"Damn the king has spoken," Cassie said, looking past a very uncomfortable Sarah, and out the window. "What happened to voting? Tell me that. Where was my input?"

"You're welcome to speak your mind," Julia said. "We always want your input."

"Right, sure you do," Cassie seethed. "You already made up your minds. You just sees more white people to Klan up with. What I sees is more mouths to feed. More people for me to step and fetch for. What do they have? Huh? What do they bring to the group? Any of you a doctor? Or a soldier? Do you gots any guns?"

"Just the one," Neil said with a sinking feeling. Cassie was right, the three of them didn't bring anything to the table. "It's empty. We only had five bullets and we used them up."

"And we're not doctors," Sarah said. "I was a pharmacy

rep and Sadie was in high school and Neil only worked on Wall Street. And none of us can fight, at least not like you, Ram."

"Hold on, Sarah!" Sadie stormed. "What do you mean none of us can fight? Did you not see Neil with his axe? He was fucking heroic just now saving your life, and no, I'm not going to watch my tongue, not if bad words is all you can notice. Jeeze! Open your eyes. Neil's been fighting zombies without a gun for days now. Let's see anyone else do that."

"It was just a few of them," Neil said, not wanting to give anyone the impression that he was some sort of badass, which was laughable on its face. "And it was only four days."

"You see?" Cassie went on. "All they gots is their sorry ass selves."

"It impressive enough for me," Ram said. "Five minutes without a gun, I'd be pissing myself. Lucky for you we can help. We have plenty of ammunition for your M16, and extra guns, though they are just handguns. Still they're better than nothing."

Cassie began to splutter at the idea of Ram giving up their weapons, but then Julia spoke in a low voice that had them all leaning in to her: "Cassie, you need to stop. You're demonstrating the classic self-fulfilling prophecy to a T. You're so worried that we will form as a group and kick you out that you are pushing us away. It's a classical form of behavior, making true what would normally be false."

"She's a psychologist," Ram explained to the now-quiet car—which only had the quiet deepening.

"Don't worry, Cass," Sadie said patting the black girl on the shoulder. "I'm crazy too. I don't know the psycho-nut job word, but I'm the world's worst follower. I ran track because I had friend who did it. I got into Goth because a friend got into Goth, and at the same time I had a friend who was into *Hello Kitty*, so beneath my black clothes I always wore Hello Kitty underwear. That's messed up, right?"

"I'm the world's worst mother," Sarah said, in a low voice. Sadie's confession was clearly designed to make Cassie comfortable with Julia's off the cuff diagnosis, while Sarah's had the car going quiet again.

"I'm almost OCD," Neil said, quickly. "Or I was. I would go around in the summer at night and check the garden hoses to see if I left them running. I even did it when it was raining. I used to always double check my locks, which didn't do me a lick of good since I'd open my door to a criminal if she looked lost."

This last had been directed at Sadie, who added, "Oh yeah, I was burglar because this guy was doing it and it seemed cool. I robbed Neil."

"I've got some sort of hero complex," Ram said. He had been smiling as he said this, but it disappeared. "And I deserted my friends and left them to die," he whispered.

Julia took a deep breath and patted Cassie on her knee. "You see? We all have problems and we all have fears and we all make mistakes. It's what makes us human. But what makes us good humans is that we don't turn people away who need our help, not when we have so much and they have nothing. I'm with Ram. I vote that they can come."

"I'd like to go to the CDC," Neil said. "We were just going to hide out somewhere and wait on a cure, but I'll only go if Sarah and Sadie want to go as well." Sarah nodded and gave Neil a small smile.

"I only want to go if we get our own car," Sadie said, trying to stretch out on top of all of the gear. "And if I can curse."

Neil shook his head. "Then we're leaving you. If I hear anything more than poop, fart or wiener coming out of your mouth, you'll be in big trouble."

Chapter 41

Ram

Kentucky

In the few hours left before sunset, they accomplished very little in Ram's view.

They had arrived at the town of Cape Girardeau, where they found an intact bridge. Mysteriously, it looked as though it had been purposefully blocked with cars stacked three high across the roadway.

"They were probably trying to block the path of the zombies, but from which direction I couldn't tell you. It could be like this all the way to New Orleans," Neil said, inspecting the cars. "Maybe if we had some long rope or a chain we could pull a couple of cars apart so we could drive across?" Ram glanced back the way they had come. There was a town back there where he was sure they could find a towrope but he suspected it was full of zombies.

"I bet there's a good dozen hardware stores back in town that would carry what we need," Ram said, not liking the idea; not after what had happened in Amarillo.

Julia was in tune with his thoughts. "And there are how many thousands of zombies there as well? I don't think it's a good idea to go rooting around in any town that size. Even if you found a rope I don't know if the Bronco can pull three cars like that."

"I say we get a new car," Sadie put in as she stretched her slim legs. Ram raised his eyebrows at the suggestion. She pointed across the bridge. "There are a bunch of houses over there. I bet we can find a car that'll do for us. Or maybe even two."

"What about gas?" Ram asked. "I bet they're all sucked dry. And even if they aren't there's still the battery to worry about."

The girl shrugged a single shoulder. "We have gas in this car and a battery. We can pop out the battery and bring a gallon of gas with us. There's a car right there," she said pointing at a minivan at the other end of the bridge. "We could have that one running in five minutes."

This seemed like a good plan. Armed with loaded M16s, but lacking the knowledge of hotwiring a car, Sadie, Neil, and Cassie climbed over the blockade of cars and made their way to the minivan, while Sarah and Julia transferred the gear from the back of the Bronco to the other side of the obstruction.

Ram, still limping, climbed to the top of the barricade with his SAW and sat watching all around, keeping an eye on a few stiffs who had been drawn to the movement on the bridge.

"How are they doing?" Sarah asked after a few minutes, nervous for her friends.

Ram squinted at the minivan and noticed for the first time that no one was around it at all. He struggled to sit higher. "I don't see any sign of them."

"They're gone? What do we do?" Julia climbed up to stand on the lowest car. "Should we keep unloading?"

"Yes. No matter what happens the Bronco is probably done. Maybe they saw a better vehicle, a bigger one...oh shit!" The distinctive thin crackling of M16s could be heard from the direction they had been staring. "Get your guns and check your ammo. And I'll need another box up here."

Down at the far end of the bridge he saw figures running—it was the two girls. There was no sign of Neil. "Who is that?" Sarah asked, but she knew and there was a whine of fright to her words. "Where's Neil? Where is he?"

He wasn't there, nor was he struggling to catch up. Instead, behind the girls, came a mob of lurching, swaying beasts.

At two-hundred yards, Ram opened up with the SAW, walking the tracers from the far left so that he wouldn't hit the girls who seemed to be flagging after the long sprint, yet still running. "Watch our six, Sarah," he ordered. "Julia, don't spray your bullets…"

"Behind us!" Sarah screamed the second she turned. Attracted by the sounds of the guns, stiffs were streaming down to the bridge from the west and the blonde started ripping 5.56 rounds into them, aiming center mass where she was most effective. This slowed the beasts down, but didn't stop them. Bullets thumped and body parts flew yet the dead only picked themselves up and kept coming.

Sarah cried for help and Julia spun and began firing as well. Even working together things might have gone horribly wrong, but just then at the far end of the bridge a huge black SUV burst onto the roadway plowing over anything that got in its way.

When she saw it, Sadie whooped in delight and stuck out a thumb as if hitch-hiking, because high up in the cab Neil could be seen grinning like a madman. He slammed on the brakes just long enough for the two girls to climb on the running boards. Moments later the truck was rumbling a few feet away from the barricade.

"We only have thirty seconds!" Neil cried out leaping down to help gather their gear.

Ram turned his SAW around and tore into the horde coming up on their rear, laying the first three rows flat before he climbed laboriously down. This bought them a few more seconds and everyone grabbed bags and gas and ammo and threw it all in the rear cargo area. Then they were all safely aboard, laughing at their escape as the huge vehicle headed east, plowing through and over the undead.

"I thought you were a goner," Cassie said to Neil.

"You can't count out my Neil," Sadie cried, joyfully, grabbing him by the shoulders from behind and shaking him. "We were in this house looking for keys to the minivan when the stiffs ambushed. We shot ourselves dry and then Neil runs up some stairs and says: Yoo-hoo! Over here!" Sadie couldn't go on—she was too tired from running, and now she was snorting and giggling.

Cassie took over the story: "He really did say that. It was so fucked up. So they chased him upstairs and there were too many for us to do anything but run." She looked over at Neil and he shrugged.

"I just jumped out a window and then ran across the street to a house where *this* was parked in the driveway," Neil said, trying to appear nonchalant. "The keys were on a key ring by the front door. It started on the first try and everything."

Sarah, who was in the back, said, "I'm just glad you're alright. I was...I was really, uh nervous for you."

This seemed to please Neil to no end and Ram had to pretend not to notice the blush that crept up the man's neck. Instead he looked out the window as they came upon a sign that read: *Shawnee National Forest*. Ram had not been in a forest such as this in ages and the closeness of the trees turned his good mood sour and gave him a bit of a bad thrill down his neck.

The place was dense with underbrush and was likely a haven to untold numbers of zombies and if they attacked there would be no forewarning like on the bridge or the open prairies of the west. The stiffs could march right up, almost invisible until they were right on top of them.

Thankfully, they drove along the forest road without incident, although, as they progressed southeast, the roads narrowed and trees pressed ever closer. Ram began to feel in his bones a sense of dread. Much to his relief, Neil made for open farmlands and found a good house to stay in for the night, though he confused them all by heading to the barn first. "What are you doing?" Julia asked giving the distant house a significant look.

"Houses are no good. I need to stretch again," Sadie said, sliding out of the Suburban. "I can't stand being cooped up like this for so long. Too bad you can't join me, Ram.

Maybe when your leg is better."

She then took off in a light skip toward the barn and in a few seconds she was loping faster over the fields, raising her fingers in a peace sign. Neil looked down at the ground and picked up a good-sized rock.

"She's found a couple," he said and then turned quickly as she squealed.

"Look at her showing off," Sarah said, coming to stand by Neil and watching the girl dashing away at her unnatural speed. "I think she must be showing off for you Mr. Ram."

Julia shook her head. "No, it's Neil she wants to impress."

"No, I don't think so," Neil replied with a nervous laugh. "We don't have that sort of relationship."

"You do, but you just don't realize it," Julia said with a smile. "Haven't you ever heard a child at a playground cry out: *Look at me, Daddy*! That's exactly the behavior she is demonstrating. She is looking for approval from a father figure."

"Well, that's sweet," Neil said, with a quick glance to Sarah. She stood watching Sadie, happily.

"It's stupid is what it is," Cassie remarked, distinctly unimpressed. "She's gonna get herself kilt, when we got all these guns."

"I don't think so," Neil said. "Watch."

It looked like Sadie was drawing them away, but then she came back straight toward the little group standing near the Suburban. "Where's your axe, Neil?" she called to him from forty yards.

"I got this," he said holding up the rock. "You see she's separated them by speed. Now I'll just have to kill them one at a time." Sadie slowed, letting the first zombie catch up and then, just as she came close to Neil she darted off to her right. The zombie couldn't decide which way to turn: after the girl or on toward the man, and when it paused to make the decision, Neil brained it with the rock.

The next zombie was even easier to kill since it was the slow variety.

"Nice silent kill," Ram said, impressed.

"A gun would bring them down on us by the hundreds," Sadie remarked stretching her lean muscles. Ram noticed that she was barely out of breath.

"Still, I sure do feel better having so many guns around," Sarah said. "Come on. Let's see if they have anything good to eat in the house."

They explored the house and found a few odds and ends to add to their store of food, including three bottles of wine. The group drank two of the bottles as they sat nibbling at their dinner. It loosened their tongues and they shared stories of the apocalypse. Although the face of Shelton ghosted into his mind, Ram pushed it aside and told how he had tracked the original terrorists. He showed them the vial of blood, which they stared at in awe. It was more to them than just glass and blood. It was possibly their salvation.

Sarah told about how she had decided not to fly out to New York that very first day when everyone heard about the Q-zones. She told them it was the worst mistake of her life and she ended up crying on Neil; something he didn't mind at all.

Sadie and Julia talked about different family members who had turned into zombies in their own houses even as they watched. And Neil talked about the rats that ate the jerk from New Jersey.

"What about you, Cassie?" Neil asked when it came around to her turn.

"Naw."

"Come on," Sadie said, shaking the black girl's foot. "It's like taking a load off your back, or like vomiting. Everyone feels better after vomiting."

"You want vomit?" Cassie asked. "How's this? I got raped by six guys and Mister Hero over there didn't do a thing to stop it. Ram just watched like it was on TV."

"You could've walked away at any time," Ram said, stiffly.

"Hold on. This shouldn't be about blame," Julia said. "We've all been through a lot. Maybe we did things we probably shouldn't have and that we regret. Ram has apologized, and though it was still a traumatic event for you Cassie, you need to stop blaming him for it happening."

"I did some bad stuff, too. I was a thief," Sadie reminded them. "I know what I did caused people to die before they were ready. I wish I hadn't done it."

"And I was a coward," Neil said in a small voice. "There was a stranger, a girl, with me on the subway platform when the man was killed. We ran and she didn't make it. I was too afraid to even try to help her."

"And I was nearly a whore," Sarah spoke as if in a dream. Her eyes were still wet and they were far away, seeing something none of the rest could. "I was going to whore myself out to the army for food and protection."

This silenced the conversation until Cassie said, "Damn, you a cheap ho. At least they had to take it from me."

Sadie was on her feet in a flash and in her hand was a long, sharp hunting knife that seemed to have come out of nowhere. "You take that back or I'll gut you," she seethed, her dark eyes running hot.

"Try it, dumbass cracker, bitch," Cassie said easily, not at all worried. In her hand was the knife's trump card, one of the Berettas looking like night itself.

Neil got up quickly, holding his hands out to the two girls. "Put the weapons down. Sadie, give me that," he said, taking the knife from her. "And you, drop it."

"Naw, I don't think so," Cassie replied. "She pull a knife on me what do you expect?"

"I expect you to be civil," Neil shot back. "What you said is almost inexcusable."

"But she's right," Sarah said, hollow-voiced and still distant. "I was cheap. Sure, I had my parents to worry about, but I worried about myself, too. I was worse than cheap...if you knew, Neil, you wouldn't look at me the way you do." Tears streaming, she shot a glance at him in fear over what his reaction would be to her confession.

"Hey no, that's not true," he said, kneeling by her chair and looking her in the face. "Nothing even happened. You can't fret over something that didn't happen. And there's no way I'll think less of you because you *thought* about *maybe* doing something wrong. You'll have to go further than that to keep me from lo..." Now he choked on his words. "From, um...to keep me from thinking anything but good of you," he finished in a hurry, his face flushed and red.

"I suppose," she said and gave him a tiny smile. She then glanced up at Sadie. "And you. I'm so thankful that I have you and Neil on my side, but I can't have you getting hurt over something like this, Sadie. They're just words. Just mean words that...that are unfortunately true."

Sadie answered her smile with one of her own and then she turned it into an acid glare for Cassie and she was joined by Neil who said in the clipped tones of an angry patriarch, "You had better watch how you talk to the people I care about."

The episode set a damper on the evening and they soon made ready for bed. The night was chill and the group slept split apart. Neil made a makeshift tent from sheets and used all the blankets he could find for warmth and padding for his group and they snuggled up close to one another—and Ram was envious.

Ram's group of three, slept in separate sleeping bags and there was space between each. He had wiggled in close to Julia, however she was concerned with Cassie. The girl seemed to be pulling away and Julia didn't want to alienate her any more for fear that she would lash out.

However, Cassie acted cool the following morning as though the night before had been of little importance. She didn't fool Ram. Her eyes were quick to glare and her lips were always a half-second from sneering. To him it was astonishing who seemed to make her the most upset.

"So what do you think of the new people?" Ram asked as the others left to have a long talk by themselves.

"Ok I guess. Usual white folk. Whatever."

He looked at her close. "Ok? I expected you to have more choice words than that. Especially about Sadie."

"I like her the most. Shit, at least she gots some balls. Not like that Michael J. Fox lookin' motherfuckin' Neil. Did you hear them go on about him being heroic? Shit. I'm stronger than that dude."

She probably wasn't far off. Cassie was taller than Neil by a few inches and was likely close to the same weight. "And Sarah?"

"You mean the Jennifer Aniston wannabe?" Cassie laughed at her own joke. "I do declare, I almost had a man in me! Whatever will I do but cry? Shit. She and Julia are exactly why you shoulda hooked up with me. They haven't gone through nothing like what I did and do you see me cryin'? Hell no. I'm tougher than all of them put together. Shit, I'm even tougher than you."

"You are," Ram admitted. He was slowly getting better; he could feel it on a daily basis, but he was still not close to his old self. "But it's turning you like leather inside. It can't be good for you."

"You sound like Julia. She's the weakest and the worst of them all."

Ram couldn't believe his ears. "She's nicer to you than anyone! She's always on your side."

"And why is that?" Cassie replied putting a hand on her hip. "Because she thinks I'm the weak one. Admit it. She is so afraid of my poor little black mind. She afraid I'll get hurt up in here. That I'll go crazy or something. Does she treat Sadie like this? No. She condescends every time she speaks to me. She always be talkin' down to me. I hate her because she's the worst type of racist. The type that think they can relate; the type who keeps a black friend on hand so they can pull the: *Some of my best friends are black* line. Shit. Gimme a Klansman any day. At least I know where I stand: they hate me and I hate them."

"You are one messed up girl," Ram said. "With all your hate, you're going to have a tough time of it at the CDC. What color do you think the majority of their scientists are going to be? Ninety-nine percent of them are going to be white or asian. What are you going to do then? Hate everyone?"

"When you put it like that, maybe I don't want to go."

Amazingly, she was serious, but Ram wouldn't find out how serious or how deep her hatred ran for another two days. And what with the sudden appearance of a baby in their lives, he forgot the conversation and failed to notice the smoldering anger in Cassie's eyes.

Chapter 42

Sarah

Tennessee

Ram was a strange individual to Sarah. Not only was he a strong, virile man—tall, dark, and handsome—he was also a good man, a caring man and yet Sarah felt nothing for him. This she found very interesting. In the old days, if he had asked her, she would have accepted an invitation to go out with him in a snap. After her run-in with the colonel, and since a zombie apocalypse seemed the worst possible time to consider romance, Sarah had officially sworn off all men. Yet she found herself attracted to the least likely man: Neil Martin.

Before all of this she would never have gone out with him. He was cute in his way, but was so slim and small. She had always liked her men to dominate her physically. It had made her feel safe and warm. Yet here she was, standing eye to eye with this little man, and the feeling of being safe was there anyway. And so was the warmth. It made no sense, especially since she had torpedoed his advances early on. Clearly, she mused, her torpedo had turned out to be a dud, since he had continued to fall for her at a rapid pace.

Sarah suspected it might have been Sadie's near constant cheerleading for Neil that had her finally giving him a second look. Or it might have been Sarah herself, coming out of the fugue state she had been in after her parents died…after she killed her parents, that is.

Or it might have been just Neil being Neil. If this was so, what did it say about her? Clearly it showed that she had been a very shallow person back in the old days, where she had taken men based more on their looks and confidence than anything else. And what had these men been so confident about? Certainly not their intelligence, emotional maturity, or their level of commitment, which was rarely anything but average. They were confident that women were shallow creatures who wouldn't look beyond their looks or their money.

Whatever it was, she smiled now every time she thought of Neil, and the night before she had purposely nudged Sadie from her customary place in the middle of the bed and took it for herself. *I want to be warm tonight*, she had said as an excuse, to which Sadie, with shrewd eyes, had replied in a whisper, *He's all warmth*. Sadie had been right. Sarah had never in her life felt the warmth of love as she did that night, because it wasn't just Neil that warmed her, it was Sadie as well.

They smushed in to her, and cuddled her; something her husband and daughter had stopped doing fifteen years before. She didn't realize how much she missed the feeling until just then. Of course because of her torpedo, she had to invite Neil close. After only six days together she knew what sort of gentleman he was—upon his honor, he would keep a safe, platonic distance from her and rigidly maintain his station all night long.

Her invitation had been that of a second grader. She had reached out for his hand and held it, pulling it close to her chest, the upper part of her chest, right below the soft spot of her throat. He had scooted over and very tentatively kissed her once on the lips. This made her grin, and anxious that his little kiss was wrong or perhaps comical he had whispered: *What is it?* Her reply: *Right now, I'm happy*.

This was only partly true. She realized just then that she had been happy frequently in the last few days; at odd times and for little reason besides looking at him after arguing with Sadie, or nibbling at the rabbit he had cooked, or watching him scurrying around trying to make sure she was happy. He was OCD alright, but out here, her happiness was his compulsion.

All of this made her wonder why Sadie had, right from the get go, been foursquare behind the two of them getting together. Before they climbed into the Suburban that morning, she had asked her.

"Because he never judged me. Not once. I robbed him and left him to die, twice! I left him stranded in his home without food, where he would've starved to death, and then later he should've been killed by John. I knew he would be, but I was sick of John and I ran away instead of helping Neil. And he never judged me. You'd be surprised how rare that is. Ever since then we have been like this." She held up crossed fingers. "So that's it. I want him to be happy. And I want you to be happy. You won't find a better man."

It was true she wouldn't find a better man than Neil. He rolled with every punch, took what life gave him and found a way to make it better, although not for himself, but better for those he cared about. Even when confronted with the possibility of becoming an instant parent, he only nodded to Sarah, giving her free rein to make a decision, though in this she was too slow.

The group was low on water when they slipped into the quiet town of Shelbyville, Tennessee and, on a recommendation from Ram, had driven to a largely deserted office park. After killing a few zombies in a quiet manner— Neil had picked up an axe at the house they had spent the night in—they raided the offices of a phone company where they found all sorts of goodies to eat and drink.

They were just loading up, and Neil was straining under the weight of a huge water jug, when a truck was heard coming towards them, rattling and clanking as if it were losing pieces with every rotation of its bald tires. The truck turned out to look exactly as it sounded.

"Let's be careful," Ram advised, turning his SAW towards the truck. "Friendly, but careful." Everyone kept their weapons in hand until they saw that it was only an older couple and not a band of desperados. They were the opposite of thieves in fact. Where one took items by force, these people practically gave items by force.

"Hey, there," the woman said around a thickly accented tongue. "I'm so happy to see people, it's been so long. I'm Emily and that's Robert, and this is Evangeline. We call her Eve as a way to hope. You know? Like the biblical Eve."

Emily, with the truck still rocking from the quick stop, came forward with a baby that couldn't have been more than two weeks old. It was wrapped in a pink blanket and Sarah immediately felt something inside her, like a low frequency echo that shimmied up from her uterus and into her heart.

"A baby!" Sadie said going forward, automatically and without question, to take the offered child. "She's precious. Look at her tiny nose!"

Ram scratched at the stubble of his chin, glanced once at Neil, who only gave a little shrug, and then said, "It's good to see friendly people as well. You can't be certain of anything these days."

"I know," Emily agreed. "You passed our place a good twenty minutes ago and I took one look at you and thought—what nice people."

"Don't forget her bag," Robert said from the driver's seat. Emily snapped her fingers, remembering, and went back to the truck. "Can't forget her stuff," he added in a drawl.

"Her stuff?" Ram asked. He turned to the others, but the women, all save Cassie, were fussing over the baby and Neil only stood there wearing a look of growing alarm. "Why do you need to get her stuff?"

"Because, silly," Emily answered.

"A baby needs her stuff," Robert commented.

Neil came forward and after clearing his throat— uselessly as it turned out—he choked out the words, "Are you giving us this baby?" He flicked his eyes to Ram in confusion, then back to the old couple. "You can't just give away babies."

"You should see her toes, Neil," Sadie squealed. "Oh my God! They are like this big." She held her fingers a quarter inch apart. "Come see." The baby was tiny and perfect and so out of place in this new world that she seemed like something left over or forgotten, something that couldn't be. Sarah, looking at the tiny pink face, knew a longing ache deep inside. She put her finger in the baby's hand and felt it close tightly around.

The old man saw this and gave a chuckle. "Yes, she has very cute toes and what a grip, right? And you should see her yawn. Just adorable. But that's not all, she's a good sleeper," he said as though he were selling a used car and pointing out its finer aspects.

"Hold on." Ram came limping forward. "We're not in a position to take this baby."

"And we're not in a position to keep her," Emily said. She brought out a pink diaper bag and when Ram didn't make a move to take it from her she draped it on the muzzle of his machine gun. "Her mother came to us hot with the fever. She was ragged and delirious, but somehow she kept little Eve perfectly whole. She died a little later and Robert had to send her on proper."

"But..." Ram said. He had nothing to follow up his one word argument except a slow shake of his head. This did little to deter Emily.

"We took the baby on, because that's what good Christians do, but we're old and we can't nearly support ourselves in these times. A baby needs a proper mother and father to protect her. You people are strong. You could do it."

"We can," Sarah announced, firmly. "And we will." She looked to Neil then and he gave her the smile that she knew she would see.

Emily breathed a huge sigh of relief and then came forward with two more bags. These she handed to Neil. "We prayed that Eve would be placed in good hands, and God has clearly blessed her. Thank you. Take good care of her now."

Just like that they had a baby. "Do you want to hold her,

Neil?" Sadie asked as soon as the couple had driven off. Neil shook his head as if to clear it of a buzzing sound and Ram only blinked dazedly.

"I'll take her," Julia said. It was more of an urgent demand than anything else, and in seconds, the woman whom Sarah viewed as sometimes cold and scientifically aloof, had turned into a cooing, goofy-faced girl. "Who's the cutest? Huh? Who's the cutest baby ever?"

"I wouldn't get too attached," Cassie said after a single peek at Eve.

"I say otherwise," Julia said, turning hard as rock, like no one there had ever seen her. "A baby needs instant bonding. They need to be loved! They need to be protected. Don't you know anything?"

Cassie blew out a *tsk* of dismissal. "I know the weak die. That's what I know. And that little thing is as weak as they come."

"That's why she needs a mother," Julia said. "I should be her mother." This brought on a general clamor from everyone. Sarah and Sadie were loud in protest and had their own demands. Cassie laughing derisively, and Ram choked on air. Julia seemed adamant. Her lips were drawn in and her back was rigid as she clutched Eve to her breast.

Only Neil had remained quiet and now he stepped up with a quick nervous smile, trying to calm them all. "Julia may be right...no, she is right about one thing. This baby needs a permanent mother. Though who it should be doesn't have to be decided right now, or even today."

"Why can't we share her?" Sadie asked. "I mean share the responsibilities and all that."

"I'm sure we will, whoever becomes her mother, or father, will need all our help. But we have to agree on a single person who will adopt her. What happens if the group breaks up? We can't share her then, can we? It should be decided before that becomes an issue."

"How are we going to decide?" Sadie asked. "By vote?

Because I want to be considered. I have experience with babies. I babysat all the time before and I'm nice and I'd be a great mother, I think."

Sarah raised her hand. "Me, too. I'd like to be Evangeline's mother."

Out of the blue, Julia cried, "You already had a baby!" She said it as if it were an accusation. The words struck Sarah like a slap in the face and she gasped before taking a step back with both hands over her mouth. Next to her, Sadie's eyes flared, but Julia held a hand out at her, pointing. "And you have Sadie," she said in desperation. "And you have Neil. You still have a chance, but I don't. I can't get pregnant."

This brought Sadie up short and she looked over at Sarah for guidance, but before she could say anything, Cassie put in her two cents, "What about me? I could be its mother. And I don't have any man, unlike you two, so I can't get pregnant neither."

This was met with silence until Sadie said in a cold voice, "Don't expect too many votes. A proper mother doesn't refer to a child as a thing or an *it*, like you just did."

"Hold on now, this is all going too fast," Neil said. "Before we vote we need to think things through. Let's just give ourselves a few minutes to calm down. This is a big decision for all of us."

The others saw the sense in that and the group drifted apart. Julia and Ram went to sit in the truck, while Sadie took Eve and crooned to her gently. Cassie watched with a disgusted look.

Sarah was in pain and her knees felt weak. "Julia's right," she said to Neil right off the bat when they were left alone. "I don't deserve her. I had my chance and now everyone knows I'm an unfit mother."

"Slow down, please," he begged. "No one thinks that. I know I don't, and Sadie doesn't. You were just an unlucky mother. No one was allowed to drive anywhere and they closed the airports. How were you supposed to get to your daughter?"

"I could have walked," Sarah replied, grasping at straws in her misery.

"And you would have died." Neil took her hands. "And Eve would never have had a chance for you to be her mother. And neither would Sadie. That's how she looks at you."

If there was anything striking about Neil it was the blue of his eyes. They stared right down into her soul. "Are you saying you'll vote for me?" she asked. Neil nodded. "What about the rest of it? It's…it's not easy raising a child alone. A baby shouldn't just have a mother."

"Yes, I guess so," he said, slowly, realizing what she was asking. "I suppose I need to ask you the same question: what about the rest of it? Us, I mean. Are we going from holding hands to being parents? Is that what you're suggesting? How do I know this isn't some ploy to get me into bed?"

She laughed and her mood lightened. "*Us* was progressing. Only last night I discovered I wanted it to progress to the next stage, and who knows what would have happened if Sadie hadn't been there. So, no, this isn't a ploy. I want us to be a *WE* eventually. I wouldn't ask you otherwise. So…what do you say?"

He looked away, towards Julia who seemed to be in two places at once, emotionally speaking—fear and hope were working her face through a series of odd looks. Neil, grinning a sad grin, said, "I'd love to raise this child with you, Sarah. I'd love to be her father, but I don't think it would be right. The way Julia reacted just now…clearly she needs this. I don't know her so well, but it feels like she's been treading water and if the vote goes against her, she may sink."

It was Sarah who felt like she was sinking just then, as if her feet were slipping beneath the pavement. "I suppose," she said in a whisper.

Neil reeled her in, pulling her gently closer so they were looking into each other eyes. "If you are truly interested in me being father to Eve, you would also be interested in me being father to our own children, too. Can you wait nine months? I guarantee I'll give you the prettiest baby."

She dipped her head, feeling tears come up quick, but not knowing if it was disappointment she was feeling or a hope for the future; her first hope in a long while. She realized Julia was probably feeling that same hope, only she had hers pinned on this one child. Sarah's hope was for more.

"I'll vote for Julia," she said. "I've had one baby and I can have more in the future. And I have Sadie, like you said." She thought Neil would also vote for Julia, however, he did not.

After a few minutes they gathered again and Ram handed each a piece of paper and a pen. "I figured we should do this with a secret ballot," he explained.

"I don't think there's any need for that," Sarah said. "I want Julia to know I'm voting for her. She was right about everything…" Sarah had to stop as Julia rushed up and hugged her. "You'll be a great mom," she added in a whisper as the lady cried on her shoulder.

"I'm voting for Julia also," Ram announced as the two women broke apart. He handed her his piece of paper and added, "Though in a way, I'm voting for myself too."

Now it was Neil's turn, but when he stood he didn't go to Julia, instead he took his paper to young Sadie. "One day it'll be your time, and when that day comes you'll be a great mom, I know it," he said and she blushed prettily.

"Shit," Cassie said in her slow way as everyone looked her direction. "I was gonna vote for myself since I knew none of you crackers would ever vote for a strong black woman, but now I sees this will be more interesting." She went to Sadie and dropped the paper at her feet. "Now it's all tied up. Whatcha gonna do? Split the baby down the middle?"

Julia, suddenly robbed of her victory, stared at Sadie. "What are we going to do?" she asked.

Sadie lifted a shoulder in reply and then stooped to pick up Cassie's poisoned vote. For a long while she stared at it before saying, "Eve needs one mom and one dad. I can't give her that, not honestly. I vote for Julia, but in return I want your share of any pop tarts that we find for the next year. Is that a deal?"

"Yes!" Julia beamed at the girl and accepted Eve in her arms. Then like a coin flipping she turned on Cassie and snarled, "You aren't a strong black woman. I've known many strong black women–they were educated and accomplished and knew what decency was. You're nothing like them. You're broken is what you are!"

At this the girl's eyes narrowed in anger and her hand went to the gun at her hip where she always wore it. Sadie, who had learned her lesson with the knife, now produced a black pistol so quickly it seemed like magic.

Cassie snorted at the gun, as if it meant nothing and said, "I see how all you be. Don't worry, you'll get yours."

"Our what?" Sadie demanded.

"What's coming to you," she hissed. "One day it won't be four crackers and a race traitor against just one of us. Then we'll see…"

Ram jumped up and grimaced through the pain in his leg. "I'm done with her, Julia," he roared, waking the baby who began to bleat with the sound of a lamb. "I'm not going to play around with you for one more second. You have two choices and only two. If you're going to keep running that mouth of yours, then leave right now, no one wants to hear it. If you can zip it until we get to Atlanta then we'll part ways then. What's it going to be?"

Despite his anger, she only raised an eyebrow. "I'll be a good little nigger."

Chapter 43

Sadie

Georgia

Sadie was slow to put her gun away. She didn't trust Cassie, and that was partially because she understood her better than the older members of the group. Certainly not on all levels, there was no way a girl from Passaic could truly understand a girl out of Compton, but on certain fundamental points she did. Such as how come she detested Julia.

The redheaded woman was generally quiet around everyone but Ram, though when she did speak she was polite, if not shy. Except when she spoke to Cassie. Then the words that came out of her mouth fell as if from on high. She acted as though she had some great wisdom that Cassie wouldn't be able to fathom.

This sort of not-so-subtle racism was embarrassing, Sadie thought, but it seemed that she and Cassie were the only ones who even noticed it.

And that was another of Cassie's issues with the group. Ram had a low-running dislike for the girl, even before the baby had come into their lives, and he brushed off Julia's odd attitude, never once bothering to say anything. Sarah, a small town girl from Farm Country USA was completely baffled by Cassie—the way she spoke, the way she dressed, the way she rarely washed her hair, the way she seemed to have built an imaginary wall around herself like a shield. They were so completely alien to each other that neither said upwards of a dozen words a day to the other.

Then there was Neil. If given enough time Neil, would've chiseled a hole through Cassie's wall. His positive cheerfulness was infectious, something that Sadie took full credit for. He had been a turtle living a hermit life before she had stumbled upon him, and now, free of that restricting shell he had blossomed into a resourceful man of action, which was a salve to Sadie's guilt.

If anyone could've gotten through to Cassie, it would have been Neil, but, once the baby came, she seemed to be beyond help. Though he tried.

The remainder of the journey that afternoon had been difficult on the group. Eve wasn't as easy as she looked and fussed so much that Julia was in tears, thinking she was failing in some respect.

"Sometimes that's how babies are," Sarah had said. "You just have to run down the check list: is she fed, burped, does her diaper need to be changed? Is she too hot, is she too cold? Are her jammies bunched somewhere? Is she just colicky? Go ahead, go down the list. Start with a bottle."

They discovered the problem eventually when Julia went to burp the baby. "She's not a China Doll," Sarah said, laughing. "Don't tap her like you're doing a golf clap. You got to go harder than that...harder." Finally, when Julie gave her a good thump on the back, Eve belched like a man, and then promptly fell straight asleep.

This had them all grinning, all save Cassie who remained rock-like and sour-faced, sitting just behind Ram, who was in the passenger seat. Neil saw her lack of response and tried to make conversation with her, "Do you have any brothers or sisters, Cassie?" When she emitted nothing but the passing of her breath, and when the eyes of the others began to dart around at her rudeness, Neil simply spoke as if they were in an actual conversation.

"I don't either. Supposedly, I was a problem child, however the nannies never seemed to mind. That was how I was raised, by nannies on the Upper West side of Manhattan, right up until the crash of '87. Do you know what that was?" Cassie answered by looking out the window, which did not deter Neil from explaining anyway.

That was how the day went. Their going was slow and

tedious. They usually avoided any town of fifty-thousand people and up, but now the land seemed to squeeze in on them as they progressed through the tail end of the Appalachians so that only twenty-five miles separated the suburbs of Chattanooga and Huntsville, and those miles were forested with stiffs.

The first night they holed up in a liquor store with barred windows and a sturdy set of doors. The two men drank until they were silly, while, Sadie had trouble feeling her toes after her second warm beer; they seemed much further away than usual. Julia and Sarah were drunk with baby fever, and did little besides sit next to Eve and smile at her least movement. Cassie sat alone sipping from a bottle of Tuaca.

The following day they traveled at a snail's pace and only came upon the city of Rome, just across the Georgia state line, near three in the afternoon. Although it was technically a large city, they had been having a hard time finding gas and they had to chance it. It was there that they came upon their first taste of what was to come at the CDC.

Just as they skimmed the outskirts of the city a light flashed at them and Neil stopped short. "Did you see that? It was a light. Whoa, there it is again." A light from a dirt brown vehicle flicked their way. "Sadie?"

"On it," she said. Whenever there was exploring or recon work needed the group called upon the teen. Staying low, Sadie slunk along the cars parked on the side of the street, ready to tear off at the slightest sign of danger. She knew that both Ram and Neil had their M16s trained at every doorway and alley she passed.

It was a nice to have Ram backing her, and it was nice to let Neil feel needed—his ability with any weapon other than his axe was suspect—but it wasn't necessary. Since the world had died, the air had become so still that she could hear the zombies long before she saw them, and she didn't think she was in much danger.

In this case she could hear them shuffling on a side street next to the odd vehicle that had flashed them. The vehicle was clearly military, yet was so strange: it had the treads of a tank, however it was without a main gun and its design was that of a brown shoebox. On the top was what looked like a raised manhole cover and from a gap beneath a set of eyes stared out at her.

"Did you need something?" Sadie whispered to the man inside.

"There's a shitload of stiffs right over there." He pointed away from himself toward where Sadie had heard them. She lifted herself from her crouch and gave them a look over the front edge of the vehicle. There were maybe fourteen of them and probably triple that number hiding where she couldn't see.

"Do you want us to kill them for you?" she asked. It seemed a reasonable thing to do.

"What? No, we were warning you. Go back and get in your car before they kill you." She gave them a quick nod and was about to slink away when the man whistled. "Hey, my friend wants to know your name."

"It's Sadie," she answered, feeling an instant heat on her neck.

"He say's you're cute."

The heat crept up her face, but she summoned her courage and tried to look past the man and into the cramped vehicle. She couldn't see a thing. "Tell him thanks, but I can't see him so I have to assume you are a bunch of sardine people from the planet Georgia. What is this thing?" she asked and tapped the metal box lightly.

"It's an M113 armored personnel carrier and I think flirting time is over. The stiffs heard us. You better run."

They were gang-rushing her. Unperturbed she stepped back from the APC and clapped her hands over her head to make sure she had all of their attention. Only when every stiff in the alley was fully aware of her, did she run the seventy yards to the Suburban. And she did so at top speed—showing off.

"What's up?" Ram asked.

Breathing heavily, but feeling good, Sadie answered nonchalantly, "Just some soldier boys. We should ask them about how things are going at the CDC."

"Soldiers?" Sarah asked in alarm. "Maybe we shouldn't."

"These aren't the same guys," Neil put in. "Now, hold on to Eve. It's going to get bumpy." He waited until the stiffs were right on the vehicle before plowing through them and over them; he then gunned the SUV down the street and pulled up right next to the APC.

Ram rolled down his window. "Good afternoon. What can you tell us about the CDC? Is it still operational?"

The man gave Ram a look and then tried to peer into the vehicle, his eyes darting right over Cassie as if she wasn't there. Sadie leaned forward and waved, catching his eyes and she saw them crinkle up with a smile. He then turned back to Ram and said, "Yeah, but they ain't taking in any more refugees. You need to go west to Guntersville. They got some spots open. At least they did a few days back. Now you better get on going. Them stiffs are coming back." They were about to leave when the man noticed Cassie staring at him with a sneer. "What are you looking at?" he asked matching sneer for sneer.

"A sorry-ass cracker."

"Cassie!" Julia cried, outraged.

"You better put a leash on her," the man advised, turning cold. "She's in Good Ole Boy country now. We won't put up with that sort of talk. Now get."

The stiffs were already marring the paint and smearing the glass, so Neil took off. As usual he floored it to clear the area, took a couple of turns and then slowed to a crawl again, looking for cars with their gas caps still sealed. There were so many left hanging open that it was obvious someone had come through before them and had siphoned them dry.

"What the hell was that about?" Ram asked Cassie. He had sat in a gathering anger, trying and failing to calm himself. "Are you going to make enemies wherever you go?"

"Shit. We in cracker country now, Ram. You and I ain't welcome. I bet you they'd let all these nice white folk into the CDC, but we got to go to some refugee camp. You ever see white folk at a refugee camp? I ain't never seen a one unless they be the ones handing out the food."

"I vote her out," Julia said suddenly. "You were warned, Cassie. You were warned not to make any more trouble. Ram? You warned her."

His anger, which sat on his face like a mask seemed to fade as he looked out at the town of Rome. Down every street there were signs of death: burnt houses, decomposing bodies, old brown bloodstains on the sidewalks and sprayed on cars. Zombies, here and there.

"Not yet," he said. "When we get out of town. We'll find her a farm or something."

Neil cleared his throat. "Maybe we should part ways at the CDC instead. I find Cassie's behavior incomprehensible as well as deplorable, however, I think we can deal with it for one more night. We're pretty close."

"If we let her out now it would be like killing her," Sarah said. "If that's the plan you should just shoot her instead, Ram. It would be more humane. I'm with Neil, we should wait. Sadie, what do you think?"

Sadie thought Cassie was bad news. The girl had clearly been stewing in hatred for some time to be the way she was—and that meant trouble. Still the idea of abandoning her here seemed completely heartless. "I can wait. We're in the home stretch. I can feel it, like we're almost done running."

"Shit," Cassie said. "Don't do me any favors, Sadie. Cuz after Ram, you'll be next. It's just what the white man do..."

"I'd zip the lips if I was you," Sadie said, cutting her off.

"I can change my vote anytime. And I'll do it if you keep pushing." She stared out the window and shook her head for a few seconds but was so bothered by Cassie that she added, "You almost sound like you want us to kick you out. Why?"

"You saw how that dude just ignored me like I wasn't even there. I was fucking invisible to him, and that's how it always be. That's how it was with the baby. None of you even paused for a second to see if I wanted her. No one asked me what I thought about taking you guys on. I was a second class citizen before the zombies and I'm a second class citizen now. And that's how it'll be in fucking Atlanta."

"Do you even want to go?" Sadie asked. She expected the answer to be a quick no. Instead Cassie had to think it over, yet she did with eyes turned away so that only Sadie caught sight of them reflected in the glass. They were the eyes of a toad.

Their camp for the evening, according to the few road signs, was twenty miles outside of Marietta, which was just one of a gazillion little towns and cities that made up sprawling Atlanta. It was still farm country, however the farms had shrunk and were closer together, with some being little more than *Gentlemen Farms* that grew next to nothing. On the plus side, their accommodations were cozier, some of the barns being as nice as hotel rooms.

On the down side, it took some work for Neil and Ram to make their position defensible. While the sun was still above the horizon, Sadie kept watch, as Sarah and Julia took turns feeding Eve. The two men went to work on the stairs leading up to the loft. They pried out the treads and risers to a height of six feet, and set a ladder firmly in place. Next they covered up the windows with heavy blankets. Only then did they start hauling baggage up; though in this it was mostly Neil doing the work.

Cassie usually helped but she was off to herself and Ram's knee was still too tender to go up and down the ladder more than a few times and, when he did it was with a grimace on his face.

Sadie would've helped, however someone had to keep watch. Also hefting heavy loads was man's work as she saw it. "You two better hurry," she called to the men as she made her rounds. "The sun will be going down in a few minutes."

Sarah glanced up from the baby in alarm. "Neil! I need to have a *long talk* with you before it gets dark." Sadie snorted at the silly code word as Neil hurried down the ladder.

"What about you?" he asked Sadie. "Do you need to talk?"

"I'm good," she said, walking away to stroll across the soft front yard of the house.

"If anyone wants to talk they'll have to come up here!" Ram exclaimed, sweating and wincing as he went back up to the loft with another bag. "I'm not coming back down for nothing."

So they went their ways and they did so in foolish contentment. Cassie went her way as well, only she did so with revenge in her heart.

The house that came with the barn, as the group saw things, was a big one with tall Greek columns and a long drive that was bordered with straight trees that were lined up like a hundred sentries on parade. Sadie sat in a rocker on the front porch and pictured the fabulous life it must have been like living there.

"Probably like *Gone with the Wind*," she said to herself. Then, as the sun crept below the trees, she decided it was time to go into hiding as they did every night. She came around the side of the house thinking this was where she wanted to live if ever the zombies could all be killed and then suddenly she froze in place—her mouth came open and she threw a hand up to her eyes as lights blared in her face and an engine roared into the night. Someone was in the Suburban! And they were leaving! Sadie jumped back as the SUV flashed by and there she saw plainly Cassie in the driver's seat and next to her was the unmistakable silhouette of Eve's car seat.

Ram was right behind, limping like mad and pointing a rifle at the fleeing Suburban. He fired twice before Sadie screamed, "No! Don't shoot. She has Eve. The baby's in the there."

Ram ignored her and went to one knee and fired three more times before she jumped in front of him. "Get out of the way, damn it! I'm aiming at the tires." Sadie jumped back and watched as the SUV slewed to the right after Ram's next burst. Then it went down the hill and was out of sight.

"She killed Julia," Ram said, his mouth hanging open and his eyes unblinkingly large. "And she has the baby."

In a rage, beyond any ability to think, Sadie took off running. No one could catch the Suburban if she couldn't.

Chapter 44

Julia

Rome, Georgia

Julia was of two minds. One part of her dwelled on the feeling of contentment, the like she had never known. The baby was hers! She was a real mother. It was a sensation that couldn't be described, beyond the meager concept of being complete.

When she had heard the news that she was barren—a word that sounded horribly hollow and appropriate when dwelt upon—she had allowed herself to be fooled into thinking that it didn't matter. After all, men weren't judged on whether they could procreate, but only on whether they could get an erection. When it came to babies they fell all over themselves to keep it from "happening to them", while men with a vasectomy walked around as if they had won the lottery.

Julia's contemporaries, other professional women, were quick to point out how good it was for her career that she couldn't conceive. These same women looked down their noses at stay-at-home moms, saying that *they* were the women who were incomplete.

Ha! What a joke her friends were. They scorned God and worshipped evolution, conveniently ignoring their own place in it. Evolution wasn't about racking up degrees and lording them over anyone with anything less; it was about the continuation of the species. And evolutionarily speaking Julia was a dead end.

But not anymore.

She bent over the portable car seat and rubbed her cheek against the softest skin in the whole world and knew all of that was just junk. Julia had been blessed with this tiny person even if she hadn't come from her womb. Now she was a mother and now she was complete.

She was also aggravated. Cassie took up the other part of her mind and it was no wonder. Julia blamed herself for Cassie's negative attitude, at least partially. What had she said wrong? What had she done, or didn't do? These were the questions that came to her mind as she watched the black girl swinging in a tire that hung from a huge shade tree in the backyard of the house.

Eve drew her mind back to what was important by making a little noise—a sigh—and Julia smiled, feeling her soul like a hot breath inside of her. She gazed with great love at the sleeping baby, day-dreaming about holding Eve's hand when she took her first step.

When she looked up again there was Cassie, appearing almost magically, with Neil's axe raised above her head and murder in her ferocious eyes.

"Not the baby," Julia begged in a whisper, her new motherhood coming out in full force as she leaned forward, putting her arms out to cover the car seat. This left her dreadfully exposed with no way at all to defend herself, however, love spoke and overrode her sense of self that her friends had always dwelled upon. There were things so much larger.

The three words: *Not the b*aby, held the axe at bay, momentarily. "I coulda been her mom," Cassie hissed. "But you wouldn't let me."

"I'm her mother," Julia said. "Do what you want to me, but please don't hurt her."

Cassie's eyes flicked to the baby. "No way, bitch. You gonna see her die and you're gonna live with that."

The girl glowered in rage, and brought the axe back as though she were going to split a log when she was really aiming to hew the baby in two. Julia could have leapt back, instead she lurched forward and threw herself across the car seat, protecting her baby. As she felt the bite of the axe, she knew in that second of death that she was a real mother.

Chapter 45

Sadie

Rome, Georgia

Sadie saw the possibilities—the group had come off of I-41 and had taken three lefts in a row, which meant Cassie would have to retrace the route exactly—she wouldn't take a chance on Atlanta, not after committing such a horrible crime.

With fear for little Eve that was near to madness, Sadie launched herself at the forest, heading north-northeast, a direct route to the highway which was just over a mile and a quarter away. Though the dark forest was the quickest way, it was also the most dangerous; sheltering as it was innumerable zombies. These rose up, in all their fearsome horror as she passed but the girl paid them no attention: she had no time for zombies when she had a ghoul to kill.

If Sadie saw in herself one redeeming quality, it was her dogged, fierce loyalty, and it was this which propelled her at speeds she had never come close to before. She came upon the highway in just under six minutes, but still missed Cassie. A long ways down the road Sadie saw the retreating taillights.

She fell against a tree, her breath hucking out of her, tears coming in a rain, and the black pistol swinging at the end of her arm as if it were nothing more than the Power-Puff lunch box she had carried when she was in grade school. It used to nick her leg just as the pistol had.

She turned from the distant lights and pictured the pink lunch box she had carried for so long and, in her mind, she saw herself as the little girl she had been with the huge Anime eyes. She remembered running with the box swatting her leg as she beat the boys time-after-time in every race they could conceive.

All of this was better than picturing what Cassie was going to do to Eve.

"She better not do anything to..." she began, however a zombie came hurrying forward to die a second time. With animalistic fury, Sadie jammed the gun in its face and pulled the trigger. It fell in a most satisfying manner.

More zombies came and Sadie's rage was large in her. "What did Eve do to deserve this?" she asked a three-piece-suit wearing zombie before knocking him out of his one remaining shoe and sending his brains littering into the forest.

"Nothing!" she gasped and then turned one last time and jumped in her sneakers. The SUV had turned! She could see its far away headlights take a left. On impulse, Sadie began jogging after it. Then she saw the truck take another left. It was coming back in her direction on a parallel course to the highway and Sadie saw exactly where it was heading.

Just on the edge of twilight she could see a house with a barn. It had to be where she was going. Everyone liked Neil's barn concept, including Cassie. With hope lending her strength, Sadie took off running for it, while behind her trailed a legion of undead.

They would have to wait.

Cassie beat her to the house by a full minute and was nowhere in sight as Sadie came up to the SUV, which had settled in a rearward list on two flat tires; Ram's aim had been spot on.

Without hesitation she went to the driver's side door, which was not only locked, but seemed to come apart in her hand. The glass, a clear sheet one second, exploded into a thousand pieces the next, as a blast split the air behind her.

Sadie threw herself to the right as more gunshots sounded and bullets thumped into the Suburban. Blindly she returned fire, but her aim was to the stars since she couldn't chance hitting Eve. Cassie wasn't burdened by the consideration of anybody's welfare but her own and she shot her gun hot.

All Sadie could do was run to the side of the house and hide. There she had two forms of death to choose from: death under the rending jaws of zombies, or death from a bullet. "An easy choice," she said to herself. When the first stiff came up she plugged it from a range of four feet; two more went down in the same manner and then she stuck her head around the corner of the house and saw the Suburban's doors were flung wide.

Now with a bit of breathing room from the zombies, Sadie sprinted to the Suburban and glanced in—no baby. She was about to head to the barn when she heard Eve's little lamb cry coming from the house and turning in mid-step she followed the sound, holding her gun out ahead of her like every television cop ever. As quiet as a shadow, Sadie slipped across the hardwood floors, ignoring the country decor, the Hummel figurines, the fancy bone china in the dining room hutch. All of her senses were tuned to that little cry, while her body was on a hair trigger, ready to shoot the first thing that moved, only the house was still and unearthly quiet save for Eve.

The baby was crying somewhere below her and when Sadie found the basement stairs off the back hall, she had to pause despite her need to save Eve. The dark below was impenetrable and it sent a nasty trembling coursing through her muscles. "Cassie," she whispered. "I won't hurt you if you give up the baby. Cassie! Don't be stupid."

The words felt foreign to her tongue because regardless of her fear, or maybe because of it, she was in a killing mood. She might have been just a girl from Passaic, New Jersey, but now Sadie had a gun and she was more than willing to use it on Cassie. She went down the stairs into the dark, slinking low, hoping to make herself less of a target. No shots rang out. She was almost down and her eyes had become accustomed to the dark, when she found little Eve in her car seat a few feet from the bottom of the stairs.

[353]

"Shhh," she said gently, while staring all around with wide eyes. There was a dim, dim light filtering in from the tiny rectangular windows set high up in the basement walls, but not enough to see where Cassie was. She could be anywhere...or nowhere.

"Sadie, you dumb bitch," Cassie said in a whisper from up the stairs. Sadie spun, confused. Why was she up there when the baby was down here? The answer was suddenly obvious and the shaking she had tried to ignore grew stronger so that she had to hold the gun with two hands to keep it from falling.

"Here they come," Cassie said. "Can you hear all them stiffs? All this shooting has got them coming from miles."

"Cassie, please..." Sadie whispered, her voice shaking along with her body. "Let us go. We never hurt you."

"You gonna shoot it?" Cassie asked.

"It? What it?"

"The baby. Man you dumb. When the stiffs come for you, are you gonna kill it? Or let it turn into a little baby zombie?"

"I'm going to kill you, is what I'm going to do," Sadie hissed in impotent fury. She didn't dare try to go up the stairs just then, she'd be an easy target. "I swear it."

"Yeah right...oh, here they come. I left the front door open and now your guests are arriving for dinner. See ya, bitch."

Above Sadie, the floorboards began to creak and groan under the weight of many, many zombies. They weren't slow either, they were coming right for the stairs, drawn by the sound of...Eve. It was only just registering on Sadie that the baby was still crying.

"No...shhh. Eve please be quiet."

Eve's little eyes were scrunched and her face red, her tiny fingers were splayed and the zombies were coming to eat her. Sadie went down the *how to stop a baby from crying* mental check list that Sarah had told Julia in the car only the day before. Unfortunately, Sadie didn't have time to try any of those remedies.

She checked her gun...four bullets left, the sight of them, so few, left her staggered. She wouldn't be able to fight her way out and, with the baby bleating as she was, there wouldn't be a chance at hiding. There would only be death. Could she shoot the baby? If she did she would have to shoot herself next; there was no way she could live after doing such a thing.

But what was her choice besides that?

Kneeling down, Sadie turned the gun on Eve. It wouldn't stay still in her grip. It shook and shimmied, and her hand went weak and numb so that it didn't feel like her own. "Oh God, please help me," she whispered. But God did not give her the strength to kill the baby.

Then, as the beasts came into the kitchen above, she remembered a movie where a woman accidentally smothered her baby to death when she was just trying to keep her quiet. There had been soldiers near who would've killed them if they had heard.

"No, I won't," Sadie whispered, but the memory of the movie wouldn't leave and in desperation, as the zombies came closer, her hand crept out to Eve's tiny face. Sadie started to cry. "Maybe a little," she said, thinking she would just hold her hand there for a little while and it would be alright...somehow.

But then Eve grabbed Sadie's finger in her tiny hand and her grip was beautiful and miraculous, and Sadie knew she couldn't hurt the baby. Not ever. She turned the gun up the stairs not knowing what else to do, and then as she waited in misery for what was to come, Eve saved herself.

The baby's grip was insistent on Sadie's finger and she had just enough strength in her tiny muscles to pull the finger right into her mouth where she immediately went to sucking on it as if it was a pacifier. A relief, like a drug, swept the young girl, but it was short lived. The zombies shuffling about above were coming closer to the stairs. Sadie lifted the baby in her arms, making sure her finger stayed securely plugged between Eve's lips, and hurried to explore the rest of the basement desperately hoping to find another way out, because she knew the dark and a few stairs would not keep the zombies away all night.

They had heard something and wouldn't give up the hunt for hours and Sadie was sure Eve wouldn't be mollified by the finger for too long.

There was a central hallway of some twenty-five feet and from it sprouted rooms; she went to each, in a vain hope of finding a way out. All the rooms were just that: little squares with tiny box-like windows set high up. Not knowing what else to do, she went back to the stairs and saw scabby legs already heading down.

Holding back a scream she ducked into what was a storage room and in the dark kicked something. This brought the zombies quicker and they thumped down the stairs in their eagerness, making a moan that had Sadie shaking and near to throwing up. In her growing panic, she stepped back and her foot came down on something small, which triggered an idea. She dropped to one knee and felt around. In the blackness her hand found a Matchbox car; she knew it by feel alone, and she sent it skittering down the end of the hall where it rattled up against the walls. And when she heard a rush of shuffling zombie feet go by, she made a break for it.

There were more zombies in the first room where the stairs came down, but these she ignored. It was dark and the stiffs were confused and slow to recognize what she was. Up the stairs she ran, pausing only to use one of her four remaining bullets; there was a zombie halfway up and there was no getting around it.

With the gunshot, all pretence of sneaking went out the window. Eve quit her finger and didn't just cry, she wailed in earnest, but there was nothing to be done. Sadie charged up into the kitchen coming face to...the thing barely had a face and lost what it did have when Sadie used bullet number two. When it fell back, she dashed through the kitchen and into the hall where she was able to dodge around the first creature in her way, but, when another appeared, she was forced to use her third bullet.

If there had been only a single zombie at the front door she would've escaped. Sadie shot one and in a snap a second was right there. She beaned it across the forehead with the now useless pistol, and ran for the stairs to the second floor as behind zombies fell over themselves to get up at her.

And then more were on the stairs above her. She was trapped, but not alone. She had Eve who was wailing in fright...and Neil. Amazingly, he came in right after the last zombie and in his hands was Ram's SAW. Like the world's smallest action hero he let the thing rip, nearly hitting Sadie in the process. The weapon seemed to rise on its own as he shot and the rounds whipped past her, one parting her spiked hair. She dropped down, clutching Eve to her, as Neil corrected his aim and tore the zombies to shreds.

"Behind you," she pointed. There were so many that one gun wouldn't do it. He shot through the doorway clearing it momentarily and then Sadie pulled him out into the night. She nearly stumbled at the sight of the horde of zombies waiting outside. "We got to run for it," she said, despite the fact she saw that it would be useless.

"No," he said, breathlessly and staggering in her grip. It was clear that he had done just about as much running as he was capable of, besides zombies were flocking in from everywhere. Even young Sadie would have had a tough time of it.

"The barn!" he cried, and then they ran, and with their burdens neither was all that fast. Still, they made it before the zombies and found that the barn wouldn't do. There was a hayloft, however it had stairs just as neat as you please and even if they had an axe to destroy them they didn't have time to use it. "Go," he said looking sick at the sight of the stairs. "I'll draw them to me. You and Eve can escape."

The short run to the barn with Eve had proved to Sadie that running wasn't going to be an option; the baby was just too unwieldy and besides her cries would bring the zombies to them like moths to a light. "No, we'll go up. Maybe there's something in the loft that'll help." There wasn't. There was pitchfork, a rake and piles of hay. Sadie placed the baby in the hay and armed herself with the pitchfork.

"Short bursts," she said as the first zombies came up. There were so many that the stairs creaked under their weight. Neil fired—pop, pop, pop. Making sure to conserve his ammo, but it was futile. Sadie saw there were enough zombies to tear down the entire...

One thought led to another and she suddenly yelled, "Shoot the stairs! The top one, shoot it right in the middle!" Neil's eyes went wide at the idea and, as Sadie pushed the beasts back with her pitchfork, he used the SAW like a saw and tore the tread in two. Immediately the zombies on it fell backward creating havoc among them. While they tore at each other to get up, he destroyed the next stair and the next. He ran out of bullets trying the fourth stair, but it didn't matter. It came apart under the weight of the zombies and they plunged downward.

Now there was a gap of almost four feet and the zombies were stymied by it and fell through one after another. This went on for quite a while. The zombies would come up, see their dinner, race faster and then plunge through the opening to the cement below.

Sadie and Neil watched for a bit and then when it got disgusting, they retreated to the straw and made a burrow of it to keep warm. Curled up in the straw with Eve between them sucking on her finger, Sadie asked, "Is Julia really dead?"

"Yeah," Neil breathed. "It was terrible...but what was worse was you running off like that. You had me scared to death."

Sadie kissed Eve's round cheek and said, "It was worth it. But what was your excuse?"

He fumbled for words before trying, "I wanted to be a hero?"

"Some hero! You should have seen yourself jitterbugging all over the place working that machine gun. I swear you looked like you were just trying to hold on for dear life. So, how did you find me? You have no idea how scared I was."

"Ram saw where you went into the woods, and then I could hear you firing. You shot a few times and I oriented on that. When I got to the house I saw the flashes and heard you and Cassie going at it like a couple of gun Old West gunfighters. And you weren't the only one scared. Sometimes I was running right next to the zombies, it was horrible."

"But you saved us," Sadie said and then grinned. "You're my hero, Neil." She kissed him on the nose, because it was the only part of his face that wasn't cherry-red.

Chapter 46

Eric

CDC Atlanta

Eric Reidy walked around the oval perimeter of the CDC with sweat on his upper lip and a digital camera in his hand. He had been told to use it brazenly, and that if he tried to sneak pictures of the defenses he would be caught for certain.

"I can't believe I'm doing this," he whispered to himself, running a hand over his face after every picture, feeling the weight of his actions like stones piling up in his gut. "This is fucking treason."

Or it would have been if there was still a working government. He hadn't wanted to go along with the coup attempt. Stubbornly, he had tried to resist, however Admiral Stevenson had laid out his reasoning rather clearly and it had made sense at the time:

"The Secretary is criminal in her dereliction of duty," Admiral Stevenson had said as if the idea saddened him. "You have no idea how dangerous she is in her ineptness. All across the country we've lost thousands of soldiers in the last week alone, and God only knows how many millions of civilians. And if she continues on doing nothing except hiding out in the CDC, it won't be long before there's nothing left of this country."

"But attacking the CDC won't help. This is where we can find a cure, or a vaccine," Eric had stammered out a defense. "If what you're saying is true about the rest of the world being overrun then we definitely can't put the CDC at risk. It's now more important than ever."

A grave smile crossed the admiral's lips. "Not if you're just spinning your wheels and wasting precious supplies uselessly. That's exactly what's been happening with the

Secretary in charge. This is about uniting our country once again under a single leader; it's not about the CDC or finding a cure. You said yourself that it might not ever happen."

"No, we can do it. It'll just take..."

"Seven years?" Stevenson interrupted, using Eric's words against him. "I wasn't joking about only having seven months. We need leadership now or the coming winter will ravage us and maybe takes us to the brink of extinction. You need to weigh these facts Dr Reidy and look to the greater good. Yes, people will die in the short run and I wish that weren't so, but in the long run it'll be for the best."

"And what will you do with the CDC?" Eric asked. "You won't just give up on a vaccine will you?"

"Yes," the admiral admitted. The answer was like a slap in the face, and Eric actually reeled back. "Yes. For now. I'll keep some essentials on staff, but I've got to look at the bigger picture. The CDC has fifteen hundred men guarding triple their own number, while at the same time there are refugee camps of five-thousand citizens being guarded by a single company of soldiers. We have literally become a country of vagabonds and yet the great majority of our resources go to a group of scientists who may or may not produce something in seven years! Paring back the manpower at the CDC should have been done weeks ago. It's just another example of failed leadership."

The admiral wasn't wrong about the Secretary, or her leadership skills, nor was he wrong in any of his arguments, however Eric hadn't agreed to help the coup for those reasons. He had other motives: the first was the fact that there was a sense of futility at the CDC—a sense that they were just going through the motions. It was as if everyone, even the scientists, knew they were doomed as a species. It came out in their work and in their reports: there wasn't a single bright spot, nor a ray of hope in all the experiments. Had there been one, Eric would've risked his life to keep the CDC going strong.

Of course his most pressing motive was that the admiral had made it clear that Eric would be killed if he didn't help.

Therefore he took the camera, and the satellite phone, and the encrypted laptop and went back to the Secretary with false promises on his lips.

The pictures of the facility, both inside and out, were easy to come by. "For my scrapbook," he had said when asked. It was the technical information, the troop numbers, the location of air defenses and their counts, the fuel situation of the Strykers, things of that nature that took him days to ascertain.

It was difficult, but it gave him hope that the admiral was being true to his word that he was looking for a surgical operation with the fewest casualties. "I could just level the place with Tomahawk cruise missiles," he had said. "However the facility has proved its worth as a forward operating base and in these days that can't be overlooked." Eric didn't know what the man meant by that exactly, but it was a relief nonetheless.

Finally when he had all the information he needed, Eric sent his encrypted message containing every possible bit of knowledge he had come by. Then he simply waited, feeling sick to his stomach, regretting his decision and yet not regretting it at the same time. He went back and forth literally as well as figuratively, pacing his room, wondering if it wasn't too late to take it back.

That night he didn't sleep. He sat by the phone hoping to hear something, anything. At midnight the phone rang once and Eric leapt at it. "Hello? Hello? This is Eric...I mean Dr Reidy."

A voice said: "Eleven hundred hours. Maintain Emcon blackout."

Eric had a sudden panic attack over this. "I don't understand what you mean. Are you saying it'll be eleven hundred hours before you attack..."

"Don't say another word!" the voice ordered. "Eleven

o'clock tomorrow morning. Do not use the phone or the computer. Do not attempt to transmit anything. Now do you understand?"

"Yes," Eric whispered. In the next second the phone went dead and he could only stare at it for long minutes. "This is for the best. In the long run I'm saving lives and besides, the Secretary is useless. Everyone thinks so." Everyone did.

Despite his words, Eric began to pack. He had no clue where he was going, he just knew he couldn't be at the CDC when the attack happened. Nor could he be there afterwards. Of all the nonessentials he was likely the most nonessential of all. He wasn't a warrior or a scientist, he didn't own a PhD, and his only real skill was as a butt-kisser, and an opportunist, and a traitor.

Packing took surprisingly little time. For the rest of the night as the clock ticked slowly on, he sat on his bags and stared vacantly at his bed, wondering if he should tuck the corners in better. By sunrise he still hadn't come to a decision about it.

When it was finally eleven and time to go, Eric left his room with his eyes down, not daring to look another person in the face until he was at the main gate. There he lied with every part of himself: his false smile, his phony demeanor, his dishonest words: "I have to collect some samples. Yes, I'll be careful. I'll be back tomorrow. No, I should be safe enough."

And then he was through the gate where only death awaited to free him from his guilt.

Chapter 47

Ram

Rome, Georgia

Just as Eric Reidy spent his night awake, so too did Victor Ramirez, and just like Eric, Ram felt about as nonessential as a man could be. He had failed Julia and the baby. He had allowed a slip of a girl to run off into a forest teeming with zombies, and then he had watched helplessly as Neil took up the SAW and went out after her. He had tried to go himself, but his knee would not allow it and Sarah had held him back, sobbing as she did.

For a man of Ram stature, the twenty-three pounds of metal was a nuisance, but for Neil the tip of the weapon dipped after only a few seconds. He wasn't going to make it. Ram knew it and yet he didn't open his mouth to stop him from going. Neil was doing what a real man would—he was going to save his daughter.

"I was asleep," he whispered to the night. "I fell asleep as if carting around a few bags and sitting in a car all day was actual work! Fuck!" He raged at the dark and next to him Sarah put a hand to her mouth as she wept.

"Get inside," he bellowed at her. "Go, or do you want to wind up like..." Just then a gunshot came to them from the forest followed immediately by another. They both knew what those shots meant—the zombies had found Sadie. Sarah stifled a cry with her hand, grabbing her own face in her misery. Ram said, "I'm sorry. Please I didn't mean to yell. But...but you should get up into the loft."

"What about you?" Sarah asked. "You can't go after them. You're hurt. The stiffs will get you and you'll die for nothing."

Just then it didn't seem to matter to Ram if he lived or died. He had fallen so hard for Julia and so quick that it didn't make sense to him. It was as though nature, knowing that it didn't have many humans left to work with, had forced love on them and, because of where they both were in their lives, they had accepted it greedily.

Now Julia was dead. He couldn't quite grasp the concept, except that seeing her body like that hurt him worse than any pain he had ever withstood. "I should bury her. I can't wait until morning. It'll haunt me if I don't." Sarah didn't argue, instead she guarded over him as he buried Julia, and they both cried, as the far away gunfire grew in intensity. They listened, wearing matching masks of fear and of course the feeling multiplied a hundred times when the gunfire ceased altogether.

Then the night stretched out forever in silence and morning left the two of them staring at each other wondering what they were going to do and how they were going to go on with whatever was left of their lives. They were red-eyed and each second was a misery and each breath seemed like a wasted effort—but then Sadie popped up the ladder, looking fresh as though she had slept through the night.

"I need bullets and a bottle, Eve is starving like you wouldn't believe."

"She's alive?" Sarah asked in amazement, staring in open-mouthed wonder at the girl. "What about Neil?"

As if to confirm what her eyes were telling her, Sarah reached out for her, however Sadie was already past them and rooting around in the bags. Over her shoulder, she said, "That reminds me. I also need a diaper and some wipes."

"What about Neil?" Sarah demanded again.

"They're not for him," Sadie replied with a grin. "Though he almost crapped himself last night. Hell, I almost crapped myself last night."

"He's ok," Sarah whispered. "Neil is ok." She said it as though to force herself to believe something she knew couldn't be true. "He's ok. And the baby's ok...did you kill *her*? Did you kill Cassie?"

Now Sadie's mood darkened. "Not yet I haven't. If I ever see her again I will, I promise you that." This last she said to Ram, and she said it so fiercely that he felt something swelling inside of him. It was the knowledge that he wasn't alone. All during the night the feeling of being alone had crept in. Yes, he had Sarah right there, however she had drifted into another world—a world where suicide was fast becoming a pleasing option to her pain. He saw it in her eyes, the giving up. And Ram had felt alone like he had never before. It was a scary feeling as though the world was growing into a vast empty desert and he was left to stand isolated and solitary.

After Sadie dropped a couple of fresh magazines into the diaper bag along with one of the Berettas, she stood and Ram hugged her unexpectedly. It was a surprise for both of them and Sadie was set to offer her customary smart-assed comment, but stopped short when she saw the tears in his eyes.

"I didn't do anything special," she said.

"You did," Ram told her. "But I'm not hugging you for saving Eve. I'm just happy you're alive. I don't know if I could've taken it if you had died too."

Sadie gave a little awkward laugh and turned pink, but then her eyes clouded. "I'm sorry about Julia," she said. "I didn't know her very well except I knew she'd be a great mom."

Ram couldn't say anything to this; his throat had seized up at the sound of her name.

They gathered supplies and rather than making the harrowing journey through the forest which many of the creatures seemed to consider their home in the daytime, Sarah suggested loading up the farm's tractor, which sat far out in a lonely field, and driving it instead. They had encountered tractors before in their travels and discovered that most were full of diesel, however since they used gasoline they tended to just ignore them.

Now, with Ram still limping badly, it seemed the only workable plan they had to get to Neil and Eve. Sadie worried that a tractor would be way too slow, while Ram worried that he wouldn't know how to operate one. Sarah, as a farmer's daughter did the driving, and showed them what a tractor could do. It wasn't the fastest thing in the world, still it chugged along at twenty-five miles per hour, twice as fast as the fastest zombie.

Neil heard them coming from a long way off and met them with Eve in one hand and the SAW in the other. "Impressive," he said of the big green machine, when Sarah turned it off.

"Not as impressive as you," she replied and then jumped down and kissed him full on the mouth. Sadie took the baby and was about to feed her when she saw Ram staring at Neil and Sarah in anguish.

"Here, you better get used to feeding her," she said to get his mind on something else.

Ram took Eve and nearly dropped her right off the bat—beneath her pink blanket it was as though she was made of spaghetti and he had trouble arranging her in his arms as she seemed constantly ready to slip out.

"Like this," Sadie said, settling the baby in the crook of one his strong arms. "And the bottle goes in there."

"I got that part," he said, slipping the bottle into Eve's hungry mouth. "Wow, she really is going to town. I wish...I wish..." He couldn't finish his sentence as his emotions threatened to sink him. All he could picture was how Julia had held Eve and fed her.

"Yeah, I wish the same thing," Sadie said. She then patted him on the head, absently feeling the springiness of his hair as she looked down at the baby. "You can do this still, if you want to. Be the *Dad*, I mean. We'll all help. You can count on us. I'll be the crazy cousin who gets her in trouble, and Neil and Sarah can be the aunt and uncle. What do you think?"

Ram hoisted Eve to his broad shoulder, amazed at the way she drew her legs up to her chest. "She needs a new mom. In this world a baby needs both parents and a big sister. I'll be an uncle, a very doting uncle...but right now it kills me to even look at her."

Despite saying this he smiled when Eve said, "Urp."

Sadie laughed and stroked Eve's back before calling out to Neil and Sarah, "Hey, you two smooch machines, you have a baby now so you can cut it out. Ram is going to be Uncle Ram from here on."

Sarah closed her eyes, letting her forehead lean on Neil's chest. She was joyfully sad, and Ram was happy for her. He was crushed emotionally but he hadn't come unglued mentally, which was something he'd been dreading. He remembered all too clearly how that had been: the vacant mind, the uncaring eyes that saw reality as though it were a movie—as though the people around him were fake and, of course, the saturating guilt that breathed from his every pore.

Instead he knew sadness and hatred on equal levels, and beneath it he allowed himself a small joy over the fact that Eve and Sadie had lived. He was the first to push the group on to the CDC. The events of the last day had given him new purpose. Before, his main concerns in life had been little more than basic survival and the finding of happiness in a cruel world with Julia; now he was set on finding Cassie and making her pay. The very idea sent a shiver through him and had his teeth on edge, while his eyes grew sharp.

Yet he was an uncle now and he owed it to Eve to deliver the blood of the terrorist. He had no clue if it would do a damned bit of good, but he was determined to try. "Mount up people," he said. The Suburban was gone. Cassie must have taken it the night before, and so they rode the tractor and it proved a loud, but adequate vehicle. It could go practically anywhere and since they all felt that this was the last leg of their journey they pushed it to its limits.

It wasn't long before they left the fields behind and

came upon the sprawling and ill-defined metropolis of Atlanta. A map was of little help in finding the CDC, however they chanced upon another shoebox-like armored personnel carrier and Sadie was quick to volunteer to ask for directions.

She slid down the edge of the tractor and jogged over to the armored box. This one had its manhole cover thrown back and the little group watched as Sadie took down directions with a disappointed air.

"What's wrong?" Ram asked. "Did they give you attitude?"

"No, they were all just old," she said, making a face. "Here are the directions." She held out her hand and upon it was writing in blue ink. "Is that a one do you think?"

It turned out to be a seven, but it hardly mattered and they drove across the top end of Atlanta unimpeded save for a few thousand curious zombies who came out of their day places at the passing of the diesel engine—Sarah kept it floored to elude them, so the group bounced and chugged along and Eve slept contentedly, while Neil got "tractor" sick.

It was a two-hour drive at those low speeds. Still they came upon the CDC at mid-morning and they gaped all around at the piled cars and the torn fencing...and the people; they had not seen so many people in days.

Sarah was nervous because most of them seemed to be soldiers, while Sadie was the most excited because she saw teens of her age and younger. She proudly showed off Eve to anyone who wished to see, though she was equally quick to pull back if anyone put a hand out.

"Not 'til you wash your hands, proper," she insisted. Since there was nowhere to wash their hands it was all *looky-no-touchy* when it came to the baby. All the civilians in sight were waiting for an armored bus that would take them to one of the refugee camps, the sound of which had Ram looking askance, and Neil grimacing nervously.

"We're not here for that," Ram said to the gate guard. There were two gates: coming and going, and at the moment there was just one man exiting and Ram and his party were the only ones entering. "We're here to talk to someone concerning a possible vaccine. We have blood that was taken from..."

"We don't take any more zombie blood, sorry," the guard said. "If you want to go on to the refugee center then we need you to get in that line over there."

"We want to go inside," Sarah said, pointing at the shiny buildings. "We came all this way..."

The guard just shook his head. "I'm very sorry about that, but we're full. I recommend the refugee camp. It's a better alternative then trying to make it alone."

In a wrath, Ram stepped close to the guard and held up the vial of red blood. "Does this look like zombie blood to you?"

"What is it?" the soldier asked, seeing the color and raising his eyebrows.

"It's blood from a vaccinated man," Ram told him, locking eyes, hoping to convey the truth of his statement with the force of his will.

"I don't know," the guard said, slowly. "I'm not supposed to take any more blood. We get like ten vials a day." The guard then noticed the man exiting the gate and said, "Hey you! Dr Reidy, you're one of the scientists, right?"

Eric Reidy turned, afraid and jumpy. "Who me? I'm not a scientist, I'm...why? What's going on? Is something happening?"

"Just these people have some blood. You should take a look at it."

Eric shook his head, relaxing a bit. "Naw. No more blood. Make sure you don't break it when you throw it away." He turned to go, but Ram hobbled to him and grabbed him by the shoulder, turning the man around.

"Look at it," he said in a tone that demanded attention. "This isn't zombie blood. I got it from one of the initial terrorists. His name was Shehzad something. I think he was from Qatar. I tracked him down in L.A."

"Shehzad," Eric whispered. He glanced once at the vial and then looked up at the sky, scanning all around and Ram noted the sweat on his lip despite the cool of the morning. "How did you get this blood?"

"I was working with Homeland Security and we were part of the initial investigation into the terrorist attacks. Shehzad admitted that he'd been inoculated. Tell me, does that mean there's a cure in this blood?"

The man surprised Ram by cursing. "Shit! Yes. Maybe. Shit! Ok I need to get that under a microscope, fast." He began to reach for it, but Ram held it back from him.

"Oh, no you don't. We're all going in with you."

Reidy began shaking his head. "No you don't want to do that," he said, but when he saw the set of Ram's jaw, he sort of wilted and whined, "Ok, jeeze, shit. Let these people through. On my authority, let them through, I'm the Secretary's personal adjunct."

"They have to leave their weapons," the guard said. He pointed to a bin. "Leave them right there, they'll be fine."

This did not sit well with Ram, or the others. Sarah was white in the face at the idea of giving up her protection, while Sadie made a show of tossing her knife in the bin while slipping her Beretta into Eve's car seat beneath the pink blanket.

"Good, good. Now please we have to hurry," Reidy said, pulling the M16 from Neil's hands and tossing it into the bin. "It'll all be here when we get back. I hope." Then they were through the gate and rushing after Eric who jogged to the main building in front of them. "Hurry, hurry," he ordered, again looking to the skies and hustling them inside. He took them up two flights of stairs and then to an office that had been converted to a bedroom. "Wait here."

The man began to close the door on them, however Neil grabbed him.

"What's going on?" he asked. "Shouldn't we be going to a lab?"

"Not now, damn it," Eric snapped and then rushed inside the room with Neil and the others right behind. Eric gave them a pained look, as if what he was about to do was going to hurt, and then reached under a bed and pulled out a bulky satellite phone. "Hello! Pick up," he said after turning it on and going to the window. "This is Eric Reidy. Abort the mission. Abort the mission. Do not attack. We have a potential cure. Please do not attack."

He paused, waiting for a response and everyone stood gawking at him in stunned silence until Sadie said, "What the fuck?"

Neil's mouth had been hanging open, but now he seemed to wake up. "Sadie, not while you're holding the baby," he admonished.

Chapter 48

Neil

CDC Atlanta

"Tell us exactly what's happening," Neil said with a confidence he didn't feel, unless confidence generated a sensation much like wanting to piss yourself.

"We're about to be attacked," Eric said with his hand out—it shook as though it were attached to a live wire. "Give me the blood and get as far away from here as possible."

Ram held the vial close in a tight fist and asked, "By who? Who's attacking us?"

Eric turned again to the window and looked out. "The government. It's going to be a coup against the Secretary. She's in charge and she's screwing everything up. I have to stop this." With a suddenness that startled them, he ran out of the room, checking his watch as flew down the corridor. "I need Colonel Taylor! Where's Taylor?" he bawled. People shrugged and someone mentioned the Secretary. "Two birds with one stone." He laughed high in his throat as he headed to a bank of elevators and began jabbing repeatedly on the down button until one came.

"Do we go with him?" Sarah asked, stepping away from the elevator. "I don't want to be in an attack. How long do we have?"

"Ten minutes," Eric told her, getting in the elevator. "If you leave, you have to give me that blood!"

"What do we do?" Sadie stuck her hand out, holding up the doors. "I'm fricken' scared about this. If we go down with him, I'm scared we won't come back up."

"And I'm afraid ten minutes won't cut it," Ram said. "They could be early, and if there's an attack by choppers they may shoot everyone up top and ask questions later. It's what I would do."

"Then we go down and take our chances," Neil said, coming to a quick decision and pushing them through the doors. "If they're after one person, then a group of us should be safe."

"Maybe," Eric mumbled.

Sadie glared at him and then when Eve began to fuss, her face relaxed and she said, "We might need a bottle. She likes to be fed before a battle, because she's a little trooper. Yes she is."

"Not down here with all the germs," Sarah said. She held herself erect, keeping her and the baby from touching anything. Spooked and pale—her skin alabaster compared to the black she always wore—Sadie kept close as well.

"It's not the germs that'll kill you," Eric said sadly. "It's always the people. They told me that the Secretary was so incompetent that she was in effect letting people die all over the country. They told me this had to be done for the sake of the country. But there isn't a country, right? You've been out there, are we still a country?"

Just then Neil wanted to say: no there isn't a country, however his heart rebelled. Sarah was a mid-west farmer's daughter, Ram was DEA out of Los Angeles, Sadie was girl from Jersey, and Eve was a tiny southern belle. They had lived a thousand miles away from the other—and each was as American as apple pie; hard working, fiercely loyal, brave as all get out, and generous to those in need...

"Yeah, there's still an America," Neil told the man. "Though I don't know how a coup will help. It sounds like people grabbing power to me, and that's not very American."

Eric nodded in a jerky fashion. He was clearly afraid, and this only grew more pronounced when the elevator let out a pleasant: *Ding* and its doors slid open. "I need to see Colonel Taylor right now," he said, hurrying up to a couple of loafing guards. "It's an emergency."

"Slow down, Doc," one of the guards said, swiveling his chair so that his long legs blocked the way. "They've got the usual meeting of the Department Heads. I can't..."

"We're about to be attacked!" Eric cried. "Let me through this instant, or it'll be on you and not me." His wild eyes were huge in his sweating face, making him appear crazy.

"Is that right?" the guard asked, looking at all of them and only growing more concerned and confused by what he saw.

"He certainly believes it," Neil answered, speaking for the group. "He had a special satellite phone and some sort of prior knowledge of this attack. We're just here to make sure someone takes a look at this blood. It's not zombie blood."

This was a lot for the guard to digest, especially with Eric huffing down on him in an erratic manner, he reached for the phone. "Let me just call..."

Eric took off running.

The rooms beneath the CDC were of gleaming stainless steel and unsmudged clear glass and the walls were stark white, and everything was perfect, peaceful, ordered—save for the man, raving loudly in a sprint. Behind him came the guards and behind them hurried Neil's group: Sadie loping along at an easy pace in front, Sarah with the baby, Neil with the car seat and Ram limping far behind.

They turned down a long hall and Eric, empowered by his knowledge of what was about to happen, flew to the last room and barged in. "We're about to be attacked!" he shouted at the gathered Department Heads, all of whom jerked in surprise. They had been lulled into a near stupor as the usual and useless meeting had dragged on, however now they were wide eyed and attentive, making Eric even more nervous. "Attacked by soldiers; Admiral Stevenson is on his way. He cornered me last week when I was on his carrier and made me...he said you were killing people, Madam Secretary. He's coming to remove you. He knows everything. I told him how many troops you have; where they're going to be stationed, and where you will be Madam

Secretary."

The Secretary was an older woman, grey haired and sharp faced, though her recent lack of "treatments" was starting to show quickly as she sagged on the edges. Her mouth came open, but instead of saying anything she turned to the only uniformed man in the room—the Security Brigade's Commander, a colonel with the name Taylor stitched across his breast pocket.

Colonel Taylor turned his hard gaze at Eric for several seconds, assessing the man. He then asked, "When?"

Eric checked his watch again. "Seven minutes, if he's on time."

"He'll be on time. That we can count on," the colonel said in a whisper as he sat back and pictured in his mind what an attack would mean. "It's going to be a blood bath. Seven minutes is not enough time."

"Is this for real?" a man in a white lab coat asked. "We're going to be attacked?"

"Yes," Eric gushed out. "Admiral Stevenson has already claimed the Presidency for himself. He called the Secretary grossly incompetent and derelict in her duty. He's coming."

"There have been rumors," the colonel agreed, shifting his eyes downward to the tabletop. "I just never thought he would go through with it."

Eric choked out, "He is going through with it today. Practically now."

"Then what are you waiting for?" the Secretary said to the colonel. "Stop this from happening. And you two," she pointed to the guards. "Arrest him, he's a fucking a traitor. And arrest them too." By this she meant Neil and his group who were standing in the doorway. One guard went to them, though what he was going to do they didn't know because just then the colonel got up and ran from the room. He was followed by first one of the department heads and then another, and in a few seconds they were all fleeing

"We didn't do anything," Sarah told the Secretary who

had dropped back down in her chair.

"They might have what we need for a vaccine," Eric said. "Show her the blood. It's from Shehzad Bhanji one of the original terrorists. They say he was inoculated, which means there is a strong possibility that the blood contains either Killed or Attenuated forms of the..."

"Who gives a shit!" the Secretary screamed. An alarm suddenly went off in the building—incessant and whining. Eve began to cry and the Secretary made a face of disgust at the sight of the baby. She went on in a high-pitched voice. "None of that matters right now. We are about to be attacked. They're coming for me. Don't you understand what that means?"

"Yes I do, but you're wrong. A cure matters to me and to a lot of people," Eric said in anger. "I only came back because I thought you cared about finding a cure. That's what we're here for, right? To find a vaccine?"

The Secretary snapped her fingers. "Cuff him and gag him. I don't want to hear another word. And you, shut that baby up, or I'll have it gagged as well."

Sarah's eyes went to slits and Sadie stepped in front of her. "That won't be necessary," Neil said slowly, trying to calm the situation. "We have another bottle for her." Sadie dug in her bag and handed a bottle to Sarah, but not before her eyes went wide at something she saw in the bag.

The guard placed his handcuffs on Eric and then looked around for a suitable gag, but before he could find anything the colonel pushed past Ram and said in a rush, "Apaches have been spotted." When the Secretary only looked at him nonplussed, he added, "Apache gunships. They're attack helicopters. Behind them will be waves of Blackhawks and if the admiral has any sense, he'll have inserted Marines already to attack the perimeter."

"Can't you tell them to go back?" she asked.

The colonel smiled in a thin way as if he were seconds from exploding in anger at her. "No. They take their orders from Admiral Stevenson and he takes his orders from you, supposedly. That means you have to talk to him."

She blanched at this, however the colonel was insistent and dialed a number for her. The group listened to the conversation and watched as the Secretary became unglued, mentally and physically, right in front of them. Her eyes became crazed and rabid. Neil thought she was going to vomit. She made heaving motions, but managed to hold back her breakfast, and said to the colonel, "He says that he's giving me five minutes...and that he wants to arrest me. What does that mean? What are they going to do to me?"

The answer couldn't be more obvious; even Sadie, the youngest, bit her lip and remained silent. "They're going to kill you," Eric said at last, hollowed-voiced. "But you should make a stipulation first. Make him keep the CDC open. We have to make a vaccine."

"You shut up!" she yelled. "This is your fault. You did this to me. If anyone should die it's you. You're the traitor here, not me." She paused, seething and stared around at the room not seeing any of them until her eyes fell on one of the guards. "Kill him," she said in a whisper, pointing at Eric. "I'm in charge. I can make the rules and I say kill him." This was met with a wide-eyed silence.

"Are you using your powers as acting Commander in Chief?" the colonel asked in a leading manner. "You have the right to order summary executions under martial law as the legitimate leader of the United States."

"Then that's what I'm doing. Kill him..." she said pointing at Eric. She turned to the others. "And kill them too."

"What?" Neil cried, raising his hands as he stepped forward. "You can't kill innocent people. Not like this." If the guards hadn't already pulled their weapons he would have yanked the one that sat nestled in the car seat under Eve's pink blanket. Next to him, Sadie tipped him the tiniest wink and rubbed the diaper bag, suggesting there was a gun hidden there. He hoped she wouldn't try to draw it, not right then. The closest guard had his weapon pointed straight into Neil's chest.

"We haven't done anything wrong," Ram said, easing to the side with the vial of blood out for them to see. "This has a cure in it. That's all we came here for. To help people. To give you this." He held it out as though it were a gift.

The vial drew their eyes. "What do I do?" the guard closest to Eric asked.

Even the Secretary eyed the little glass tube, but at the man's question she blinked away from it and said, "Kill them. That's an order. And you, Colonel, gather your men to fight. We can't just let the admiral win. This will be a great fight. We fix this traitor, and these others and then we fight." She swung back to the guard. "Go on, kill the traitor; that's what happens to them, we kill them."

All eyes went from the vial to the disheveled scientist. He had his hands in the air and everyone could see how violently they were shaking. "Please I didn't mean..."

"Do it!" the Secretary screeched. Neil's hand crept closer to carrier, but the guard stopped him with a look.

Eric made a choking sound and dropping to his knees, hung his chin low so that his eyes were on the floor and not at the black gun pointing his way. "In the...head," he said between sobs. "I don't want to turn into one of them. I only wanted to save lives."

There was nothing more to say.

From a foot away, the guard pulled the trigger on his weapon—it flashed and bucked. With his brain shot away, Eric jerked in a fish-like spasm and then flopped to the ground on his face, showing the world the crater where his brain had been.

And then, like a robot, slow and mechanical, lacking even the most rudimentary emotions, the guard turned to Neil—the man's face was unblinking and pale as if it were his own brain he had destroyed with his executioner's bullet.

He pointed his gun once again.

"I won't get on my knees," Neil said. "I'm an American and I have rights. You remember what those are?"

The guard/robot nodded and thumbed back the hammer. There came a moment in which Neil felt his heart stop on its own. It just ceased its crazy thumping and went altogether still and it was then Ram spoke in a low voice, "If you shoot, I swear I'll break this vial. It's your only chance at a cure. Think about it. It's your only chance at a future." This seemed to penetrate the man's frozen mind and he put his hands up as if the vial was a bomb.

The Secretary watched in disbelief. "Kill him, you idiot! There is no cure, don't you understand? See? It's just blood." She went to Ram and with a speed of a striking snake, snatched the vial from his hands. "There's nothing in here but blood."

"There's no cure?" the guard asked in a little boy's voice.

"No," she hissed. "What cure is there from getting your throat ripped out? Or having your arms torn off? Our only cure is stopping the admiral. He can't be allowed to do this. He can't just kill innocent people."

"If you kill us," Sarah said, around gritted teeth. "You're the same as him."

The older woman sneered. "No. You came here with a traitor, pedaling your fake cures. You are hardly innocent, and this," she held up the vial. "Isn't going to save you." Like a baseball pitcher she cocked her arm back and let the vial fly. It zipped through the air, passing over the body of Eric Reidy to smash against the stark white wall. Glass went everywhere, blood shot out, looking like a red star in nova.

Everyone stared at the blood and knew a horrible evil had been committed. It was a sin that couldn't be undone and its repercussions sank into them: their future had been destroyed and their journey and all their efforts had been a waste of time and lives.

With a cry of anger, Sadie moved in a blur. The Goth girl ripped the pistol from the diaper bag and jammed it up under the neck of one of the guards. One beat behind, Neil dug out the Beretta from the car seat just as the second guard turned on Sadie. Neil stuck his weapon to the man's temple and said, "Drop it." They were four in a line and only Neil at the end was safe.

"You'll kill me if I do," the man said. He had huge round eyes and they were cocked far over in his head to see Neil's face.

"I won't," Neil promised. "I'm not a murderer, but I will kill you if you hurt my girl." Sadie flashed him a nervous smile, but it went haywire as she saw how close the second guard's gun was to her face.

"You can't trust them," the Secretary said. "Kill them, quick. We're running out of time. The admiral's coming."

"Jesus, lady!" the guard cried. "He's got a gun to my fucking head."

"Well, someone do something," the colonel growled. "By my calculations we have two minutes before we're attacked."

"There's only one thing you guys can do," Sadie said, after a long moment when no one spoke. "You two drop your weapons or..." Here she paused and her breath began to pick up. "Or, we all pull our triggers on the count of three."

"No," Sarah breathed out in panic. "Don't do it Sadie."

"I have to," Sadie said; she had all the color of a sheet. "You know it's them that can't be trusted. If we disarm ourselves they'll kill us. So...here goes nothing...one..."

"Sadie, please," Neil begged, but at the same time he dug his pistol into the guard's temple.

"You have to shoot him, Neil," Sadie said and then added, "Two..."

"I will," he whispered.

"Shit!" the last guard cried. "Murph! Drop your fucking gun."

The guard with Neil's gun to his head suddenly lifted the pistol from Sadie's face and pleaded, "Please, no. Don't shoot me. Here take the gun."

Neil took it with a shaking hand, while Sadie disarmed the other guard, though she looked about to faint as she did. The Secretary sat down in her chair appearing small and frail. "This changes nothing," she said without glancing up. "I am the rightful leader of the United States of America. You people can't hurt me. It would be illegal. It would be murder. Now go defend us, Colonel. "

"Yes Madam Secretary," the colonel said and made to leave, but Ram stopped him.

"I'm afraid it does change things," he said, taking one of the guns from Neil. "If you manage to hold out, Colonel, what happens to us? We'll be arrested and executed, isn't that right?" The colonel nodded reluctantly and Ram sighed. "And if you lose, how many people will die? A thousand?"

"Yes…maybe even two thousand," the army officer admitted. Ram and the colonel exchanged hard looks and then the officer gave the smallest of nods.

"Then this is for the best." Ram turned his pistol on the Secretary and said into her wide-eyed face, "For the greater good." He shot her once between the eyes; she twitched and died, and not even little Eve cried at her passing. "I take sole responsibility for her death," Ram said with finality. "Now do your duty, Colonel. Surrender your men and arrest me."

Neil turned away and went to the wall where the blood was already beginning to turn a red brown color. He pretended to study it as tears filled his eyes.

Chapter 49

Epilogue

The Atlanta Base

All four of them were arrested, five if Eve were included in their number and this was a good thing, because had they not been arrested and held for trial, they would have been sent to the refugee center at Guntersville, which was later overrun by a great army of zombies with a fearful loss of life.

They counted themselves as lucky, yet the looming trial was a weight upon all of them. They slept little and worried a great deal, especially Sadie who wasn't nearly as tough as she tried to let on. She found the cage oppressively small. Restless, she walked the ten-by-ten cell every day, stretching her legs and complaining about the need to run.

In spite of everything they stayed as cheerful as they could and looked on the bright side: they were warm and alive and still together. The time passed and it was hard to tell how long, though Eve could hold her head up and blow raspberries at the guards by the time Colonel Taylor was arrested for speaking out repeatedly against the admiral's heavy-handed methods.

Things grew especially grim after the colonel "confessed" to the killing of the Secretary of Health and Human Service and was executed by firing squad. Since the little group was among the few who knew the actual truth, Ram surmised that it wouldn't be long before each of them was forced to make their own confessions and were killed as well.

It seemed a very likely thing, but not two days later the USS Harry S Truman, the admiral's flagship, exploded in a giant fireball. His coup was ended with a countercoup, which in turn led to an assortment of counter-counter-coups until the remaining hodge-podge of military forces set up veritable city-states where generals reigned with all the power of petty kings.

And all the while, the five of them sat in their makeshift cells, until it was practically forgotten what they were incarcerated for. Thankfully Eve, with her giant blue eyes and her tiny button nose, made such an impression with the guards that they were looked upon favorably and when word got out there was a baby being held as a prisoner, the group was taken before a general none had ever seen before.

"This is the baby I've heard about?" he asked. "May I hold her?" He was a kindly sort of man with short grey hair and wore a uniform that had been starched to such a degree that he seemed bulletproof.

Still Sadie said, "Only if you wash your hands."

Since the general had benefitted from the Secretary's death and had never liked the admiral in the first place, he didn't hold a grudge and released them as soon as Eve went red in the face, grunted twice and filled her diaper. "She's all yours," he said quickly, handing her back. "Good luck."

Things had changed greatly at the CDC during their stay in jail. For one it was no longer called the CDC. It was simply called either the Atlanta Base or just Atlanta. And gone were the multitude of scientists. Some stayed, but for the most part the others drifted away when actual work was expected of them. The base had been expanded to include the buildings and grounds of nearby Emory University, and for the most part, as winter turned to an early spring the base was beautiful.

It was a thriving community of both men and women, numbering close to three thousand people. Neil's family was welcomed, mostly because Eve was such a novelty. Very few babies had lived through the initial stages of the apocalypse, and children of all sorts were considered somewhat of a prized possession.

Sarah and Neil decided immediately that they wanted to

stay. The base was secure and the general seemed a good and fair ruler; overall it seemed an ideal place to raise children. Although Sadie liked Atlanta well enough, she stayed mainly because she couldn't stand the idea of ever leaving her apocalypse parents.

Ram was different. He chaffed all through March and by the time the Dogwoods began to flower he shouldered his pack and kissed his friends good-bye.

"I'm going north," he said in a vague reply to their questions. "Just to see what's what. I'll be back, I'm sure." The truth was that his heart was restless. It held the ghost of a woman he had loved and the thirst for revenge. Cassie was out there—and she deserved to die. Often he had dreamed of her and in those dreams she was a faceless hate.

"Bring me back something nice," Sadie begged. "Like the Liberty Bell, I've always wanted one."

"Is that all?" he asked, with a laugh. "Just a thousand pound bell? Not the crown from the Statue of Liberty?"

"Or a shot glass from the Empire State Building, one or the other. I'm going to miss my Uncle Ram."

"Me, too," Sarah told him. "What I want is for you to bring yourself back when you're done setting your heart to rest." She hugged him fiercely, while Neil was quiet and shook his hand solemnly.

"Good luck," he said. "And keep your powder dry...wait. Is that a real thing or a sexual metaphor?"

Ram couldn't help but smile at the man, or at any of them really, however he knew, as he went through the gates, that smiling didn't always equate to happiness. Sometimes it was only a mask to hide pain. So Ram smiled his fake smile one last time and then turned to begin his hunt.

The End.

Peter Meredith

*

Author's Note:

A quick word about The Apocalypse and the warning posted in the front of the book. I am unfazed by people calling me a racist--out of dozens of evil characters one is black and that makes me racist? Nor do I care about the cries of sexism or misogyny-- are these people unaware of the millions of women around the world who prostitute themselves for far less compelling reasons than basic survival?

No, this is concerning the military and how it's members are portrayed in this novel. As a Coast Guard brat and the son of a career officers, and as a veteran myself (82nd Airborne, 5th Mash 86-91) I have great respect for our military. For the most part they are proud, honorable men and women who serve God and country like heroes. In The Apocalypse I tried to visualize what would happen to our soldiers if there was no country left to fight for and if the intangible God was replaced by hell on earth.

History would suggest they would take on the aspects of their leaders: the same union army that was slow and plodding under McClellen turned into a beast under Grant. Napolean took a bunch of pro-revolutionary idealists and turned them into royalists in a matter of months.

In this narrative the army doesn't turn into a bunch of murdering rapists, they behave pretty much as their leaders do. General Fairchild's soldiers fight with dogged tenacity, retreating slowly away from the eastern seaboard. Lieutenant Mathers and his men head off into Manhattan on a suicide mission without question. Private First Class Marshall Peters of the 82nd is depicted practically without officer oversight and he fights to the best of his ability before his position is overrun.

Only in the men of the Island do we find a real breakdown in morals, sparked once again by the leader: Colonel Williams. I know each of us would like to think they would never, ever debase themselves in such a way as those soldiers did, yet I feel confident to say none of us have ever been in a unit that had suffered upwards of 90% casualties during months of prolonged, intense fighting. It is conjecture of course, but people have broken down under less duress and there are, sadly to say, plenty of instances of abuse throughout history.

If you would like to discuss this further, the best forum for that is on Goodreads.com where people gather to banter this sort of thing back and forth. I would love to hear your opinions.

Finally, on a self-serving note, the review is the most practical and inexpensive form of advertisement an independent author has available in order to get his work known. If you could put a kind review on Amazon and your Facebook page, I would greatly appreciate it.

Peter Meredith

The Story Continues...

The Apocalypse Survivors is not an uplifting tale of heroes and heroines. Get that out of your head right now. It's a tale of survival. It's a tale of dried blood beneath your nails, of new pain, of gnawing hunger and unrelenting loneliness, of fear and hatred, and yes, of courage.
In The Apocalypse, the great majority of the men and women who fought with honor, with a sense of duty and loyalty, gave their lives for others, leaving those without honor to flourish and rule. Their rule is not marked by decency or civility, but by wicked brutality.
Yet, in some very rare cases, the kind and the noble survived. These hardened survivors learned to live among the undead, but now they must learn how to stay alive among creatures that are far more monstrous: their fellow man.

Fictional works by Peter Meredith:

A Perfect America

The Sacrificial Daughter

The Horror of the Shade Trilogy of the Void 1

An Illusion of Hell Trilogy of the Void 2

Hell Blade Trilogy of the Void 3

The Punished

Sprite

The Feylands: A Hidden Lands Novel

The Sun King: A Hidden Lands Novel

The Sun Queen: A Hidden Lands Novel

The Apocalypse: The Undead World Novel 1

The Apocalypse Survivors: The Undead World Novel 2

The Apocalypse Outcasts: The Undead World Novel 3

The Apocalypse Fugitives: The Undead World Novel 4

Pen(Novella)

A Sliver of Perfection (Novella)

The Haunting At Red Feathers(Short Story)

The Haunting On Colonel's Row(Short Story)

The Drawer(Short Story)

The Eyes in the Storm(Short Story)